DEADLY GAMES

BY

LINDSAY BUROKER

⊷ EMPEROR'S EDGE SERIES ⊶

BOOK THREE

Edited by Shelley Holloway
Cover and interior design by Gene Mollica Studio, LLC.

DEADLY GAMES

CHAPTER 1

In the predawn light, Amaranthe Lokdon charged up the worn travertine steps of the ancient stadium. Her thighs burned, her calves ached, and sweat streamed into her eyes.

"Idiotic," she muttered to herself between strained breaths. "Deranged...masochistic."

A dark, round shape blurred out of the shadows. Instinctively, she lifted her hands and caught the heavy, sand-filled ball to keep it from slamming into her chest. Barely. She wobbled, the weight threatening to knock her onto the stone benches, but she compensated and continued upward. With a last burst of energy, she hurled the ball back to the shadowy figure that had appeared at the top of the stairs.

Amaranthe kept her hands up, thinking he might throw it again, but he propped it against his hip and waited. Legs trembling, she reached the top step and forced herself to stand up straight instead of collapsing in a sweaty, exhausted heap.

"Dedicated," Sicarius said.

"What?" she asked when she caught her breath. Stars still lurked in the deep blue sky, and she could not make out his face, but it would not have hinted at his thoughts anyway.

"Your list," he said.

Amaranthe waited for him to expound. He did not.

"You think I'm dedicated for being here, an hour before dawn, training with you? Even though I told everyone to take the week off because we've been working so much lately?"

"Yes."

Figuring her pride had kept her on her feet a respectable length of time, she sat down on the closest bench.

"You don't think I should be following my own orders and enjoying a relaxing week? I could be sleeping in or maybe planning for a day at the beach. It is summer, after all, and the weather is finally good. Yet I'm here with you, torturing myself. You don't think I'm crazy?"

"In general, or for training?"

She scowled suspiciously at him.

A clank drifted up from the sand-covered floor of the arena below. A yawning man in city worker's overalls shambled out of a maintenance door carrying a lantern. He headed toward the towering machine that controlled the Clank Race, a steam-powered obstacle course with a tangle of climbing walls, swaying nets, rocking platforms, and swinging axes. The contraption occupied half of the arena floor inside the running track, and boxing and wrestling rings took up the other half. The worker patted his pockets, cursed, and walked back inside.

"The athletes will show up soon to start training," Amaranthe said. As a junior, she had competed in a smaller version of the Imperial Games, and she missed training for something as innocent as medals and honor. "I suppose we should go."

"Yes." Sicarius offered a hand.

Surprised, she gazed at it for a couple of seconds before clasping it. He pulled her to her feet gently and held the grip for a moment.

Amaranthe swallowed. A couple of months earlier, he had admitted he cared for her, but he had also said it would be a bad idea for them to act upon such feelings. Outwardly, she had agreed with him; inwardly, she kept hoping he would be overcome by emotion—or she would settle for lust—and tug her into his arms for a passionate kiss. Unfortunately, she could not remember having too many men overcome by lust because of her presence. Perhaps it was because she always wore her hair in a practical bun and donned utilitarian clothing more suitable to mercenary life than an evening out. Anyway, Sicarius wasn't the type to be overcome by...anything.

He released her hand without a word and led the way down the steps. Amaranthe trailed him, wondering if she had imagined that pause. They followed a railing toward steps leading down from the elevated tiers of seating.

Sicarius stopped before he reached the stairs. A young woman climbed into view, blond hair and freckled skin illuminated by a pair of gas lamps burning on the landing. Though she wore the loose white togs of one of the athletes, she clenched a short bow in one hand and had an arrow nocked with the other. Her head turned from side to side, eyes searching the arena below.

A throwing knife appeared in Sicarius's hand.

"Wait," Amaranthe whispered, slipping past him.

Fear whitened the woman's knuckles where she gripped the bow—this was no hardened bounty hunter.

Amaranthe held her hands out, palms up, and walked toward the landing. "Greetings."

The bow jerked in her direction.

Amaranthe dropped to her belly, wincing as the hard edge of a travertine step rammed her chest. A clink sounded as the arrow skipped off the railing. Amaranthe sprang to her feet, hoping to reach the woman before she could reload.

Sicarius was already behind the woman, a knife pressed against her throat. The bow clattered to the stone floor.

Amaranthe flung her hand out, saying, "Don't," but Sicarius had already paused, waiting to see what she wanted to do. A few months ago, he would not have. He simply would have killed someone—anyone—who dared lift a weapon in his direction.

Amaranthe straightened her shirt and walked forward. "Care to explain why you're shooting at the shadows? In particular, the portion of shadows I was occupying?"

Rings of white shown around the young woman's blue irises. She opened her mouth a couple of times but did not manage to speak. She could not be more than eighteen or nineteen, and with that pale skin she was not likely a Turgonian.

Amaranthe waved a hand toward Sicarius to suggest he could loosen his grip. He did not.

"He'll only kill you if you don't talk," Amaranthe said.

"Accident," the woman whispered, a faint lilting accent marking the word. "I was tense. My sister...someone took her."

"Oh? Like a kidnapping?" Eagerness thrummed through Amaranthe, revitalizing her tired limbs even more than being shot at had. Was there some trouble afoot? Something her team could handle? Something that could earn them attention— *good* attention?

"Kidnapping." The woman started to nod but winced when the movement drew blood. Sicarius kept his knives sharp enough to split the hairs on a flea.

"Let her go, please," Amaranthe told him. "I do believe that's a client."

Though Sicarius had drawn the woman back into the shadows, to stay out of the light on the landing, Amaranthe had no trouble reading the cool expression he leveled her way.

"What?" she asked him. "It's not as if you were going to spend the week sunbathing at the beach."

Sicarius released the woman, but he did not put away his dagger. As soon as she was free, the girl clasped a hand to her throat and lunged away from him.

"We might be able to help you," Amaranthe said. "My name is Amaranthe. What's yours?"

"Fasha," she said, still holding her hand to her neck. She eased closer to Amaranthe while throwing uneasy glances at Sicarius. "Are you...athletes?"

"We're swords for hire," Amaranthe said.

"Mercenaries?" Fasha tensed. "Lowlife dung-crawlers that work for the highest bidder? How do I know you're not the people who took my sister?"

"We don't work for the highest bidder, and I'm reasonably certain I haven't mingled with dung lately. You?" Amaranthe raised her chin toward Sicarius.

He said nothing.

"He hasn't either," Amaranthe said. "He's quite fastidious." When neither person commented, she cleared her throat and got back on topic. "We work for the good of the empire, taking on missions that the emperor would approve of in the hopes of—" getting the cursed bounties off their heads, she thought, "—winning his favor. In fact we—"

Whistling came from the arena. The worker had returned, a box of matches in hand, and he was veering toward the furnace.

"But perhaps we should discuss it elsewhere," Amaranthe murmured.

She led the way into the shadows outside the stadium. Despite her criticism of mercenaries, Fasha picked up her bow and followed. Sicarius disappeared, but Amaranthe trusted him to stay nearby. More than anybody, he knew how good she was at finding trouble.

Voices sounded—two male athletes walking past the stadium a few dozen meters away. Amaranthe chewed on her lip. The idea of a mission excited her, but it would be foolish to linger at Barlovoc Stadium after sunrise. Though a week would pass before the Imperial Games themselves started, enforcers were already patrolling the barracks and training areas to keep the peace amongst the athletes. That thought made her wonder why Fasha had not sought out the law for help.

"Can you tell me what happened?" Amaranthe asked.

"My sister and I are here from Kendor to compete. This is the first year your Games have been open to outsiders."

Amaranthe nodded. She had read the article in *The*

Gazette and knew Emperor Sespian was responsible for that. Though monetary rewards had never been a prize in the empire's biennial competition, every young citizen dreamed of competing and winning. Also there had been instances of superb athletes sweeping the events and being granted a ticket into the warrior caste, something usually reserved for outstanding wartime performances. A foreigner would not be eligible for that, but the newspaper article had mentioned a citizenship prize for those who wished it—an offer that had traditionalists grumbling in cider houses across the city.

"She didn't come back to the barracks last night," Fasha went on.

Amaranthe's shoulders drooped. That was it? The girl had only been missing for a few hours? "Maybe she found a handsome young man and spent the night with him."

"No. She's been training too hard for this. She may celebrate after it's all over, but for the last week she's been in bed early and up before dawn to train. Keisha is good. Very good. She's won every race back home. She even beats the men in anything over a hundred meters. She's utterly serious about winning here."

"Did you try going to the enforcers?" Amaranthe asked.

"Yes, late last night. I returned from my evening run, and Keisha wasn't in our room. Right away, I knew something was wrong. I went to the men who guard the barracks, but they were derisive. They said nothing got past them. And they threatened to throw me in jail when I mentioned..."

Amaranthe straightened, her interest returning. "The Science?"

"You...know about the mental sciences?"

"My team has had run-ins with practitioners before."

"Oh!" Fasha's clothing rustled as she brushed Amaranthe's shoulder with a pat made clumsy by the darkness. It was an enthusiastic pat though. "Maybe you *can* help. The enforcers told me it's forbidden to talk about magic—that was their ignorant word for it. Two breaths later, they told me magic doesn't exist. If it doesn't exist, why would it be forbidden to speak of it? Ignorant heathens."

"Yes, the empire's stance isn't entirely logical," Amaranthe admitted. "What did you actually sense? Are you a practitioner yourself?"

"No, but there's a shaman in our tribe, and you come to recognize the Science being practiced when you grow up around it. I sensed...a definite residue. I believe something was done to my sister so she'd be easy to steal away."

Amaranthe tapped her fingers against her thigh. "I'd like to see your room. I used to be an—" she stopped herself from saying enforcer, since that might not breed confidence in the girl, "—an investigator. Is it private, or are there others staying in there?"

"We paid for a private room."

"Any windows?" Amaranthe supposed she would have to admit she was a wanted woman at some point and that she could not stroll past enforcers without risk of being recognized and captured—or shot.

"No, it's a little room on the inside of the building."

"Near a backdoor, by chance?"

"No...." Fasha sounded puzzled. "Does it matter? We can bring guests in."

"My comrade and I are wanted by the law."

Fasha's lips formed an "Oh," but no sound came out.

Amaranthe eyed the brightening sky. More and more athletes were on the road leading past the stadium, and the barracks would be an active place. "Don't worry about it. I'll think of something. Let's go."

Amaranthe had taken only a few steps when a dark figure appeared at her shoulder. She jumped despite the fact she ought to know better by now.

"We're going inside the barracks?" Sicarius asked.

Now Fasha jumped and sidled several steps away. The

brightening sky revealed Sicarius's unexpressive angular face, his fitted, black clothing, and the variety of daggers and throwing knives adorning it. Fasha fingered her bow.

"It's fine," Amaranthe said. "He's my most trusted ally."

"That'd be more comforting if you hadn't just admitted to being wanted by the law," Fasha said.

"You didn't think you'd find a Science-savvy mercenary team in the empire without a few eccentricities, did you?" Amaranthe asked.

"The barracks," Sicarius repeated, cutting out whatever reply Fasha might have made.

"I'll sneak by the enforcers and check it out," Amaranthe told him. "I won't be long. You can wait outside. If they try to drag me off to Enforcer Headquarters, you can be nice and provide a distraction so I can slip away. A non-death-causing distraction."

"The last time you went into the enemy camp while I waited outside," Sicarius said, "someone threw a blasting stick at me."

"As I recall it was *at* the position you'd recently vacated, but, thanks to your hyper-vigilance, fast reflexes, and quick mind, you evaded the attack and were long gone when the cliff top crumbled."

Amaranthe smiled, hoping to tease a light response out of Sicarius, something that might show Fasha he had a side that was not entirely dark and scary.

Birds twittered in the branches of trees lining the road. Thunks and whistles of steam came from within the stadium, signifying the Clank Race gearing up.

Finally, Sicarius spoke. "I see. Your plan is to flatter your way past the enforcers."

Amaranthe's smile did not fade. "If the plan doesn't work, maybe so."

She left Sicarius to the shadows and led Fasha to the athlete complex, a mix of permanent structures and brightly colored tents set up to house visiting competitors from across the empire. Men and women jogged or bicycled past, some heading off to train, others stopping at the food pavilions first. A steam carriage chugged past, rumbling up a circular drive to the majestic travertine lodge reserved for warrior caste athletes. Enforcers guarded the front door of the women's barracks. Amaranthe mulled over how to get in and out before full daylight came, making it easy to recognize faces.

Instead of veering in that direction, she angled off the main road toward a pair of dome-shaped brick buildings: men's and women's bathhouses. Smoke wafted from the chimneys, signifying the floors and pools were already warm.

"You wish to bathe before investigating?" Fasha asked.

"I could use it." Amaranthe plucked at her shirt, still damp from the stair-running session. "But, no."

She headed for the entrance of the women's bathhouse—no enforcers guarded those doors.

Steam wrapped about them as they headed in, obscuring visibility, but Amaranthe had visited the complex before and knew the layout. She slipped into the dressing room, found no one inside changing, and plucked someone's white togs out of a niche.

"You're stealing people's clothing?" Fasha asked.

Already changing, Amaranthe thought about spouting some justification about it being for the good of the empire, but she never would have bought that from a thief when she had been an enforcer. Oh, well. "Sandals, too," she said.

On the way out, she grabbed a few towels. She wound one around her hair, draped another across her shoulders, and handed Fasha a third. She found a satchel and hid her own clothing and her knife—the closest thing to a weapon she had brought for the morning training session—inside.

"Two lady athletes returning from the baths to change before breakfast," Amaranthe said.

Fasha sniffed at her. "Let's hope the enforcers' sense of smell is as poor as their sense of magic."

"Your Turgonian is quite good," Amaranthe said instead of responding to the dig.

It occurred to her that this could be a setup. What if some early-rising enforcer had spotted Sicarius and her training and, knowing he could not take them on in the open, arranged a trap? More than one bounty hunter had attempted to get close by feigning an interest in hiring them.

"I'm the daughter of a chief," Fasha said. "I've been educated."

"What did you say your sister's name is again?"

"Keisha."

"And she's how old?"

"Sixteen."

"Why don't you tell me more about your tribe and why you're here competing," Amaranthe said, heading toward the barracks.

Fasha's brow crinkled, but she complied. Amaranthe listened to the story and asked more questions as they walked, seeking inconsistencies or hesitations that would suggest the woman was making it up as she went. Everything sounded plausible, though, and by the time they neared the barracks, Amaranthe decided she was being paranoid.

Two men with short swords and crossbows stood guard on either side of the front door. She did not recognize either—since Barlovoc Stadium was located on the southern end of the city, there was little chance of her running into someone she had worked with—but that did not mean they would not recognize her. Though her wanted poster did not decorate the city as profusely as Sicarius's, it was out there.

Amaranthe adjusted her towel wrap and climbed the stairs. "You didn't run here last year, so you don't know," she told Fasha, "but the sand on the track doesn't feel very well packed. It might make it easy to lose your footing."

"Uhm, yes, maybe so," Fasha said. "Do you think..."

One of the enforcers grabbed Amaranthe's arm as she tried

to walk through the door. Cursed ancestors, she had hoped to at least get inside to snoop about before being caught.

"What are you doing with her?" the enforcer demanded.

Amaranthe blinked. "What?"

The enforcer, a young man who could not be more than a year or two out of the academy, pointed at Fasha while scowling so fiercely he threatened to snap a tendon in his neck. "She's a Kendorian."

Ah, of course. There must be quite a few annoyed with the new policy, allowing foreigners into the Imperial Games.

Amaranthe shrugged. "She's running in the same events as I am."

The second enforcer, whose rumpled uniform and bleary eyes might have meant he had been on shift all night, stabbed Fasha in the shoulder with a finger. "She was out here, spouting about magic last night. We ought to have thrown her in the wagon. And any imperial woman who colludes with her as well."

Amaranthe groaned inwardly. She had never seen Sicarius laugh, and she did not want the first instance to come because she was foolish enough to get arrested for someone else's crime.

Fasha lifted her chin. "I've done nothing wrong. You ignorant Turgonians should be ashamed of yourselves for heckling athletes."

"Ignorant?" The first enforcer reached for the handcuffs dangling from his belt hook. "You—"

Amaranthe pushed Fasha back and glided between the enforcers. She lifted a hand to her lips and whispered out of the side of her mouth, "I'm on it."

"Er, huh?" The enforcers shared perplexed looks.

"Watching the suspicious foreigner," Amaranthe murmured. "She came to the track babbling about kidnappings and magic. As if either would happen at such a well-guarded venue."

The wrinkled foreheads smoothed. "Oh. Of course, that's right."

"You gentlemen can't go inside the women's barracks," Amaranthe said, "but I can. *I* can watch her and let you know if she does anything suspicious."

"Yes, yes, right," they murmured. "You let us know."

They drew back and nodded for her to go inside. Fortunately, Fasha kept her mouth shut and did nothing to antagonize the men as they passed, entering an open bay dominated by two long rows of bunk beds. A few held slumbering figures, but most had been vacated. Women in various states of undress chatted and tended to their morning ablutions.

"That was embarrassing," Amaranthe said, as she and Fasha walked down the aisle.

"That your people are so ignorant about magic?"

"That those enforcers fell for that. Academy standards must be slipping." Amaranthe waved toward the bay. "Where's your room?"

"Down there." Fasha pointed toward a hallway at the end.

Conversations ceased as they passed. Amaranthe wondered if she had made a mistake coming in with a foreigner. She might have acquired information more easily if she chatted with people independently. One of these women might very well have something to do with the kidnapping. Another plot to oust outsiders?

The sound of running water came from latrines farther down the hallway. Amaranthe would check that direction later. The back door ought to be guarded similarly to the front, but perhaps someone could have escaped with a prisoner through a window, especially if some magic had rendered the prisoner unconscious. She shook her head, reminding herself she had not yet determined if anything was truly amiss. Even if Fasha's sister had been a daughter of the warrior caste, the enforcers would not have started searching for her after only one night missing.

Fasha pushed open a door that lacked a lock. They walked into a simple room with footlockers, two narrow beds, and a chest between them doubling as a side table. Two tea mugs and a bag of nuts rested on top next to a low-burning kerosene lamp.

Amaranthe turned the flame up.

"I looked around to see if she left a message." Fasha lingered in the doorway. "But I didn't touch anything otherwise."

"What did you sense exactly to make you think the Science was involved?" Amaranthe poked about, looking for anything out of place. She dropped to her belly to peer under the beds, and her towel wrap flopped off her head.

"It's hard to explain. Like a residue in the air."

One of the tea mugs was half full. Amaranthe sniffed the herbal concoction. "Is this hers or yours?"

"I'm not sure. They're from yesterday morning, I think."

"Hm." That would be a slow-acting drug if it had taken all day to go into effect. Amaranthe wished she had more of a feel for what was and was not possible in the realm of magic. She might have to find Akstyr and come back to—

"Has anyone seen Anakha?" a woman asked in the hallway.

A black-haired, bronze-skinned Turgonian woman strode past the door, bumping Fasha without noticing. She strode out of sight, but Amaranthe followed her to the bay.

"Anyone?" the woman asked again. "Anakha? Tall woman with more muscles than the men."

"Haven't seen her since yesterday," someone said.

"She never came to bed."

Murmurs of assent came from others.

"Great grandmother's bunions," the original speaker growled and strode through the bay and out the front door.

Amaranthe returned to Fasha. "Have you heard of any other kidnappings?"

"No."

"This Anakha, she's Turgonian?"

"If she's who I'm thinking of, yes. There're only a few of us from outside of the empire."

"Huh." Amaranthe scratched her jaw. If this other missing woman had disappeared in the same manner as Keisha... it would stomp out her theory of this being a plot against foreigners.

She spent another ten minutes searching the room, hoping to find something that would justify this trip into the barracks, but she found nothing, not even dust balls. "I better get going. I'll come back tonight or tomorrow night and bring one of my men." Assuming Maldynado had not taken Akstyr to some week-long brothel experience to celebrate their vacation. Only Books had spent the night at their latest hideout. Even Basilard, not a notorious brothel-goer had been gone when Amaranthe awoke. "If you need help before then, you can find me in the locomotive boneyard. It's near the tracks, two miles south of here."

"You live in a...junkyard? Is that what boneyard means?"

"Temporary lodgings."

Amaranthe took the towels, prepared to create another bath-house-inspired costume, but, when she left the barracks, nobody stood guard at the top of the steps. She did not see the enforcers anywhere. A shout almost made her misstep and tumble down the stairs.

"Sicarius!" a male voice cried. "He went that way! Enforcers! That way!"

Amaranthe groaned. *What* was he doing?

The early morning sunlight brightening the city did not reach the alley where Basilard stood on a half-rotted wood stoop before a door. Gang graffiti marked the chipped and broken brick walls around it, and rusty bars protected a window closed off with oilskin rather than glass. A homeless man snored on a stoop farther down while a mangy dog pawed through excrement dumped on the ancient cobblestones. This old neighborhood was not on the city sewer system, as the smell attested.

Thanks to the knives at his belt and the scars covering his hands, shaven head, and face, Basilard doubted anyone would bother him. He was more concerned about dealing with the woman inside. A sign dangling from rusty hinges read *Apothecary*.

Basilard lifted a fist to knock, but paused. A bushy tuft of greenery sprouting from a crack caught his attention. Soroth Stick? Like dandelion and lizard tail, the Turgonians treated the plant as a weed, but he hopped down from the stoop and plucked several leaves. They made a tea that soothed cramps, and, given how much training the team did, such a beverage was often necessary for replenishing the body.

Since he did not have the foraging satchel he carried in the wilderness, he tucked the leaves into an inside pocket in his vest, with a mental reminder to wash them well before using them. Given this dubious locale, they had probably been peed on. By multiple species.

Basilard returned to the stoop, but he cast his gaze about, wondering if the grungy alley might host any other edible plants.

Stop it, he told himself. No more procrastinating. As grandpa used to say, "Cleaning a fish don't get any more pleasant for having put the task off."

He took a deep breath and knocked on the door.

A part of him hoped no one would answer. Not many of his people lived in the Turgonian capital, and he had not sought any out since Amaranthe and Sicarius had killed the wizard who had bought Basilard years ago. Nor had he had the freedom to visit anyone during his tenure as a slave. He had never come face-to-face with the Mangdorians that played a part in the city water poisoning a couple of months earlier, so this would be the first he had met since... He swallowed hard at the memory of a young man he had killed in a pit fight engineered by their owners. He had killed many in those forced battles, since it had been the only way to preserve his own life.

The sound of footsteps came from within. A lock thunked, and the door opened.

A stooped woman with graying red hair squinted at Basilard. An Eye of God necklace hung around her neck, and his breath caught. He had expected an apothecary, not a priestess. She peered up and down the alley before addressing him.

"You must be here for my herbs," she said in heavily accented Turgonian. Her gesture encompassed his scars. "Come in, come in. My services are very affordable. I don't use no magic though, so don't expect that." She glanced up and down the alley again.

Basilard guessed that meant she could use the mental sciences, but would not risk it if there was a chance the locals would find out.

He followed her into a one-room dwelling partitioned into sections for sleeping, meal preparation, and work. The pungent aroma of dozens—hundreds?—of drying herbs thickened the air. She gestured for him to sit on a faded sofa, and he ducked beneath bundles of leaves hanging from the ceiling to perch on the edge.

"What's your problem?" She sat on a stool beside a desk piled high with flasks, tins, and tools. "You're in pain from your scars? I've seen pin cushions less poked up."

Basilard shook his head and touched the knot of scar tissue on his throat, the wound that had stolen his ability to speak.

"No voice? I can't fix that. No herb can repair damaged vocal cords."

He lifted his hands, but did nothing except hold them in the air at first. As soon as he signed, she would know he was Mangdorian. As far as he knew, the hand code his people used on the hunt—which Basilard now used to speak to his comrades—was not employed anywhere else in the world. He had brought pencil and paper, too, because there were few female hunters amongst his tribes, and she might not understand the code well. Maybe he should simply write his message. But she would find out he was Mangdorian sooner or later, since he had come to discuss their people.

He signed, *I seek information. Do you understand me?*

Her eyes widened, and she drew back so quickly she almost fell off the stool. "You're Mangdorian?" She eyed his scars. "Those are knife wounds, aren't they? Did someone do that to you...as punishment?"

He had not expected her to guess he was not responsible for them, that he may not have violated God's mandates of peace and pacifism. Could he lie to her? And avoid her condemnation? Maybe if she had been a simple apothecary, and not worn the necklace of a priestess as well. He could not lie to a holy servant. Besides, he told himself, this was a one-time meeting. Her opinion of him did not matter.

I was a slave, he signed. *I was forced to fight for my life. Many times.*

The priestess dropped her chin to her chest, clutched the bronze eye on her necklace, and whispered a prayer he had not heard in a long time, but one that he remembered well. It asked for God to pity him and give strength to his family because his actions had condemned him.

Basilard sighed. When she looked up, he signed again, *I seek to help our people. I need information on a man who might have wronged Mangdoria somehow.*

"How would you help our people?" She frowned. "By killing this man?"

He hesitated. *I would rather not, but if he has committed crimes against us, I feel it would be my duty to act.*

Her frown deepened, and he realized she was struggling to follow his words. Over the last few months, he had added signs to his people's sparse hunting code, so he could speak more completely with Amaranthe and the others, but, of course, outsiders would not know the gestures he had made up.

I wish to do good, Basilard signed. *If I...help our people, maybe*

God will forgive me.

The priestess straightened, her back as rigid as a steel bar. "God does *not* forgive killers. You have condemned yourself to the darkest circle of Ethor, young man. Nothing you can do in this life can make up for it. That you would even consider killing someone to avenge a wrong proves how far you have fallen."

Basilard closed his eyes. He had just met the woman. Her opinion should not matter, but he knew it was a reflection of the same opinion his family—his *daughter*—would share should he ever return home. And it was an opinion he feared held far too much truth.

I need to know.... Have you spoken to any other Mangdorians in the city? Have you heard anything about a man called...

He grabbed his paper, knowing she would not know his made up sign for the name, and scrawled it for her. His fingers surprised him by trembling. Maybe he did not really want to know the answer. What would he do if his suspicions proved correct?

Still frowning, the priestess read the name. "Sicarius? The assassin?"

Yes.

Her lips puckered in disapproval, whether for Sicarius or for Basilard, he did not know. "What would you do with this information if I told you. Attempt to kill him?"

His heartbeat quickened. *There is something to tell?*

Her pucker deepened.

Basilard leaned forward. *I must know.*

"You should leave this place. The blood on your hands taints my home."

Basilard gripped the sofa's faded floral armrest so tightly his fingers ached. She watched his hand warily, perhaps anticipating violence from a man such as he. Condemned or not, he would not threaten an old woman. He forced his fingers to loosen. How would Amaranthe talk this lady into giving up the information? By giving her what she wanted? What did she want?

If he has wronged Mangdoria, he should be...dealt with. Our people cannot do it without damning themselves, correct? If I am already condemned, then I'm the logical choice to avenge the tribes.

In truth, Basilard did not want to pick a fight with Sicarius. For one thing, he doubted he could win. For another, he did not dislike Sicarius, not the way Akstyr and Books did. Sicarius was cold and impossible to know, and he expected everyone to train as stringently as he did, but Basilard had not found him cruel or vindictive. Hard but fair, he would say. But, that moment in the shaman's cave, when Sicarius had destroyed that Mangdorian message before Basilard or Books could read it.... That had raised Basilard's suspicions. Since then, he had thought often of the moment and wondered what the assassin was hiding.

"You do not treat your soul with respect," the priestess said.

If nothing I do matters... Basilard shrugged.

"Very well. The rumor is Sicarius killed Chief Yull and his family."

Basilard flopped back so hard the sofa thumped against the wall. Crumbled dust from the herbs drying overhead sifted down to land in his eyes. He barely noticed it. Good-hearted Chief Yull, the man Basilard had dreamed of working for as a boy, back when he had thought to become a forage leader and chef. Basilard's gut twisted. And there had been sons. *Young* sons. Jast and Yuasmif.

He closed his eyes. Why had he snooped? Why had he asked for this information?

And, now that he had it, how could he do anything *but* kill Sicarius? Or die trying.

CHAPTER 2

Dawn had come, and Amaranthe felt conspicuous as she sidled up beside one of the enforcer vehicles. She could not count on darkness to mask her wanted-poster features any longer, but she could not leave without knowing if something had happened to Sicarius.

Several men stood between two lorries with smoke drifting from the stacks. The enforcers spoke in hushed tones, and she struggled to eavesdrop over the hissing boilers and idling machinery.

"...Sicarius doing here?"

"...missing girls?"

"...men will catch... Already wounded him."

Wounded? Amaranthe's jaw sagged open. Surely not. Not by enforcers.

One of the men frowned in her direction, and she knelt to tie a shoelace. She dared not linger. It sounded like Sicarius had not been caught yet. What stunned her was that he had been seen at all. Though it was true he did not usually favor costumes, he had a knack for remaining unseen, especially at night. It rattled her beliefs to think he could have stumbled into someone he shouldn't have—and reacted too slowly to keep that someone from raising an alarm.

When Amaranthe had spent as long tying her shoe as she could without attracting attention, she jogged toward a pair of oaks spreading shade over the men's barracks. Not wanting to return to their hideout without knowing Sicarius was safe, she stopped where she could watch the enforcers.

Birds chirped overhead. The smell of cooking eggs wafted from a vendor's nearby tent. Early morning sun slanted through the oak's lower branches and warmed the back of her neck. It was not a sound but the disappearance of that warmth that alerted Amaranthe to someone behind her.

She turned to find Sicarius, hands clasped behind his back, the sunlight limning his short blond hair. No sweat dampened that hair and no dust smudged his black clothes. He certainly did not look like a man who had been on the run.

"What're you doing?" She glanced at the enforcers.

He had placed himself so a tree hid him from their view, but the sunlight and the people walking all about made Amaranthe feel exposed and vulnerable.

"Standing," Sicarius said.

"Where have you *been*? Why did you let the enforcers see you?"

"I did not."

"You find him?" someone called near the vehicles.

Amaranthe grabbed Sicarius's arm. "We have to get out of here. You can explain later."

They jogged toward a swath of trees separating the stadium and grounds from the main railway tracks that ran alongside the lake and through the city's waterfront. Amaranthe intended to push straight through and follow the rails to their hideout, but Sicarius veered north as soon as they were under cover.

"This way." He slipped down a narrow path clogged with shrubs and brambles.

Amaranthe winced as enthusiastic thorns snagged at her togs and attempted to tug her stolen satchel from her shoulder. "I hope you're leading me to a place where answers will present themselves."

Not only did Sicarius not respond, he maneuvered through the grasping foliage more deftly than she and soon disappeared.

Amaranthe ducked a branch at poke-her-in-the-eye height and, figuring Sicarius was out of earshot, added, "This *might* be worth it if you were taking me to a secluded nook where a picnic basket, blanket, and jug of fresh juice awaited."

Black clothing appeared through the leaves ahead. Amaranthe pushed past a rhododendron and stepped into a claustrophobic clearing only a few feet wide. At first, she could see nothing beyond Sicarius's back. When she realized he was pointing at the ground, she eased around him, almost stepping on a man's hand.

"So..." she said, "no picnic basket."

As usual, Sicarius ignored her non-work-related comments. "While you were inside," he said, "this man ran out of the trees near the stadium, and someone shouted 'That's Sicarius.' The enforcers took off after him. He raced through a crowded area where a sergeant with a crossbow shot him in the back. He evaded his pursuers and crashed through here, but then collapsed." Sicarius pointed at a crossbow quarrel protruding from the man's back. "It pierced a lung."

Amaranthe crouched, all thoughts of picnics gone. The dead man wore black, had short blond hair, and wore a bandana over his face. She touched a tuft of hair still damp with sweat. "This looks dyed."

"My color, yes."

"So, someone's impersonating you. Someone who couldn't have known we'd be here at the same time. Is someone trying to blame you for a crime? These kidnappings perhaps?"

"Unknown."

She stood and frowned at Sicarius. "When I recruited you for my team, I didn't fully realize how many people there were scheming up plots that involved you."

"Regrets?" he asked.

Amaranthe almost said something flippant—how often did he set himself up so nicely for teasing?—but a faint variance to his usual monotone made her think the answer might matter. It seemed impossible. She always figured she needed him on her team far more than he needed her. Ancestors knew he had saved her life more times than she could count. But maybe he had come to care about what she thought of him.

She sighed and patted him on the arm. "Nah, you know I like a challenge. Let's get back to the hideout and see if we can hunt down the others. I seem to have granted a vacation prematurely. I think we're going to need everyone in on this."

"Agreed," Sicarius said.

Morning sun burned into the rusted hulls of decommissioned rail cars that filled the vast boneyard. Heat radiated from them, some as yet unscathed by the years and others so rusted each wall was a see-through latticework. The occasional shiny bits glinted, throwing rays into Amaranthe's eyes as she passed. Weeds rose from cracks between faded and broken bricks that lined the ground, suggesting the area had once had a nobler purpose.

Sicarius had disappeared as soon as they neared the boneyard, and Amaranthe weaved through the aisles toward their hideout alone. Unfamiliar coughs and voices echoed from different parts of the field, a reminder that more groups than hers called this place a home, however temporarily. Cigar stubs, some filled with tobacco and some with more potent leaves, littered the bricks. Bloodstains were nearly as frequent. The boneyard had the benefit of not being visited often by enforcers, but that also made it a place Amaranthe would not have chosen to visit alone at night.

She turned down a dead end and stumbled. Maldynado

lounged in a chair he had scavenged from one of the passenger cars. His face was tilted toward the sun, his eyes were closed, his hands were clasped behind his head, and he was…naked.

"Maldynado," Amaranthe groaned.

"Oh, hullo, boss." He neither rose nor adjusted his position to hide anything; he simply sprawled there, like a cat in a sunbeam.

"What are you doing?"

"Vacationing."

Amaranthe pulled a towel out of her satchel and draped it across his waist as she walked past. "I see you've set yourself an ambitious itinerary."

"You said to relax. I'm relaxing." He scratched an armpit. "I've been thinking."

"Profound and philosophical thoughts?"

"Naturally," Maldynado said. "For instance, I figure we should have a team uniform."

"A uniform?"

"Clothes that make us look like a stylish and cohesive unit of elite combat professionals."

"Something like what Sicarius wears?" Amaranthe asked.

"He's far too monochromatic and plain to be considered stylish."

"I see. Well, let me know what you come up with." She peered into the cars she and her team had claimed, a set of three that were less rusted than most. They framed a dead end and created a private camp spot. "Anyone else about?"

"Akstyr's off somewhere being secretive and magicky, and Books left at dawn, excited about spending a day at the library—that is pathetic, by the way."

"Basilard's not around?"

"Haven't seen him since last night."

"I hope he shows up today. I want to take everybody in and investigate Barlovoc Stadium. Something's going on, maybe something important."

"Important enough to interrupt our vacation?"

"Absolutely," Amaranthe said. "This has the potential to attract attention high up. This could be the one."

"Uh huh, when you're done rubbing your hands together and plotting gleefully, think about what you're going to wear for your date tonight."

"My what?"

Sicarius chose that moment to finish scouting and walk into camp.

"You know what I'm talking about," Maldynado said. "Lord Mancrest. I've been trying to get you to meet him for weeks, but you keep saying, 'wait until we have some time off.' Well, you gave us time off."

"All right, but not tonight. This is more important than—"

"I already set it up," Maldynado said.

Sicarius's expression was cool as he drew near, but she did not know if it was due to the conversation topic or Maldynado's lack of attire.

"I told him you were free and that you'd meet him tonight," Maldynado said. "He said he'll take you out to a nice dinner. His family has money, so you should mine that vein for all it's worth. When was the last time you had something fancy? Get the priciest cut of meat."

"Maldynado..."

"He's a gentlemen. Probably won't even expect you to warm his sheets afterward. Unless you want to, of course. I don't think you've blanket wrestled with anybody for as long as I've known you, so you must have some urges that are aching to be sated."

"Maldynado!" Amaranthe should not have blushed, but she was all too conscious of Sicarius standing a few paces away.

"Wear something nice," Maldynado said. "He's expecting you at *The Gazette* building at six."

"I'm not... Did you say *The Gazette*?" Amaranthe wanted to object, since she'd already been planning a night of snooping, but the chance to go into the city's largest newspaper office and chat up the boss *was* appealing. At the least, she could find out if the journalists had heard about anything fishy going on at Barlovoc Stadium. Developing a relationship with Mancrest could prove useful long-term as well. If she could convince him her team was working for the good of the empire, perhaps he would publish something nice—like the truth. "All right. I can send you fellows ahead and come to the grounds afterward. No self-respecting snoop sneaks in before midnight anyway."

"Excellent."

Sicarius said nothing, but his gaze was less friendly than his daggers. When she met his eyes, he jerked his chin toward the old rail car that served as the group's parlor. She clambered inside after him.

The wide opening lacked the sliding door it would have had during its service days, and Sicarius walked to the far end, presumably wanting a private conversation. Crates, battered lanterns, and a couple of old strategy games with missing tiles comprised the furnishings. It would be silly to keep anything valuable inside since vagrants roamed the boneyard. Amaranthe missed the days of having a safe home to return to at night, one where she could keep treasured belongings...like books and dinnerware. When she had been an enforcer, she had never thought she would think of her simple, one-room flat as a luxury.

Sicarius leaned against the far wall, arms crossed over his chest. Sun slanting through holes highlighted rusty rivets on the floor, her purloined broom and dustpan, and the utter lack of humor on his face.

"Problem?" Amaranthe wondered if he might be the teeniest bit jealous at the idea of Maldynado setting her up on a "date." She, of course, had only professional interest in this man and would tell Sicarius that if he asked. She wished he *would* ask, since that would imply his admission about caring meant caring in a romantic way. Well, romantic might not be the exact word to use when describing Sicarius's feelings, but something of that nature anyway.

"Deret Mancrest wrote the story condemning us as Sespian's kidnappers," Sicarius said. "Prior to that, he wrote other articles about me and encouraged the emperor to siphon more forces into capturing me so the army could put me in front of a firing squad."

"Oh." Amaranthe sank down onto a crate. Not jealousy after all. Sicarius just hated the man for condemning him in writing. "So he's the one who called you abhorrent and degenerate and me an accomplice."

"You remember the adjectives used to describe me and not the author?"

"Well, I'm not warrior caste. All those 'Crest' names blend together in my mind."

"It would be unwise to visit him," Sicarius said.

"If he's a friend of Maldynado's he—"

"He may have requested the meeting to arrange a trap."

"For you?" Amaranthe asked. "Wouldn't he have asked you out to dinner if that were the case?"

The sun did nothing to warm Sicarius's dark eyes. "You have a bounty on your head as well."

"Yes, I know. But..." She stood and grabbed the broom. "He may actually be exactly what we need. If he has a years-long record of deriding you—in writing—and he could be... converted, he could become an asset to us." She swept as she spoke, angling dust into a pile. "If we can convince him you weren't behind Sespian's kidnapping, and you've worked for the good of the empire on several occasions since then, his favorable opinion of you would carry a lot of weight. With a single story, he could make the entire city question all they've heard about you." She held the dustpan aloft and smiled. Yes, that sounded like a good plan.

Sicarius stared, as unexpressive and unmoving as marble.

"You know..." Amaranthe dumped her dust pile outside

and returned to face him. "It's hard for me to maintain my vigor and enthusiasm for leading you when you do nothing but stand there and ooze disapproval at me."

"Not at you," he said.

"If your disapproval is aimed at Lord Mancrest, he's not here to receive it. And if you're irked at Maldynado... I think he's only looking to receive a sunburn on his nether regions right now."

"I will go with you tonight."

"Er, to the eating house?" She imagined him wearing his black clothing and knife collection, looming over her shoulder while she tried to woo this Lord Mancrest over dinner and wine.

"To the newspaper building. To see if it's a trap."

"Ah." She supposed she could send him to the stadium after they verified Mancrest was not up to anything duplicitous. "Very well. We'll take Maldynado, too."

Sicarius strode to the doorway, hopped down, and disappeared.

"No, no." Amaranthe lifted a hand. "You needn't let me know you think my idea has promise. It's been nearly three months since the last time I almost got myself killed, so I'm brimming with self-confidence. I don't need bolstering."

Wind whistled through the boneyard, stirring dust and providing her only answer.

She finished tidying the rail car before climbing out to find Maldynado had left—to put on clothes, she hoped—and Basilard had returned. He sat in the vacated chair, arms draped over his knees, while he stared at the earth. The sun gleamed against his shaven head, highlighting the briar patch of scar tissue marring his scalp.

"Problem?" Amaranthe asked, thinking he appeared glummer than usual.

He flinched when she spoke, and she wondered what he had been thinking about. He only shook his head.

Amaranthe dragged a crate over so she could sit beside him.

"I'm glad you're here. You know that vacation I promised? We may need to work this week after all."

He did not react, did not even twitch a shoulder.

"Do you mind going with Books and Akstyr to do some nocturnal investigating tonight?"

This time Basilard did shrug. If it had been Akstyr, who had just turned eighteen, she might have understood the moody response, but Basilard usually gave people more respect and showed interest when she discussed missions.

"I've heard that talking about problems makes one feel better. I can keep confidences if you want to divulge any dark secrets." Amaranthe smiled, intending it as a joke, but Basilard studied her through narrowed eyes, as if he knew of the secrets in her life she had failed to keep. Or perhaps the ones she had kept and shouldn't have. Could he have found out about Sicarius's past in Mangdoria?

She shifted from foot to foot until she realized that made her look guilty. She forced herself to stop and clasped her hands behind her back.

You wouldn't understand, Basilard signed.

She let out a slow breath. That did not sound like something that had to do with revenge or deep-set anger.

"Maybe not," Amaranthe said, "but the nice thing about talking to other people is they don't have to do anything for you to feel better. They might just nod and grunt a few times. The feeling better part comes from speaking of the burdens you've been holding inside, things that weigh upon your soul." Hm, that sounded preachy. She decided she wasn't old enough or wise enough to mother these men, so bowed her head and backed away, intending to leave Basilard alone.

He stopped her and lifted a hand, swiping two fingers toward his chest.

"I don't know that sign yet," she said.

"Soul," he mouthed, and she understood since she'd just used the word. *Turgonians believe in soul?*

Amaranthe drew closer again. "Some do. The old religion speaks of an eternal soul that lives on after you die. All of our references to spirits and fallen ancestors come from that. Though Mad Emperor Motash worked his entire life to declare the old ways dead and atheism the only acceptable belief, er, disbelief, many still believe in guidance from ghosts of the past."

When you die, your soul goes where?

"Agormak, the Spirit Realm, supposedly. Although, through various ceremonies, dead ancestors can be called upon for advice, and people have claimed to see them in our realm."

No hell?

"Not like your people believe in, no. Though some say cowardly acts, especially suicide, destroy the soul, rendering it unavailable for consultation. One wonders what those priests were drinking when they sat around and thought up the rules."

Basilard's eyes widened, and Amaranthe winced. She forgot how much Mangdorians valued their religion and used its tenets to guide their lives.

"I'm sure your people's religion makes more sense than ours," she said by way of apology, but she worried she was sticking her foot deeper into her mouth. A stricken expression twisted Basilard's face. Yes, she was quite sure her big toe was brushing a tonsil. She coughed. "It's possible I was mistaken when I said talking to someone would make you feel better."

He snorted. It might have been a semi-amused snort. She hoped so.

Basilard considered her again, and she tried not to squirm. His eyes were not narrowed this time, but withholding Sicarius's past crimes in Mangdoria gave her a reason to feel guilty next to him, and she never forgot that.

Why The Emperor's Edge? he signed, surprising her.

That surprise must have shown on her face, for he clarified, *If you believe your soul safe, why risk your life over and over, trying to impress the emperor? Is it just for a pardon?*

"It's partially about clearing my name and partially about... trying to give happiness to someone who means a great deal to me. Also, it's about wanting a place in the history books. I used to think I could find that through being the first female enforcer to reach... Well, that's not going to happen now. Maybe it was never going to happen as long as I was following someone else's path, but now I've got my own path, and I believe again that I can make history." She chuckled. "It's all kinds of hubris, I know, but that's the imperial way. You either gain immortality through having children or you earn it by becoming someone history remembers. Despite Maldynado's attempts to set me up with a man, I have a feeling my odds of achieving the latter are better right now."

Basilard smiled briefly, but it did not reach his eyes. *I understand. It's good that you are making your own trail. I fear that's not an option for me. I believe my destination is chosen.*

"I thought you'd decided to work to end the underground slavery in the empire and to make things better for your people."

He poked a brick with his toe for a moment, shrugged, then stood. *Thank you,* he signed and went into the sleeping car.

Amaranthe sighed, not sure if she had helped, or that she knew how to help him.

A steam whistle blew, and workers streamed out of factories. Positioned between the industrial district and the shops and studios of the northern waterfront area, the old *Gazette* building overlooked one of the canals that flowed through the city. From the mouth of an alley across the waterway, Amaranthe, Sicarius, and Maldynado observed men exiting, shucking their single-breasted jackets and frock coats to walk home in the warm air.

Though evening had come, the sun still shone, offering

few shadows to cloak the alley. The idea of heading along the broad waterfront street and over the wide canal bridge made Amaranthe uneasy. This was part of her old patrol route, and any enforcers she ran into here would recognize her.

"It's not going to be a trap," Maldynado said. "I know this fellow. We used to fence together back before he took a spear in the hip at Amentar. He earned a medal of valor because he was leading the attack to save some border town and risked his life to save a bunch of children. He's a good, noble man."

"Good, noble people are the types who feel obligated to turn in outlaws," Amaranthe said, drawing an approving nod from Sicarius.

"He'll expect you to come in through the front," Sicarius said. "I'll see if there's another entrance."

He went down the alley instead of walking out the front, presumably choosing a route that would keep him out of sight.

"He'll probably find us a third-story window to crawl through," Maldynado muttered. "Look, I've had brandy with Deret twice since I became an outlaw. He hasn't turned me in yet. *And* he doesn't look down on me because I'm disowned. He's one of the few who don't."

"I'm sure he's a fine fellow," Amaranthe said. "We're just being cautious."

While they waited for Sicarius to return, the traffic leaving the front of the building dwindled. A pair of enforcers strode along the timeworn cobblestone street lining the canal, and Amaranthe eased deeper into the alley. An ordinary patrol, she told herself. Nothing that suggested they were conveniently around to play a role in a trap being sprung.

She nibbled on a finger, wondering if she was letting Sicarius's paranoia get to her.

"This way." Sicarius appeared at her shoulder.

Maldynado was the one to jump. "Always sneaking up on people," he muttered under his breath.

Without a word, Sicarius led them through the alley and

around the building to a ladder leading down to a ledge along the canal. Keelboats and cargo rafts floated up and down the waterway, but nobody paid attention to Amaranthe's team. The pilots were too busy navigating past houseboats, skiffs, and each other to watch the foot traffic.

Sicarius stopped at the base of one of the city's newer steel bridges and gripped one of the support beams. Legs dangling, he swung from handhold to handhold, like a monkey skimming through the treetops.

Amaranthe and Maldynado exchanged incredulous looks.

"Is he joking?" Maldynado asked. "Why can't we walk across the bridge?"

"Training?" Amaranthe guessed.

Sicarius, midway across, paused and peered back over his shoulder. "The top of the bridge is visible from *The Gazette's* upper windows."

"So?" Maldynado said.

"It would be unwise to let them see us coming." Sicarius returned to the climb, apparently considering the discussion over.

"Does he truly believe someone is sitting at a window, watching the bridge for your arrival?" Maldynado asked. "I didn't tell Deret you were *that* cute."

"Thanks," Amaranthe said dryly.

Sicarius had already reached the other side. Glad she had rejected Maldynado's suggestion that she wear a dress for the night, Amaranthe hopped and caught the girder. A couple of keelboats were coming; she had best not delay.

The smooth, cool steel did not make the most ideal handhold, but she navigated it without trouble. Sicarius's frequent obstacle-course runs had given her experience with awkward moves that relied on upper body strength, and she could perform as many pull-ups as the men. As many as Books and Akstyr anyway.

She landed with a grunt on the other side, and Maldynado soon plopped down behind her. Sicarius jogged a few meters and stopped above a storm-water-runoff grate on the canal wall beneath the ledge. Thanks to the recent dry weather, nothing flowed out of it. When he crouched to wait for the river traffic to dwindle, Amaranthe groaned.

"We're not going in there, are we?"

Sicarius dropped to his belly, fiddled with a lock, and opened the grate. He rolled off the ledge, twisting to land on his feet inside a tunnel that led inland from the canal.

"I think you're right," Maldynado said. "He's doing this because he can't pass up a chance to torment, er, train us."

"Come," Sicarius said, his voice sounding hollow in the concrete passage.

Amaranthe was starting to get the feeling he had a reason for this circuitous route, so she slithered off the ledge and into the tunnel without answering Maldynado. After sighing dramatically, he followed her. Sicarius closed the grate behind them and jogged into the darkness.

"I forgot to bring a torch," Maldynado said. "I wasn't aware you'd preface your date with a spelunking expedition."

Amaranthe headed up the tunnel at a slower pace, keeping one hand on the cool cement wall for guidance. Though dry, the surface sported frequent lumps of indeterminate fuzzy or squishy—or fuzzy *and* squishy—growth. She wiped her hand often, wishing she had a glove.

Fortunately, their subterranean trek did not last long. Light appeared ahead—Sicarius lifting an access cover. He slithered out before Amaranthe could ask where they would come up. Trusting him to guard the top, she jumped, caught the lip, and pulled herself out.

Sicarius crouched in the shadow of a steam lorry stamped with the newspaper's name. The travertine of the old *Gazette* building rose behind it. They were on the back side rather than the front, and no windows gazed out upon the alley. Closed loading bay doors loomed nearby, but nobody was shipping papers out this time of day.

Maldynado clambered out of the tunnel, and Sicarius closed the manhole cover.

"We did all that just so we could go in through the loading bay?" Maldynado asked.

"No." Sicarius pointed at a vent under the eaves of the four-story building. Before they could debate with him, he grabbed a ceramic drainpipe and started climbing.

Amaranthe shook her head in bemusement. "And you thought he'd settle for a *window*."

Maldynado groaned. "You *did* tell him this isn't one of our morning training sessions, right?"

Amaranthe headed for the drainpipe, wondering if she should put her foot down and say this was too ridiculous and that they would go in through the loading bay. Then something hard poked into the bottom of her shoe. She lifted her foot to check for a chunk of gravel. It wasn't a rock that had prodded her though; a shiny metal rifle ball rested in the groove between two cobblestones. A dark, fine powder sprinkled the ground. She swiped her finger through it and sniffed. Black powder.

"You're right." She picked up the rifle ball. "I don't think this *is* a training session."

Within city limits, firearms were forbidden to all except the military. Though it was true that gang members and criminals risked enforcer ire to carry pistols now and then, it was rare to see evidence of their use.

"Attic entry it is," she said, grabbing the pipe.

Maldynado issued another dramatic sigh. Sicarius had already unfastened the vent and disappeared inside. Amaranthe clambered up, amused that what would have once seemed an impossible climb did not cause her to break a sweat. She did have to perform an acrobatic lunge to launch herself from the pipe to the vent opening, but she had mastered the art of not looking down some time ago. She shimmied through and landed on a dusty, wood floor littered with owl pellets and rat droppings. Grimacing, she removed a kerchief from a pocket and wiped her hands.

Sicarius waited inside, close enough that he could have helped if she had needed it. He never presumed she would though. She liked that he trusted her to take care of herself, but it would have been considerate if he'd kept her from stepping in the dubious pile of... Was that *bat* guano?

Thanks to Maldynado's broad shoulders, he had more trouble squeezing through the vent opening. He grunted and pushed and cursed Sicarius's ancestors and finally plopped onto the floor.

Sicarius took the lead again, padding through a dusty maze that sprawled before them. Boxes and bundles of yellowed newspapers rose to the ceiling, creating twisting aisles that often ended without notice. Most of the clutter in the attic was what one might expect, though a stuffed grimbal head sat inexplicably under one window.

Sicarius's route led them to a trapdoor. He pressed his ear to the wood, then lifted it. After peering about, he dropped out of sight. Amaranthe waited for his signal, then followed him through.

As soon as she landed, she heard voices coming from below, but she could not make out words yet. No lanterns burned, but enough evening light angled through the windows to illuminate the area. They were on a broad balcony filled with book-laden shelves. The floor vibrated from printing presses at work somewhere below.

When Maldynado joined them, Sicarius headed toward the balcony railing. Before he reached it, he waved for them to drop to their bellies. On elbows and knees, Amaranthe crawled to the edge.

Two stories below, in a vast workspace open to the ceiling, rows of desks stretched from wall to wall. Only one was occupied. A man with dark, wavy hair sat before a stack of papers, head bowed, pencil scrawling, while a second fellow paced around him. The first wore civilian clothes, a cream-colored shirt and forest green vest, and he seemed to be doing his best to ignore the mutterings of the other. The second man had the same hair, though shorter, and wore black army fatigues, complete with a sword and pistol hanging from his belt.

Amaranthe squinted but could not make out the rank pins on the man's lapel.

"A lieutenant," Sicarius whispered, and she wondered when he had come to know her so well that he could guess at the thoughts behind her squints.

Maldynado wriggled up beside them. He pointed at the man at the desk and whispered, "That's Deret."

"Trap?" Amaranthe flicked a finger at the officer.

"Maybe not," Maldynado said. "I think that's Ferel Mancrest, one of Deret's brothers. There's an older one, too, but I think he's a captain. Ferel's probably in town for the Imperial Games and visiting his little brother."

"So he stopped to load a weapon in the alley?" Amaranthe whispered.

"Hm."

Down below, the officer leaned his hands onto the desk. "You said six, didn't you?"

"That's what Maldynado said." Deret kept working without looking up.

"That disowned drunken gigolo," the officer growled. "You'll be lucky if he gives her the right directions to find this place."

Maldynado's eyebrows rose. "*Drunken?*" he mouthed.

"Just don't shoot me with your grandiose plan," Deret said. "The army has already damaged me enough." He flicked a hand at a cane leaning against his desk.

"Don't be bitter because my C.O. didn't consult you. You let me know about her. You did your part."

"Wonderful."

"You don't need to be here. We'll—" The officer broke off and faced the balcony.

Amaranthe tensed, prepared to back away from the railing, but his eyes focused on something on his own floor. A soldier jogged into view, a rifle in hand. He saluted and clicked his heels together as he came to attention.

"Sir, Corporal Dansek checking in, sir. No change in status. The target has not been spotted yet. The men remain ready."

"Very well. Dismissed."

"The *men?*" Amaranthe whispered, turning an incredulous eye on Maldynado. "This *is* a trap."

Sicarius leveled a dark stare at him as well.

Maldynado's eyes widened. "I didn't know."

Amaranthe scooted back, gesturing for the others to follow her. They retraced their route in, not stopping until they reached the back alley again. Maldynado muttered to himself all the way out.

"I can't believe he'd betray my trust like that," he said.

Sicarius took a few steps toward the alley entrance, but Amaranthe caught his arm.

"Wait," she said. "Let's talk about this."

"You're not going in," he said, more an order than a question.

"Going in, no. That wouldn't be too smart if there's a squad of soldiers waiting to capture me."

"Then what is there to discuss?"

"This man could still be the ally we want him to be. It'll just take more work than we thought to sway him to our side." Amaranthe smiled.

"Dear ancestors," Maldynado said. "You already have a new scheme in mind."

"Nothing big. Maldynado, I need you to do a little shopping, then you can meet the others at the stadium and let them know we'll be late. Sicarius and I will be arranging a kidnapping."

Maldynado scratched his head. "A kidnapping that requires... shopping?"

"One must be prepared." Amaranthe smiled again.

CHAPTER 3

"What are all these slagging enforcers doing here?" Akstyr slouched against a tree and glowered at the grounds where athletes mingled, roaming from the barracks to the baths and to various eating and shopping tents.

Books stood beside the tree as well, though he was scribbling something in a notebook and paying little attention to the scene before them. As far as Basilard could tell, serious training had ended for the day, but the evening was young enough that few of the athletes were heading for the barracks. More enforcers than one would expect patrolled the grounds.

"We're not going to be able to investigate a cigar butt without getting spotted," Akstyr went on.

In the fading light, Basilard exaggerated his signs so Books and Akstyr could read them. *We're only supposed to see if magic is being used. We don't need to get close or talk to anyone.*

"Cursed enforcers will bug me just because of my brand." Akstyr lifted a fist to display the arrow mark scored into the skin on the back of his hand. That seemed less likely to get him harassed than the greased ridge of spiky hair bisecting his head and the baggy mismatched clothing any enforcer would assume he stole—probably correctly.

"Then keep your hands in your pockets," Books said.

Where should we start? Basilard asked.

"I believe I'll observe from here," Books said. "You two lads are young enough to pass as athletes, but with my gray hairs, nobody will believe I'm in the competition."

Basilard lifted his eyebrows, amused at being called a lad. He was close to thirty-five and had a bald spot it would take a beaver pelt to cover. All the scars made the hair on the sides grow in patchy, so he simply kept his whole head shaven.

"That and the fact you can't walk more than ten steps without tripping over something," Akstyr said.

"I'm not *that* clumsy." Books tucked his notebook into a pocket.

A gaggle of young women Akstyr's age walked past, their sleeveless togs displaying enough flesh to stir one's imagination. Akstyr straightened and touched his hair, as if to ensure it was still suitably spiky.

Basilard signed a comment for Books, *I'm surprised your empire lets girls compete. Larocka and Arbitan did not have women fight.*

"They're permitted to enter the running events and the Clank Race," Books said. "Not wrestling or boxing. Women have never been allowed to fight in the empire. As to the rest, the historical precedent is interesting. In the old days, warrior caste men would come to the Imperial Games to hunt for brides. The women who won the events were presumed to be most likely to birth sons who would become superior warriors. The original awards ceremony involved interested men coming out to compete for the winners. Bloodshed was often involved. Sometimes death. I understand there are some warrior-caste men who still come with the intent of shopping for brides, but the women are less likely to be interested these days. They want to start shops or wide-ranging businesses, using the status and honor they gain from their victories to assist in their endeavors. We live in a fascinating time, I must say."

"Look at the chest on that one." Akstyr pointed at a woman trotting to catch up with comrades. "I'd watch her run a race anytime."

"Fascinating for some of us anyway," Books muttered. "Akstyr, why don't you go look for magic. That's why we're here, right?"

Akstyr shrugged and ambled off.

Basilard had wanted to talk to the younger man alone and saw his chance. *I'll go, too, and see if all these enforcers are here about the missing people or Sicarius.* Amaranthe had briefed Basilard, Books, and Akstyr on the morning's events.

He jogged to catch up with Akstyr, and they took the path that meandered around the grounds. A nervous flutter teased his gut, and he did not start a conversation immediately. If he guessed incorrectly, and Akstyr tattled on him, he would be a dead man.

They avoided the crowded areas as they walked. Basilard could not tell if Akstyr was checking for signs of magic use or simply ogling female athletes. They veered into the shadows to avoid a pair of enforcers marching in their direction.

"They're all over the place," Akstyr said when the men had passed, "and as annoying as flies on dung."

Perhaps it's because Sicarius was supposedly spotted this morning, Basilard signed, seeing a chance to bring up the topic he wanted to discuss.

"I guess," Akstyr said. Unless one was talking about the mental sciences, he was a hard man to draw into a conversation.

Basilard tried again. *I wonder why that man impersonated Sicarius. Especially when it only got him killed.*

"Because he was stupid," Akstyr said.

Someone paid him perhaps.

"Not enough."

Yes, even if the enforcers did not kill him, Sicarius himself might have...for having the audacity to impersonate him.

"Probably."

Basilard gritted his teeth. With the conversation going nowhere, he decided to drop it, but then Akstyr gave him a lead-in.

"I hate him sometimes."

Sicarius?

They stepped into the shadows behind a food tent to avoid more enforcers.

"Sometimes he kind of seems all right," Akstyr said. "Like he stood up for me once when we went to see my old boss, but I think that was on account of Am'ranthe and not because he cares if I live or die."

Likely, Basilard signed, but he did not know if Akstyr could see his hand codes in the gloaming light.

"But I hate when he climbs all over our backs just because we aren't good enough at his dumb exercises. I want to be—" Akstyr caught himself and lowered his voice. "Well, you know what I want to be. I don't care about running and swords and obstacle courses. You can't object though or he threatens you. He's such a cold bastard."

Basilard drew Akstyr around the side of the tent where there was more light. Raised fire pits illuminated tables and benches where men and women chatted over tea and cider.

He lifted his hands to sign the next question. A bead of sweat dribbled down his spine. *Do you ever think of...collecting his bounty?*

"Oh, dead deranged ancestors, yes." Akstyr laughed. "Don't you?"

The blatant admission surprised Basilard, and his fingers hung still for a moment before he could sign a response. *Maybe.*

"Bas, you don't know how bad I want to get out of this balls-sucking sinkhole of an empire. I'm tired of having to hide all my...interests, and I can't find anyone to teach me, and people here would shoot you just for—" Akstyr's voice tightened, and he cleared his throat.

Basilard had not realized how passionate the boy was about learning the mental sciences.

"If I had a million ranmyas," Akstyr said, naming the price on Sicarius's head, "I could get out of here. I could go to Kendor or the Kyatt Islands and hire a teacher, and nobody would care 'cause it's *normal* there."

Basilard nodded. Though money would do nothing for his predicament, it made sense to encourage Akstyr's fantasy if he wanted him for an ally.

"But it'd be a dumb move," Akstyr said. "He'd kill you in a heartbeat if he thought you were serious about it. And how would you get him anyway? He never sleeps, and he won't eat anything we cook unless he's seen everyone else eat it first."

Yes, Basilard had already considered the fact that he prepared more meals for the group than anyone else. He knew of numerous herbs that could incapacitate or even kill. But Sicarius never ate his stews or soups, nor did he drink anything besides water. Basilard was not sure if it represented paranoia or simply dietary preferences. He'd never seen Sicarius eat anything except fruits, vegetables, nuts, and plainly prepared fish or meat. Basilard thought he *might* try something Amaranthe offered, but his stomach turned at the idea of using her to get to him. It would devastate her to be the instrument of his death, and Basilard did not want to hurt her.

One would have to be extremely careful, Basilard signed. *Perhaps there's some...magic?*

Akstyr's forehead furrowed. He glanced around—three times—then lowered his voice. "Are you actually thinking of doing this?"

Maybe.

"What'd he do to you? I thought you got along with him better than anyone except Am'ranthe."

Basilard debated whether or not to share his reason. Akstyr would care nothing about the deaths of the Mangdorian royal family—he probably wouldn't even be outraged at the idea that Sicarius had killed children—but he might understand why Basilard would be committed and trust him not to back out or cross him.

Remember that note in the Mangdorian shaman's hideout?

"Yes," Akstyr said.

I recently learned that fifteen years ago, Sicarius was the one responsible for the assassination of my rulers.

"Oh. Huh." Akstyr stuffed his hands into his deep pockets and prodded a tuft of grass with his boot. "If I found a way to make him sleep, would you do the deed?"

Yes.

"And I'd get half the money?"

You can have it all.

Akstyr's eyes bulged. "Really?"

Yes.

"Well, maybe we could look into things a little. You gotta swear not to say anything to anyone though. Maldynado and Books wouldn't get on this locomotive."

Agreed. You make same promise?

"Oh, I'm not saying a word."

As they left the side of the tent and the tables full of happily chattering people, Basilard wondered if he had taken the first step down a path that would result in his death. The idea of death terrified him, especially since that priestess had confirmed he had no chance of avoiding eternity in Ethor, but shouldn't he at least go out striking a blow of justice for his people?

Amaranthe nibbled on a fingernail. She hid in the shadows behind a street vendor's cart while she waited for Maldynado. Almost a half of an hour had passed since he disappeared into the busy market. She needed to get back before the Mancrests left the *Gazette* building.

Though twilight had settled in, the throng of shoppers had yet to wane. Gas lamps shone light onto the vegetable stands, smoked meat carts, and tables displaying candles, soaps, and flower bundles. Across the street from Amaranthe, a man and woman were selling freshly roasted walnuts and almonds doused in cinnamon and sugar. Her mouth watered, reminding her it had been a long time since breakfast.

Maldynado ambled into view with bulging canvas bags draped over both arms.

Amaranthe stared at the sizable haul. "You were just supposed to get flatbread and cheese," she said when he joined her. "Maybe a cheap jug of applejack."

"You do *not* know how to prepare a romantic dinner." He poked through his bags. "I got you red wine, Anduvian rolls, quiche, fresh herbs and greens, carrots, parsnips, cider vinegar, and walnut oil—you can make a lovely salad. Oh, and cedarwood scented candles. Those promote stamina." He wiggled his brows.

"First off, I'm not romancing the man. He tried to turn me over to the army tonight. Second, how did you get all that? I only gave you five ranmyas."

"That's right, you did." Maldynado rearranged the bags, fished in a pocket, and pulled out a five-ranmya bill. "Here's your change. I got it all for free. Samples, you see, on account of the lavish spread my mother is planning. If she likes what she tries, she'll put in a huge order for her annual summer tea party."

"This is the mother who hasn't spoken to you in a year?" Amaranthe asked.

"Closer to two." Maldynado winked and started loading bags onto her arms, but paused midway through. "Maybe I should go with you and help set things up. You're a capable woman in general, but I'm not convinced you have the necessary experience to seduce a man."

"I'm not *seducing* anyone." She took the remaining bags

from him. "I'm just trying to talk him into listening to my story and publishing the truth about our adventures."

"I got you today's copy of *The Gazette*, too. You might want to see if he's got an article in it. Then you can talk to him about it. Men love it when you're interested in their work. And sports. Do you know anything about the athletes entering the wrestling? You could—"

"*Thank* you, Maldynado." Amaranthe did not quite manage to keep the exasperation out of her voice. "I've got to get back before he leaves the office."

"You're certain you don't want me to come?"

"I'm certain."

"At the least, I feel I should go along and punch him in the nose a couple of times for betraying me and trying to ensnare you. That's not a gentlemanly thing to do."

"No need. Go check on the others. Books will be bored without you." Amaranthe strode away at a brisk pace before he could burble more.

"That *is* true," was the last thing she heard him say.

With the bags in hand, she headed toward the canal where she had left Sicarius watching the *Gazette* building. Though she appreciated Maldynado's enthusiasm for planning her evening—sort of—his shopping trip had taken her away for longer than expected. If Lord Mancrest left before she returned, Sicarius was supposed to follow him and find out where he lived, but Amaranthe worried that sending Sicarius off after a man he loathed might not be wise.

Deepening twilight made it easier to travel without worry of being recognized, and she was almost jogging by the time she reached the canal. Lamps brightened the street paralleling the waterway, but shadows obscured the alcoves and alleys. She headed for the niche where she had left Sicarius, but a figure stepped out of a doorway before she reached it.

Two figures. One threw back the hood of a lantern with a clank, and light flared.

Amaranthe squinted and stepped back.

Two enforcers stood before her, one a sergeant holding a sword and the lantern, and the other a young private aiming a repeating crossbow at her chest.

"Can I help you gentlemen?" she asked, hoping they had not identified her for certain yet. Across the canal, the windows of the *Gazette* building were dark. If the Mancrests had left, Sicarius would be gone, too, following Deret home. No chance for help.

"Former Corporal Amaranthe Lokdon," the sergeant said.

So much for not being identified.

"We were told you might be in the area tonight."

Idiot, she cursed herself. She should have assumed Mancrest would tip off the enforcers as well as his brother in the army.

"Who?" Amaranthe asked innocently. "You must have the wrong person." It was worth a try. She hefted the shopping bags. "I'm heading home to prepare a dinner for the young man who's courting me."

Footsteps sounded behind her. Steel rasped—a sword being drawn—followed by the thunk of a crossbow lever being set. She peeked behind her, verifying that two more enforcers stood less than ten paces away. One she recognized, Corporal Riek, a man she had worked with before. Not good.

The sergeant snorted. "Who's courting you? Sicarius?"

"We know who you are Lokdon," the crossbowman in front of her said. "You worked with us until you turned traitor."

Right, no chance of convincing them they had the wrong person.

"Do it," the sergeant told the crossbowman.

The weapon came up, quarrel aiming at Amaranthe's chest, and the meaning of "do it" became clear.

"Sicarius," Amaranthe blurted.

"What?" The crossbowman and the sergeant looked around.

Amaranthe might have taken the moment to run and fling herself into the canal, but it was a dozen paces away, and the two men behind her surely had her targeted.

"Sicarius *is* in the neighborhood," she said. "And he's more of a reward than I am, isn't he?"

The sergeant scowled at her. "We're not in this for a reward. Taking down criminals is our job, a job *you* once shared."

"I know you wouldn't be granted a monetary reward," Amaranthe said, glad she had him talking. Talking to her was far superior to shooting her. "But surely promotions have been offered." She remembered how much the promise of a promotion had meant to her once—it was the reward Hollowcrest had dangled to get her to go after Sicarius all those months ago.

The men exchanged glances. Soft murmurs came from the enforcers behind her.

"Out of curiosity, has a promotion been offered for me?" Amaranthe said.

"Killing you, or bringing you in, is worth a positive commendation," the sergeant said.

"And Sicarius?"

"A promotion to captain."

If not for the bags in Amaranthe's hands she would have propped her fists on her hips. "I'm only worth a positive mark in your record, and getting *him* can leapfrog you straight to captain?"

The crossbowman laughed. "Jealous?"

The sergeant glared at him, and he forced his features into a more professional expression. That's right, Amaranthe thought, chat with me, laugh at me, and think I'm a friend and not someone you want to kill....

"Look," she said, "I don't want to die tonight. I know you gentlemen have no reason to believe it, but I wasn't the one who kidnapped the emperor. I helped free him in fact. You should be looking up an outfit called Forge."

The sergeant was shaking his head, and he lifted a hand, as if to give an order. Yes, that tactic was worthless.

"But regardless," Amaranthe blurted, rushing to out-speak the man, "I can take you to Sicarius. In exchange for my life. I'll show you his latest hideout."

"You wouldn't betray an ally."

"Come, now, if you believe I betrayed the empire and the enforcers, why would you think I wouldn't turn in an assassin? It's not like he's a friendly, cuddly fellow who I share a deep, meaningful relationship with."

Though it was her intent, it saddened her in a wry way that the argument seemed to sway the men. At the least, they nodded in agreement. Who could have a meaningful relationship with a callous assassin?

"We can't let you go, Lokdon," the sergeant said.

"And we don't have enough men to take down Sicarius," the crossbowman said with a shudder.

The sergeant glared at him again.

"You don't have to let me go," Amaranthe said. "Just don't shoot me. Take me to the magistrate, and I'll plead my case to him. I'm sure you'll still get your commendation. And then there's the potential of that captaincy...." She met the sergeant's eyes. He would be the one who would make the decision—and who stood to earn the reward. "Big pay increase, huh? And an honor as well. It's true Sicarius is a dangerous man, but he won't likely be there right now. It's night...the time when he does his work. I can show you his hideout, and you can come back tomorrow with more men. Attack him while he's sleeping."

"I don't know...." The sergeant scratched his jaw.

She had him. She sensed it. A little more, and she could sway him.

"Wasn't he seen on the Imperial Games grounds?" Amaranthe asked.

The sergeant's chin came up. "This morning, yes. What was he doing there? Do you know?"

"I'm not privy to all his whims," Amaranthe said, "but if he *did* have some mischief planned..." She shrugged. "I'm sure you'd feel bad if he hurt someone there, and you knew you'd had the chance to take him down before it all happened."

The sergeant glowered. He had to know she was trying to manipulate him, but her argument was persuasive—she hoped.

"If I agree to take you to the magistrate," the sergeant said, "and to have you show us this hideout, will you give me your word you aren't walking us into a trap?"

"A trap?" How could she be walking them into a trap, when they'd been the ones to ensnare her? She almost blurted, 'Of course,' but stopped herself. If Sicarius saw her being escorted by these men, he would attack them without thinking twice, and he might kill somebody. She frowned at her thoughts. *Might?* Sicarius *would* kill somebody.

"I'm aware of what happened to Corporal Wholt and his team when he tried to arrest you," the sergeant said coolly.

The crossbowman scowled, finger tightening on the trigger of his weapon. She wished nobody had mentioned that incident. They would be more wary while escorting her now.

"They tried to kill me," Amaranthe said. "That whole night was...unfortunate."

"I'll say," the sergeant said. More murmurs came from the men behind her. "Your word. You're not walking us into a trap?"

Strange that her word meant something to him. She lifted her chin and announced loudly—loudly enough Sicarius would hear if he was nearby, "You have my word I'm not walking you into a trap."

She hoped that was true. Fortunately, he had not made her swear she would not try to escape. That was more on her mind, and she had better do it before Sicarius showed up. Having more enforcer blood on her hands would be intolerable. She could not pretend she was some noble hero working for the good of the empire if her actions resulted in dead citizens.

"Check her bags," the sergeant said.

"Want to carry them for me?" Amaranthe asked the young

private who came forward to rifle through them. She hoped he would be less likely to confiscate them if she made it sound like it would be a favor. "They're getting heavy."

"Carry them yourself, outlaw," the private said.

Good.

"Just food and wine, sergeant," the private announced.

"Wine?" came a speculative inquiry from the crossbowman. "Maybe we should confiscate that."

"Focus on your duty," the sergeant told him in a clipped tone. "Get going," he said to Amaranthe.

With two enforcers marching behind her, crossbows trained on her back, and one man on either side, Amaranthe led the way down the street. She doubted she could meander through the city for long before they grew suspicious about her ability to take them to this fictitious hideout.

She considered her surroundings, searching for inspiration. Couples walked past, hand in hand, enjoying the pleasant evening. Now and then, crowds of university students or off-duty soldiers sauntered down the street, their voices boisterous with drink. Everyone turned curious eyes toward the enforcer procession as it passed, but nobody gave Amaranthe anything to work with.

She decided to stay on the street paralleling the canal. If no better option presented itself, she might be able to distract her captors long enough to sprint to the side and jump in. Of course, she might also get her back peppered with quarrels if she tried that tactic. Even if she made it in, the gas lamps from the street shone onto the water, creating yellow pools that provided enough light for a crossbowman to see a head pop up and to shoot at it.

Ahead lay the bridge her team had crossed under earlier. She thought of the grate Sicarius had unlocked. He had closed it, she remembered, but nobody had bothered to re-lock it. If she could get to it, maybe she could sprint through that tunnel and out the other side, then lose the enforcers in the city. How, though? Jump into the canal, swim to the grate, open it, climb in, and run? That seemed like an eternity where she would be a target to the crossbowmen—if she could get past them long enough to jump over the railing to start with.

Most of the boat traffic had dwindled with twilight's arrival, though a keelboat floated past now and then. Lanterns lit up one heading upriver, with six pole-bearers striding along the sides in sync, pushing the vessel with their long staves. It would float under the bridge before long. If Amaranthe slowed her pace, she might be able to time a trip over the canal at the same time as the keelboat passed below.

"Hold up, please." Without waiting for permission, she lowered the bags to the ground and made a show of shaking out her hands. "These are heavy." She moved a couple of items from one bag to the other.

A boot thumped against her backside. "Get going."

She picked up the bags one at a time, watching the approach of the vessel. That should do it.

"This way." Amaranthe headed for the bridge. "He's in the attic of a factory over on Sankel Street."

The enforcers followed without comment. Her heart lurched into double time as she considered the escape. She might very well get herself shot. Or she might break a leg jumping off the bridge. Or they might simply follow her and capture her. This was foolish. She should wait for a better opportunity. But there might not be one.

They started up the bridge as the keelboat approached.

A harsh smell wafted through the air. She sniffed, trying to identify it. Varnish.

She eyed the houseboats tied on either side of the canal. It was hard to tell in the dim light, but she spotted something that may have been brushes, drop cloths, and a tin of varnish on the deck of a floating home.

Between one step and the next her plan changed.

Amaranthe slipped a hand into one of the bags, hoping

Maldynado had been complete with his shopping. What good were stamina-promoting candles without matches to light them?

As they reached the apex of the bridge, the sergeant moved a step closer, a shrewd gaze upon her. He must have noticed the keelboat and guessed at her plan.

Well, she had a new plan now. Down at the bottom of the bag, past the vegetables, wine bottles, and candles, she found what she sought—a couple of sturdy wooden matches. While thanking Maldynado for overly thorough shopping, she slid them out.

When they passed the apex without Amaranthe attempting to leap onto the keelboat, the sergeant's attention shifted forward again.

She found a round tin can in the bag. Some fancy spread? It didn't matter. As they neared the bottom of the bridge, and the floating home in the process of being refinished, Amaranthe tossed the item down the slope.

"Oops," she said, "dropped something."

She bent, as if to try to catch it before it could roll away, and launched a backward kick into the enforcer who had been walking on her right. At the same time, she jabbed an elbow into the sergeant's gut. Without waiting for them to gather their thoughts, she vaulted over the railing.

Though she anticipated the drop, it stole her breath. With the water low this time of year, she fell twelve or fifteen feet before hitting the roof. She rolled to keep from breaking an ankle, but got tangled up with the shopping bags, and an ill-placed stove vent made the landing even more painful.

Shouts sounded above. A crossbow quarrel thudded into the roof.

Amaranthe scrambled over the side, landing on the deck near the finishing equipment. She found the varnish and unscrewed the tin.

Thumps came from the roof—the enforcers following her down.

"Over here!" one shouted.

She dumped the varnish all about and struck a match. She dropped it in the liquid and darted around the corner of the house. Flames flared to life behind her.

"Wait, don't go down!"

"She started a cursed fire!"

Amaranthe hurled a deck chair into the water under the bridge, hoping the enforcers would think the splash resulted from her diving in. As she eased around another corner, she silently apologized to the poor homeowner whose house she was vandalizing. Maybe she could send money later.

"Did she go overboard?"

"I heard a splash. There!"

"Somebody get a bucket! This fire is—" The order broke off in a round of coughing.

Hoping they were all peering into the water under the bridge, Amaranthe slipped up a ladder leading to the ledge along the canal. She skimmed through the shadows to the grate. It remained unlocked. She eased over the side and alighted in the tunnel.

When she leaned out to pull the grate shut, she glimpsed the fire she had started, and she gaped. The flames had spread to the wall and roof of the home. The intensity of the light illuminated the canal and turned the water a burnished orange. People on the street were gathering. If the enforcers did not give up their search and send someone to alert the Imperial Fire Brigade, the owners of that house would lose everything.

She pulled the grate shut, pausing to lean her head against the cold bars. "Dumb move," she whispered. Yes, she had escaped, but at what cost? She didn't have the kind of money it would take to reimburse the homeowners.

Amaranthe straightened, and a wine bottle in the bag clunked against the iron bars. How she had managed to keep the silly groceries with her she did not know.

She turned her back on the canal, and the devastation she had wrought, and ran up the tunnel.

In the alley behind the newspaper building, she checked both directions before crawling out of the passage. Careful to do it quietly, she eased the manhole cover back into place. She stood, then jumped with surprise when she found a shadow looming next to her.

"It's me," Sicarius said before she could think of flinging a shopping bag at him.

"Thank the emperor," she breathed. "We need to go." She trotted to the nearest street.

"Yes." He fell into step beside her, and they headed away from the canal. Shouts rang out behind them—people yelling at others to help or run for the fire brigade. "I saw the enforcers," he said.

Great. Another witness to her arson, though he would probably approve of such tactics. That didn't make her feel better.

They jogged past rows of factories, dormant for the night, and crossed into a residential neighborhood. Several blocks into it, on the edge of a park, Amaranthe dared to stop to catch her breath and collect herself. She dropped the canvas bags, hardly caring if she damaged something. The bottle of wine rolled out and bumped to a stop against a tree root.

"What happened after I left?" she asked. "Did you follow Mancrest?"

"Yes. An army lorry rolled into the alley and picked up two squads of soldiers. The Mancrests left out the front. They parted ways, and I followed the journalist to his house." Sicarius eyed the shopping bags. "You still wish to speak with him?"

"Yes." Amaranthe snorted. More than ever she needed to make friends with Mancrest. "I need someone to squash the front-page headline I foresee hitting the papers tomorrow: Notorious Criminal Amaranthe Lokdon Commits Arson on the 17th Street Canal."

"That can be arranged," Sicarius said, though he hesitated before saying it, as if he was not certain they were thinking of the same way that deed could be done. Good guess.

"Not with threats of pain," Amaranthe said. "Or actual pain."

He said nothing.

She crouched, putting her back to an oak, and looked up at him. Streetlights burned at both ends of the park, but full night had fallen, and darkness hid Sicarius's face. His black clothing made it hard to pick him out, even a few feet away.

"Out of all the enforcers you've...killed..." She had a hard time saying that. Whatever happened, she had still been an enforcer for nearly seven years, and it was painful to think of harm coming to her old colleagues. "Out of all of them, did you ever start the fight? Or was it all just a matter of them trying to kill you?"

"If I perceived them as a threat, I eliminated them."

"But you never saw a couple of patrollers strolling down the street and decided, oh, yes, there need to be fewer enforcers in the world, so I'm going to leave the shadows and stick a knife in their backs?"

"You know I did not," Sicarius said, a hint of reproach in his normally emotionless voice.

"I know. Sorry. I'm just trying to figure this out." She dropped her head in her hands and dug her fingers into her scalp. She liked to think she was bright, but maybe she was just delusional. She ought to have been able to escape without wreaking havoc. If she truly were smart, she would not have been captured in the first place. But as long as they worked in the city, and went out and about to pursue missions, it seemed unlikely she could successfully avoid the enforcers every minute of every day. She needed them to look the other way, but her stomach clenched at the idea of blackmail or any strong-arming. "How can I make them understand that I'm on their side and they don't need to try to capture me, no matter what the bounty says? I feel like we made some progress with that water scheme, but again so few people know we were involved. And every time something like this happens—" she waved back toward the canal, "—it's a step backward. I'm not sure they'll ever forgive me for what happened to Wholt and those other enforcers." She thought of her discussion with Basilard and wondered if she was delusional for believing she could find a place in the history books as a hero. "Maybe I should give up on heroics and become a villain. The money's better, I hear, and you're a fine example of how easy it is to become notorious. *You're* probably guaranteed a place in the history books."

She sighed and dropped to her knees to grab the wine bottle and shove it back in the bag. "All right, I'm done whining. Thank you for listening."

In the dim lighting, she did not at first notice when Sicarius grabbed one bag and extended a hand for the second. She gave it to him. She was cursed tired of carrying the things anyway. Maybe he knew that. He surprised her by offering his hand again, this time to grip her arm and help her up.

"Hm," she said. "If I'd known it would result in you carrying things for me, I'd have moaned and complained to you more often."

"Easy?" he said as they headed off down the tree-lined street.

"What?"

"You think it's easy to become notorious?"

"Well." She managed a faint smile. "You make it look easy."

"Huh."

CHAPTER 4

"Top floor, eh?" Amaranthe followed Sicarius to one of only two doors in a short hallway. The one they stopped in front of was made of stout oak and featured a hand-carved image of a spear-toting man hunting a bear alongside a tree-lined river.

"Yes," Sicarius said.

Since Mancrest was warrior caste, it made sense that he would have the resources to own a flat that took up half of the floor. What surprised her was that he lived in a neighborhood full of university students and modest-income families, in a building that lacked a doorman in the lobby to keep out riffraff. Maybe as a journalist, he favored being in the heart of the city.

Amaranthe took the grocery bags from Sicarius. "Thank you. Do you want to wait outside while I—"

"No."

"No?"

"He may have a limp, but he's a former officer. He'll be a dangerous opponent."

"No doubt," Amaranthe said, "but I'm not planning to fight him. Also, I find it difficult to...sway people to my way of thinking when you're holding knives to their throats. That tends to render one unwilling to believe my entreaties of friendship."

Sicarius's only response was to knock on the door.

"You have an amazing knack for being almost personable one moment and, er, yourself the next."

He said nothing.

Uneven footsteps and the rhythmic thump of a cane on a hard floor sounded on the other side of the door. Sicarius took up a position against the wall. She wanted to tell him not to jump out and put a knife to Mancrest's throat, but the door opened too soon.

Amaranthe had a glimpse of short, wavy brown hair, a strong jaw, and spectacles before Mancrest realized who she was and reacted.

He jumped back, whipping his cane up. A click sounded, and the wood flew away from the handle. Amaranthe dropped the groceries and flung an arm up to block the projectile, but Sicarius blurred past her.

He caught the flying cane and tackled Mancrest. Something—steel?—clattered to the floor.

In the half of a second it took Amaranthe to realize she could lower her arms, the skirmish was over. Mancrest lay sprawled face-first on the floor with Sicarius on top, pinning him. She cringed. At least knives were not involved. Yet.

"Good evening, Lord Mancrest." Amaranthe picked up her bags and the hollow husk of the cane. She spotted the handle attached to a rapier on the floor inside the threshold. Sword stick. "I thought we had a dinner date. Was my invitation received in error?"

Having his face pressed into the floor muffled his response.

"Pardon?" Amaranthe stepped inside, closing the door behind her. "Sicarius, would you mind letting him up, please?"

Sicarius yanked him to his feet, keeping Mancrest's arms pinned behind his back. A pained grimace twisted Mancrest's face, and his spectacles dangled from one ear.

Amaranthe waved for Sicarius to loosen the hold. He did not.

"I apologize for being tardy at your proposed meeting place," Amaranthe said, "but there appeared to be a squad of soldiers lurking inside. What do you suppose they were doing there?"

Mancrest glowered and said nothing.

"Maldynado seems to think you're an honorable fellow," Amaranthe said, "and even knowing that you arranged to have me captured, or killed I suppose, he still thinks I should talk to you." Actually, according to Maldynado's candle selection, he thought they should do more than *talk*.

"I *am* honorable," Mancrest said, voice strained as he fought to stifle grimaces of pain that flashed across his face. "That's why I tried to arrange your capture."

Sicarius stood a couple of inches shorter than Mancrest, but Amaranthe had no trouble meeting his eyes over the bigger man's shoulder. "Let go," she mouthed.

At first he did not, but she held his gaze for a long moment, and he finally searched Mancrest for other weapons and released him. Mancrest took a couple of careful steps away from them, trying to hide his limp, but the stiffness of his movements gave it away. He positioned himself so his back was no longer to Sicarius.

Amaranthe assembled his sword stick and extended it toward him. Mancrest considered it—and her—for several long seconds before accepting it. He rested the tip on the floor, though he did not lean on it.

Despite what must be a permanent injury, he appeared fit. The rolled-up sleeves of his creamy shirt revealed muscular forearms. As Maldynado had promised, Mancrest had a handsome face, though what might have been pain lines creased his eyes and the corners of his mouth, making him appear a few years older than he probably was.

"I guess it's good I didn't dress up for you then." She hefted the bags. "Hungry? Mind if I find some plates?"

"Depends." Mancrest was spending more time watching Sicarius than her. "Will three be dining or just two?"

"Ah, I believe my provisions were gathered with a pair in mind." She gave an apologetic shrug to Sicarius. "Maldynado did the shopping."

Sicarius wore his usual guess-my-thoughts-if-you-can mask, though she sensed he did not approve. Of dinner or the entire situation? She did not know.

"Where shall I set up?" she asked Mancrest.

Masculine leather chairs and sofas, a desk, and a gaming table occupied the main room, but nothing looked like a dining area. A half dozen doors marked the brick and wood walls, none of them with any enlightening ornamentation that proclaimed, "Kitchen this way."

Mancrest jerked his head toward one in the back. "In there."

At least he was cooperating. That was a good start, right?

Amaranthe headed for the door. As she passed through, she noticed she had picked up a shadow.

"I don't think he's going to try anything right now," she whispered to Sicarius who was already taking up a post against the wall beside a long dining table made from a single thick slab of wood. "He must be curious about what I have to say. He's a journalist, after all."

Mancrest stepped through the door, veering the opposite direction from Sicarius.

"May I get you a drink?" he asked, pointedly not looking at Sicarius or including him in the offer.

Amaranthe pulled out the wine bottle. "Just a corkscrew."

Mancrest examined the bottle. Checking the label to see if it met with his refined warrior-caste palette? No, she realized. He was seeing if the seal had been broken.

"Nothing's poisoned. If we wanted you dead, that would have happened by now." She did not nod toward Sicarius; she didn't figure she had to.

"Oh, yes, I'm sure your assassin could have arranged that," Mancrest said, "but I figured you might have a lesser punishment in mind and have arranged for some gut-wrenching vomiting or emergency movements from the other end."

"You must have courted some vindictive women," Amaranthe said.

Mancrest grunted, set the wine bottle down, and headed for a door that presumably led to a kitchen.

"Plates, too," Amaranthe suggested.

Sicarius detached himself from the wall to follow.

Mancrest paused and stared at him. "Unless you know where I left my corkscrew, I don't need your help."

Sicarius followed him into the kitchen anyway, probably thinking Mancrest might have a pistol or two on the premises. If she ever did go out with a man for non-work-related reasons, she would have to figure out a way to leave Sicarius home. Of course, if he'd ever deign to take her out for non-work-related reasons, that would suffice as well.

Amaranthe laid out Maldynado's food choices, trying to arrange the bread and pastries in such a way that one might not immediately notice their battered state. Given what these groceries had gone through to arrive here, she was happy nothing was poisoned with varnish.

She had forgotten Maldynado stashed a newspaper in a bag, too, and she glanced over it. Mancrest did have an article on the front page. Apparently the winners of each of the events in the Imperial Games would be invited to dinner with the emperor.

"Wish I could enter," she muttered. With all the training the team did, she was more fit than she had ever been. Though she had never been tall enough to have a chance at the sprints, where the long-legged women excelled, she had won medals for the middle- and long-distance races as a junior. Unfortunately, any race she ran these days would end with enforcers taking her into custody—or worse.

A crash sounded in the other room—a big one.

Amaranthe lunged around the table, a vision of Sicarius mashing Mancrest with a meat cleaver stampeding into her head. She shoved the swinging door open. A drawer lay on the floor beside a butcher-block island; cutlery and silverware scattered the travertine tiles. One wicked serrated knife had somehow struck a cabinet door with such force that it protruded from the wood, handle still quivering.

Sicarius had Mancrest bent over the island, his cheek smashed into the butcher block, his arm chicken-winged behind his back, fingers jerked up so high he could have braided his own hair, were it long enough. Maldynado would have had an innuendo-laden comment about the men's positioning. Amaranthe only propped her hands on her hips and said, "Problem?"

"No," Sicarius said.

"Yes!" Mancrest cried. "I was just trying to get silverware out."

"Is it possible you're being a touch jumpy?" Amaranthe asked Sicarius.

He kicked something on the floor behind the island. An ivory-handled pistol skidded across the tiles and bumped against the fallen drawer.

Amaranthe picked it up. The hammer was cocked. She lifted the frizzen, and powder poured out of the pan.

"I forgot it was there," Mancrest said, voice muffled by the fact his cheek was still mashed against the butcher block.

"Really?" Amaranthe asked, prepared to give him the benefit of the doubt.

Mancrest hesitated. "No."

Given the situation, his honesty surprised her, however belated.

"Care to tell us where the rest of the loaded firearms in your flat are?" she asked.

"Not really," Mancrest said.

"Then I guess Sicarius will have to follow you around all

night, hovering over your shoulder while you eat. Breathing down your neck. Sharing your salad. Hogging your croutons."

That might have drawn a snort from Sicarius had they been alone, but with someone else present, he gave no hints of emotion, and she could not guess what he was thinking. Probably that he did not want to be there. Perhaps that he would like to finish grinding Mancrest's face into the island.

"Do you actually think I'm going to sit down and dine with you?" Mancrest asked.

"Standing is an option, if you wish," Amaranthe said. "Where are the other firearms? I'll be more comfortable eating and chatting with you, knowing it's unlikely you'll be able to shoot me between courses."

"Parlor room desk drawer," Mancrest said, "and in the latrine above the washout."

"Thank you. I'll...did you say latrine?"

"A man feels particularly vulnerable with his trousers around his ankles." Mancrest tried to pull his arm free—a futile attempt. "Would you mind calling off your attack dog? I can't feel the blood in my fingers."

Amaranthe nodded at Sicarius. "Want to go check on those firearms?"

He did not move.

"Or I could check," she said. "Let him wriggle his fingers, will you?"

Amaranthe trotted through the rooms, wanting to find the weapons and come back to rescue Mancrest before lack of circulation lost him any digits. She found the pistols and returned to the dining room. Mancrest sat in a seat—not the head of the table—with Sicarius at his back, arms crossed over chest in one of his typical poses. Amaranthe handed Sicarius the pistols, which he unloaded, then tossed into a corner.

She slipped into an upholstered seat at the head of the table, a throne of a chair that made her feel slight. The hand-carved feet resembled cougar paws and the rest of the detailing also evoked a predatory feline feel. None of this man's furnishings had been produced in a factory or by anyone other than a master woodworker.

Mancrest, arms also crossed over his chest, glowered at her, and Amaranthe wondered how much force had been involved in seating him.

A gold-and-silver corkscrew rested on the table by the wine. She opened the bottle and poured two glasses.

"Your dog isn't drinking?" Mancrest asked.

Amaranthe fought to keep a scowl off her face. While she could understand Mancrest being irked with Sicarius, her instinct was to come to his defense. She doubted the barbs would bother him, but they bothered her. "Sicarius is my partner in our endeavors. I'd appreciate it if you didn't belittle, dehumanize, or otherwise deride him. Given the stories you've printed about him, I believe he's showing admirable restraint in not killing you."

"He's a cowar—assassin, and I've done nothing but print the truth."

Hm, maybe that correction was a sign of progress. Or maybe he was gentlemanly enough not to purposely irritate a woman.

"At least one of the stories you've printed is an untruth," Amaranthe said. "We did not kidnap the emperor last winter. In fact, we saved his life."

Mancrest snorted. "I interviewed witnesses that say you were there and that Sicarius had an axe over the emperor's head when the guards stormed in."

"He was lifting the axe to cut the chains binding Emperor Sespian to a dispensary of molten ore, a situation set up by Larocka Myll and Arbitan Losk, the former heads of the Forge organization. You've heard of them, I trust?"

Mancrest's face grew as hard to read as Sicarius's. Since he was not scoffing, she decided to press on.

"Arbitan was a Nurian masquerading as a Turgonian businessman, and he was the creator of the monster that was killing people all over town last winter. That was little more than a distraction, though, so he could plot against the emperor. And he almost succeeded. Sicarius saved Sespian's life."

Mancrest snorted. "Oh, please."

Ah, there was the scoff.

"We also thwarted Forge's attempt to pollute the city water a couple of months ago," Amaranthe said. "That epidemic you wrote about as well."

"You're claiming that, too?" Mancrest laughed. "The entire army went up there. *They* handled that."

"They cleaned up after we did all the work, including killing a half a dozen makarovi that had butchered everyone in the dam."

Amaranthe stood before Mancrest could voice another statement of disbelief. She untucked her blouse and displayed the scars on her abdomen. Showing unfamiliar men—or *any* men—her midsection was not something she did often, and the wounds were not exactly unquestionable evidence that her story was true, but she figured it might prove worth it. His eyebrows flew up and his mouth sagged open. The reaction did not leave her with the triumphant feeling she had expected; rather it reminded her that she would have ugly scars for life. Though she might be focused on her goals and was not usually one to worry about vanity, no woman wanted a man to be horrified when she showed some skin. She tucked her blouse back in.

"Of course, if my plan had been better thought-out, I might not have been mauled, but fortunately I had talented people to dig me out of trouble." She smiled at Sicarius and caught him staring at her abdomen.

He lifted his gaze to meet her eyes, and for once she was glad she could not read his face. She could not imagine the long look being for anything other than pity or perhaps guilt over not having kept her from that fate, and she did not want either from him. Ancestors knew that whole debacle had been a result of her questionable-at-best scheme, one he had tried to talk her out of, and she had nobody to blame but herself.

"Naturally, I don't expect you to take my word as truth," Amaranthe said, "for any of these events, but I'd like to think *The Gazette*, should it be proved to be in error, would print a retraction." She gestured to the forgotten meal and wine. "Shall we dine?"

"Huh?" Mancrest glanced back at Sicarius, then stared at her.

"Problem?" Amaranthe asked.

"I...When you started talking about those stories, I assumed you were here to threaten me and force me to print something more to your liking." He checked on Sicarius again, who was doing a good imitation of furniture at the moment. "Or is that activity still forthcoming?"

"No, I'd rather eat now if you don't mind. I've had a busy night." She tore a chunk of bread, admiring the flaky crust and soft interior—a tasty change from the rice-based flatbread more common in the empire. A small tin held freshly smashed peanut butter. It never warmed enough in their satrapy for peanuts, so the import was a rare treat. She smeared some on the bread, and her mouth watered in anticipation. Though Maldynado had nearly walked her into a trap, she could forgive him since his shopping had proved so thoughtful. She lifted the piece of bread and offered the traditional before-meal salute, "A warrior's health."

Mancrest had been watching her, and, after she took a few bites, he prepared a plate for himself.

Amaranthe lifted her bread toward Sicarius. Though she knew he would not accept the invitation, she would have felt awkward eating without offering him something. He gave a single minute head shake.

"You're not what I expected," Mancrest said.

"What'd you expect?"

"Given you're a rogue enforcer and who you work with

now—" Mancrest jerked a thumb over his shoulder at Sicarius, "—someone draconian and pugilistic."

"You think Maldynado would spend time with someone like that?"

"If that someone had nice breasts, yes."

Amaranthe chuckled. "Perhaps so. By the way, did Maldynado tell you who he wanted you to meet, or did you guess?"

"Is he going to be in trouble if you find out he did tell me?" Mancrest sipped from his glass of wine—he had apparently decided it was safe to drink—and watched her over the rim of the glass.

She had a feeling she was being tested. "That might earn him an extra stair-running session."

Two vertical lines formed between Mancrest's eyebrows. "Stair-running? Like exercise?"

"Yes."

"If it'll get him extra work, then maybe I should say yes." Mancrest smiled for the first time that night. "But, no, he just said he knew a nice girl I should meet, someone who was working too hard and needed to have more fun." He raised his eyebrows. "I figured out the rest on my own. People have noticed who he's running with these days. His family is vocal in expressing their disappointment and quick to point out that this demonstrates why he deserved to be disowned."

So, they had earned enough notoriety that everyone who knew Maldynado knew he was a potential avenue to her and Sicarius. She would have to remember that.

Mancrest sipped his wine. "How do you get Maldynado to climb stairs? We used to fence together, and he was always too unambitious to put any serious effort into his training."

"We aim to be a fit group. It helps with defeating the evil doers of the world. At the least, it helps if you're fast enough to outrun them. We're all up well before dawn for distance work or obstacle courses, and there's usually weapons training in the afternoon or evening."

Mancrest sputtered and almost spilled his wine. "You can convince Maldynado to get up before dawn?"

Behind him, Sicarius stirred. He pinned Amaranthe with a hard stare. Not enthused about her sharing information on when and where they trained? She raised her fingers and nodded once. He was right. Mancrest was not someone to be trusted yet.

"I didn't think even breasts could convince him to get out of bed before nine," Mancrest continued, not noticing her exchange with Sicarius. He did glance at her chest, as if wondering if something special might be going on down there. Uh huh. Right.

"That's not how I motivate the men," Amaranthe said dryly. "And I'm sure it would take someone prettier than I to finagle them into doing things by that method."

"Oh, I don't know." Mancrest smiled for the first time. "You're pretty enough. I'd like to see you with your hair down. It looks like you have a few waves that don't want to be confined."

"Uhm. Maybe another time when I'm sure escaping soldiers and enforcers won't be a part of the evening activities."

Mancrest's smile widened. "Is that a request for a second date?"

"Er." She was rescued from having to avoid Sicarius's gaze by the fact that his eyes were boring into the back of Mancrest's head. "We'll see. Why don't you tell me more about your recent story?" She laid the newspaper on the table between them. "The emperor is going to dine with the winners of all the events?"

Yes, that was good. Talking about work. Sicarius wouldn't glare disapprovingly then, right? And maybe she could even get some useful information out of her new contact.

With that in mind, she spent the rest of the dinner chatting with Mancrest about the Imperial Games and avoiding such fraught topics as hair. He had not heard of the kidnappings, so she managed to pique his interest with those tidbits. Though he made no promises in regard to Forge or retracting stories, by the end of the evening, she had hope that she might make an ally out of him one day.

🙢〜🙠

After almost an hour of wandering the grounds, Basilard and Akstyr found something. Rather Akstyr found something, and Basilard waited while the younger man knelt in the grass behind the bathhouse examining it.

What is it? Basilard signed.

Head bent low, Akstyr did not see the question.

Basilard nudged Akstyr's arm, drawing the younger man's gaze, and repeated himself.

"It's too dark back here," Akstyr whispered. "I can't see your fingers."

Basilard waved toward a glass globe lantern hanging from a post and took a couple of steps that direction, but Akstyr did not follow. His head was down again, his eyes focused on some tiny object in his hand. Something magical? That was the only thing Basilard could think of that would explain Akstyr's fascination—especially since it was too dark to examine much with eyes alone.

He headed to the lantern, figuring Akstyr would come show him his find sooner or later.

The number of people enjoying the summer evening had dwindled, but people still ambled along the trails. Voices drifted from the men's and women's bathhouses every time someone opened a door. Athletes strolled back to the barracks in pairs and groups, all friends now, but that would likely change once the events started.

The faint scent of blackberries lingered in the evening air. Basilard patted himself down, found one of his collection bags, and followed his nose toward a bramble patch in the shadows.

Frenzied grunts coming from nearby bushes made him pause, thinking someone might be embroiled in a battle and need help. His cheeks warmed when he realized it wasn't the sort of battle from which one wanted to be extricated. He supposed he should move farther up the path and give the enthusiastic grunters their privacy, but a post-coital chuckle made him freeze. That laugh sounded familiar.

Basilard plucked the lantern from its wrought iron perch and returned to the bushes. He parted the branches, lifted the light, and revealed...

"Oh, hullo, Basilard." A nude Maldynado propped himself up on an elbow.

A young woman squealed, snatched a grass-stained towel off the ground, covered herself, and sprinted toward the women's barracks. Judging by the speed her long bare legs managed, she was one of the athletes, a rather embarrassed one.

You have the night off? Basilard signed, an eyebrow raised.

"Not exactly." Maldynado stood, brushed grass off himself, and started retrieving clothing. A shoe from under the bush, a belt from the grass, and—how did that shirt get ten feet up in that tree? "The boss sent me to find you fellows and let you know she'd be late. I hunted all over and didn't see you. I did see that exquisite young lady coming out of the baths all by herself, though, and she appeared lonesome so I struck up a conversation, asking if she knew how in the old days women used to compete at the Imperial Games to win the eye of eligible warrior-caste bachelors, and did she know I was warrior caste—I left out the part about being disowned naturally—and would she like to..."

There were times Basilard dearly missed having undamaged vocal cords. He would have liked to bark an, "Enough," to cut Maldynado off. It was bad enough few people outside of his team could understand his sign language, but his scars and lack of height ensured no Turgonian women looked upon him with kind—or lascivious—eyes.

Akstyr trotted over, which fortunately resulted in Maldynado bringing his story to an end.

"Look." Akstyr held his hand out, oblivious to the fact Maldynado had yet to find his trousers.

Basilard lifted the lantern, wanting to see what had occupied the younger man's attention so thoroughly. It looked like...

"A cork?" Maldynado asked. "You've been here for two hours and that's all you've found?"

"A cork with the residue of something Made," Akstyr said. "A powder or maybe it was a liquid in a vial. I need to do some research." He snapped his fingers. "That Nurian book I have has a section on potions, powders, and airborne inhalants. Oh, but I'll need Books to help me translate it. Where is he?" Akstyr looked around and blinked in surprise when he noticed Maldynado's state of undress. "Why are your crabapples hanging out?"

"*Crabapples?* More like Mountain Generals." Maldynado made gestures with his hands to denote the size of the largest local apple.

"Uh, whatever." Akstyr nodded at Basilard. "Books?"

Back that way, last I saw. Basilard pointed toward the other side of the grounds.

"All right, tell Am'ranthe we may have something." Akstyr waved the cork and jogged off. "I'll grab him and go back to the boneyard," he said over his shoulder.

Excited about his find, he sprinted away almost as quickly as Maldynado's conquest had. A nervous thread wove through Basilard's belly. Akstyr had promised he would share nothing of their discussion with anyone, but losing track of the young man made him uneasy. Also, this left Basilard alone with...

"So, Bas." Maldynado slung an arm over his shoulder. Thankfully, he had located his pants and put them on. "Looks like we found what we needed to find tonight. We ought to be able to head off and have a few drinks now, eh?"

Is Amaranthe still coming?

"Later, I think. She got held up." His easy-going smile faded. "Deret tried to set up a trap to capture her. He used me to get to her."

Alarm coursed through Basilard. *Is she all right?*

"She's fine, or was when I left. Sicarius figured it for a trap before we went in. She's going to visit Deret for dinner and still might get in trouble that way. You know how she likes to take risks." Maldynado lowered his arm and swatted a tree branch brushing his hair. "I helped buy her groceries, but I'm irked at Deret. I always thought him a decent fellow. Sure, I could see him feeling compelled to set the enforcers on Sicarius's tail, but the boss doesn't deserve that bounty."

Agreed, Basilard signed. *We shouldn't drink if she's coming here. She might expect us to be working.*

Maldynado shrugged. "We can't find magic stuff."

Let's check the stadium for anything suspicious. We haven't yet, and the athletes should have stopped training for the day.

His prediction proved true, and nobody occupied the arena or the tiers of seating surrounding it. Lanterns burned at periodic intervals, providing enough light for walking. He and Maldynado did a lap of the track, though Basilard did not know what to look for. Without Akstyr's nose for magic, they would have to search for mundane clues.

It took Maldynado only a few minutes to grow bored of investigating. He wandered into the middle of the arena where the furnace powering the Clank Race still burned. Someone must have been out training recently.

Maldynado threw a couple of levers. Gears turned, pistons clanked, and a moan of releasing steam sounded as the massive machine powering the obstacle course started up. While the wood and metal structure remained stationary, the moving parts created a strange sight in the darkness. Arms and spindles rotated and turned, propelling sharpened axes and battering rams out to thwart someone crossing spinning logs and tiny moving platforms. In more than one spot, bloodstains spattered the sand beneath the contraption.

Anyone ever die at your Games? Basilard signed.

"Oh, sure," Maldynado said, "but I think there are more injuries in the wrestling. Most of the people crazy enough to do this thing are agile as foxes. But, yes, someone dies most every year, and others lose arms and legs. People get careless when they're trying to earn the best time." Maldynado tapped a paper stuck to the side of a support post. "Looks like some cocky athletes have posted their times already. Hm." He eyed the machine speculatively.

What?

"Want to try it?"

What? Basilard signed. *After you just told me it's killed people?*

"Come on. Odds are good Sicarius is going to make us try it at some point anyway." Maldynado mimicked Sicarius's stony face and monotone to say, "Good training." The serious facade lasted almost a second, before he grinned and said, "Doesn't it look fun?"

Basilard eyed the swinging blades, clanking machinery, and the puffs of steam escaping into the darkness with soft hisses. The long lost boy in him admitted it might be enjoyable. They were not competing with anyone, so they did not have to sprint through recklessly.

"Ah, you're tempted, aren't you?" Maldynado grinned and trotted over to a giant clock, its hands visible even in the dim lighting. "Let's see, how do we time ourselves.... Here we go. Loser buys the winner drinks tonight. Ready? Go!"

Maldynado threw a lever on a giant time clock and darted up a ramp leading into the course.

What? Basilard had not agreed to the terms, but he sprinted after Maldynado anyway. They did not get paid enough for him to buy drinks for that bottomless gullet.

He raced up the ramp to a wooden platform seesawing up and down. Two spinning logs stretched ahead. Maldynado had taken the left, so Basilard ran right. He darted across as fast as he could, staying light-footed on the rotating wood, knowing that going slow or with tense muscles would be more likely to cause a misstep.

He caught up with Maldynado at the next platform.

"Look out," Maldynado barked.

Half expecting the warning to be a trick designed to slow him down, Basilard almost missed the man-sized dummy swinging down at him on a series of ropes. Spikes protruded from all of its wooden sides.

Basilard flung himself to his belly. The dummy swung past, the draft stirring the hairs on the back of his neck.

When he rose, Maldynado was already jumping onto a rope that dangled from a beam. Something—spikes?—protruded from the ground beneath.

Basilard growled and chased after Maldynado. After the rope climb, they had to traverse along pegs sticking out of the beam, thirty feet above the ground. A net took them to the next obstacle. Tiny circular platforms, some only a few inches wide, rotated about while axe blades and battering rams swung out of the darkness. Basilard jumped and darted, relying on instincts more than thought. By luck more than design, he reached the next seesawing platform before Maldynado. He clambered up a mesh wall, over a beam, through a rope swing course, and finally hurled himself into a net where he scrambled to the bottom and toward a ten-foot wall.

He burst over that last obstacle and sprinted to a finish line, beating Maldynado by several seconds. He staggered a couple of weary steps and collapsed in the sand to rest.

Stars had come out overhead, though they were not as bright as those he had once known in his mountain home. He inhaled deeply; here, surrounded by grass and trees, the air was cleaner than in the city core, but it still smelled of burning wood and coal. A homesick twinge ran through him, an aching for a life to which he could never return.

"Great time, Bas." Maldynado stood by the giant clock. "You were as fast as some of these athletes. Pretty impressive considering this is your first time doing it. Of course, I would have beaten you, but I was a touch weary from my earlier vigorous exertions."

Basilard was about to sit up when a dark figure loomed over him. Sicarius.

The flickering illumination from a lantern hanging on the obstacle course frame cast his face half in shadow, half in light, enhancing his hard, angular features. When he stared down, Basilard struggled not to cringe or show any nervous reaction. Sicarius could not know what he and Akstyr had been discussing earlier. He had just arrived.

"What's going on, gentlemen?" Amaranthe's voice came from a few paces away. "Finding anything interesting?"

Basilard jumped to his feet and faced her, glad for the excuse to turn his shoulder toward Sicarius. He had sensed Sicarius's suspicions toward him since the incident in the shaman's hideout, and now he knew why. He must suspect Basilard would one day find out about his crimes in Mangdoria. That wariness would make it all the more difficult to surprise him.

"We found out Basilard can run the Clank Race as fast as some of these pampered athletes," Maldynado said.

"Oh?" Amaranthe regarded him with more interest than Basilard thought the statement warranted. "That might be perfect," she said, talking more to herself than him.

What? Basilard signed.

"It seems the winners of each event get to have dinner with the emperor. That'll be...thirty-six people, but most of those youngsters won't have anything to talk about."

Maldynado smirked. "I like how you talk about youngsters as if your twenty-six years make you venerable and wise, boss."

Basilard smirked, remembering her memorable birthday party at the Pirates' Plunder.

Amaranthe, eyes bright, continued her vision without

acknowledging Maldynado. "Those young athletes will likely be cowed by Sespian's royal presence. If you won, you could angle your way in there and talk with him about your people, about the underground slavery that still exists in the city."

Basilard almost sank back down to the earth. Was that possible? For him to win an interview with the emperor? In one night, could he truly bring awareness of the slave problem to Sespian? Basilard glanced at Sicarius, abruptly regretting his vow to kill the man. That was a task he was not sure he could carry out without being killed himself. Maybe it could wait until after the Imperial Games? But perhaps his mind was spinning too quickly. What were the odds of him actually winning an event? Against agile young athletes half his age?

"You could take Books to translate for you," Amaranthe said.

"Most men would prefer to take a woman on a dinner date with the emperor," Maldynado said.

"Well, if Basilard could find one that could translate for him, I suppose. I'm too notorious to show up at such a venue these days. But anyway, Basilard are you interested in entering? Sicarius can help you train."

I can train on my own, Basilard signed swiftly.

Amaranthe gave Sicarius a bemused smile. "I guess nobody else appreciates your stair-climbing sessions the way I do."

Sicarius did not respond. Their relationship—if they could be said to have one—baffled Basilard. She treated him like a friend and confidant, and half the time he did not even respond when she spoke to him.

"Where are Books and Akstyr?" Amaranthe asked.

"They went back to the hideout," Maldynado said. "Akstyr found...I don't know. Bas, did we decide it was a cork?"

Magic, Basilard signed.

"Oh?" Amaranthe asked. "Related to the kidnappings?"

"I'm not sure precisely," Maldynado said. "I was looking for my pants at the time."

Amaranthe opened her mouth, then shut it, probably deciding she was better off not knowing. "Have there been any more kidnappings?" she asked. "Are the people who disappeared last night still gone?"

Three total, Basilard signed. *Two foreigners and one Turgonian man from a different...place.* Though he had added a lot of signs, giving his language versatility amongst the group, saying "The Chevrok Satrapy" was beyond him for now, but Amaranthe nodded understanding, and he went on, *The enforcers I overheard are starting to accept that something strange is going on. They're blaming Sicarius since he was sighted this morning.*

"*Supposedly* sighted," Amaranth said. "I wonder if we can find out who sent that fellow and what he wanted to accomplish. Basilard, I apologize, but my reason for wanting someone from our team in the Imperial Games isn't entirely selfless. I'm hoping an insider might be more likely to hear about what's going on. Maybe they'll even target you for one of the kidnappings." She bounced on her toes, then caught herself. "Sorry, that should probably not excite me."

I'll take solace knowing you'd be just as happy if you could pose as an athlete and get kidnapped.

Maldynado snorted. "That'd make her even happier."

"Basilard, you'll need someone to play the role of trainer and translator," Amaranthe said. "Akstyr and Books may be busy, so..."

Maldynado slung an arm over Basilard's shoulder. "I'm always happy to spend time at the stadium and watch all the fine...events."

Just keep your pants on, Basilard signed.

Amaranthe opened her mouth again, shut it again, and shook her head.

"No promises." Maldynado winked.

CHAPTER 5

An ice wagon trundled across the grounds, selling blocks to vendors who turned them into chilled tea and strawberry juice. Amaranthe thought about buying a glass of the latter, but the midday sun left few shadows for wanted women to hide in. Clad in white athlete togs again, she was sitting on a bench on the edge of the grounds with a wide-brimmed sun hat pulled low over her eyes while she waited for Fasha to meet her. Sicarius had pointed out that night meetings would be safer, but Amaranthe wanted to listen in on the local gossip. The trail leading from the stadium to the baths and barracks wound past her perch, and she had already overheard quite a bit.

"...need more guards," a woman with sweat-dampened bangs told her comrade as they strolled past.

"The enforcers aren't admitting to anything," the other woman answered. "They're saying nothing's going on, that the missing athletes probably went home."

"Oh, sure, they trained all year, and then just went home before the competition even..."

The women walked out of hearing range. Amaranthe bent her head to study the short list of names on a notepad in her lap. Five athletes were missing now: two foreigners, including

Fasha's sister; and three Turgonians, one a local, and two from other satrapies. She recognized the local man, a warrior-caste wrestler, because they were the same age and had competed in the junior events at the same time. What eluded her was the common theme. All of the missing people had disappeared in the middle of the night from their barracks or, in the wrestler's case, a private room in the lodge.

"You should pay attention to your surroundings when you're in a public area," Sicarius said from the shrubs a couple of feet behind the bench.

Amaranthe stifled her usual twitch of surprise and did not lift her head, wondering if she could wheedle her way out of a lecture. "I knew you were on the grounds."

A long moment passed before he answered. "You are assuming that you're safe, simply because I'm in the area?"

"You know I'm not at my most attentive when I'm plotting and mulling. I've come to trust you'll keep an eye on me."

"That's reckless," Sicarius said. "I'm your colleague, not your bodyguard, nor can I guarantee your safety since I cannot walk about freely here. If you must study papers in a public area, you should scan your surroundings every fifteen seconds, ensuring you are aware of the movements and interests of everyone within a radius of at least... Why are you smiling?"

Actually, it was more of a grin. "You called me a colleague," Amaranthe said. "I'm flattered."

"You are not taking my admonishment seriously."

"I am, too," Amaranthe said.

Another pair of athletes was approaching, so Amaranthe left the bench to join Sicarius in the foliage. Mischievous branches tugged at her hat and rained leaves onto her shoulders. She dusted them off. As much as she liked the idea of nature, it was difficult to maintain a tidy appearance when surrounded by it.

"I'm just bad at admitting out loud that I'm wrong about something," Amaranthe added.

"A character flaw you should correct."

"Likely so." She lifted her notepad, intending to ask his opinions about the names, but he surprised her by continuing.

"It would bother me if you died while I was attending to biological needs."

Amaranthe's grin returned at the admission. "It would bother me if I died then, too. Or any time." She handed him the notepad. "These are the people missing thus far. One disappeared three nights ago, two the night before last—that was when Fasha's sister went—and one last night. I'm trying to figure out what the common link is. After talking with Fasha, I figured it might be another ploy against foreigners, but we now have more Turgonians missing than outsiders. The wrestler, Deercrest, has won often, so I could see him being targeted as someone to get rid of. Though it's not honorable to make opponents disappear, it's certainly not without precedent in the history of the Imperial Games. But the other four are young no-names. One isn't even old enough to compete in the regular events; he was entered into the junior Clank Race."

"Perhaps they are promising contenders for this year's competitions," Sicarius said.

"How would a kidnapper know? The qualifiers don't start until tomorrow. Sure, some people post their practice times, but most don't, and the best athletes often only compete hard enough to make the cut in the early rounds." Amaranthe leaned against a tree. "Besides, who would want to get rid of multiple good athletes? I could see rigging your own event, or your child's event, but why wrestling, running, *and* the Clank Race?"

As was often the case, Sicarius did not answer, but she knew he was listening.

"Could it be a gambling scheme?" she mused. "People bet on the events, and some people bet a *lot*. Is someone trying to set things up so they can guess the winners?"

"With athletes disappearing days prior to the race, the odds will be adjusted accordingly."

"True, it'd make more sense to kidnap someone the night before, or minutes before the event if you wanted to upset the odds-makers." Amaranthe took the notepad back and tapped it. "Still, it might be worth talking to some of the bookmakers."

Male voices sounded on the path in front of the bench. She parted the branches as a trio of muscular young men walked past. They did not wear athletes' togs, but instead the sleeveless overalls of miners. That was odd. Most local companies only gave workers the final two days of the Imperial Games off because they were considered a holiday in the capital. Even if one man had finagled a day off somehow, it seemed unlikely a group could have managed the same. Mining outfits were particularly stingy with leave, as Amaranthe well knew. She had seen little of her father when she was growing up. Yet here these men were, wandering about, a day before the qualifying events were to start and a week before the holiday finals.

"*They* are not bookmakers," Sicarius said.

The branches rustled as Amaranthe released them. "No, I know. I was just thinking..." She paused as the possible connotations of his comment slid over her. Was he displeased to have caught her ogling handsome young men? No hint of consternation marked his face; maybe she had imagined his words had underlying meaning. Besides, he knew she would happily ogle him if he gave her more opportunities. "I'm going to follow those men. I have a hunch."

His eyes narrowed slightly, but all he said was, "There are numerous enforcers about."

"I know. I'll stay out of trouble."

"Doubtful."

"Just don't wander off for too long at a time to attend biological needs."

Amaranthe tossed him a wink and slipped out of the brush without waiting for a response. She tugged the brim of her hat low over her eyes. It did a decent job of hiding her features, especially considering most enforcers were men, and her five-

and-a-half feet put her face below their eye level, but she had best not chance getting too close.

She trailed after the miners at a distance, keeping other people between her and them. One had a rolled up newspaper and a small leather-bound journal protruding from back pockets. That piqued her interest even more. Most miners only had the mandatory six years of schooling and started working young, so it was rare to find one who was comfortable looking to books or newspapers for information.

A bent, old woman stepped out from the courtyard of an eating tent, and the miners stopped abruptly. She leaned on a cane and wore her gray hair in buns on either side of her head — hardly a formidable-looking person, but the young men darted back the way they had come, nearly running into Amaranthe. She hopped off the path to let them by. They must have been in their twenties, but they tore away like truant children avoiding a school teacher.

"I saw you, Rill and Stemmic," the old woman hollered after them, "and your mother will hear from me. You being off work this many days, you ought to be helping her out."

The men ran into the stadium and disappeared from view, but Amaranthe barely noticed. That woman's voice... It was familiar. Something from her childhood.

She squinted at the old lady, and it took a moment to place her. She was the mother of a friend of her father's, and Amaranthe had stayed at her flat once as a girl when Auntie Memela had been sick.

The woman had stopped yelling after the young men, but she continued to stand there, leaning on her cane and grousing under her breath. Though Amaranthe was curious what the exchange had been about, she found herself hesitant to go up to the woman. She had avoided everyone from her old life since becoming an outlaw, in part to keep them out of trouble, but also because she did not want their pity or condemnation. Once she found her exoneration, she could reconnect with old comrades.

But this was different. This might be some sort of lead.

Amaranthe girded herself and strode up to the woman. "Hello, ma'am?" She decided not to mention her name. What were the odds that the woman would remember her? "Do you need any help? Did those boys do something to you?"

The woman tilted her head and squinted up at Amaranthe, peering beneath the hat. "Amaranthe Lokdon?"

"Er, you remember me?"

"I remember you." Her face was difficult to read. No hint of a smile stretched her lips. "I see you remember me, too."

"Yes, but you look the same."

"That's good. I think," the woman said.

"Wasn't I only seven or eight the last time we met?"

"Yes, but I've recently seen your face decorating a poster."

"Ah." Amaranthe tugged her hat a little lower, reminded of the public nature of the place.

"I imagine your father would be horrified."

"Yes, ma'am. I imagine so."

"He wanted so much for you, *sacrificed* so much."

"I know, ma'am. I'm trying to...make amends now."

"By loitering around the stadium grounds in the middle of the day? Are you betting on the events or something?"

"No, I—" Amaranthe cleared her throat. She would be here all day—or until someone caught her—if she stood around, explaining her every action. "I was wondering about those miners. Don't they have work?"

"Indeed so. *They're* not outlaws."

"Then why aren't they at work?" Amaranthe asked, pushing the dig aside.

"Some scheme of Raydevk's. I haven't the faintest notion of what, but they've been down here all week. My grandson is racing. That's why *I'm* here. There's no reason for young, able-bodied souls not to be laboring during the workday."

"Yes, ma'am. Ah, is that the Foreman Raydevk my father knew?"

"No, his son. Elder Raydevk passed on last year, Black Lung, same as your da."

"I'd like to talk to Raydevk," Amaranthe said. It was a long shot, that off-work miners roaming around with journals had anything to do with the kidnappings, but she had no better leads. "He has a place in the city, doesn't he?"

"Not one he'd like me to direct some outlaw to, I'm sure. You thieving these days, too? He's got a wife and two sons, and he scarcely makes enough to keep them fed. He doesn't need any more trouble than what he's already schemed up."

"No thieving, ma'am. If it matters, I was wrongfully accused, and I'm trying to clear my name. But now that you bring it up, I think I've been to Raydevk's flat. Doesn't he live down by the railway tracks?" She was guessing, but most of the low-income housing was down there, near the Veterans' Quarter. "In that building on..." She wriggled her fingers, as if searching for the information in her head.

"Nelview?" the old woman said.

Amaranthe snapped her fingers. "Yes, that's it. It's right by that eating house, isn't it? The..."

The woman snorted. "I'd hardly call The Brewed Puppy an eating house. If you don't stick to drinks, you're like to get sick in there."

"That's true enough," Amaranthe said, conjuring a map of that part of the city in her head. "And Raydevk's flat is on the second floor, right?"

The woman opened her mouth, but snapped it shut again and gave Amaranthe a shrewd look.

"Never mind," Amaranthe said. "I'll find it. Thank you for your time."

She hustled away, hoping she could escape before the woman shouted any parting messages, but her words followed Amaranthe anyway.

"You'd better not thieve from him, girl. Your father's spirit must be twisted in knots, knowing what came of you."

A pair of athletes walking past from the other direction gave Amaranthe quizzical looks. At least they weren't enforcers.

"Crazy old grandmother," Amaranthe told them with a chuckle and hustled toward the stadium.

She wanted to find the miners and see if they might give her more information on this "scheme," but a knot of people blocked the entrance to the stadium. A bare-chested man hopped onto a bench, his oiled muscles gleaming, a wooden megaphone held to his lips.

"Sicarius, we know you're out there!" he shouted.

Amaranthe tripped and almost fell over.

"I, Erton Garthcrest, challenge you," the man went on. "If you're half the man the rumors say, come and prove it. Enter the wrestling and see if you're my match!" He finished by thumping his fist against his muscled chest, which was so puffed out that he looked like he could tip over backward and fall off the bench at any moment.

The bystanders cheered at the short speech. Amaranthe wanted to go around and into the stadium, but the cheers went on. "More," someone hollered, "Bring out Sicarius," and that started a chant of, "Sicarius, Sicarius." This drew more people to the scene.

The entire episode had an orchestrated feel to it, and Amaranthe thought about creeping closer to see if she could identify the ringleader in the crowd, but several enforcers trotted out of the stadium and headed for the group.

Amaranthe eased off the path. With the enforcers extra alert to trouble, this wasn't the time for her to roam about inside.

She headed for the shrubs where she had last seen Sicarius, but did not find him. She continued on toward the greenbelt, figuring he would have gone that way. They had been following the railways from the boneyard to the grounds the last couple of days.

Before she had taken more than three steps into the trees, Sicarius's voice came from behind the brush.

"You found trouble," he said.

"I had nothing to do with those people calling your name," Amaranthe said. "It seems you're a popular fellow around these parts."

"Too popular."

"Yes, it's suspicious. Think someone is trying to get you to make an appearance?"

"Unknown." He gazed toward the stadium, though foliage hid the crowd from view. Perhaps at the enforcers' behest, the shouts of "Sicarius" had stopped.

Amaranthe summarized her conversation with the woman for him. "I want to find this Raydevk's flat, but let's check in on Books and Akstyr first. It's hard to imagine Turgonian miners coming up with a scheme that involves magic, but I'd like a better idea about what we're dealing with, just in case. Unless you want to go off and start training for the wrestling event?" she asked, since his gaze was still toward the stadium. "Did that fellow with the megaphone tempt you?"

Sicarius looked at her as if he suspected her of having received a brain-damaging head wound. "It would be foolish for me to go anywhere near the stadium once the Imperial Games begin, certainly not into the arena."

He turned his back on the grounds and led her deeper into the woods. They passed a human-sized statue of an arachnid that must have once had a head, for it was hewn off with the granite stump now fuzzed with moss. Another victim of Mad Emperor Motash's mandate to decapitate all statues from the old religions.

"True," Amaranthe said, "but some men have egos that demand they prove themselves whenever challenged."

"That is why they are dead, and I am not."

"I guess that explains your longevity." She grinned. "I knew it wasn't a matter of your amiable, warm-hearted nature endearing you to people."

That comment received no look at all, and he said nothing

during the trip back to the boneyard. With that much silence surrounding Amaranthe, her mind was left to its own musing, and, not for the first time, she wondered why Sicarius's name kept coming up here—and why someone would risk impersonating him. She also wondered what had happened to Fasha to keep her from meeting Amaranthe.

"Questions," she muttered to herself. "Nothing but questions."

"What are you doing? I thought you were going on two more runs before taking a break. Your timing is still off on those swinging axes."

Basilard flopped onto his back, hot sweat streaming down his cheeks. Maldynado stood over him, fists propped on his hips. The Clank Race whirred and hissed behind him. Most of the other athletes had left, though a young man was timing himself on sprints up the nets.

You're a worse taskmaster than Sicarius, Basilard signed.

"That's because you don't seem motivated. You have to win to have dinner with the emperor. I thought that mattered to you. You want to talk to him on behalf of your people and slaves in the city, don't you?"

Basilard sighed and rolled to his knees. If he attacked Sicarius, he would not live long enough to win anything. Unless he succeeded. And if he did, Amaranthe would kick him out of the group, and he'd have no one to translate his wishes to the emperor anyway.

"Why don't you get some water?" Maldynado said. "Then we'll do another round."

Basilard stumbled to his feet with thighs rubbery from the previous twenty runs. *We?*

"We," Maldynado said. "We're a team. You run the Clank Race, and I stand over here with the pocket watch and cheer you on. I think it works well. I'm..." His eyes shifted to watch something over Basilard's shoulder. He frowned.

Basilard turned around to follow Maldynado's gaze, but did not recognize the man approaching. He wore simple, but tailored clothing and a wide-brimmed beaver hat. Walking with a cane made his gait uneven, but it slowed him little, and he appeared hale. Folded spectacles hung from his shirt collar, a pencil protruded from the band of his hat, and he carried a pad of paper under his arm. He strode directly toward Maldynado and Basilard.

"What do you want, Deret?" Maldynado growled.

Basilard wondered if he should know this person.

"I'm working on a story." The man gave Basilard a curious look before focusing his attention on Maldynado. "Interviewing athletes. Trying to figure out what's going on around here with the missing people."

Ah, this had to be the journalist Amaranthe had gone to see the night before. Mancrest.

"You could apologize for trying to kill my boss when I promised her you'd take her out to dinner and show her a nice evening," Maldynado said.

"You neglected to mention she was a notorious outlaw," Mancrest said.

"Seems you figured it out on your own. I'm lucky you don't turn me in."

"For two hundred and fifty ranmyas? Why bother?"

Maldynado's fingers curled into a fist.

Basilard waved to get his attention. *Perhaps we should not irritate this man since there are enforcers around and he knows who we are.*

Maldynado sniffed. "I'm not going to irritate him. I'm not going to talk to him at all." He turned his back on Mancrest and pointed at a couple of young men resting in the shade of the Clank Race's massive furnace and boiler. "Those two look like your most promising competition, Bas."

Basilard kept an eye on Mancrest. If Maldynado's dismissal bothered him, he did not show it.

"I have information for your...what is she to you exactly?" Mancrest said. "A former lover? I can't imagine you trying to arrange a courtship for someone you were currently involved with, but it's also impossible for me to imagine you getting out of bed to exercise before dawn at the behest of a woman you have no feelings for. It is equally impossible for me to imagine you living in close quarters with a woman and not sleeping with her, or attempting to sleep with her."

During this spiel, Maldynado had slowly turned to face Mancrest again, and he eyed the other man with suspicion. "Bas, was there an implied insult to the boss in there, or is he just insulting me?"

I...think the latter, Basilard signed.

"All right." Maldynado's shoulders lowered, and he unclenched his fists. "That's nothing unexpected then. What do you want me to tell her, Mancrest?"

"What is she to you?" Mancrest asked.

"My employer."

"You've never gotten up early for an employer before." Mancrest eyed Maldynado up and down. "You look like you're in the best shape of your life."

Maldynado brightened swifter than the night sky presented with a lightning flash. "I am! Look!" He dug his shirt out of his trousers to display the lean ridges of his abdomen.

Basilard rolled his eyes. *There aren't any women around to impress.*

He caught a similar eye roll from Mancrest. Maybe the fellow wasn't so bad after all.

"Maldynado..." Mancrest sighed.

"Look, she's my boss and a friend, all right?" Maldynado lowered his shirt. "And..." He prodded the dusty clay earth with his boot. "She's twenty-six."

Huh? What did Amaranthe's age have to do with anything?

At first, Mancrest appeared as perplexed, but then his lips formed an, "Oh."

"Tia's age," Maldynado said. "And real adventurous and quick to smile. She's a good girl, and she doesn't deserve that bounty, and she probably only has it because Sicarius is in the group. She thinks he's useful, and I guess he is, but nobody's going to pardon us as long as he's around."

Basilard studied Maldynado's face, wondering if he might have another ally to turn against Sicarius. Surely if the whole group wanted him gone...

"Yes," Mancrest said. "I wondered about that. If you're not sleeping with her, is *he?*"

"Listen, Deret. This isn't one of those smutty Aleeta Dourcrest novels your mother has lying all over the house. We're a professional team of mercenaries. Elite even. Nobody's sleeping with anybody." He hesitated and whispered to Basilard. "They're not, right?"

I don't think so.

A hint of relief lightened Mancrest's face, and Basilard thought the man's interest in Amaranthe curious, especially given that he had tried to turn her over to the army.

"Didn't my mother catch you reading one of those novels when you were over to play in the pond with me and my brother?" Mancrest asked.

"No."

Mancrest folded his arms over his chest.

"Well, fine, maybe. I wanted to know what women like, and some of that information has proved useful to me over the years."

Ask what he wants to tell Amaranthe, Basilard signed, hoping to keep Maldynado from wandering off track.

"Right," Maldynado said. "Just tell us what you want. We have training to do."

"You're not entering an event, are you? While nobody is going out of the way to turn you in for that measly bounty,

I'm sure if you were right here in front of everybody on race day, even the enforcers could bestir themselves to walk the ten meters to the finish line to lock you up."

"I'm not racing." Maldynado pointed at Basilard. "He is."

"Oh?" Mancrest asked. "No bounty on your head?"

Basilard ran his fingers over the scarred flesh of his scalp. The sweat had dried, leaving his skin dusty and warm beneath the sun. *No.*

"Surprising. You look..." Mancrest shrugged, perhaps thinking better of offering what could only have been an insult.

"Thugly?" Maldynado suggested.

Basilard frowned at him.

Maldynado slung an arm over his shoulder. "Basilard's a good fellow. Only fights when he hasn't got a choice. And besides, who would waste money putting out a bounty for a foreigner?"

Basilard removed Maldynado's arm.

"I understand Amaranthe is researching the kidnappings here, too. I want to exchange notes with her," Mancrest said.

"Does that mean you believe what really happened when the emperor was kidnapped?" Maldynado asked.

"It means...sometimes present deeds count for more than past actions."

Basilard shook his head wistfully, wishing that were true. Neither man caught his movement. He missed being a more viable part of conversations. He missed...mattering.

"Anyway," Mancrest said, "I'm interested in what she knows about the missing people. Tell her I'd like to meet her at—"

"You don't get to pick any more meeting places," Maldynado said.

"Fine, what do you propose?"

"I'll tell her you'll be at Pyramid Park two hours before midnight."

"That sounds like a good place to get your head thumped in and have your purse stolen," Mancrest said.

"Not with Sicarius around."

Mancrest snorted. "He's just as likely to thump my head in as a pack of gang kids."

"Quit whining. You're warrior caste, not some defenseless kitten." Maldynado pointed a finger at Mancrest's nose. "And if there are enforcers lying in wait, we'll know not to trust you. And you better believe Sicarius will do more than thump on you, too."

"Any chance you can tell him he's not invited?" Mancrest asked.

"I'll pass on your message, that's it." Maldynado shooed the other man away. "We've got training to do."

As soon as Mancrest left, Maldynado asked, "Think we can trust him?"

Doubtful, Basilard signed.

"Think that'll keep Amaranthe from meeting up with him again?"

Doubtful, Basilard signed again, this time with a wry twist to his lips.

Maldynado sighed. "That's what I thought."

CHAPTER 6

Before they entered the boneyard, Sicarius stopped Amaranthe with a hand on her arm. He pointed at plumes of black smoke wafting into the sky ahead of them. Overgrown blackberry bushes and the rusted carcasses of locomotives hid the source.

"Bonfire?" Amaranthe guessed.

"No. Listen."

Amaranthe closed her eyes and cocked an ear in the direction of the smoke. Despite the homeless and hunted that camped in the boneyard, quiet ruled there, except for the cicadas that favored the trees on the southern end. She and Sicarius were at the northern entrance, though, closest to the city, and she heard nothing beyond chirping birds. A working train rumbled by to the west, following the tracks along the lake and into Stumps. Wait. She listened harder. Maybe that was not a locomotive, and maybe it was not far enough west to be on the tracks.

"Steam carriage?" she asked. "No, I can't imagine anyone wealthy enough to own one spending time here. Enforcer wagon more likely."

Amaranthe took a step in the direction of the smoke, intending to check it out, but Sicarius had not released her arm.

"Don't you want to investigate?" she asked. "Or did you want to stand here and fondle my arm for a while?"

He released her. "I was alerting you to the potential of trouble so we could avoid it."

"So...no interest in arm fondling, eh?"

She expected him to ignore her or perhaps sigh. Instead, he said, "Were that my goal, your *arm* wouldn't be my target."

Amaranthe blinked. "Why, Sicarius, is it possible you have a playful side beneath your razor-edged knives, severe black clothing, and humorless glares?"

"I will lead." Sicarius headed into the boneyard. "Make no noise."

She was the one to sigh, but she followed him anyway. One day, after they finished their work and made peace with the emperor, she was going to drag him off some place where it would be impossible to train and the only acceptable activity was having fun. She had heard of tropical islands in the Gulf where the inhabitants welcomed everyone with bead necklaces and feasts. Even Turgonians were supposed to be allowed, so long as they did not come to conquer.

Sicarius did not choose a direct path to the smoke. He circled through weed-choked aisles between rows of boxy freight cars. Nobody stirred in the shadowed interiors, not with enforcers around.

Sicarius climbed the rusty side of an early model locomotive. Salvagers had torn away the siding, removed the wheels, and scavenged any engine parts light enough to carry.

Crouched in the shadow of the smokestack, Sicarius waved for her to come up. She clambered to the top. They were closer to the source of the smoke now, and she glimpsed the top of a steam wagon between rail cars a couple of aisles over. It gleamed with familiar red and silver paint. Enforcers.

Something clanged, like a baton striking the metal side of a car.

"See any more?" a man called.

"We probably got the wizard already," came another male voice.

"The ones we've chained say it's not them."

"Of course they're not going to *admit* it, patroller. Not when the punishment is death."

"They're all gang thugs. They're probably going to get a death sentence anyway."

"The lady said the wizard was *young*."

Amaranthe mumbled, "What has Akstyr done?"

Sicarius said nothing.

She had seen enough. She jumped down, her feet stirring a cloud of fine dust when she landed. It tickled her nose, and she pinched her nostrils shut. The last thing she needed was to alert the enforcers to her presence with a mighty sneeze. Sicarius alighted beside her, somehow not kicking up any of the dust covering the sun-faded bricks.

"Let's warn Akstyr and Books," she whispered and headed into the maze. Warn wasn't exactly what she wanted to do with Akstyr. Kick might be a better verb. Maybe he had a good reason for doing something that had made someone think he was a wizard, but she doubted it.

Their hideout lay a half a mile to the east, close to the far boundary of the boneyard, and she hoped they would have time before the enforcers made it over there. Between the hundreds of rail cars and the narrow, cluttered aisles of junk and weeds between them, the area would not be easy to navigate with a steam wagon. Of course, she and Sicarius had been gone all day. The enforcers might have already been to their hideout. That thought stirred worry in her gut, but, no, even if they had searched her section of the boneyard, their words implied they had not captured Akstyr yet.

Amaranthe relaxed when she heard familiar voices.

"I did *not* mistranslate it," Books said.

"Well, it's not working," Akstyr huffed. "I tried three times."

"Perhaps the error is not with the translation but your interpretation."

"Are you calling me inept, old man?"

A clang reverberated from within a rail car.

Amaranthe and Sicarius turned down the dead end to their hideout. Books stumbled out of the "parlor" car with a palm pressed to his temple. She'd thought the men were past the point of engaging in fisticuffs if she was not around to mediate, but perhaps not.

"Did Akstyr hit you?" she asked. Maybe she *should* let the enforcers find him.

Books waved an acknowledgement of their arrival and said, "Not exactly. His concoction emitted fumes that caused me to lunge away and smack my head on the wall."

Sicarius climbed the nearest car and crouched on the roof, standing watch.

Since it appeared Books would recover, Amaranthe gave him a pat on the shoulder and went straight to business. "There are enforcers searching the boneyard for a young wizard with a gang brand."

Akstyr stuck his head out of the rail car. The usual spiky queue he styled his hair into had sagged, leaving a limp carrot top dangling on either side. Soot and blue goo stained what had started out as a baggy white shirt. A faint smudge decorated his upper lip.

"What?" he asked. "Why?"

"I thought you might know," Amaranthe said, reaching for her kerchief. "Been performing your arts on anybody outside of our group?"

"I wish he wouldn't perform them on anybody *inside* the group," Books muttered, his hand still clutched to his temple.

"Uhh... I don't know what you're talking about," Akstyr told Amaranthe.

"Positive?" she asked.

Akstyr shoved his hands in his pockets. "Yes."

"What about that girl you were talking to this morning?" Books asked.

Akstyr scowled at him. "I can't talk to girls?"

"She was comely and well-dressed," Books said. "Maybe warrior caste."

"What're you saying? That no good-looking girls would talk to me?"

"Essentially." Books lowered his hand and curled a lip when his fingers came away bloody.

Amaranthe glanced up at Sicarius, not sure they should be wasting this time with the enforcers nearby. He wriggled his fingers in one of Basilard's signs. The predators were closer, but not yet a threat.

"Akstyr," Amaranthe said, "what you do with your talents is your choice, but doing it where the group is hiding out can get us all in trouble."

He bent his head and kicked at a weed thrusting from beneath one of the rusted car wheels. "I just wanted to make some money on the side. You don't pay us hardly nothing, and I've got expenses. I don't just drink and whore like Maldynado. I've got to buy books and components for researching now." He jerked his elbow toward the car without taking his hands out of his pockets.

"Understandable," Amaranthe said. "Next time..." She approached him with the kerchief. The smudge above his lips was bugging her. Since his hands were occupied, she figured she could clean it off before he objected. She dampened it and swiped it beneath his nose.

"What're you doing?" he balked.

"Cleaning that smudge," she said.

"What smudge? There's no smudge."

"No, there's definitely something there." Despite his protests, she managed to give it a good rub.

"Amaranthe, you're tormenting the lad," Books said, though his eyes glinted with amusement.

"Huh," she said. "It won't come off. Oh, it's hair."

"It's *not* hair." Akstyr stepped out of reach. "It's a mustache."

"I don't see anything," Books said.

"That's because you're senile." Akstyr lifted his nose and smoothed his upper lip to show it off. "Anyone can plainly see that it's coming in nicely. I've been working on it for several days now."

"I see," Amaranthe said. "A bit on the wispy side still."

"Wispy and invisible," Books muttered.

She shook her head and settled for wiping some of the goo off of Akstyr's face and shirt. He sighed deeply under this torture.

"As I was saying," Amaranthe said, "next time, just come to me if you need help purchasing items that can benefit the group. I'll find a way to get the money."

"And don't be a dolt and bring your...clients here," Books said. "What'd you do for her anyway?"

Amaranthe wondered that, too. And how had the woman known to find Akstyr? Honored ancestors, he didn't have flyers out around the city, did he?

"Healed her," Akstyr said.

"Nothing appeared to ail her," Books said.

"Look, it was her toenail, all right? Some fungus. It was all black and nasty. Could we not talk about it? This isn't exactly what I dreamed about when I started studying this stuff. It's embarrassing. I wish I could go to Kyatt or somewhere that I could study real Science and learn to do interesting things."

Leave the empire? Was that the goal to which he aspired? Amaranthe supposed she could understand that, given the danger his studies brought him here, but she would have to keep an eye on him. If he planned to leave, he probably did not care about exoneration or accolades from the emperor. The day might come when his goals were at odds with hers.

"Well..." Amaranthe rested a hand on her belly. "I've found

your healing skills to be *quite* interesting. And useful. In a thank-you-for-saving-my-life kind of way."

Akstyr grunted.

"And please update your flyers to make sure people know you'd rather visit them than have them visit here," she added.

"I don't have *flyers*."

"Update whatever your promotional method is," Amaranthe said. "Now, tell me about your research. Did you find anything?"

"Oh!" Akstyr clambered into the rail car.

"I didn't mean to send him scurrying away," she murmured.

"We found a fine yellow powder inside a divot in the cork," Books said. "It was visible only with a magnifying glass."

Akstyr popped back out again, a hefty tome balanced in his arms. He held it open, displaying weathered pages full of foreign text comprised of sweeping curlicues and complicated symbols. Amaranthe could not imagine writing a page in the ornate script, much less an entire book.

"What language is that?" she asked.

"It's Nurian," Books said, "though a calligraphy version. It was most difficult to translate, and it did not help that someone was impatiently breathing down—"

"Just look at the picture." Akstyr tapped the page.

Several yellow dots were sprinkled around a homely brown root with more kinks and snarls than a hair ball.

"That's the powder that was on the cork?" she asked. "It comes from that root?"

"This *might* be the powder," Akstyr said. "I'm...not real experienced at identifying things yet."

"An understatement." Books massaged his temple.

"If this is the right powder, the root it's made from can make you sleepy if you eat it. But wizards have tinkered with it, and there's a recipe here for enhancing its effects, so it can knock someone out completely."

"Is it put in food or water?" Amaranthe asked.

"It can be, but it's so fine that people have also made blow tubes and breakable capsules for distributing it in the air. Breathing it can be enough to knock you out."

"So, it's Nurian?" Amaranthe thought of Arbitan Losk. Was it possible another Nurian had come to the capital with a plan to disrupt the empire? Or to get at the emperor somehow? Tradition mandated he would be at the final days of the Imperial Games, and there was that dinner.... She did not know how disappearing athletes might be used against him though. Could someone be getting the competition out of the way so a particular loyal athlete would make it to the end to get close to the emperor? For an assassination attempt? But, if so, why bother to kidnap so many people, across multiple events?

"Maybe." Akstyr tossed his head, flicking hair out of his eyes. Thanks to his errant experiments, it had the same snarls and tangles as the root today. "Maybe not. The root is from the Nurian continent, but it's actually the Kyattese that made the powder and have done most of the experimenting with it."

"They wouldn't attack the empire, though," Amaranthe said. "Or would they? They're supposedly a peaceful folk with academic tendencies, but we did try to conquer them a couple of decades ago. Could they be harboring thoughts of revenge?"

Akstyr looked around. "Are you still talking to me? 'Cause I dunno about that stuff."

"No, just thinking out loud. Books?" she asked, thinking to draw him into the conversation—he had wandered away and seemed to be looking for a cloth for his cut.

"Anyone home?" Maldynado's voice came from the distance.

Amaranthe winced at the loudness of it.

"We've got news for—ouch!"

She jogged out of the dead end to find Sicarius standing

before Maldynado and Basilard. Maldynado was clutching his shoulder.

"Lower your voice," Sicarius said. "Enforcers are nearby."

"You could have started with that instead of throwing a rock at me," Maldynado muttered. He spotted Amaranthe and said, "Mancrest wants to meet with you."

Sicarius glared. Maldynado was lucky he had waited until after the rock throwing to deliver this information.

"You arranged another meeting for me?" Amaranthe asked. "Are we certain enforcers and army officer brothers won't be involved?"

Maldynado thumped his chest. "*I* set the meeting place this time. Tomorrow night, Pyramid Park. Nobody could possibly ambush you there."

She snorted and looked at Sicarius, thinking of their first meeting. He hadn't exactly ambushed her, but he had appeared behind her as if by magic. She still did not know how he had gotten there without using the only set of stairs leading to the top. He appeared to be too busy glaring at Maldynado to ask just then.

"All right," Amaranthe said. "Did he sound...interested in hearing more from me? Did you arrange things again, or was it his idea?"

"His idea," Maldynado said. "He wants to talk about the kidnappings, but he sounded interested in you. And wanted you to leave Sicarius at home." Maldynado winked. "I think you charmed him. Maybe he's ready to take you to dinner."

If Sicarius's glare grew any frostier, it would leave icicles dangling from Maldynado's lashes. Or perhaps an ice spear thrust between his eyes.

"It's likely another trap," Sicarius told Amaranthe.

"This Mancrest thing isn't the priority now," Amaranthe said. Eager to change the subject, she added, "I'd like you gentlemen to get out of the boneyard before the enforcers amble through. Please assist Books and Akstyr in their research. Sicarius and I have something to do tonight and may be back late."

"Nothing that will make Deret jealous, I hope." Maldynado snickered, as if he had made some fabulous joke.

The building trembled as a locomotive rumbled into the station down the street. From the darkness of The Brewed Puppy rooftop, Amaranthe watched a tenement building across the street while she waited for Sicarius to join her. The stench of burning meat wafted up to her, mingling with an omnipresent thick yeasty smell oozing from the building's pores, and Amaranthe judged the old woman's dismal opinion of the eating house's quality to be accurate.

With her elbows propped on a low wall and a spyglass raised to her eye, she checked each window, searching for a man with a woman and two young boys. She did not know if she would recognize Raydevk based on a vague memory of the man's father, but if she found the right combination of people...

She paused. Could that be it? Beyond a third-story window, a woman sat, knitting on a couch in a clutter-filled, one-room flat. Toys littered the floor at her feet. While Amaranthe was trying to judge if the carved wood blocks and automata represented boys' or girls' playthings, two youngsters scampered into view from behind a room partition formed by furniture draped with clothing. They chased each other around the woman's chair, but an upraised hand and word from her halted that. She thrust a finger toward another clutter-partition, this one with a curtain hanging on a rod to delineate a door. The children disappeared into the dark space. Their sleeping area, Amaranthe assumed.

Voices sounded below as a couple exited the eating house, and she shifted her elbow to move the spyglass from her eye.

Something gooey made her sleeve stick. She drew her arm back with a grimace and picked off tar.

She yawned and glanced around her rooftop perch, thinking of Sicarius's warning to check her surroundings frequently. Moonlight gleamed against a stovepipe and provided enough illumination to confirm nothing stirred nearby. No doors led to the lower levels of The Brewed Puppy—she had climbed up via a drainpipe—and she doubted anyone except Sicarius would sneak up on her. She returned her attention to the brick building across the way.

"Is he there?" came Sicarius's voice from behind her.

Amaranthe almost dropped the spyglass.

"Not yet," she said, putting her back to the wall so she could face him.

It took her a moment to pick him out, standing in the shadows of a chimney. Had he just arrived? Or had he been testing her? Seeing if she would notice him before he announced himself? And why did she always feel like he was an army instructor, bent on training her to be a better soldier?

"You found a uniform?" Amaranthe asked.

He glided out of the shadows, soundless, like a haunting ancestor spirit. The moonlight did not reveal the color of his outfit, but it appeared less dark than his usual black, and she thought she detected familiar silver piping and buttons. A boxy cap covered much of his blond hair.

"Yes," he said.

She touched his sleeve when he knelt beside her, and her fingers met the familiar scratchy wool of an enforcer uniform. She wore hers as well, the only article of clothing she had retained from her old life.

"Did you...uhm, where'd you find it?" Amaranthe had asked him not to maul anyone for a uniform, though he did tend to do things his own way.

"Clothesline."

"Oh, good." Her hand bumped an enforcer-issue short

sword hanging from his belt. He had not found *that* on a clothesline, but it was a typical part of the uniform, so she decided not to ask. She wore one, too, as well as handcuffs. She pointed at the window she had identified earlier. "I think I've spotted the wife and children. Maybe we should…interview her before the husband gets home." Yes, "interview" sounded friendlier than interrogate. "She might know what he's up to. I can talk to her, see what I can learn, and you can snoop and see what you can learn."

"Too late," Sicarius said. "The husband has arrived. Or an enthusiastic lover."

"Huh?" Amaranthe lifted the spyglass to check on the flat again, but jerked it from her eye as soon as the scene came into focus. "Ugh. I don't want to walk in on that."

"They'll stop." Sicarius started for the drainpipe leading to an alley below.

"Maybe we should wait until they're done," Amaranthe said.

"Why?"

"I'm sure he'll be in a better mood afterward. Would you want to be interrupted in the middle of…stoking the furnace?"

He said nothing. He probably thought it ridiculous to worry about such a thing.

"We'll just wait here and…" She groped for a way to pass time that would not make Sicarius balk. Chat? No. Draw a grid and play Dirt Defender? No, not enough light. Emulate the people across the street? Hah. Sure.

"Watch?" Sicarius said when her silence went on.

"What? No! I used to arrest people for that."

Grunts drifted up to the rooftop. The lovers had clambered out of their window and were undressing each other on the fire escape. That was one way to avoid waking the children, Amaranthe supposed. Though the neighbors might not appreciate it.

"We could discuss the team uniform," she said, joking.

"The what?"

"Maldynado thinks we should have a team uniform."

The long silence that followed said plenty about his opinion of the idea. She collapsed the spyglass, tucked it into a pocket, and moved away from the edge of the roof so she could not be seen from the fire escape. "We'll just take our time getting over there," she said.

"The plan?" Sicarius asked.

Yes, it would not be as easy for him to snoop with two adults in the room. "Back to the original." Amaranthe patted a pocket that held a forged document neatly folded into quarters. "It seems we have the magistrate's permission to search the premises."

"If they recognize one of us?" Sicarius asked.

"I doubt they will. Miners don't get much time off to roam the city and peruse wanted posters."

"If your source is correct, this one does."

"We'll adjust the plan if need be," she said.

"It would be far simpler to go in, grab him, and force him to answer questions."

"Sicarius..." Amaranthe hung her head. "Sespian is never going to want to get to know someone whose solution for every problem is torturing people. I know it's efficient, but I don't think he's someone who can respect a man who isn't humane."

"Humane," Sicarius said flatly.

"Yes. At least in one's actions. Nobody can be judged for what's in his thoughts, eh?"

"And the *humane* thing to do is to disguise ourselves as enforcers and lie to these people to obtain answers."

Er, she hated it when she was trying to be morally superior and someone pointed out that her idea was only slightly less sketchy. "I think it's a...humane option, yes. If all goes well, nobody will be hurt. Is it ideal? Perhaps not, but I don't know of an ideal situation. I'm beginning to think our circumstances preclude those. But maybe it's always been that way. If the legends are anything to go by, being a hero doesn't mean being perfect. Being a hero means overcoming those imperfections to do good anyway." There that sounded plausible. Or pompous. Was she truly comparing the two of them to the great heroes of old? "Anyway, I think Sespian is far more likely to admire someone who eschews the easy solution, however efficient, in favor of the one that does no harm. I'm sure of it."

Sicarius said nothing at first, and she winced in anticipation of a cold reaction. Surely the philosophizing of a twenty-six-year-old woman could only make him snort in derision. Inwardly anyway. He would never deign to be that expressive outwardly.

"I see," Sicarius finally said. "And are you?"

"Am I what?" she asked. Her own thoughts had sidetracked her.

"More likely to admire someone like that."

Huh. Did he *care* what she thought of him? Enough that he might make a humane decision instead of a practical one? For her? She found herself reluctant to test that hypothesis, for she might be disappointed—and hurt—if it proved false down the road. "I know it's the nature of women to try and change men, but you don't have to do anything on my behalf. I'm just trying to help with Sespian. In my arrogance, I think I'm more like him than you are, and I may have more insight into what would make him...interested in knowing you."

"Not arrogance. Fact. They've completed their coitus. Let's go."

Amaranthe blinked at his abrupt switching of topics, but she recovered and jogged after him. They skimmed down the drainpipe, waited for a couple of locals to enter the eating house, and crossed the street to the apartment building. She slipped past Sicarius to open one of the double doors and step inside first.

Nobody occupied the shabby parlor, and half of the gas lamps on the walls were out. She headed for a hallway at the back. Doors lined both sides, and the staircase she sought rose at the far end. A faded gray runner had collected so much dirt, she barely recognized the repeating sword pattern. She did know it had been one of the early themes woven on the first steam looms, making it a testament to the rug's age.

At the base of the stairs, she stopped near one of the working lamps, intending to check Sicarius's uniform. She trusted him to get the details right, but she needed to know if he had any rank pins or badges that would mark him her superior. If so, she would have to amend her spiel to pretend she was taking orders from him. But, when she saw him in the light, she froze and stared.

Clad in the crisp, clean lines of a gray enforcer uniform, he looked...good. Handsome, yes, but heroic, too. Not like some assassin who lurked in the shadows, ready to jab a dagger into someone's back, but like someone noble who helped people.

It's just fabric, girl, she told herself, but the thoughts brought a lump to her throat nonetheless. What might he have been had his childhood been different? Normal.

"Something inaccurate?" Sicarius asked.

"No." Amaranthe cleared her throat. "No, you've got it right." She lifted a foot and placed it on the first stair, but paused again. "Do you—or *did* you ever want to be something else? For an...occupation? When you were a child maybe?"

Anyone else would have given her a perplexed frown over such a random question. He...gazed at her without a hint of his thoughts. Floorboards creaked in a room nearby. A muffled conversation went on behind a door. In the hallway, he neither moved nor spoke. She searched his eyes. Did he spend even half as much time wondering what she was thinking as she did wondering what he was thinking?

"Never mind," Amaranthe said. "I just meant you'd be... believable as an enforcer."

She headed up the stairs.

"A soldier," Sicarius said quietly.

Amaranthe halted. "You daydreamed of being a soldier?"

"When it was necessary for my focus to be elsewhere, I thought of it occasionally."

He caught up with her and kept climbing, perhaps considering the conversation over. *Focus to be elsewhere.* As in to block out the pain of some torturous childhood training session? He did not expound, and she did not ask. She matched him, and they ascended the steps side by side.

"Like Berkhorth the Brazen?" she asked, wanting to leave him with better thoughts than of some past need to will his mind elsewhere. "The third century general who was so gifted with a blade that an entire city surrendered en masse when they saw him walk up with a single squad of soldiers?" They rounded the second-story landing, and she kept talking, warming to the idea of Sicarius as the legendary hero. "The man so fearsome that none of the soldiers guarding that city realized his squad was covered in blood and wounds and had only a single, battered sword between them because they'd just escaped capture and torture?"

Sicarius slanted her a faintly bemused look. "Starcrest."

Her toe bumped a step, and she caught herself on the railing. "Fleet Admiral Starcrest? Really? I picture you more as a warrior general than a brilliant naval strategist."

They reached the third floor and another empty hallway.

"You believe I lack intelligence?" Sicarius asked.

Amaranthe jerked a hand up. "No, no." It had been some time since he had thrown a knife at her, and she did not want to give him a reason to consider it again. "It's just that...ah, you lose to me three out of four times when we play Strat Tiles."

"Because you cheat."

"How do I cheat?" she asked, trying to read his face to see if he was irked or merely giving her a hard time. She never should have given him permission to tease her.

"You talk," Sicarius said.

"Talking isn't cheating."

"It is when you seek to wheedle my strategy from me under the guise of learning from my greater experience."

She blushed. She hadn't realized he saw through that so easily. Though it had worked.... Several times.

"I should be flogged, no doubt," Amaranthe said.

A rare gleam of humor entered his eyes. "Perhaps."

Amaranthe counted doors until they reached the flat she had been observing, the one she hoped belonged to Raydevk and his wife. The building could very well house other families with two young sons.

She pressed an ear against the door before knocking; she did not wish to interrupt a second round of lovemaking. Voices murmured, male and female, the words too low to make out. They did not sound ardor-filled.

She knocked. Out of habit, she straightened her uniform and patted down her bun. Looking the part of a professional enforcer might no longer be a requirement, but some tics failed to die.

The door opened, and a moon-faced woman leaned into the gap. When she spotted the uniforms, her eyes bulged. Even a rookie could have interpreted the guilty we're-caught expression.

Amaranthe stuck her foot into the gap, lest the woman's first instinct be to slam the door shut and lock it. The woman stepped back, but bumped against one of the piles of furniture, boxes, and clutter that were used to delineate separate spaces in the single room.

"Peaceful evening," Amaranthe greeted. "I'm Corporal Lokdon." The name was sewn on her name tag, so she dared not change it, but she said it quickly on the chance the woman read the newspapers. Amaranthe nodded to Sicarius. "And this is Corporal Jev." Or so his uniform said. "We have a few questions for your husband, ma'am."

"Who is it, Pella?" a man, presumably Raydevk, asked. "One of the boys? They weren't supposed to come until nine." He snickered. "Or is it old Ms. Derya complaining that the fire escape isn't a suitable place for sex play? Again."

Since the woman—Pella—seemed stunned with indecision, Amaranthe pushed the door open. The smirk on the miner's face dropped. He held a book—a journal?—in his hands, and he hid it behind his back. Yes, the guilt hung in the air like smog around a factory. Though that meant it was probably good that she had come, it also made her fairly certain these weren't the masterminds behind...anything.

"Mister Raydevk?" Amaranthe asked. "We have a few questions for you."

"I've done nothing illegal," he said.

"Good." She smiled. "Then we'll be able to finish quickly."

"Uh, right." Raydevk eyed several of the cabinets and clothing-draped stacks. Seeking somewhere to stash his journal?

"Mind if we come in?" Amaranthe asked.

Sicarius invited himself in, slipping past Amaranthe to stand inside the doorway. Pella stepped, no, stumbled backward. Hm, Amaranthe might find Sicarius's appearance heroic in the uniform, but he still intimidated others. The cold unwavering stare perhaps.

"Thanks," Amaranthe said brightly. She strolled in and displayed her warrant oh-so briefly to Pella. "Corporal Jev has orders to search the premises. I hope this won't inconvenience you terribly."

"Search?" Raydevk's voice squeaked. "What for?" His eyes darted about in his head, searching again. Still trying to get rid of that journal? He focused on a credenza in a corner by a cook stove. "Can I get you a drink?"

"No, thanks," Amaranthe said.

Regardless, he darted for the credenza, opened a door, and withdrew glasses and a bottle of applejack. "I'll just have a taste, if you don't mind."

Loosening one's tongue was not a particularly good idea

for a liar—a possibly criminal liar—faced with enforcers, but Amaranthe saw no reason to object. Raydevk met his wife's eyes, widening his own in some signal.

"Why are you folks here?" Pella asked.

"A group of miners has been implicated in a conspiracy against the athletes at the Imperial Games," Amaranthe said, trying to surprise reactions out of Pella and Raydevk. She did not truly expect these people to have much—if anything—to do with the kidnappings, but one never knew. "The missing athletes, to be precise."

Pella glanced at her husband and rushed to say, "We don't know anything about that."

Raydevk had his back to everyone, ostensibly preparing a drink, but he froze at Amaranthe's words. He jerked his head at Pella and she burbled on, giving some story about the men winning time off at a company lottery and simply going to the Games to relax.

Amaranthe barely listened. She was watching Raydevk. Still fiddling with his drink, he tried to hide his actions as he set the journal on the credenza and opened it. He coughed to cover the noise he made ripping the top sheet off. He used the movement of returning the bottle to a shelf to slip that page into his pocket.

"Corporal Jev," Amaranthe said. She trusted Sicarius had seen the inept legerdemain and hoped he interpreted her head tilt as would-you-be-so-kind-as-to-retrieve-that-for-me. "Begin the search."

Sicarius gave her a hard look, no doubt wondering why they were dickering around instead of simply taking what they needed. She flicked her fingers, hoping he would play along a little while longer. These people were not experienced criminals, and they would likely give her everything they knew without the need for force.

"You're not going to disturb the children, are you?" Pella asked.

Amaranthe had forgotten they were sleeping behind one of the walls of clutter. She trusted Sicarius with her life, and she resented that doubt curled into her at the idea of sending him in to deal with a couple of kids on his own, but what he had shared of his history did not lead her to believe he would be good with them. Granted, the order to dump decapitated heads on the floor with five-year-old Sespian watching had been Emperor Raumesys's command, but still.

"We'll check them last," Amaranthe said. Together. She hoped Sicarius did not read the reason for her hesitation in her words. She trusted him. She did. She just figured that even at his most innocuous, he would scare children.

"Mister Raydevk, where do you work? Black Peak?" she asked while Sicarius went through shelves and drawers in the room.

"Yes." He took a swig of applejack, though he had appeared more relaxed before the alcohol touched his lips.

Yes, Amaranthe definitely wanted that paper. "Then it'll be easy enough to check up on this story about a lottery and winners."

Raydevk froze again, the amber liquid to his lips. He recovered and shrugged. "I imagine so."

Pella scraped her fingers through her hair and chewed on her lip.

"You and other miners have been seen at the Imperial Games a number of days this week," Amaranthe said. "Care to explain what you're doing there?"

"Just watching the athletes and enjoying my time off."

Amaranthe decided to try talking about herself instead of asking questions. It might put the man at ease and make him more likely to slip with his comments. "It's fortunate you got that much time off. My father was a miner. He never received more than a couple of days off in a month." Though he had once come all the way into the city to watch Amaranthe's race even though he had to get right back on a train to make it to work the next morning.

"He die young, did he?" Pella asked.

"Yes," Amaranthe said. "It's a hard life, I know."

"Got that right," Raydevk said.

"Can't blame people for wanting to better their lot," Pella said.

"Is that what you're doing at the Games?" Amaranthe asked.

"I told you," Raydevk said, quick to speak over Pella, Amaranthe sensed, "I'm just down there to enjoy my time off."

"I'd think you'd want to spend more of that time with your family."

"Don't you judge me." Raydevk scowled and pointed a finger at her face. "I take care of my family real good."

"I'm sure you do," Amaranthe said.

"Then what exactly are you accusing me of?"

Sicarius paused at the curtain leading to the children's sleeping area. His ear was cocked. Had he heard something?

"The boys are sleeping in there," Pella said. "No reason to go in."

Amaranthe could not tell if she was hiding something, or simply did not want enforcers scaring her children.

Sicarius pushed the curtain aside. A five- or six-year-old boy stumbled out and collapsed at his feet. Someone listening at the "door," apparently. Eyes round, the boy stared up at Sicarius.

"Are they here?" a young voice queried from the darkened sleeping area. Soft thumps sounded—bare feet running across a thin carpet. "Ma, you said we could come say, 'Hello,' when Uncle Drovar came." A boy younger than the first charged out of the room as he spoke, and he would have crashed into Sicarius's leg, but Sicarius lifted his foot, removing the obstacle.

When the boys realized they had strange visitors, in intimidating uniforms no less, they grew quiet and slunk over to their mother. She lifted a finger, as if she might send them right back to bed, but Sicarius slipped into the vacated area. A light came to life. A good time to search, but Amaranthe wished he would get her that note first. He would be a smoother pickpocket than she.

"Mister Raydevk," Amaranthe said, "you're not accused of anything yet, but it's clear you're not telling the truth. If you don't answer my questions honestly, we'll be authorized to take you to the magistrate for further questioning. Are you sure you don't know anything about the missing athletes?"

"I don't know anything."

The older of the two boys left his mother's side to peer into the sleeping area.

"If you *did* know something," Amaranthe told Raydevk, "and it led to the arrest of those who spawned the plot, it's possible we could work a deal where your punishment was waived."

Raydevk hesitated, but only for a second. He spread his arms wide. "What would a miner have to do with kidnappings?"

"I only said athletes were missing, not that they were kidnapped," Amaranthe said. "How do you know someone is taking them?"

"Er, I don't. I mean, the newspapers said that, didn't they?"

"No."

"Just a guess, then," Raydevk muttered.

The boy peering into the sleeping area leaned in further. "What are you doing, mister?"

His mother stepped around the younger one and stretched out a hand to grab him, but the boy slipped inside.

"Do you want to see my models? I have an imperial warship, the first steam ferry, and Da's friend made me a replica of the city's ice breaking ship."

Amaranthe figured Sicarius would ignore the questions, but he was pragmatic to the point where he probably wouldn't think twice about tying the boy up to keep him out of the way. She stepped toward the curtain to make sure nothing like that happened, but knocks at the door made her pause.

Raydevk cursed under his breath. His wife winced.

"Problem?" Amaranthe asked.

"No," Raydevk said. "Wrong address."

Nobody said anything for a moment, but then the knocks came again—multiple fists striking the wood. "Ray, what's the hold up? You two entertaining the neighborhood from the fire escape again?"

The wife's face flushed red, and even the miner had the sense to appear mortified.

"Why don't you let that wrong address in?" Amaranthe asked. "Maybe they know something about the missing athletes."

"Come on, Ray, we have to go. Meeting starts in ten minutes."

"Meeting?" Amaranthe smiled even as Raydevk cursed. She supposed she should not feel pleasure at watching someone's lies falling apart, but fate usually tormented her, so it was nice seeing someone else have trouble.

"I...uh...I'll just answer that," Raydevk said.

He backed toward the door, watching her as he went, and she sensed he meant to try something. He wore no weapons, but he might have one stashed in the flat. A small table with a drawer leaned against the wall near the door. Amaranthe eased behind the sofa, figuring she could duck for cover if need be.

Raydevk reached for the doorknob, though, not the drawer. "You gentlemen will have to come back another time," he said loudly without taking his eyes from Amaranthe. "There's an enforcer lady here who's talking to me about—" He flung the door open and darted into the hall. "Run!"

Surprised, Amaranthe did not react immediately. The coward had left his wife to deal with the enforcers while he ran off with the boys? The wife gaped at the open door, as startled as Amaranthe. All the men had taken off, and footsteps thundered in the stairwell at the end of the hallway.

"Si—Corporal Jev," Amaranthe called.

Sicarius strode out.

"I need you to follow that..." The grinning boy riding Sicarius's leg and clutching a toy boat made her pause. Well,

Sicarius hadn't tied the child up. That was good. "Our miners are off to a secret meeting. If you could extricate yourself, I'd appreciate it if you'd find out who they're meeting and where."

Without a word, Sicarius unwound the boy from his leg, deposited him on the sofa, brushed past Amaranthe, and slipped out the window. He vaulted over the fire escape rail without bothering with the ladder.

"How come that man can't talk?" the boy asked.

"He can talk. He's just not the chatty type." Amaranthe eased around the sofa toward the door. She doubted Pella would run off and leave her children behind, but there was no need to tempt her. As she was shutting the door, her hand brushed her pocket, and something inside crinkled. She slipped her fingers in and slid a piece of paper out—the note Raydevk had stashed. When Sicarius had been close enough to him to retrieve it, she did not know, but she itched to unfold it and read it.

"My brother isn't chatty either," the boy said.

Conscious of the mother's gaze upon her, Amaranthe slid the note back into her pocket. She would check it later.

"He liked my boat," the boy added.

Amaranthe wondered how that deduction had been made if Sicarius hadn't said anything. "I'm sure he did. It's very nice."

"Marl, Denny, go back to bed," Pella said.

Marl, huh? Amaranthe wondered if Books would be flattered to know a boat-loving toddler shared his name.

"Where did Da go?"

Pella dragged her hands through her hair. "I don't know. Just go to bed, please." She shoved them toward the curtain and sank down in a chair.

Amaranthe thought that "I don't know" sounded authentic, but she perched on the sofa across from the woman, intending to find as many answers as she could. "Ma'am, mind answering a few questions?"

"Do I have a choice?" Her bleak smile held no humor.

"Not really, no." Though she had a good memory, Amaranthe

withdrew a notepad and a pen. It might help her appear official. "Do you know what he's involved with? He's not responsible for kidnapping athletes, is he?"

"No, no, he wouldn't do that. I don't even know why..." Pella shrugged. "I'm not sure what he's up to."

"It's strange that he's home for the week, isn't it?"

"Yes, he never gets this much time off. He...I shouldn't be betraying his trust to you, should I? A good wife is supposed to keep the books and her husband's secrets."

"You do know," Amaranthe said, "that the law no longer requires a woman to go to jail with her husband if he's convicted of a crime, right? Unless she's found to be an accomplice...."

"I'm no accomplice! He shows up here, takes all our savings, and promises me it's for the greater good. That we won't have to worry about anything in the future. That it's worth living in poverty today if we can live like emperors tomorrow. I don't know what I'm supposed to make of that. He won't tell me more. Just says not to worry about it. I'll have to work for our reward, but it'll be worth it in the end."

"You'll have to work for it?" Amaranthe tapped her pen against the notepad. That did not sound like a gambling scheme. Unless Raydevk meant his wife would have to work, taking care of kidnapped prisoners. But, no, she did not know about them, and some had been missing for days, so she would have been recruited by now if that were her task.

"That's what he said."

Amaranthe leaned back. A broken spring beneath the sofa cushion prodded her in the butt. Though she feared she would get little more information, she spent another fifteen minutes questioning Pella.

"I'm not going to jail, right?" Pella asked when she walked Amaranthe to the door at the end. "Whatever he's gotten tangled up with, it wasn't my idea. I'm a good, loyal citizen. I swear it. And my boys are, too. They need me."

A guilty twinge coursed through Amaranthe—this woman

had doubtlessly committed fewer crimes than *she* had. She forced a smile and gripped Pella's shoulder. "If what you say is true, you've nothing to worry about from the enforcers."

Her husband was another matter.

The building's parlor remained empty, so Amaranthe stopped beneath a light to check the note.

Two columns of names were written in sloppy, barely legible handwriting that an imperial code-breaker would have struggled to decipher. She recognized three out of the five, and one of them was Sicarius.

A chill ran through her. Had Raydevk known who Sicarius was all the time? He hadn't shown any signs of recognition when Sicarius stepped through the door. And Raydevk hadn't been that great at hiding any of his other thoughts. Surely, he would have given something away.

Sicarius's name was at the top of the left-hand column, one with three entries in it. Deercrest, the missing wrestler, came under him, and Amaranthe did not recognize the third. The top name on the second column belonged to Fasha's sister Keisha. The other two looked like Borsk and Allemah. Maybe.

Amaranthe pocketed the note again and stepped outside. She debated whether to wait on the sidewalk in front of the building, return to the hideout, or go back up to Pella and see what her reaction would be to the name, "Sicarius." Her gut squirmed, knowing she had sent him off to spy on people who apparently wanted him for some nefarious reason.

She headed back into the building, adjusting the stiff collar of her enforcer uniform as she climbed the stairs again. It was scratching her neck more than she remembered—maybe the fabric was reminding her she no longer had any right to wear it.

When she reached the flat and lifted her hand to knock, the door stood ajar. Strange. She would have thought Pella would lock everything up and put the children to bed after the incident.

Amaranthe pushed the door open. Darkness shrouded the room, but she sensed what she would find even before she brought in a lantern and searched. Pella and the children were gone.

CHAPTER 7

Basilard urged his legs to greater speed, though the darkness made the footing treacherous. He snorted. Even by day, the footing was treacherous.

He reached the end of the swinging platforms, leaped onto the last wall, pulled himself over, and dropped the ground. He sprinted the last ten meters to the finish line.

A soft clack sounded as Akstyr stopped the watch. He held it up to one of the few gas lamps still burning. "Just over two minutes. Nice. You're going to be a real competitor. Imagine how speedy you'll be when it's light enough to see."

It will be easier to avoid the swinging axes, Basilard signed with a nod toward the dark, deadly shadows swaying back and forth.

Akstyr squinted, and Basilard could tell he struggled to read the hand signals in the dim lighting. When Akstyr had told Maldynado to take the night off, that he would work with Basilard on his "training," Basilard had assumed the young man wanted to speak about Sicarius—perhaps he had some idea?—but thus far Akstyr had not mentioned him. Basilard should bring it up. This was his quest after all.

As if sensing his intent, Akstyr whispered, "I was thinking about that powder. If it's what I think it is.... Am'ranthe tell you the details?"

Basilard drew closer to the light, so his hand signs would be visible. *Yes.*

"If we could get some..."

A creak sounded behind them, and Akstyr jumped a foot, spinning in the air to face the sound. The maintenance fellow who manned the obstacle course's furnace strode from a doorway in the stone wall below the first tier of seating.

Akstyr chuckled nervously. Basilard touched his arm and nodded, indicating they should walk. The man would be powering down the engine for the night anyway, so training was over.

You suggest finding the kidnappers and colluding with them? To get some of the powder? The thought did not sit well with Basilard. Though he had no reason to love the athletes attending the Imperial Games, he had no reason to wish them ill either, and he did not care for the idea of working against Amaranthe.

"No, I wasn't thinking about that," Akstyr said, keeping his voice low as they walked. "Am'ranthe wants me to go investigate apothecaries tomorrow, to see if we can find out if a local sells the stuff and if someone suspicious has been buying it up. If I get a chance, I'll buy some while I'm there. Then we just have to figure out how to use it on Sicarius, and you can..." He sliced a finger across his throat.

Basilard swallowed. Even if he was no longer the model Mangdorian, he shrank from the idea of killing an unconscious man. But at the same time, he could not foresee downing Sicarius in a fair fight. He had never even drawn blood when they sparred. Basilard had a measure of talent when it came to knives, but Sicarius had...*erkt mahlay*. That was the Kendorian term for it, and one his people used as well. Literally, snake blood. Figuratively, the ability to strike, not just with the speed of a viper, but with a snake's utter lack of hesitation and remorse. Even knowing what he knew about the man's crimes, Basilard would hesitate. He knew he would. Sicarius would not.

Basilard massaged the bridge of his nose with his thumb and forefinger.

"You're not backing out, are you?" Akstyr asked.

No. I'll do it.

"Good."

Amaranthe stood on top of the rail car, her back to the rising sun. A thousand metallic objects in the boneyard reflected its rays, and her eyes already ached from staring across the expanse.

Clanks sounded below her—one of the men climbing up. The others spoke in low tones around the fire pit below. Basilard was cooking eggs, and the appealing scent wafting up should have pleased Amaranthe, but she was busy worrying.

Books's head poked over the top of the ladder. "Breakfast is almost ready. A particularly fine one. The men are in a celebratory mood because they got to sleep in and nobody dragged us off to exercise before dawn."

Great. Sicarius was missing, and that caused a celebratory mood. Maybe Amaranthe should have led an exercise session, despite his absence.

Books clambered up beside her. "No sign of him yet?" He nodded toward the metal-filled vista.

Amaranthe shook her head once.

"I'm sure he's fine," Books said. "He's always disappearing to do...whatever it is he does when he disappears."

"Not when he's on an assignment for the team." Amaranthe sat down on one of the crates Maldynado had dragged up while claiming that a person could stand watch just as well sitting down as he could fully upright.

"He's probably trying to fulfill his assignment then. Perhaps he's chanced onto something good and needs to observe it before reporting back."

"Perhaps." Amaranthe rubbed her eyes. She had lain awake most of the night, waiting for Sicarius's return, and, as the hours had dwindled on, she had begun to question herself for sending him after the miners. They had seemed innocuous enough, but that was before she read the note with his name on it. And before the family had disappeared, leaving her with no link to the miners. "I should have let him do it his way, Books."

"Would that be a way that involved killing, torturing, or otherwise maiming people?"

"I bet he could have gotten the answers we needed by applying force that didn't do permanent damage." She poked at a splinter of wood sticking out of the crate. "Instead I got sanctimonious and said it would be better to fool the miners into talking to us by dressing up as enforcers. If we'd done it his way, we'd probably have been finished in ten minutes, and we'd know who we were up against by now."

"I'd be uncomfortable working for you if you chose his way very often," Books said.

"Well, my way isn't getting the sword polished."

"Why do you say that? We've accomplished noteworthy tasks under your leadership."

"Because we've been lucky. No because *he's* gotten me out of trouble. My crazy ideas have almost gotten me killed a half a dozen times now, and I've landed the whole group in dire situations more than once. My schemes seem so tantalizing and shiny when they first come to mind, and then I jump off the dock without checking to see if the lake's gone dry. I should stop and get Sicarius's opinion first—and listen to it and think about it. I should get *all* of your opinions. What good is a group if you don't utilize everyone to his fullest?"

Books grunted and sat on a crate opposite from hers.

She eyed him. "This would be the appropriate time for you to say something like, 'Amaranthe, you're being too hard on yourself....'"

"Oh? I thought we'd had a conversation like this before, and you told me the woman wants to rant while the man nods and grunts in agreement."

"That was a little different." She tried to smile for him, but could not, not when she remembered the events that had led up to that conversation with him on a frozen dock outside of a cannery. That night, Sicarius had *helped* her by slaying a squad of enforcers and her old partner. "You're right though. Sicarius's ways of doing things are too macabre for the group and our goals. But mine are..." She propped her chin on her fist. "What do you think, Books? I value your opinion."

"I don't think we'd have accomplished what we have without your ideas. Don't get rid of them, and don't stop being..."

She waited for him to say "crazy."

"Creative," Books said.

Well, that was nicer than crazy.

"But..."

Amaranthe braced herself. She *had* asked.

"You lack prudence," Books said. "I suspect it's a combination of youth and the fact that, until recently, you lived your life under strict rules, first as a child obedient to your father and your school teachers, and then as an enforcer, obedient to superiors and indeed in charge of enforcing laws yourself. For the first time, you have utter freedom, and it's natural for you to struggle to find a way that works. We all say we crave freedom, but the truth is many people hang themselves without the structure society imposes. Nobody's done what you're trying to do, so there's no precedent, no guideline to follow."

"That is true," Amaranthe said.

"Since that's the case, you should think twice and consider all possible outcomes before embarking on a plan that could get you, or someone else, captured."

"It's not as if that's always foreseeable."

He raised his eyebrows. "Are you sure? You have a tendency to wander into the enemy camp to chat with the head villain."

"I don't..." She stopped, since his eyebrows were threatening to crawl up to the top of his scalp and leap for the sky. Yes, she had done exactly that with Hollowcrest, the wizard Arbitan, and the shamans from Mangdoria. And now she had sent Sicarius off to spy on what might be the head villain.

"You do," Books said, "and I understand why. You get a lot of information from talking to people, and you're smarter than average, so you probably believe you can get yourself out of any trouble you get into. When I was a professor, I found that bright people sometimes make the worst students. They don't want to simply do the assignment; they want to add creative flair and sophistication, and they make things so complicated that they fail to finish on time."

"What did you say to those challenged-by-their-own-creative-flair students?" Amaranthe asked. "How did you teach them more...prudence?" She smiled, thinking he would appreciate that she used his word.

His face grew long though, and he shook his head. "I couldn't teach them that. Only experience could. There are a lot of platitudes that suggest age makes us wise, but the truth is it's *losing* that teaches best. Making mistakes. Failing. Some people are wise enough to learn from the mistakes of others, but most need to experience failure first hand. You may need to lose something important before the lessons of life sink in." He grimaced, perhaps thinking of his son and his own past.

"I liked it better when you were just grunting," Amaranthe said.

"I'm sorry, but you asked—"

She lifted a hand. "I know. I did. Thank you. I'll think about your words. And I hope they're not prophetic. I'm not ready to lose anything, especially not one of you."

"Well," Books said lightly, "if you *had* to lose someone, Sicarius would be the least missed."

Amaranthe stared at him, stricken.

"Er." This time he raised an apologetic hand. "Sorry. It was a joke. A poor joke."

"He's the only reason I'm alive, Books. He saves my life again and again, and I repay him by sending him off to be abducted or killed by whatever nefarious magic-hurling zealots are swiping athletes from the Imperial Games. Who *does* that to people they—" Amaranthe stopped herself from finishing the sentence, certain Books would be horrified by a proclamation that she loved Sicarius. She cleared her throat and switched subjects. "I'm hoping he's only detained, but I feel it'd be best to go forward on the assumption he's in trouble. If that is the case, I'd like to *prudently* extract him from it." She dug out the note they had swiped from the miner's pocket. "We lose nothing by working toward that goal, since I'm guessing, if he *is* missing, he's where the rest of the athletes are."

While Books studied the note, she wondered at her own words. *Rest* of the athletes? It was applicable, if not official. Sicarius might not have ever competed in a public venue, but she had little doubt, even older than most of the field, he would be at the top if he did enter. Maybe this had nothing to do with the Imperial Games at all. Could it be someone was rounding up the most physically gifted men and women around and using this event to shop for likely candidates? Sicarius's reputation could place him at the top of such a list even if the people doing the shopping had not seen him perform.

If her theory were true, to what ends would someone want these people? To create some sort of mercenary army? An elite force? She curled her lip at the idea. That was her *own* fantasy for the Emperor's Edge. Aside from perhaps the wrestlers, the other athletes who had been taken were not necessarily warriors. Being able to run fast or maneuver through the Clank Race did not mean one had studied fencing or unarmed combat.

"Any thoughts?" she asked Books.

"Horrible penmanship."

"You better give me more than that if you're going to save me from doing something imprudent." She smiled.

"Oh? You have an idea?"

"I was just ruminating on the common link between the names I know. Superior athleticism."

"Why don't you let me go to the stadium with Basilard today? I'll see if I can get a copy of the list of entrants and match these two unknown names. If it turns out they, like Sicarius, are not athletes that might give us more to go on."

"Agreed," Amaranthe said. "If we can figure out exactly why these people were taken, we might be able to get a bead on *who* might want to take them. Akstyr's going around to the apothecaries in the city to see if any of them has that root in stock and if they remember anyone buying it recently. If you finish early, you and Basilard can join up with him. He may need help researching and finding all the apothecaries."

"Huh, and I thought it was going to be a light work day," Books said, but he smiled, and she suspected he was happy for the chance to do research.

"I'll take Maldynado and go back to the miner's flat to see if the family is back or if anyone has information on where those men meet. Maybe if we work this from both ends we can find the kidnappers' lair somewhere in the middle."

"Assuming we are dealing with kidnappers and not someone who merely wants to kill irritatingly gifted people," Books said.

She stared at him. "This would be a case when a grunt or a nod would have been more appreciated."

"Oh. Sorry."

CHAPTER 8

Under the light of day, the brick building where Raydevk and his wife lived seemed poorer. Every few minutes, a train chugged through, shaking the ground. Surly men hunkered in doorways, drinking from ceramic applejack mugs stamped with the Three Legged Dog logo, a homely mark for the satrapy's cheapest distillery. Some said the outfit used the bruised worm-filled apples left in the orchard grass after the other distilleries had their pick.

"Charming neighborhood," Maldynado drawled after a gaunt old man stepped out of an alley, buttoning his pants. Amaranthe hoped all he had been doing in there was peeing.

As she and Maldynado approached the building, they stayed near the wall, so the wife, Pella, would not see them coming if she glanced out the window.

"This is the kind of place Sicarius takes you for evenings out, eh?" Maldynado added.

"Actually, I took *him* here," Amaranthe said. "And got him kidnapped. I'm not a very good date."

They reached the front door, and Maldynado held it open for her.

"Fortunately, Deret likes an adventure," he said.

"Is there some reason you're intent on matching us up?" she asked as they headed up the stairs.

"He's a good man, mostly, and you're a good woman, mostly. And he's in a position to help us reach our goals, so that doesn't hurt. Maybe he's not in love with you yet, but I'll wager you could talk just about any man over to your side, given time. I mean, emperor's warts, you've got *Sicarius* working for you."

Her lips twisted into a dry smirk. "Getting people to go along with my schemes and getting men to fall in love with me aren't the same."

"Sure, they are," Maldynado said as they stepped out onto the third floor. "You just make the former your priority. If you tried as hard to woo a man into bed as you did to woo me into joining your mission, you'd never sleep alone."

Amaranthe speculated on the idea of putting effort into "wooing" Sicarius, but shook the notion from her head. She had more important things to focus on. She hoped Pella had returned home, so she could question her.

Two doors away from the flat, Amaranthe halted and stretched her arm across the hallway to stop Maldynado as well. An uneasy feeling raised the hairs on the back of her neck.

The door to the family's flat stood open. Gouges marred the wood of the jamb near the lock, and splinters littered the floor beneath.

"Think Sicarius is in there?" Maldynado whispered.

A thump sounded inside, like a drawer closing.

"You think *Sicarius* would leave evidence of entering or make noises once inside?" she whispered back as she slipped her short sword from its scabbard.

"Er, no."

She would like to think it was he, that perhaps he'd spent the night tracking the miner, lost him, and come back to question the wife, but Amaranthe doubted it. She eased forward, sword in hand, stepping lightly on the hall's threadbare runner.

A faint rasp of steel sounded as Maldynado drew his rapier and followed her.

Before she could peep around the doorjamb, footsteps came from within. Heavy footsteps. A scruffy young man strode out, carrying a canvas tote stuffed so full the contents threatened to burst through the material. When he saw Amaranthe and Maldynado, he threw the tote at them and bolted down the hallway in the opposite direction.

Amaranthe turned her shoulder, but Maldynado lunged and caught the bag before it hit her.

"Get him," she said. "Bring him back."

Amazingly, he dropped the bag and sprinted down the hall without stopping to make comments about how hard she worked him for so little pay.

Another thump came from inside. Amaranthe peeked past the door, did not see anyone, and eased into the room, her back pressed against the wall. Several of the purposely arranged clutter-piles-turned-into-walls had been tipped over. Food cans, cooking utensils, and clothing scattered the floor. All the cabinet doors were open on the credenza where Raydevk had stored his applejack. One dangled from a single hinge. No bottles of alcohol sat inside the cabinets now.

Footsteps came from the corner of the room near the window, but one of the partitions hid the area. A curtain hanging from a rod marked the "doorway." Amaranthe eased closer and peered around it.

A man knelt before a dresser, shoveling clothing and knickknacks into an apple crate on the floor. His back faced Amaranthe. The hilt of a dagger poked up from his belt, but she did not see any greater weapons on him. No thoughtful consideration went into the items chosen for the crate, and she suspected they had stumbled across a mere burglary.

She crept forward and pressed the point of her sword against the back of the man's neck. "Aren't thieves supposed to ply their trade at night?"

The man froze for a heartbeat, then dove forward into a roll. He twisted and came to his feet, facing Amaranthe. His hand went to the dagger, only to find it missing. Bewilderment widened his eyes.

Amaranthe held up the blade and raised her eyebrows. "Mind if we skip further attempts at complicating my day? If you tell me how you found out this place was vacant, I imagine I can look the other way over this robbery."

"Velks!" the man shouted.

"I see, you wish to complicate my day."

"Velks!" he cried again.

A grunt sounded in the living area. The man gave Amaranthe a you're-in-trouble-now look, to which she shook her head sadly. This fellow, barely older than a boy, judging by the thinness of the goatee he aspired to grow, did not seem too bright.

When his comrade, Velks presumably, came to stand beside Amaranthe, his arms were twisted behind his back, courtesy of Maldynado who loomed behind him. Velks appeared little older than the first young man, and they shared a squareness of face. Brothers?

"Got him, boss," Maldynado said.

"Tie them up, please," Amaranthe said.

"Gently or roughly?"

"Neither!" Velks blurted with a heroic attempt to twist free.

Maldynado yawned, unperturbed by the slender man's efforts.

"Yes, neither." The younger man eyed Amaranthe's sword, but with Maldynado blocking the exit, he did not attempt anything physical.

"That depends," Amaranthe said. "Are you working for someone I shouldn't annoy, or are you independent... entrepreneurs?"

The old enforcer in her hated the idea of turning her back on a crime because the criminals were working for a gang leader or another influential underworld figure, but she had spent the last few months trying to establish connections with a few of those types, and she would look the other way if it meant keeping contacts happy. If they were independent thieves, she saw nothing wrong with trussing them up and sending a tip to Enforcer Headquarters so they could be collected.

"We're working for Sicarius," Velks said.

For half a second, Amaranthe thought he might be telling the truth, that Sicarius had sent them back to hunt for clues or some such, but she caught herself. That was wishful thinking, a hope that Sicarius was about and on the mission. Even if this man's eyes had not darted up and to the left when he spoke—according to Sicarius, that was a tell for many folks when they were lying—the story was implausible. Before he met her, Sicarius had always worked alone. He would not use errand boys.

"Yes, that's right," the younger brother said. "We know him real well, and he'll assassinate you if you bother us."

"Assassinate you for certain," Velks said. "He owes us a favor on account of us taking him out for drinks last night."

"You lads aren't very good at this," Maldynado said. "So, boss, gentle or rough for the tying?"

"Actually..." Amaranthe eyed the clothing strewn about the floor. "I believe they'd like to clean up their mess first. Take their weapons and help them find a broom."

"Clean?" The thieves exchanged incredulous looks.

"Yes," Amaranthe said. "It's a type of work. Like stabbing people with knives, but with less blood involved."

Maldynado shrugged and patted down the first man for weapons. "As long as I'm not the one waylaying the dust balls, I don't care."

While he monitored them, Amaranthe searched the room. One of the thieves tried to flee for the door when Maldynado thrust a feather duster into his hands. Maldynado pounded an unapologetic fist into the man's nose, convincing him to suffer the task without further escape attempts. He wiped at a trickle of blood with his sleeve and glowered at Amaranthe.

"I thought you said cleaning didn't involve blood," he growled.

"I said it involved less blood than stabbing people, not no blood," she said without looking up from the desk drawers she was rifling through.

Fifteen minutes of searching did not reveal anything interesting. She checked the tote the first thief had been carrying out when she interrupted them, but it contained only valuables, modest ones commensurate with the income level of a miner.

Amaranthe drummed her fingers against her thigh and considered the thieves again. "Did you gentlemen take anything out of here before we found you?"

"No."

Maldynado grabbed Velks by the collar and hoisted him up to his tiptoes. "Are you positive?"

"Positive!"

"Were you looking for anything when you broke in?" Amaranthe asked.

"No, just stuff to fence. We live downstairs, saw the family leave last night."

She watched his eyes, but nothing in his face implied he was lying. The other one nodded, and he, too, appeared sincere.

"What lovely neighbors this place has," Maldynado said. "Go out for the night, and they're in your flat, pawning your silverware before lunchtime the next day."

"Have you noticed any men coming and going, visiting this flat?" Amaranthe asked.

"You mean the other miners?" Velks asked.

"Yes. How long has that been going on?"

The brother lifted his feather duster. "Why should we answer all these questions? What's in it for us?"

"I could restrain myself from punching you again," Maldynado said.

"Now, now, no need to be brutish," Amaranthe told him while considering the thieves thoughtfully. "If the flat is cleaned up and everything is put back, I don't think there's a need to tell the enforcers you were here. *If* you answer my questions."

"You were going to tell the enforcers?" Velks asked. "You're thieves, too, aren't you?"

"No, we're investigators."

Both brothers' brows furrowed. She imagined them trying to figure out if "investigators" were people who were legally on the premises or not. She decided not to clarify.

"About these miners," she said, "how long have they been visiting?"

"Seen some of them before," Velks said, "but they only started coming all the time last week."

"Did they stay here when they met, or did they start here and go someplace else?"

Velks shrugged. "How should I know? We didn't sit up here with our ears pressed to the door."

The brother snapped his fingers. "But that one time, when we were sitting on the steps, hoping to get a look up girls' dresses when they went up, we did hear them say something, remember?"

"Don't tell people about that," Velks hissed.

"About what they said?"

"About the dresses, you idiot."

Maldynado leaned a hand against the wall and shook his head. "Not too bright, are they?" he mouthed to Amaranthe.

"You never tried that tactic?" she asked.

"I never had to resort to such desperate measures. Women couldn't wait to lift their dresses when I was around."

Amaranthe kept from rolling her eyes — she *had* encouraged him by asking after all — and turned back to the thieves. "What'd you hear them say?"

"They were going with Raydevk to meet a girl at a fountain," Velks said.

Oh, yes, that was a priceless gem of information. Still, if the men had all been going together, maybe it had been more than a tryst. "What fountain?" she asked.

Velks glanced at his brother who only shrugged. "They didn't say."

Amaranthe asked a few more questions, hoping she might tease more out of the would-be burglars' heads, but they proved feeble resources at best. While they finished cleaning, she searched every last nook of the flat, even going so far as to thump at floorboards in case any covered a hollow storage niche.

She knelt, doing a last check of the areas beneath the beds, when Velks spoke again. "Can we go?"

"We cleaned everything and put everything back that we took," his brother said. "We even got rid of those gummy food stains that we were *not* responsible for."

"We even did the windows!" Velks added.

Maldynado snickered. He was lounging on the sofa, playing with a sliding puzzle block in which one had to find appropriate niches for various war implements. Apparently the thieves had not made an escape attempt in a while.

"Yes, you may go." Amaranthe returned the dagger she had taken from them and surveyed the flat. It sparkled. Huh. "Gentlemen?" she added, stopping them in the middle of a sprint for the door.

"What?" Velks asked, shoulders hunched.

"You do good work. Perhaps you should consider a career in the cleaning services."

"*Cleaning* services?" Their mouths gaped open.

"Men don't clean, they fight!" one said.

"And they run over imperial enemies with giant steam trampers and they tear down massive fortifications with those brilliant new rammers." Velks sighed longingly.

"Are you two planning to join the military?" Amaranthe asked, thinking they appeared old enough—Akstyr's age at least.

Maldynado yawned and gave her a why-are-we-spending-so-much-time-here look as he thunked a puzzle piece into place.

"Maybe." Velks shrugged.

Probably a no then. "Madame Rawdik on Fourth runs an industrial cleaning outfit. They have a steam pressure washer as big as a tramper. If you worked for her, you could probably ride it."

Two sets of eyes grew round. "Really? I didn't know there was such a thing."

"If you decide to apply for a job, tell her that her old school friend Amaranthe says you do good work."

Their eyes remained wide, and they exchanged gapes with her. It wasn't *that* much of a favor. Had nobody ever vouched for them for anything before?

"Thanks," Velks said, and his brother nodded and scampered out the door. Velks hesitated, his face screwed up in concentration. "I don't know if it helps, but those miners also said...the girl they were seeing had...fire hair? Fiery hair. And she was worth pounding like a steam hammer. I listened to that part, on account of, well—it was about a woman."

"I see," Amaranthe said. "Thank you."

The young men left, and Maldynado thunked a final piece into the puzzle before tossing it onto a chair. "How'd you know?" he asked.

"Know what?"

"That they had more information."

"I didn't." She winked. "I just like to reform wayward youths whenever possible."

"That's very noble. I bet Deret likes noble women."

"Don't start with that again, or I'll try to reform you."

"I'm hardly a youth."

"But you don't argue against needing reform?" Amaranthe headed for the door.

"Not really, no." Maldynado opened it for her. "What's next?"

"We have Akstyr update his search. He's not just looking for that powder at the apothecaries; he's asking clerks if they remember a sexy red-headed woman coming in and doing the shopping. That's far from a normal hair color in the empire."

"Ah, Akstyr will be doing the work? Excellent." He followed her into the hallway.

"Oh, no, we'll be searching the neighborhood and contemplating all the fountains within a two miles radius."

Maldynado stopped walking and flopped against the wall. "*All* the... This is Stumps! There are almost as many fountains in the city as there are headless statues."

"There aren't *that* many," Amaranthe said.

"There's one at every intersection."

"Every other intersection, at the most."

"That's still a *lot*. And just because these people *met* at a fountain the other night doesn't mean they'll be loitering nearby now."

"I know. It's not much to go on. I'll think on it while we watch Basilard compete this afternoon."

"Yes." Maldynado snapped his fingers. "And we need to get there early. No fountain searching on the way. What if someone tries to kidnap him?"

"I doubt anyone knows who he is," Amaranthe said, amused at how quickly Maldynado could start scheming his way out of work. "He entered with his Mangdorian name, didn't he?" Even if people knew a "Basilard" ran with Sicarius, nobody in the city would know his real name.

Maldynado snickered. "Not exactly."

"What do you mean?"

"You'll see."

Basilard hopped up and down and swung his arms. He was one of six athletes left in the staging area, and he did not think anyone else appeared as nervous as he. Though it was the first day of events, and only a third of the benches in the stadium were filled, Basilard could not help but feel as if thousands of eyes watched him. Already, he had visited the washouts beneath the stands three times, both to urinate and to throw up.

He remembered being nervous before the pit fights, but not this nervous. Strange, considering his life had been on the line there, and people had shouted and jeered from above, calling out for bloodshed. Maybe it was because he had more to win here. It wasn't just an extension of his own existence, but a visit with the emperor and a chance to speak for his people. If he did not get himself killed trying to take out Sicarius first. He growled at himself, annoyed with the situation. He never should have gone to visit that priestess.

Basilard distracted himself by studying a large blackboard near the furnace. So far, two people had beaten the best time he had recorded with Maldynado or Akstyr. He hoped daylight—and the exhilaration of the moment coursing through his blood—would help him improve. To go out in the first round would be a shame.

"It's all right," a familiar voice said. "I'm his coach."

"You don't look like a coach. You look like a professor."

"Why, thank you," Books said.

Basilard lifted a hand toward the young man tasked with keeping intruders from bothering the athletes in the staging area. He let Books through with a suspicious glower.

Books weaved past other athletes swinging their arms and stretching in the sandy pit. "Greetings, Basilard," he said. "Are you prepared for your event?"

Yes.

"Good." Books unfolded a piece of paper. "I found those other two names. They are indeed athletes here. One is a male boxer and one a female entered in the Clank Race." He considered the men surrounding them. "Did the women already compete?"

Earlier this morning.

"She's not missing yet—she's the only one on that list who isn't. The boxer disappeared last night. If we could find the girl and watch her, perhaps we could get a glimpse of the kidnapper."

Books?

"Yes?"

I race soon. I must concentrate.

"Oh. Yes, of course. Do you want me to watch, or leave you alone?"

Stay. Cheer. He lifted an arm and imitated some of the enthused people in the stands.

"I've not attended many sporting events," Books said. "Is that arm-pumping action required?"

Absolutely. Basilard flashed a grin.

"Clapping won't suffice?"

Clap for others' performances. Cheer for me.

"Ah, very well."

"Temtelamak?" the man queuing the athletes called.

Basilard lifted an arm, then told Books, *That's my imperial athlete name.*

Books's eyes widened. "Temtelamak? *Why?*"

Thought enforcers would recognize 'Basilard,' and Maldynado said my Mangdorian name didn't sound fierce enough.

"Did he tell you who Temtelamak was?" Books lowered his voice to mutter, "I'm surprised that uneducated buffoon knows that much history."

A mighty warrior.

"A moderately famous general, yes, but he was notorious for his bedroom exploits, not fighting. He had seven wives at the time of his death, all near different forts and outposts where he'd been stationed. None of them knew the others existed. I believe there were copious mistresses as well."

Basilard shrugged. *It's Maldynado.*

"Yes, he doubtlessly thought it'd be amusing. We'll see if

the emperor finds it so, should you win the event and get your chance to meet him."

Could make an interesting conversation starter.

Books opened his mouth to say more, but a scream of pain interrupted him. One of the athletes had stumbled in the axe crossing and fallen off the moving platforms. He rolled in the sawdust, one hand grabbing the opposite triceps. Blood flowed through his fingers and stained the wood chips. A medic trotted out to help him off the field while the people in the seats roared. Whether they were supporting the noble attempt or cheering at the sight of blood, Basilard could not guess.

"Perhaps you should have entered a running event," Books said, eyeing the bloodstained sawdust.

If he were tall and lanky and fast, that might have been an option. For Books's sake, or perhaps to reassure himself, he simply signed, *One less competitor now. Besides, I had no trouble with the axes on the practice runs.*

"Yes, but is it not different when a thousand gazes are upon you, and there's something at stake? Suddenly, sweat is dripping into your eyes, your hands are unsteady, your senses are over-heightened, and—"

Basilard gripped Book's arm. *You're not helping.*

"Oh, pardon me."

"Temtelamak," the call came again. "You're up now, or you'll forfeit if you're not ready. You coming?"

Basilard chopped a quick wave at Books and jogged forward. On his way, he glanced at the chalkboard. The top seed had run the Clank Race in 1:55 with the fifth coming in at 2:03. The top five advanced to the finals, and there were four more runners after him. He had best target a sub two-minute time, which would put him in third. That ought to be enough.

Easier said than done, he thought, as he walked to the starting line. The giant axe heads swinging on their pendulum arms appeared far more dangerous by the light of day. Their steel blades gleamed in the sun, and Basilard no longer had to imagine their ability to draw blood, since crimson drops spattered more than one of the platforms.

After taking a deep breath, he stepped to the line and nodded his readiness to the starter.

Though nobody in the stands could know who he was, or care, cheers went up, regardless. Memories flooded his mind. He thought of his nights in the pits, fighting before an audience who craved blood. The pain and anguish he had experienced there. The comrades he had been forced to kill so he could go on living.

Nausea stirred in his stomach again, and those memories almost overwhelmed him. It's merely a race, he told himself. He was not here to hurt anyone.

A hammer hit a gong, signaling the start of the run. Thanks to his wandering thoughts, he lost a split second, and he cursed himself even as he sprinted up the ramp to the spinning logs. He sprang across them, bare feet navigating wood hot beneath the sun. Most of the other athletes wore shoes of some kind, but he could grip and scramble up obstacles more easily with toes available. He skimmed across the moving platforms, ducking and weaving the swinging axes.

He launched himself at a rope hanging from a beam. Below, a bed of three-foot-long spikes glistened in the sun. Basilard caught the rope and zipped up it. Thanks to Sicarius's training, *that* was an easy obstacle.

No, no thanking Sicarius, he told himself. And no thinking about anything except the clock he had to beat.

When he reached the top of the rope, he thrust himself toward the first of several pegs sticking out of the beam. Sweat slicked his palms, and his hand slipped free. Basilard flailed with his other hand and, by a stroke of luck, caught the peg before he fell. His heart hammered in his ears. The thirty-foot drop to the spikes would do more than put him out of the competition; it would kill him.

The crowd roared shouts of encouragement, and, for the first time, he grew aware of them. He wished he hadn't.

He caught the next peg, a couple of feet to the right, and swung from handhold to handhold, his feet dangling below. The pegs started in a straight line, but then zigzagged up and down, requiring strength and agility to maneuver through them.

Basilard reached the end and swung his legs to the right, catching a net stretched between two massive wooden supports. He skimmed halfway down to the ground, found the opening in the middle, and slithered through to land on a platform. One of his bare feet, just as sweaty as his palm, slipped on the smooth wood boards. He caught himself, but not before he rethought the wisdom of going shoeless.

Ahead of him, the small circular platforms moved, some linearly back and forth and others in orbits on mechanical arms, like those that rotated wheels on a train. The axes swung like pendulums.

He launched himself onto the first platform, planning his route on the fly. An axe whistled by behind him. If he had hair, the breeze would have stirred it. He did not look back or slow down. Basilard danced to the next platform, then the next. Some were barely four inches wide. Even without the axes slashing through, they would have been difficult targets.

Here, his bare feet helped. His toes wrapped over the edges, and he launched himself from spot to spot. At one point, he dove under an axe for a chance to skip two platforms ahead.

Thousands of people gasped at once as the blade skimmed past, an inch above his shoulder blades. He got his feet under him again and leaped the last couple of feet to the solid platform on the far side. Two more walls, net climbs, and a sprint across a spinning log, and he reached the ramp on the far side. Though weariness burned in his thighs, he sprinted the last few meters and catapulted over the solid wall, pulling himself up and over without using his feet. Relieved to be done, and out of some notion he should finish with a flourish, he leaped into the air as he passed the finish line, doing a somersault before landing by the timekeeper.

Cheers erupted, and he grinned. Those people would root for any good showing, but knowing they appreciated his athleticism, instead of his ability to stick knives into people, made him grateful.

The cheers went on longer than expected. An attendant was already painting his time on a sheet on a giant pad of paper that could be spun to show both sides of the stadium. 1:53.

Basilard gaped. That put him in first place.

A high-pitched, enthusiastic whistle floated down from the seats near the stadium entrance. He glanced over in time to see Books swatting Maldynado in the back of the head, nearly knocking a hat off, one with a white plumed feather of ridiculous proportions. Though Basilard could not read lips, he caught the gist of Books's words, "Quit drawing attention to us, you big oaf. We're wanted men."

Amaranthe stood with them, too, her broad-brimmed sunhat hiding her face to some extent. A lump formed in Basilard's throat. They—especially Amaranthe—were risking a chase from the ever-present enforcers to be here to root for him.

He did not want to call attention to them, so he merely nodded that direction before accepting a towel from a boy garbed in attendant's yellow and white. Basilard swabbed sweat out of his eyes and off his scalp.

"Congratulations on your time, sir," the boy said, eyeing the briar patch of scars crisscrossing Basilard's head. No imperial child would shy away from a man covered with old wounds, but even here, in the militaristic empire, he was an oddity. "There's lemonade in the athletes' lounge. I'll show you."

The promise of a cold drink enticed him. Besides, it was better not to go straight to Amaranthe and the others, not when enforcers might be watching. Still wiping himself off with the towel, he headed for the shady rooms beneath the tiers of spectators. He had never had lemonade before coming to the empire—importing a perishable item from hundreds of miles to the south was an impossible feat for his people—but he admitted a fondness for the drink, and he was salivating in anticipation when he entered the shady concrete corridor.

He padded into the interior, his eyes adjusting to the dim lighting. Just as he was wondering if it was strange that nobody else occupied the passage, something stirred the hairs on his arms. Magic?

When he glanced over his shoulder, he saw only the towel boy strolling after him. With dark hair and tan skin, he appeared a typical Turgonian youth, not anyone who might have access to the mental sciences.

A few feet ahead, something tinkled to the floor. Glass.

Immediately, Basilard thought of the cork Akstyr had found, the cork that had restrained a vial full of knock-out powder.

He backed away and stumbled into the boy, but the youth made no move to stop him.

Basilard's mind spun. Had his fast time made him a new target? Could these kidnappers work so quickly?

He would not linger to find out. Though he could see no one in the corridor, he continued backing toward the entrance, ready to defend himself if necessary. Before he had gone more than a few steps, a strange lethargy came over him. The fatigue that had turned his legs leaden at the end of the Clank Race was nothing compared to the heaviness that flooded them now. Heaviness and numbness.

His steps turned to stumbles, and then he could not feel his bare feet coming down on the cement at all. He lost his balance and tipped backward. The ground came up far too quickly for him to turn the fall into a roll, and his head cracked against the hard floor.

Shapes drifted out of the shadows and coalesced into men looming over him. Basilard could not lift his arms, could not do anything to defend himself.

His instincts forgot he could not speak, and he tried to scream for help, but no sound came out. One of the men grabbed Basilard's head and slipped a bag over it. Darkness swallowed him, and he knew no more.

The last of the competitors finished the Clank Race, and the timekeeper painted the results for all to see. 1:59. Nobody had beaten Basilard's score. Amaranthe smiled to herself, tickled that he had done so well against younger and taller competitors, men who had trained all year for this event. Albeit, the exercise sessions they endured with Sicarius could be no less arduous than anything those athletes inflicted upon themselves.

Her smile faded at the thought of Sicarius. Guilt sat in her belly like an undigested meal; it was wrong to idly watch the Games while he was missing.

"What's he doing down there for so long?" Amaranthe murmured.

She wanted to collect Basilard and start investigating the fountains near Raydevk's flat. They did not have many hours before her meeting with Deret. She was tempted to cancel that, but he might have information about the kidnappings she did not. Surely a journalist had as many informants in the city as the enforcers did.

"He's a contender for the trophy now." Maldynado removed his hat to scratch his head and nearly poked Amaranthe in the eye with the ostrich feather. "I bet he's getting mobbed by women who want to grease his snake tonight."

Amaranthe gave him a sidelong look. "The way your mind works is unique."

"Not amongst men," Maldynado said.

"Amongst *some* men," Books said.

Amaranthe fidgeted and watched the tunnel entrance through which Basilard had walked with the towel boy trailing behind. Several minutes had passed, and neither had returned to the arena.

"The towel boy hasn't come back," she said.

"What?" Maldynado asked.

Even if Basilard had decided to find the latrine or change out of his white togs, the boy should have returned to attend to the remaining competitors. Why had he followed Basilard, anyway? No boys had accompanied any of the other athletes.

"I think Basilard's in trouble," she said.

"What?" Books asked.

"He's been gone too long." Amaranthe wondered if it signified paranoia that neither of them seemed concerned. "Do either of you two 'coaches' want to try to go down there? See if you can get into that tunnel?" Amaranthe eyed a pair of enforcers stationed where they could keep spectators from wandering into the arena to bug the athletes. "I'll go outside and see if I spot anything suspicious."

"Which of us should—" Books started.

"Either. Both. I don't care." She was already maneuvering through the packed benches toward the aisle, worrying that they had wasted too much time. How long would it take to drag an unconscious man out through a back door? "Maybe I'm overreacting," she muttered under her breath. "Maybe it's nothing."

Though she said the words, they did not keep her from pushing past spectators and running down the stairs. At the bottom, she reluctantly slowed down, aware that a sprinting woman might draw the enforcers' suspicions.

Only when she reached the stadium exit did she break into a run. Maldynado caught up with her.

"Books is going in since Basilard already vouched for him today."

"Understood," Amaranthe said.

They ran off the path to follow the curve of the stadium's outer wall. Twenty meters of neatly trimmed grass stretched away from the structure before trees and shrubbery started, hiding the locomotive tracks in the distance. Amaranthe scanned the leafy green canopy, searching for the telltale smoke trail of a steam-powered lorry. Anyone in the kidnapping business would need a getaway vehicle.

"I don't see anybody," Maldynado said.

"Me either."

Intermittent metal doors marked the outside wall, too many for her and Maldynado to watch. Amaranthe took a guess at which one corresponded with the corridor Basilard had gone down and tried it. It did not budge, nor did it have a lock on the outside one might pick. A single pull-bar handle rose from a sea of brass rivets and steel.

"No way to pick the lock, huh?" Maldynado asked.

Amaranthe knelt to examine tracks in the earth. Dozens, if not hundreds, of people had been in and out of the door that day, so they told her little. A dirt trail led to the wider road ringing the stadium.

"We're smart though," Maldynado said. "We ought to be able to figure a way in."

"Got an idea?"

Amaranthe touched a long gouge in the earth. Was it her imagination, or did that look like the sort of mark that might be left if a couple of men were dragging another?

"Lots of ideas." Maldynado grabbed the pull-bar and heaved for all he was worth. Muscles strained beneath the thin fabric of the back of his shirt, but the door did not budge. He released it with a growl, then kicked it.

"Watching your mind work is always a pleasure," Amaranthe said.

"Because it's unique?"

"Something like that." She pointed at the gouge. "I think they may already have him."

She trotted to the opposite side of the road and examined the ground. If kidnappers had dragged Basilard out of there, they would not have stuck to the main path where witnesses would be many. Even now, a pair of female athletes was jogging along the road, warming up for the upcoming races.

Half-crouching, half-walking, Amaranthe searched for unusual prints. Too bad Basilard was the one missing; he was a great tracker.

"Afternoon, ladies." Maldynado swept his hat from his head and dropped into a low bow when the athletes approached.

Amaranthe expected him to ask them to accompany him somewhere for drinks or other activities, but he stayed on task.

"Has either of you seen anything suspicious out here?" he asked.

One of the women eyed Amaranthe, who was still poking at the earth, looking for tracks, and asked, "Aside from you two?"

"Yes." Maldynado offered a sparkling smile, the kind known for making the most standoffish ladies swoon, and the women's visages softened. One blushed. "Anyone dragging an athlete across the grass, for instance," he said. "Or a towel boy roaming around where he shouldn't be?"

"Oh!" The blushing girl sidled closer to Maldynado and laid a hand on his forearm. "On our last lap, we did see a young boy standing at that door." She pointed to the one Maldynado had tried to open. "It looked like he was beckoning to someone in the woods. I didn't see anyone, and he ducked back inside when he spotted us." She gazed up at Maldynado and batted her eyelashes. "Does that help?"

Amaranthe shook her head in bemusement. At times, Maldynado could be downright useful.

"Tremendously, dear," he said. "Thank you."

"We should go, Reeva," the girl's companion said. "Our race starts soon. If you don't want me to win again, you should probably be there to compete against me."

"Win again?" Reeva released Maldynado and propped her hands on her hips. "You only won *last* time because that stupid warrior-caste girl tripped and took me down with her."

"On second thought," her comrade said, "you should stay here and go off with him." She resumed her jog, heels kicking up dust on the dry path.

Reeva pouted at Maldynado. "I have to go. Would you like to come watch my race? It starts soon. And then afterward, perhaps we could have an iced tea in the garden."

"Why, I'm quite tempted, my lady," Maldynado said.

Amaranthe gripped his arm. "No, he's not. Our friend needs us." She jerked her chin toward the trees.

The girl scowled at Amaranthe. She ignored it and tugged Maldynado along.

"Sorry, miss," he called to his newfound friend. "I'm not the sort to put my own pleasure above a friend's needs. Not a good friend's, anyway."

Amaranthe led the way into the trees, and Maldynado caught up with her. She was debating whether to look for tracks or go straight through to the railway when voices drifted to her ears.

Somewhere ahead of her, men spoke in urgent tones. She picked up the pace, though she stepped lightly, not wanting to be heard. She held a finger to her lips, and Maldynado softened his own footfalls.

"...got him," someone said ahead of them. "Go, go."

Machinery ground and clanked. An engine starting? Amaranthe sniffed and caught a whiff of burning coal mingling with the earthier scents of the woods.

She gave up stealth and ran full out, dodging trees and trampling through dry brush. Her hand strayed toward her belt, where she often wore her short sword, but it wasn't there. Right. She'd decided a woman with a sword would stand out at the stadium. At least Maldynado had his.

The chugging of machinery floated through the trees clearly now. It sounded more like the great pumping pistons of a locomotive rather than the smaller engine of a carriage. But nobody had a train for an escape vehicle. She hoped.

The woods thinned ahead with sunlight streaming through a gap in the canopy. The railway tracks?

The sounds of the machinery were moving away from her. More, the distinctive clickety-clack of a car moving on rails joined with the chugs. No doubt now. She was listening to a train.

Amaranthe sprinted the last ten paces, burst out of the trees, and scrambled up the raised ballast bed supporting the train tracks. Twenty meters away, a combination locomotive-carriage was rumbling toward the city. Puffs of gray smoke wafted from a short stack. Though doors on either side held windows, the carriage had moved too far away for her to see through them. For a second, she thought of running after it, but it picked up speed even as she watched. No, she would never catch it.

Growling, she kicked at the gravel between the wooden sleepers.

Branches snapped and brush rustled, announcing Maldynado's exit from the woods. Amaranthe pointed at the carriage dwindling in the distance.

Maldynado blew out a low whistle. "What a beauty. An expensive conveyance for a private owner to pay for, too. My father talked about getting one for the family businesses at one point, but we never did."

"So our kidnappers are well-to-do," Amaranthe said. "Or they stole it from someone well-to-do."

"Always a valid vehicle acquisition strategy." Maldynado threw a wink at her, no doubt thinking of the times they had borrowed enforcer wagons as a means of creating a distraction.

She could not muster a response, not with a second man now missing. Amaranthe squatted on the tracks, elbows on her knees, head hanging. If she had thought Basilard would be a target in the middle of the day, she never would have suggested he enter the competition. Well, not exactly true. She would have had him enter with the intent of using him as bait to lure the kidnappers, and she wouldn't have been sitting hundreds of meters away in the stands when it was time to spring the trap.

"Did he ever run the Clank Race that quickly in your practice sessions?" Amaranthe asked.

"Nah. He got under two minutes once, but who knew he'd have the fastest time today?"

"Strange that the kidnappers went after him right in the middle of the day when all their other abductions have been at night. Did they know he didn't sleep in the dormitories? Maybe this was to be their last abduction, and they figured it didn't matter if someone saw them at work. Maybe they weren't planning on targeting him at all, but he beat the person they had in mind so they switched—"

Crashes sounded in the woods from whence Amaranthe and Maldynado had come. She drew her knife and jumped down to take cover behind the four-foot-high ballast bed. Maldynado knelt beside her, a rapier in hand. This one had an opal gem on the pommel, and silver runes running up and down the steel blade.

"How many swords do you have?" Amaranthe whispered.

"Only thirteen. That covers most of my ensembles."

The thrashing continued, closer now. Books raced out of the foliage.

Amaranthe started to relax, but the expression on his face stopped her. As he ran toward the tracks, he glanced over his shoulder twice. The second time, he tripped over a rock and nearly tumbled head long into the gravel.

"Time to depart," Amaranthe said. She climbed up to the wooden sleepers and waved for Maldynado to follow. "Books," she said, but he had already seen her.

He scrambled up the ballast bed and joined them on the railway.

Amaranthe raced along the tracks, boots striking the wooden sleepers with each stride. She wanted to obscure their trail by running on a surface that wouldn't leave telltale footprints, but only for a moment. "How far behind are your pursuers?"

"Not...far," Books panted.

A steam whistle screeched in the distance, a train heading for the city. Good. Maybe it would cut off pursuit.

"This way!" a male voice shouted from the woods.

Amaranthe led the way off the tracks, jumping from the gravel to the weeds lining the edge of the woods, hoping not to leave prints in the dusty band in between. Maldynado and Books, with their longer legs, made the leap easily. The team weaved through the trees for a hundred meters, then came out on the paved trail that ran along the lake, the trail Amaranthe and Sicarius had run together so many times.

The ache that formed behind her breastbone had nothing to do with her running efforts. He hasn't even been gone a day, she reminded herself. Nothing to worry about yet. Besides, they were going to find him. Basilard, too.

Thousands of footprints trampled the dusty red clay of the trail, and her fear of pursuit faded as she and the men continued along it.

"What happened?" Amaranthe asked Books.

"Basilard wasn't back there," he said.

"We know."

She explained the towel boy and the rail carriage as they continued running. Popular beaches sprawled between the trail and the lake, many occupied with naked children running, playing, and swimming about. It was a workday, and most adults who could steal time away were at the Imperial Games, but a few nannies attended the youths. One voluptuous and quite nude woman waved to Maldynado who puffed out his chest and smiled back.

"Well, there's one witness to our passing," Amaranthe muttered. "Who was chasing you, Books? Enforcers?"

"Yes, I saw that towel boy, and I tried to apprehend him. He pulled this out of his pocket." Books plucked a vial filled with a golden powder from his own pocket and held it out for Amaranthe. "He tried to hurl it to the ground to, I presume, knock me out. I was quicker than he and stopped him, but he started screaming, and enforcers surged into the tunnels. One thought he recognized me as a criminal—can you imagine that?—so I had to run."

Amaranthe took the vial. With that much of the powder, perhaps Akstyr could give her more information on it—confirm whether it was the one from his book or if it had other properties.

"*You* bested a ten-year-old boy?" Maldynado asked Books. "All by yourself? Why, I'm impressed."

"Impressing a small mind is an insignificant task." Books lifted a hand, pointing toward a beach. "Is that Akstyr?"

Amaranthe almost dismissed the possibility without looking—Akstyr was supposed to be investigating apothecaries—but they *were* getting close to the boneyard. The shirtless figure lounging on his back in the sand had a familiar spiky hairstyle, too....

"Yes, it is," Maldynado said. "How come he's got the afternoon off?"

"He doesn't." Amaranthe checked behind them to make sure no squad of enforcers was huffing and puffing down the trail after them, then veered past three rows of stands stuffed with bicycles.

Akstyr saw them coming and sat up, a sheepish grin on his lips. Children hollered and yelled in the shallows. Though this particular beach was far from residential neighborhoods, it sported sand instead of rocks, making it popular.

"I checked a whole heap of apothecaries and didn't learn anything about your red-headed woman or the powder," he rushed to say, probably trying to head off a lecture. "Some of the older clerks knew about the powder, but they said you can't get it in the empire."

"How many apothecaries are in 'a whole heap'?" Amaranthe asked.

"Bridger's on Second and that little foreign-owned one in the Veterans' Quarter, and...uhm..."

"Two?" Books said. "Two constitutes a heap? I'll send a note to the publishers of the Titanus Imperial Dictionary so they can update the entry."

"Ha ha," Akstyr said. "Look, I was going to check some more after I relaxed a little."

Amaranthe held out the vial Books had retrieved. "We got a sample of the powder."

Akstyr took it and held it up to the sun. "Oh, brilliant," he breathed. His eyes narrowed, and calculation gleamed in them.

Amaranthe noted his expression. Did he think he could sell the powder for a handsome profit?

"Where's Basilard?" Akstyr asked. The hand holding the vial drifted toward his pocket.

"He was kidnapped after a stellar performance on the Clank Race." Amaranthe reached out and caught Akstyr's hand before he could pocket the vial. She pried it out of his fingers. "I'll keep this for now."

He reached for her hand, and an objection seemed on his lips, but he caught himself. "Sure, whatever. Not like I need it for anything."

Uh huh. Which assured her he did. She would have to keep an eye on him.

"What do you mean Basilard was kidnapped?" Akstyr asked. "Weren't you there? How could someone take him when you were watching?"

"He was in the athlete area," Maldynado said. "We were spectators."

"And we'd appreciate it if you didn't imply we were negligent," Books added, his back straight and stiff.

"Fine, but we need Basilard," Akstyr said. "He's important for...stuff."

"Yes," Amaranthe said, her own eyes narrowed now as she considered Akstyr. "Yes, he is." It was hard for her to believe

Basilard would be a part of some scheme of Akstyr's, but she *had* noticed the two talking together more this past week than ever before. "We're going to get him back. Sicarius, too. I need to hunt down a map and make some notes."

"A map of city fountains?" Maldynado asked, watching her warily.

"Perhaps," she said. "You can help me. Books, are you up for a research assignment? Want to see if you can find a record of that rail carriage?"

"Of course," he said.

"This isn't turning out to be a very good vacation," Maldynado observed.

"I agree," Amaranthe said, as they padded onto the dusty trail.

Chapter 9

Amaranthe examined the map under the soft light of one of the gas lamps lining the city block around Pyramid Park. She had a lantern along as well, since the bone-yard was black at night, but this provided better illumination.

Books leaned over her shoulder, also studying the map, while Akstyr humored Maldynado in a game with the catchy title of "You Pick a Letter and I'll Say a Woman I've Slept with Whose Name Begins with That Letter."

"Z?" Maldynado asked. "That's easy. Zevinika and Zela."

"This isn't any fun. You could be making these people up," Akstyr said.

"Well, traditionally two people alternate names of women they've slept with, and the name one person says has to start with the last letter of the name the other person said."

"How is that more fun?"

"It'd be more fun for *you* because you could reminisce on past loves as well," Maldynado said, "but since I know you've a dearth of experience in that area, I chose to modify the game so you could play."

"Real thoughtful of you."

"I know. You're welcome."

Attempting to block out their chatter, Amaranthe pointed at

the seven fountains circled on the map. "These are the closest to the miner's flat," she told Books. "Since they said they were meeting at *the* fountain instead of the Fourth and Loom Street Fountain or some such, that seems to imply it was a nearby location they were all familiar with. What do you think?"

"I think we may want to focus on the rail tracks instead." He tapped the hatched line on the map. "That locomotive headed into town, but, given its clandestine purpose, I doubt it ever made it to the station where its arrival would have been logged. There are a limited number of stubs it could have turned up before then. A hideout might be located along one of those routes, as kidnappers wouldn't want to carry famous athletes through the open city for far."

"True, but they could have transferred their cargo to a steam carriage."

"If they did, they might have left evidence behind, or someone might have seen them," Books said. "There are only six possible stubs before the station and only two near the fountains you circled."

Amaranthe would not get her hopes up, but she said, "It's worth checking out."

"Since these are residential neighborhoods, there are limited places where one could store a number of kidnapped athletes," Books went on. "I doubt anyone would choose a flat surrounded by nosy residents, so we can narrow our search to abandoned buildings or perhaps those with large basements with exterior entrances. If we split our team up, we could check the buildings along both of these stubs tonight."

"Agreed," Amaranthe said, "though I hate the idea of splitting up when we're already missing two people. I don't want to lose anyone else."

"I'm surprised nobody's tried to kidnap me," Maldynado said. "I'm at least as good of a find as Basilard and Sicarius. It's obvious these kidnappers aren't basing their choices on looks."

"We believe they're basing their acquisitions on athletic prowess," Books said.

"I have that, too. I should have entered an event, so I could get noticed."

"Are you actually jealous that you weren't kidnapped?" Amaranthe asked.

"Not jealous. I just think they're shortsighted if they didn't consider me."

"Why would you care?" Akstyr asked. "They're probably getting tortured and forced to do unpleasant stuff."

Amaranthe winced. She did not need to hear about those possibilities, not for her men. Her *friends*.

"I would have entered if not for the bounty on my head," Maldynado said.

"It's not like anyone ever tries to collect your bounty," Akstyr said. "It's not worth it."

"That's not true. Just the other day a bounty-hunting miscreant tried to apprehend me. I was lucky to escape with my life."

"Is that the child I saw chasing you through the boneyard with a slingshot?" Amaranthe asked.

"What? No! Er. You saw that?"

Amaranthe drew her pocket watch. "A quarter past ten. If Lord Mancrest doesn't show up in five minutes, we're going rail-carriage hunting."

"It's that late?" Maldynado asked. "That's not like him."

Amaranthe picked up her lantern and headed for the gated entrance to the pyramid. It was set into a wall around the corner from the steep stone stairs leading to the ancient dais. The gate ought to be locked—the woman who owned the property ran tours during the day and presumably wanted to keep the tacky souvenir merchandise inside safe—but maybe someone had left the door open and Mancrest had gone in to wait. It seemed unlikely, but it did not hurt to check.

"What's that?" Maldynado asked.

Amaranthe squinted at a shape on the ground under the gate. She stepped closer, holding her lantern aloft. At first she had no idea what the object might be because it was squished beneath the metal frame. Then recognition jolted her.

"Mancrest's hat," she said.

Maldynado grabbed a metal handle, turned it, and swung the gate open with a soft creak. A stone tunnel led away into darkness.

"Think someone snatched him?" Akstyr asked.

"Our kidnappers?" Books scratched his jaw. "How would they know he was here? And why would they want him? Mancrest, with his cane and spectacles, doesn't fit into the same category as the superb athletes they've abducted thus far."

"He was a decent duelist before he got hurt," Maldynado said.

"We going in after him?" Akstyr asked, his tone suggesting the idea held no appeal for him.

"Amaranthe?" Books asked. "What do you think?"

She was standing, head down, chin in her hand as she considered the hat. "I think...if Sicarius were here, he'd say this is a trap."

"Set by Mancrest?" Books asked. "Or the kidnappers?"

"Do we believe there's any connection between Mancrest and the kidnappers?" Amaranthe did not. "He hasn't covered them in the newspaper, other than to say some people are missing. I'm skeptical they'd be aware of him."

Maldynado picked up the hat. "If that bastard tried to get me to set you up again, I'll..." He squinted at something inside the hat, then held it close to Amaranthe's lantern. "That looks like blood."

Amaranthe closed her eyes, trying to decide whether she wanted to devote more time to Mancrest when her comrades were missing. If he *was* in trouble, rescuing him might endear him to her, but she found the location of the hat suspicious.

It couldn't have been better placed if someone wanted her to find it.

"Books," she said, moving away from the gate, "do you know another way in?"

"Hm, I believe so." Books stroked his chin. "I researched the pyramid extensively when I wrote a paper on the civilization that lived around the lake two thousand years ago. They were a fascinating people, primitive and cannibalistic, but surprisingly advanced insofar as literacy and mathematics. They worshiped a—"

"Books," Amaranthe said. "I'd like to have time to look for Sicarius and Basilard tonight. The entrances?"

"Ah, of course. There's an underground entrance coming up from the ancient tunnels beneath Stumps, but the installation of the city sewer system destroyed a lot of those passages. Oh, wait. I recall a reference to a trapdoor under the dais up top."

Amaranthe nodded, remembering how Sicarius had appeared up there without using the stairs. She had wondered if there might be a door up there somewhere.

"And it connects with this tunnel?" She pointed through the gate.

"I believe so. The passages do wind around in there, and I can't promise to be an unerring guide, but I have some memory of the layout from the maps in the texts I... Where are you going?"

Already heading for the stairs, Amaranthe waved toward the top of the pyramid. "Up. You can keep talking on the way if you want."

"But it's not a requirement," Maldynado said, jogging after her.

Books muttered something to Akstyr about his knowledge not being fully appreciated. Akstyr responded with his usual, "Whatever."

When Amaranthe reached the top, she hunted around for signs of the trapdoor. Sicarius, she remembered, had appeared behind her when she had been near the stairs, looking down. She knelt and prodded around the base of the altar, which still sported the headless statue with its two wings, clawed feet, and furry torso.

"Did your studies tell you how to open this trapdoor?" Amaranthe asked Books.

"Not that I recall," he said.

"You can recite the dates of each reign of every emperor since Dorok the First," Maldynado said. "Why can't you remember something useful like this?"

"Historical tomes rarely advise people on how to break into ancient structures through unguarded entrances," Books said. "I believe they like to discourage the pillaging of goods inside."

"We're not pillaging anything," Maldynado said.

"Unless there's something good to pillage," Akstyr said. "Is there?"

"Not that I'd tell you about," Books said.

Amaranthe groped about the stone floor. The lantern light did little to illuminate the subtle nuances in the ancient blocks, but her fingers found dents and divots. She poked a few and nothing happened. She moved to the two rear columns supporting the roof covering the altar.

Her knee clunked against a bump, and she winced. She investigated the object, a slightly elevated triangular stone. She—and her knee—found it suspicious that it stuck out when nothing else did. Amaranthe tried pulling and pushing it. Neither worked. Maybe a turn? She rotated it to the left, as if she were unscrewing a lid on a jar.

The floor disappeared beneath her.

Amaranthe dropped into darkness with a startled squawk. Though surprised, she twisted in the air, moving quickly enough to get her feet beneath her. The landing jarred her, but she softened her knees enough that she did not injure herself.

Unfortunately, her lantern did not survive the fall unscathed. It had gone out as it dropped, and clanks and clatters echoed from the stone walls as it bounced several times, then rolled to a stop in the darkness. Close, dusty air wrapped about Amaranthe, intruding upon her nostrils. It smelled like vermin had died nearby. Maybe other things as well.

"Amaranthe?" Books called from above. "Are you...well?"

She had their only lantern—well, the darkness had it at the moment—but she could make out the men's silhouettes as they leaned over a three-by-three-foot hole in the ceiling. She opened her mouth to respond, but a sneeze assailed her nostrils instead.

"Is that a yes?" Books asked.

"Yes. Looks like I found the trapdoor."

"Looks like," Maldynado drawled.

"We can't see anything," Books said, leaning forward and patting around the trapdoor entrance. "How far down are you? Is there a ladder?"

"Maybe ten or twelve feet, and I don't know. I'll see if I can relight the lantern. After I find it."

Amaranthe knelt and swept her hands across cold, smooth stone. Cool air whispered past her cheeks. Above ground, it had been a warm summer evening, but down here, she shivered in her thin trousers and half-sleeve shirt.

It took a few moments to find the first wall, and she determined she was in a room, not a corridor. Some sort of preparation area for priests performing ceremonies on the altar above?

She found the lantern. A soft thump came from behind her.

"Who—" she started to ask.

"Me," Maldynado said. "Can't let a girl wander around a dark pit by herself."

"You can if you don't know if there's a way out," Akstyr said. He and Books waited above.

"Want us to go grab some lanterns?" Books asked.

"Let me see if I can get this one relit first." Amaranthe patted her pockets down. "I have matches." Somewhere.

"Is one lantern sufficient lighting for pyramid spelunking?" Books asked, his tone implying he hardly thought so.

"It's a long jog to the boneyard and back." Amaranthe struck a match and lit the lantern. "And I think you should join us since you're the pyramid expert. Akstyr can stay out there in case we..." Got themselves hopelessly lost or trapped by the enemy? No, she shouldn't say that. Too demoralizing. "Need backup," she finished.

The lantern light revealed a chamber filled with cobwebs and layers of dust that made her long for the giant steam-powered cleaning machines she had described to the thieves in the tenement building. Rows of niches on the walls had long since been emptied of their contents, though cobwebs cloaked them like cocoons, and one could almost imagine this place still held ancient treasures.

"Not very likely when we're in the middle of a city with a population of a million," Amaranthe told herself.

"That's why I came down," Maldynado said.

"To treasure hunt?"

"No, to keep you from talking to yourself. That's a sign of a lonely, disturbed mind." He drew his rapier and swiped at a cobweb curtain dangling above a narrow, low-ceilinged stairwell leading down. "This way, you can pretend you're talking to me."

"Oh, good." She turned her head toward the trapdoor again. "Books, are you coming? We need your insight."

"Since I so rarely hear those words, I'd best join you."

"We'd crave your insight more if you gave us less of it," Maldynado told him. "They say scarcity creates desire."

"I'm heading down," Amaranthe said. The men could snipe at each other all night if she let them.

She drew her short sword, but waited for Books to shimmy over the side of the hole, dangle from the lip for a moment, then drop down. He landed in an easy crouch. She smiled. He might not realize it, but Sicarius's training had brought

Books a *long* way in the last six months. Whether one had natural aptitude or not, constant repetition and an unrelenting taskmaster did tend to encourage improvement.

A couple of steps down the stairs convinced Amaranthe to return her sword to its sheath. The narrowness and steepness made her want to brace herself on the wall as she descended, and the lantern seemed the more important thing to hold aloft. Blackness swallowed the bottom of the stairs, but she imagined the fall could be long and far should she lose her balance.

"What kind of tiny-footed people built this place?" Maldynado asked after a bout of cursing when one of his boots slipped.

"Actually," Books said, "it's quite fascinating. The Pey'uhara, the first lake dwellers, were—"

"No, no, never mind," Maldynado blurted. "I didn't mean it. I don't want to know."

"It's a shame you prefer to wallow in a mire of ignorance when knowledge floats by within reach," Books said.

"Isn't it?"

"Let's practice our stealth mode," Amaranthe said. "In case there *are* kidnappers or trap-setters about."

The men mumbled sheepish apologies and fell quiet.

Silence surrounded them, stirred only by the soft padding of their feet and their own breaths. One could forget a modern city lay less than a block away.

The soft flame of the lantern revealed a short landing below with three options. To the right and the left, more stairs descended. If they continued straight ahead, they would enter a narrow corridor. A low stone ceiling promised much ducking for Maldynado and Books should she choose that route.

Amaranthe stopped on the landing. "Have we gone far enough to be at ground level?"

"I don't think so," Books said.

He touched cryptic hieroglyphs carved into the wall. One looked like a dog mounting another dog, but she supposed that was her imagination. Nothing so crude would be represented in two-thousand-year-old glyphs.

"Also the tunnels at the floor level are wider and easier to navigate. I believe that corridor leads to the Graveyard of the Fallen Enemies." Books lifted a finger, perhaps wanting to explain the place more thoroughly, but he glanced at Maldynado and said no more.

"Doesn't sound like a place we need to visit," Amaranthe said.

"Is that a dog humping another dog?" Maldynado pointed to the hieroglyph she had noticed. Leave it to him to have a mind at least as crude as hers.

"Actually, yes," Books said. "It's a sign of dominance. These people were letting everyone know they had dominated and vanquished their fallen enemies."

"Dominance, eh?" Maldynado said. "If you say so."

"Left or right?" Amaranthe asked. "Any thoughts?"

"Not from me," Books said.

"There's an uncommon event," Maldynado said.

Amaranthe lifted the lantern and examined both stairwells. The right held fewer cobwebs, and soft gouges and stirrings on the dusty steps might be footprints. "It looks like that way has seen traffic more recently."

When no one disagreed, she led the way downward again. The stairs did not descend far before they reached a T-section with wide corridors.

A faint rustle came to Amaranthe's ears. Her imagination? She dimmed the lantern in case it was not.

The blackness to the left seemed less absolute than the blackness to the right.

Nothing on the smooth granite floor would be an obstacle for their feet if they moved forward in darkness, so Amaranthe signaled to her men with a finger to her lips, pointed, and dimmed the lantern the rest of the way.

Darkness swallowed them. She waited for her eyes to

adjust to the gloom. There was not enough light for her to see anything except that it was less dark in one direction than the other, but that would have to be enough.

A hand reached out and found her shoulder. Maldynado's, she guessed, because he had a tendency to be less tentative than Books when touching people, especially female people. She hoped Books had a hand on Maldynado's shoulder as well. She did not want to lose anyone down here.

With one hand on the wall, she felt her way down the corridor. She found an edge—a corner. The light increased when she turned down the new passage, though she could not see its source.

"...longer?" a male voice asked ahead.

Amaranthe halted. The grip on her shoulder tightened in warning.

She turned an ear toward the passage, but whatever response the question garnered was too quiet for her to hear. She tried to decide if that had been Mancrest's voice. It had not sounded familiar, but it was hard to judge anything from one word.

"Want me to check it out?" Maldynado whispered in her ear.

"No," she whispered back. Basilard would be the first to tell Maldynado he was not the stealthiest man on their team. She pressed the lantern into Maldynado's hand. "I'll go. Stay here. Fetch me if I get myself in trouble."

His snort was soft, but audible. She patted him on the chest, then eased her short sword free and continued down the passage. Toe before heel, she walked, making sure there was nothing on the floor that might crunch or be kicked before committing to each step.

Cobwebs brushed at her face, and she stifled an urge to sneeze again. It was hard to sneak up on someone while discharging dust from one's nostrils.

As Amaranthe walked, she let her fingers graze the wall, and she twitched in surprise when they found a gap, then bumped against metal. She slid her hand up and down it. A bar. One of many. Some kind of gate?

She continued on, passing several of the wide gates, and finally reached a corner with the warm yellow of lantern light glowing beyond it. Trusting the darkness to hide her, Amaranthe eased her head around the edge. The illumination, several lanterns' worth, came from inside an open gate. From her angle, she could not see inside, but impatient mutters and shuffles came from the cell beyond.

The snippet of conversation she had caught implied there were at least two people waiting in there, but the noises suggested more. Four or six maybe.

She eased around the corner and tiptoed closer. Stacks of boxes came into view first, the closest stamped with the words "souvenir hats." Ah, the gates represented shop fronts. She must be nearing the main pyramid entrance.

Another step took her close enough to see past the boxes and into the room. A man in black soldier's fatigues leaned against the wall, his elbow propped on the muzzle of a rifle.

"Maybe we should turn out the lanterns," someone opposite of him said.

"We're three turns from Mancrest," someone else said. "She won't see the light."

"Until it's too late."

Soft snickers followed that oh-so-witty line.

"Unless Sicarius is with her."

That stopped the snickers. A nervous shuffling followed.

"Word from the enforcers is that somebody's got him."

Amaranthe curled her fingers into a fist. How had the enforcers found out? Did they know something she didn't?

"I'll believe that when his head is on a pike in Mariner Square," the man in view said.

Clothing rustled—a shrug? "I heard the enforcers were told to send word to the emperor to get the bounty money together, because his dead body would be delivered after the Imperial Games."

It was just talk, Amaranthe told herself. Rumors.

"Enough chatter," an unseen man said. "This is an ambush, not barracks cleaning day. Nobody's paying you to trot your lips."

The soldier Amaranthe could see sighed and turned his eyes toward the corridor. She stopped breathing. If enough lantern light seeped out of the room for him to see her...

He frowned and squinted in her direction.

Amaranthe slipped a hand into her pocket. Her fingers found curved glass.

The soldier took a step her way.

Before she could debate the wisdom of the move, or the danger to herself, Amaranthe held her breath, thumbed the cork off, and tossed the vial through the metal bars. It skidded beneath the soldier's feet, and he jumped.

She scurried back, not sure what the range was on the powder, or if it would even do anything without some sort of magical preparation.

The soldier charged into the corridor.

Amaranthe spun and ran. The darkness ahead kept her from sprinting, but she hoped she remembered the layout better than the soldier.

Only her outstretched hand kept her from smashing her face into the wall at the first turn. So much for memory.

Heavy footfalls followed her, but it sounded like only one or two pairs of boots, not the entire squad of soldiers. If only a couple of the men chased her, she and her team ought to be able to take care of them. They could separate —

"Oomph," she grunted, hitting another wall.

Left turn this time. One more corner, and she should run into Maldynado and Books.

Before she finished the thought, she ran into another obstacle. Not stone this time, clothing and flesh.

"Boss?" Maldynado whispered.

"Yes, sh."

The clomping footfalls of a soldier rang out as the man rounded the corner. Amaranthe turned to face him.

In the darkness, she could see nothing. The rhythm of the soldier's run faltered and slowed. He must sense he was close, or maybe it was something else. The powder? His steps were heavy, almost labored. He made no attempt to stifle the sound of his advance.

The gait slowed and grew uneven. Amaranthe bent her knees, sword ready. A loud thud came from ahead, no more than a pace away. Something clattered to the floor.

Silence fell.

A flame flared to life. Maldynado held the lantern high, illuminating the dust-and-cobweb-cloaked tunnel—and the unmoving soldier at their feet, his rifle a foot away from his outstretched hand.

"Huh," Maldynado said.

"You killed him?" Books stared at her.

"No, at least I don't think so. I threw that vial you took from the towel boy into their room." She knelt down, intending to check his pulse, but a soft snore rumbled from the man's lips.

"Ah," Books said.

Amaranthe took the soldier's rifle, then patted him down. She found keys on a clip at his belt and removed them. "Anybody have rope we can use to tie him up?"

"Not me," Maldynado said.

Books spread his open hands. No rope. Hm.

"I need to come better prepared for these meetings with men," Amaranthe said.

"Yes," Maldynado said, "you never know when rope will come in handy on a date. Lots of reasons to tie people up."

Amaranthe chose not to contemplate his statement. She pointed to the soldier. "See if you can use his belt and pants or something, and then follow me. There are more men. I'm hoping they're sleeping, too."

Not sure how long the powder might last, Amaranthe jogged back down the corridor toward the cell. She did not know the dissemination range either. That thought made her slow down. Would it still be active, or did it wear off shortly after release? She would feel idiotic if she ran in to check on the soldiers and passed out on top of some man's chest.

She thought about waiting for Maldynado and Books to catch up, but maybe it was best to go in alone. If she did pass out, maybe they would realize it and avoid the mistake. Or they'd collapse on top of her on top of the soldier.

"Over-thinking things," she muttered, though she dug a kerchief out of her pocket and wrapped it about her nose and mouth before continuing.

She peered through the gate and counted five soldiers sprawled on the floor amongst overturned boxes and tipped lanterns. A couple had taken steps toward the exit, but most had collapsed where they stood. The vial, now cracked, gleamed where it had come to rest against the wall. The powder had disappeared, turned to smoke and vanished.

Amaranthe decided not to risk getting close enough to investigate further. She checked the keys she had taken from the soldier. A fob read *Polga's Pyramid Tours*.

"Let's hope Polga has the power to lock and unlock the gates," she said.

"Talking to yourself again?" Maldynado asked as he and Books strode around the corner.

"No." Amaranthe tried one of the keys in the lock. "I knew you'd be here to hear me."

"The other soldier is sufficiently trussed up," Books said.

"Albeit, he'll find it a bit drafty in here without his pants," Maldynado said.

"They're the only thing that could be used to tie his ankles together and bind them to his wrists," Books said.

"I'm not judging you," Maldynado said. "That, given the opportunity, your first thought was to strip a handsome, young soldier of his pants doesn't bother me."

"You're odious."

"They were setting up an ambush," Amaranthe said. "Perhaps we should stop talking until we've subdued the bait."

The fourth key she tried turned in the lock. Good. She closed the gate and secured the soldiers inside.

"Do we believe the bait is Mancrest?" Books whispered.

"We'll see."

She debated whether to continue forward with the lantern dimmed, but decided the bait would expect her, so she might as well come in as anticipated. There just wouldn't be a squad of soldiers ready to charge in and capture her.

She pulled her kerchief down around her neck, and she, Maldynado, and Books followed the corridor to a ramp that angled downward, then turned at the bottom. More hieroglyphs adorned the walls down here, though she did not spot any more dogs engaged in carnal activities.

The corridor widened and angled to the right. Light came from ahead. More gates marked the walls, and cells—shops— lay behind them. A mix of tacky "adventuring hats," pyramid-related paraphernalia, and history books adorned the shelves.

The light ahead of them was coming from one of the shops. Amaranthe cut off her lantern and approached on silent feet.

She stopped at the gate. She did not see anyone inside, though a candle burned on a merchant's counter, the flame sputtering on the wick, and a hint of beeswax tinged the musty air. Racks of cheap factory-made clothing stretched along the walls.

A low groan emanated from the back of the shop. Ah, there was their bait.

A man lay on the floor, his back to them, wrists and ankles tied with a fat rope. Perhaps it had been chosen for its visibility—one could not miss it, even from the corridor. The wavy brown hair on the man's head was a familiar hue and length.

Amaranthe lifted her eyebrows toward Maldynado. He nodded. Yes, it was Mancrest.

The gate stood open. Amaranthe slid her hand into her pocket, wrapping her fingers about the cool metal keys. Though she meant to abandon stealth in a moment, she did her best to withdraw the fob quietly.

"Evening, Lord Mancrest," she said as she selected the key that had worked on the other gate. The number of shops—and locks—they had passed suggested one key opened multiple doors. "How'd you get yourself tied up there?"

The muffled response was unintelligible. He did manage to twist about so she could see a gag blocking his mouth.

"Disgusting," Maldynado muttered. "What proud man of the warrior caste stoops so low as to act as bait in a stupid trap?"

"Ssh," Amaranthe whispered, then raised her voice. "Are you in danger, Lord Mancrest? Who tied you up?"

Again, the gag muffled his response, but she caught the gist this time, "Help, come untie me."

"I don't think so." Amaranthe shut the gate, slipped the key into the lock, and turned it with a resounding thunk.

Mancrest sat up, eyes wide. His "what're you doing?" was easy to understand.

"Getting annoyed with your donkey manure, old boy," Maldynado said.

"What?" Mancrest said, still playing the game.

Was it possible he had not arranged this, and he was actually imprisoned? No, soldiers would not tie up someone from the warrior caste without permission.

"We have comrades to rescue," Amaranthe said. She found a rough corner on one of the stones on the opposite wall and hung the key ring on it. "I imagine you can find a couple of clothes hangers, twine them together, and fetch that on your own with a little patience, assuming your binds aren't particularly tight and you can free your hands. I wouldn't count on the soldiers rescuing you. They're incapacitated at the moment."

"Especially the one without pants," Maldynado said.

"*Will* you stop bringing that up?" Books asked.

"Probably not," Maldynado said.

"Let's go, gentlemen," Amaranthe said. "We have work to do."

Mancrest's shoulders heaved and his face screwed up as he wriggled his hands behind his back. His bonds fell free, and he yanked the gag out of his mouth.

"Wait!" He tore away the ropes at his ankles, leaped to his feet, and sprang to the gate.

Books jumped back. Amaranthe watched Mancrest's hands to make sure he did not reach for a pistol or dagger beneath his shirt. Maldynado leaned against the opposite wall and yawned.

Mancrest grabbed the bars of the gate. He tried to open it, failed, and gaped at her. "You locked me in?"

"You were planning to ambush us," Amaranthe said, not surprised but chagrinned to realize Sicarius had been right, that Mancrest could not be trusted to do anything except turn her over to the enforcers. "I think my response is quite generous."

He curled his lip and opened his mouth, as if to argue, but closed it again and took a deep breath. "What about my men. Are they...unharmed?"

"I think so. We used what the kidnappers have been using to knock people out, and I locked them in."

"Who's going to let us out?" Mancrest asked.

"Surely someone else is privy to your plan and will come look for you eventually."

"My brother. After he gets off work tomorrow."

"Long time without a latrine nearby," Maldynado said, still leaning against the wall, arms crossed. "But you deserve to marinate in your own pee overnight."

Mancrest ignored him. Hands gripping the bars, he told Amaranthe, "It's my duty and obligation to capture criminals if I have a chance."

"Our duty sometimes lands us in unpleasant circumstances." A fact she knew well, since following duty was what had set her on the path that resulted in her becoming an outlaw. She nodded toward the key ring. "I can make it easier for you to unlock yourself, if you tell me what you know about Sicarius's capture and the kidnappers in general."

Mancrest's shoulders drooped, and he leaned his forehead against a bar. He chuckled ruefully. "When I imagined how tonight would end, it involved me questioning you about what *you* knew, not the other way around."

"He should have come up with a more clever ploy then," Books said out of the corner of his mouth to Maldynado.

"For once, we agree," Maldynado said back.

"Was this interrogation you imagined happening here or at Enforcer Headquarters?" Amaranthe asked.

"Fort Urgot," Mancrest said.

"I've been questioned there before. I don't care to arrange another visit. Are you going to provide the information I requested, or not?"

"What will you do with the information?"

"Rescue my men and stop the kidnappers from whatever it is they're doing," Amaranthe said. "Given the nefarious nature of the disappearances, I doubt it's wholesome."

"Why are you bothering?" Mancrest asked. "I understand your comrades are missing, but you were involved in this before that, were you not?"

"I want exoneration, so I help the empire when I can. Now, speak." She gave him her best icy-cold-Sicarius stare. Given the hours she had wasted coming to Pyramid Park, it was not difficult to muster.

Still leaning his forehead against the bars, Mancrest considered her. His eyes flicked downward, taking in her newly acquired rifle. "I suppose I should be grateful you haven't killed me for my attempts at trapping you."

"I wouldn't do that," Amaranthe said.

"*I* might," Maldynado said. "Since you keep using me to get at her. Street licker."

"No," Mancrest said, holding Amaranthe's gaze. "I'm beginning to see that. I don't know who has Sicarius, only that an anonymous message came into Enforcer Headquarters, informing them he'd been captured and would be delivered dead by the week's end."

Amaranthe's breath caught. A steam tramper stomped all over her theory that these kidnappers were collecting superior athletes to turn them into soldiers. If they intended to kill Sicarius in a few days...

She closed her eyes. Then she had a few days to find him. *That* was what she needed to focus on.

"Also..." Mancrest slipped a hand into a pocket and pulled out a folded piece of paper. "One of the rookies brought me this advertisement for approval. Someone mailed it in with scrip from a mining outfit."

Amaranthe's ears perked. Mining outfit?

"I disapproved it. *The Gazette* doesn't accept ads for just *any* business, certainly not anything that sounds like a spiel from a pitchman's oiled tongue, and we don't take scrip for payment either. Later I realized it came in a couple of days before the first abduction. It could be unrelated, but..." He spread a hand, palm up. "Perhaps not."

Curiosity piqued, Amaranthe took the paper from him. Before it had been folded, it had been crinkled, as if it had spent time in a wastebasket. Books peered over her shoulder at it.

Foreman got you down? Do you deserve more? A home on the Ridge? A say in the government? It's all possible. Invest in your future now. Enquire at the Imperial Tea House.

"Interesting," Books said. "Perhaps a recruiting letter that was intended to gather more miners?"

"Raydevk didn't seem too bright," Amaranthe said. "I could see him trying to recruit people for criminal activities in a newspaper."

Mancrest's grip tightened on the gate bars. "Raydevk? That's the name I got when I checked at the tea house. *Is* this tied in with the missing people?"

"It's possible." Amaranthe handed the note to Books to study further. For all she knew, he could do some handwriting analysis to identify likely culprits. "We had a run-in with some miners. What else did you learn at the tea house?"

"Little," Mancrest said. "Despite the lofty name, it's run by the same people that own half of the mines in the mountains, and it's something of a slum establishment for lowly workers who can only pay in company scrip."

"I know it," Amaranthe said, her tone cool. "My father used to go there when he was in town."

"Oh."

"Smooth tongue there, Mancrest," Maldynado said.

"Yes, uhm, they picked me out as warrior-caste right away," Mancrest said, "and nobody answered my questions. I was trying to find out where the fellow lived and what he was selling."

"Perhaps we'll check it out later," Amaranthe said. "We have another mission tonight."

"If you find out anything," Mancrest said, "and you need any help..."

"Oh, sure," Maldynado said. "You've only tried to lure us into traps twice. Let's arrange another meeting. Maybe the third time, you'll figure out how to get us."

"I understand why you might not be quick to trust me," Mancrest said.

Amaranthe snorted.

"But—" he lifted a finger, "—if you seek exoneration, then you'll want me there to witness your magnificent capture of the perpetrators. As a man from the warrior-caste, I would also be obligated to report the truth as I saw it."

She watched his face, trying to decide if he was eager for a story or if he simply wanted another chance to ensnare her. If he had gone to this tea house, then it might indicate the former. But Maldynado was right. She'd be an idiot to give him another chance to betray her.

"I'll think about it," Amaranthe said. "Gentlemen." She nodded to Maldynado and Books. It was time to go.

They started down the corridor, but Mancrest cleared his throat.

Ah, the keys. Right.

Amaranthe removed them from the protruding stone on the wall and dropped them on the floor in front of the shop.

"Didn't you say you'd let me out if I shared what I knew?" Mancrest eyed the keys. They were closer but still too far for him to reach.

"I said I'd make it *easier* for you to unlock yourself," Amaranthe said. "Now you'll only need one clothes hanger instead of two. Good night."

She, Maldynado, and Books headed out. Midnight had to be growing near, and they had much work to do.

CHAPTER 10

S oft rain pattered onto the cobblestones and railway tracks alongside the street. Amaranthe pedaled up the waterfront, trying to hover above the damp bicycle seat in an attempt to avoid a wet backside. Maldynado rode alongside, his knees nearly clunking his own chin with each revolution—he had been unable to find a taller model left on the communal rack and had refused a couple of larger bicycles that appeared "too feminine." That it was well after midnight and no one was around to see him riding did not seem to matter.

He also balanced the soldier's rifle across the handlebars. Tonight, it might be worth risking the unwanted attention of being spotted with firearms in the city. Amaranthe wore a pistol on her sword belt, opposite the blade. A light jacket hid the firearm, and Maldynado could always toss the rifle if potential witnesses spotted them.

They pedaled through darkness punctuated by puddles of light from gas lamps. On the other side of the tracks, water lapped at the pilings of docks, many supporting towering warehouses, all dark this time of night. Amaranthe supposed they would not luck across one with a brightly painted sign that read, "Kidnapped athletes stored here." This time of year, the docks saw a lot of traffic and would make a poor hideout for those engaging in felonious activities.

"There's the spur." Maldynado pointed at tracks veering inland, away from the main line. The wet steel gleamed under the influence of a corner street lamp.

"Let's check it," Amaranthe said.

She turned onto the street, glad to leave the bumpy cobblestones for a modern cement avenue. A hill loomed, though, and Maldynado grumbled under his breath, something about it being less work to carry the small bicycle up the incline than to pedal.

Warehouses continued for the next few blocks, and commercial and residential tenements rose beyond that. Amaranthe doubted they needed to search that far up the hill.

"What are we looking for exactly?" Maldynado asked.

"A door large enough to hide that rail carriage." Amaranthe yawned. She was starting to feel the lateness of the hour. "Though freight cars are sometimes shunted up the sidings, they don't spend the night. Our kidnappers have to be able to hide their conveyance when they're not using it."

"A *lot* of these doors are big."

"But are they big with railway tracks leading beneath them?"

"Ah, not all. Just..." Maldynado pointed. "There's one."

Amaranthe parked her bicycle against the brick wall of a building on the opposite side of the street. They were between lamp-lit intersections, so shadows would hide them from anyone looking out a window. Not that she expected to chance upon the villain's hideout in the first place they checked, but one never knew.

A couple of blocks up the hill, a ponderous steam vehicle rolled onto the street with twin lanterns lighting its way. It had the girth of a rail car itself, and swinging mechanical arms stuck out of the upper portion of both sides, like a pair of bug antennae. A stench reminiscent of burning hair wafted down the street ahead of it.

"What is that hideous thing?" Maldynado had also dismounted and leaned his bicycle against the wall.

"You've never seen a garbage steamer?" Amaranthe asked. "How can you have lived your whole life in the city without seeing one?"

"I don't know." He clasped a hand over his nose. "I tend to run the other way when I smell a stench like that in the middle of the night."

The vehicle trundled to a stop and a soot-caked man with a greasy beard and hair in need of scissors hopped out. He grabbed a couple of ash cans in an alley and dumped them into the back. He opened the door to an incinerator that burned independently of the firebox powering the boiler. The contents of a bronze waste bin went into the flames.

"Why don't you take a look at that building?" Amaranthe waved to the one they had stopped to check. "I'm going to talk to that fellow. If he works at night, he may have seen something suspicious on his route."

"Be careful," Maldynado said. "He looks dangerous, like he doesn't see daylight too often. Probably not women either."

"So, he'll be happy to see me."

"He'd be happier if you were in something less...well, less. What happened to the disguise I got you before we went into the mountains?"

"The one that showed more skin than most people reveal in the public baths? Sicarius didn't like it."

"First off," Maldynado said, "you shouldn't take fashion advice from someone whose wardrobe is monochromatic. Second, he didn't *like* it? How could a male not like seeing an attractive young female in that outfit? Whatever is wrong with that man is no small thing."

"I'll let you tell him that when we find him."

Amaranthe waved him toward the building and jogged up the hill.

"Hello," she called to the man, not wanting to startle him.

A second fellow sat in the cab of the vehicle, and she lifted a hand in greeting toward him as well.

The garbage collector nearly dropped the can in his arms when he spotted her. He glanced over his shoulder, perhaps thinking she was speaking to someone else.

"That's a nice looking steamer," Amaranthe said as she drew near. She fought the urge to crinkle her nose, not entirely sure all the foul smells came from the vehicle.

He scratched his tangled hair, probably trying to figure out why a woman was running up to him in the middle of the night. "Yup, yup 'tis."

"I was wondering what those arms do." She pointed at the articulating antennae-like devices.

"Yup, yup, they're for fetching big pieces outta hard-to-reach spots. See them claspers at the end?" The man went on to detail dozens of features of the vehicle, which turned out to be a brand new model. After a barked warning from his co-worker, he continued to work while he talked.

Amaranthe walked beside him and grunted encouragingly from time to time, figuring they were bonding. The man ought to think her less odd if they had established a rapport before she started pumping him for information.

"Yup, she's a real fine lady." He finished by patting the vehicle on the side. "You want to ride along a spell?"

"Tempting," she said, "but I'm on a quest."

"Oh?" He scraped his fingers through his tangled beard.

"I don't suppose you've seen a fancy black rail carriage rolling through this neighborhood late at night? It would have been in the last two..."

She trailed off, since he was already nodding.

"Seen that beauty a couple of times. That's a custom job. Ain't no factory-made model, no, ma'am."

"Did you see it on this street?" she asked.

"Naw, over on West Monument. Saw it rolling out of the old fire brigade building a little after midnight a few nights back."

"Monument, good, thank you." A nervous flutter disturbed her stomach. That was the direction she had sent Books and Akstyr. "I don't suppose you're heading over that way?" she asked, thinking of the proffered ride. It would be faster than the bicycles if she could convince these fellows to detour from their route—and not pick up trash on the way.

"Naw."

"Any chance you could be *convinced* to head that way?"

"Well, my partner drives, so reckon I gots to ask him." The man held up a finger, then swung up to address the person manning the controls.

While they conversed, Amaranthe looked for Maldynado. She could signal him to stop searching the buildings off this spur if she spotted him, but nothing stirred on the street. A muggy breeze whispered off the lake, bringing harder rain. Another reason to switch from bicycles to covered conveyances.

"...take that long," her scruffy ally was saying.

The only word Amaranthe caught in the response was "teats." She arched her eyebrows. The fellow might be invoking the ancient imperial platitude about the unfairness of suckling on a dog's rearmost teats, or he might be referencing her chest. Neither sounded promising.

"...nice girl," Scruffy said. "...not going to do that."

"Nice?" the response came, voice louder. "Nice girls don't roam the streets at two in the morning. They're home with their fathers or husbands."

"Ssh. I'm not asking her..."

No, this did not sound good at all. She took a step forward, thinking she had better handle the negotiating, but Scruffy swung down and faced her first.

"Sorry," he said, "but Chalts figgers we're going to get took down by our boss if we delay our route that much, so it's got to be real worth the hollering at." He shuffled his feet and prodded one of the vehicles fat tires. "He says we'll do it if you show us—show him—your, uh..."

"Emperor's warts, Scuv, we'll be here all night if you talk."
The second man leaned out of the cab so the lights on the
vehicle illuminated his face. He was comelier than his scruffy
comrade, but that did not make Amaranthe appreciate his
request more. "Pull up your shirt and show us some teats, and
we'll give you a ride."

While she had paid greater prices for things before, she
doubted a mercenary leader striving to build a reputation for
competence should entertain such an offer. She unbuttoned
her jacket, intending to show them her pistol rather than any
skin.

"She's going to do it!" Scruffy whispered in an aside to his
comrade.

"Told you," the other muttered. "She probably—oomph!"

Without further warning, the man flew out of the cab and
crashed to the street at his comrade's feet. A familiar figure slid
into the vacated seat—Maldynado. The soldier's rifle rested
across his lap.

"*I* haven't even seen under her shirt," he said, "so there's
no way you two shrubs are going to get a show." He gave her
a wide-eyed significant look, as if to ask what she had been
thinking by unbuttoning her jacket.

Amaranthe smiled and lifted the garment to display the
pistol.

"Ah, right." Maldynado wriggled his fingers. "You coming?
I'm sure I can drive this."

"You want to *steal* it?" She eyed the garbage workers.

Scruffy was helping his comrade to his feet amidst much
groaning.

"I just wanted a ride," Amaranthe added.

"Aw, come on, boss," Maldynado said. "I haven't gotten to
abscond with an official imperial vehicle since we molested
those soldiers up at that secret lake."

"We didn't molest them, we helped them." Amaranthe
rubbed her face. It was so difficult to establish a reputation

for being a doer of good. "These two gentlemen were going to give us a ride. I don't think we need to steal their vehicle and get them in trouble."

The man Maldynado had thrown out lunged for the cab, his hand balled into a fist and drawn back to throw a punch. He halted mid-swing when the rifle whipped up. The cold steel muzzle pressed against his forehead.

"I don't think we want these fellows riding along with us," Maldynado said.

The driver backed down, arms raised. "Told you she wasn't nice," he muttered to Scruffy.

"What did I do?" Amaranthe asked.

Both men glared at her. Maldynado grinned. Yes, this might have gone past the point of salvaging with words. She took out her pistol. Though she did not point it their direction, she made sure they saw it.

"You two have any rope in there?" she asked Scruffy.

"Spare winch cable."

"Can you get it, please?"

He shrugged and unlocked a box near the front wheels. He pulled out a large spindle of metal cable.

"Thanks," Amaranthe said. "Now, you two sit over there, back to back, please. I'm going to tie you up."

"What?" Scruffy balked.

His comrade scowled. "*Definitely* not a nice girl."

"Actually, I thought this would keep you gentlemen out of trouble," Amaranthe said. "Better to be incapacitated by deadly bandits than simply wander back to headquarters without your truck, right?"

"Oh," Scruffy said. "Like a *lot* of bandits, right?"

"At least six, I should think," Amaranthe said.

He sat on the cement. After a glower at Amaranthe's pistol, his grumbling comrade did the same.

"Want me to beat them up a bit?" Maldynado asked. "To add verisimilitude?"

"No time." Amaranthe finished tying the men and joined Maldynado in the cab. "They can smash their heads against each other's faces if they feel the need to add physical evidence to corroborate the story."

Maldynado threw a lever. Gears turned, pistons pumped, and the truck lurched backward, flattening an ash can.

Amaranthe groaned. "Why do I find it so difficult to be a law-abiding citizen these days?"

Maldynado shoved the lever the other direction, causing the vehicle to roll forward. "Is there a law against smashing people's trash cans?"

"Imperial City Code 174 covers it. There are numerous pages on vandalism."

"It can't be vandalism if it's done by accident." Maldynado fumbled about, and they veered toward a stone wall.

"No, no, use the turning arm!" came a cry of advice from the bound men.

Maldynado located the controls and turned the vehicle to the left. He angled toward an intersection. "Good thing you didn't gag them."

"Yes, they'll be in big—*bigger*—trouble with their boss if we wreck their vehicle." Amaranthe realized her hand was gripping the side of the cab with clenched fingers.

"Nah, I've got it now." Maldynado pushed the vehicle to full speed. "We'll be there in a few minutes. This is fun. Far better than riding that ridiculous bicycle."

Wind drove rain droplets through the open side, and moisture spattered Amaranthe's cheeks. She was already regretting her choice. That theft would be reported, and the enforcers would match it to her once the workers described her. She should have handled the situation better.

"Quit it," Maldynado said.

"What?"

"Self-flagellating. I heard what that man said; you got the location of the rail carriage. We wouldn't have gotten that if you hadn't gone up to talk to them. And it's important to get over there quickly in case Books and Akstyr have already found it and are on the brink of getting themselves in trouble."

Amaranthe wiped water from her cheeks. "You're wiser than you let on most of the time. In fact, you usually hide it well."

"It's late. I'm not at my best." He nodded toward an upcoming intersection bisected by rail tracks. "There's our street."

He turned the corner and rolled over a streetlamp in the process. It snapped from its cement post without hindering the sturdy truck. Amaranthe dropped her face into her palm.

"Oops," Maldynado said.

Smoke teased Amaranthe's nostrils, distracting her from a mordant response. She sniffed at the air outside the window. It did not smell like the coal burning in their furnace.

"Uh oh." Maldynado pointed down the street.

Flames licked around the edges of a window in a building a block ahead. A building with an oversized statue in the shape of a hydrant out front—the old fire brigade.

A sleek black steam carriage trundled up the hill, coming their direction. It was a street model, not one for the railways, but it had a similar style to the other one. A chauffeur perched on the bench of the carriage, hood drawn to shield him from the rain. Face forward, he avoided looking their direction. Lamps burned inside the carriage, but dark curtains hid the contents.

"Crash into them," Amaranthe said.

"What?" Maldynado blurted.

"Nobody who lives around here can afford a personal vehicle, and somebody started that fire." The carriage was drawing even with them, and it would be too late to stop them soon. "Crash into them!" Amaranthe reached toward the controls.

"All right, all right." Maldynado jerked the vehicle to the left.

The garbage truck rammed into the side of the carriage. Metal crunched, and the impact threw Amaranthe against the back of the cab. That did not keep her from scrambling out, pistol in hand.

She had expected the crash to force the carriage to stop, but the chauffeur only turned his vehicle away, trying to extricate himself from the garbage truck. The curtains stirred, and Amaranthe caught a glimpse of red hair. Her heart leaped. Their foreign woman.

Maldynado kept mashing the garbage truck into the carriage, trying to pin it against the brick wall of the closest building.

"What are you doing, idiot?" the chauffeur shouted.

Amaranthe sprinted around the garbage truck and jumped onto the driving bench. The carriage lurched and wobbled, rattling the perch like a steam hammer. The chauffeur spun toward Amaranthe, his hand darting for a weapon.

She pressed the pistol against his temple. "I don't recommend that tactic. Why don't you stop the carriage?"

He snarled at her and did not obey. She shoved his hood back with her free hand. He had the olive skin and brown hair of a Turgonian. A scar ran from his ear to his jaw, a mark that would have been memorable if she had seen it before, but she had not. He did have the short hairstyle soldiers favored.

"Stop the vehicle," Amaranthe repeated, putting more pressure on the muzzle pressed against his temple.

"Very well." The man grabbed a lever.

Steam brakes squealed, and the abrupt halt nearly threw Amaranthe from the bench. She gripped the frame and would have been fine, but the chauffeur took advantage. He launched a kick at her ribs. She dodged, avoiding the majority of the blow, but it upset her balance. Before she toppled off, she grabbed his leg and took him over the edge with her.

They tumbled toward the street. Amaranthe twisted in the air and landed on top of him. She caught his wrist, yanked it behind him, and slammed his face into the wet cement. He groaned and ceased struggling. With her knee in the chauffeur's back, she patted him down and found the weapon he had been reaching for, also a pistol. She stuffed it inside her belt.

Steel squealed behind them.

Amaranthe rolled to the side and jumped to her feet, afraid someone had started the carriage again. Getting run over was never a good plan.

Neither it nor Maldynado's vehicle was moving though. The noise came from one of the garbage truck's articulating arms. It had latched onto a flue on the carriage and was lifting the back end of the vehicle into the air.

"They're not going anywhere now," Maldynado called, leaning out of the cab and grinning.

A carriage door opened. Something glinted.

"Look out," Amaranthe called.

A shot rang out.

Maldynado yelped and ducked out of sight.

Not sure if he had been hit or not, Amaranthe left her man and sprinted for the opposite side of the carriage. She grabbed the door handle, thinking to surprise those inside if they were watching Maldynado, but it was locked. The dark curtains were still drawn, and someone had extinguished the light inside.

Amaranthe was debating about using her pistol to smash through the window when footsteps sounded to the rear. She peered around the end of the carriage. Books and Akstyr were running toward her, swords drawn.

She waved for them to cover the back of the carriage, in case the people inside jumped out and ran in that direction, then she left the locked door and eased around the front. The chauffeur was sprinting toward an alley. She ignored him, figuring the important people were inside.

Using the front of the carriage for cover, Amaranthe leaned around the corner, her pistol ready. The carriage door dangled open.

Books hunkered by the front of the garbage truck, using

it for cover while he pointed a pistol at the open door. Akstyr had gone to the far side of the carriage in case the riders tried to escape that way.

"Come out," Amaranthe said. "We have you surrounded."

Something tiny flew out from within, and Amaranthe jumped back. Glass hit the cement and shattered. Smoke poured from a broken vial.

She fired into the few inches of open doorway. She did not expect to hit anyone, but maybe it would make them think twice about throwing anything else outside.

"Is that—" Books started.

"Back up," Amaranthe called over his question. If this was the stuff that knocked people unconscious...

Though she backpedalled several meters, the smoke billowed outward at an alarming rate. It soon smothered the street and hid both vehicles. An acrid scent stung her nostrils and eyes. She fumbled to reload the pistol, but had to stop to dash away tears that blurred her vision. At least she did not feel woozy or sluggish. This was some new concoction with a different—horrible—smell from the yellow powder.

She wiped her eyes again.

Movement stirred the smoke. She lifted her pistol, but did not fire, not when it might be one of her men.

Amaranthe listened, expecting telltale footfalls. Surely, the occupants intended to use the smoke to camouflage their escape.

Though the vehicles had stopped moving, their engines still rumbled and clanked. But then she heard something different. A clatter. Something hitting the ground.

She dropped to a knee, left arm supporting her right hand to steady it for a shot. She waited, searching the smoke through bleary eyes.

A boom shattered the night. Its force hurled Amaranthe backward, and her head cracked against the cement street. Pain exploded in her skull, and black dots danced before her eyes. Rain pelted the street around her. No, not rain. Pieces of metal tinkling and clanking to the ground.

A shard gashed her cheek, eliciting new pain, and she rolled over, wrapping her arms over her head. Something slammed onto the street inches from her face. She found herself gaping at a detached portion of the articulating arm.

"Up, girl," she told herself, forcing her mind into gear.

Pain lanced through her at the change in position, but she shoved her feet under her anyway, and turned toward the crash site. Smoke still hazed the street, and the air stank. Her first thought was that one of the boilers had ruptured, but perhaps the people in the carriage had thrown some sort of explosive.

Two tall figures strode toward her, their features masked by the smoke and night shadows.

Amaranthe had lost her pistol in the fall. She yanked out the one she had taken from the chauffeur.

"It's us," Maldynado said.

"Are you all right?" Books asked.

Amaranthe lowered the weapon. "Yes. Did you see anyone? Did you *capture* anyone?"

Given that they dragged no prisoners between them, the latter seemed unlikely, but Akstyr wasn't accounted for yet. Maybe he had had better luck.

"Sorry, I was busy getting shot," Maldynado said.

In the poor lighting, she could not see if he was bleeding, but the way he reached for his temple and then lowered his hand to check it made her suspect so.

"Can you walk?" Books asked. "I think they set the fire in that building down there. If so, they must have been trying to hide something, to destroy evidence perhaps."

Before he finished the words, Amaranthe forced her legs into a jog. "Let's check it. Where's Akstyr?"

The back of her head sent a pulse of pain through her skull with each step. She probed her scalp gingerly, and her fingers met dampness. What a night.

"I'm not sure," Books said. "I saw him racing into an alley. I think it was him. He must have seen someone."

Amaranthe thumped her fist against her thigh, torn between wanting to race after him to make sure he did not get in trouble and wanting to investigate the building before the flames burned away any evidence that might be inside. "Which alley?" she asked.

Books hesitated, then pointed at one a half a block down the hill. Amaranthe veered toward it, but when she reached the mouth, she could not see anyone. Several alleys opened to the left and right before the main one emptied onto a street a block away.

"Could be anywhere," she muttered.

"Let's check the building," Books said. "I'm sure he'll be fine."

Amaranthe was not, and she did not want to lose any more men, but she let Books lead her away. Maldynado had stopped to gawk at the wreckage revealed by the clearing smoke. Warped and charred, the vehicles slumped like candles melted down to stubs. Though warehouses and commercial buildings filled these blocks, Amaranthe doubted that explosion would go unreported for long.

Shaking her head, she followed Books to a tall, double-door entrance—one large enough to accommodate a railway carriage. Smoke poured out, and he had pulled his shirt up over his nose. Flames continued to burn at the ground-level window, and fire danced behind the upper floor windows now, too.

Even before Amaranthe stepped inside, dry heat blew over her face. The rail carriage sat in the middle of an open bay. Flames crackled and danced along the wooden ceiling high overhead, but the fire had not damaged the carriage yet.

She rifled through a pocket and found the kerchief she had used earlier in the night.

"The flames have likely compromised the structural integrity of the building," Books said.

"That's his way of saying we're stupid to go inside, right?" Maldynado asked.

"I believe so." Amaranthe went in anyway, heading straight for the rail carriage. Hot air and light assaulted her already beleaguered eyes, and tears streaked down her cheeks, cool against skin flushed from the heat. "Spread out and search this floor."

A board fell away from the ceiling and thudded to the cement ahead of her. Flames licked the charred wood. She ran around it and circled the carriage, hoping one door would be open. None were. She tugged her jacket off, wadded it up to insulate her hand, and reached for the handle.

The heat seared her flesh even through the cloth barrier, and she yanked the door open as quickly as possible.

A ceiling beam snapped, and half of it dropped, smashing onto the engine of the rail carriage.

Amaranthe gulped. Wisps of charred paper and wood floated in the air, and even with the kerchief over her mouth and nose, hot fumes seared her lungs.

Using her boot, she nudged the door open wide. Nothing rested on the carpeted floor or black-velvet benches on either end. A shirt or jacket hung over the back of one though. Amaranthe doubted it would reveal anything useful, but she lunged in and grabbed it.

"Amaranthe!" Books yelled.

She jumped out of the carriage. "What?"

"Over here," he called from the far corner of the bay, somewhere behind the carriage. "You're going to want to see this."

"I'm not so sure about that," Maldynado said.

Amaranthe eased around the carriage and spotted the two men behind a low wall that partially hid a bank of standing lockers. Books was staring at something on the ground, his face twisted in a horrified rictus.

Maldynado backed away, his expression grim. "I can't look at that."

Amaranthe took a deep breath and joined Books.

The woman's body on the ground did not surprise her, but its nudity and the scars gouging the torso did. Though the smell of burning wood — burning *everything* — dominated the building, she caught a whiff of blood, and her stomach twisted into a knot, threatening to eject its contents. Amaranthe took a deep breath and sought to find detachment, at least enough to study the body and figure out what it meant.

The scars seemed systematic rather than the result of sword or knife fighting. Some were stitched and partially healed while others appeared more recent. Though blood saturated the blonde hair, the face was oddly unmarred.

A jolt of recognition went through her. It was Fasha, the woman who had first alerted Amaranthe to the kidnappings. Either that, or the missing sister was a twin, but given that Fasha had failed to show up for their last meeting...

"Some of those scars." Books coughed and cleared his throat. "Some of those look like they're over the reproductive organs."

Amaranthe stared at him. "What are you saying? Someone removed her organs?"

"It seems likely someone did *something* to them."

Another beam snapped, and burning shards of wood fluttered to the floor.

"We ought to get out of here," Maldynado said from a few feet away. "I'm sure you two can further discuss the creepiness of this whole situation outside."

"Good idea," Books said, stepping past Amaranthe.

"Wait, we should remove the body," she said. A doctor could tell them more about the cuts and if anything was...missing. "Can you help me —"

A massive crack boomed above her head. Burning boards plummeted toward her.

Amaranthe leaped back. Someone's hand gripped her collar and yanked her further. Charred wood and rubble from the floor above buried the body and hurled smoke and ash into the air.

The rag about her mouth did little to keep fine particles from invading her throat. Coughs wracked her body, and she bent over, trying to find air. The heat and fumes brought dizziness, and blackness encroached upon her vision again.

More wood snapped overhead. An arm snaked around Amaranthe's waist, and she found herself slung over someone's shoulder.

"Help you get out of here?" Maldynado asked in response to her request. "Why, yes, yes I can."

When Amaranthe opened her mouth to protest, another series of coughs sent spasms through her body.

"You approve?" Maldynado said. "Excellent."

Despite her reluctance to leave without the body, a surge of pleasure raced through her when they stepped outside and cool night air replaced the heat of the building. Rain splattered the back of her neck, and she didn't mind it one bit.

"Dear ancestors," Books said, "what a mess."

"Me?" Amaranthe croaked.

"I believe he's referring to the crash you instigated," Maldynado said.

He had not set her down yet. Amaranthe, butt in the air, torso dangling down his back, twisted her head to the side to view the tangled metal carnage in the middle of the street.

"Take a good look," Maldynado said. "I want you to remember this the next time you bother me about running over a street lamp."

"Are you planning on destroying more street lamps?" Books asked.

"Oh, I think that's a given as long as we work for the boss here."

Amaranthe opened her mouth to tell him to set her down, but motion up the hill stopped her. A vehicle had turned onto the street and was rolling toward the crash. Night made it impossible to make out details, but she could guess at the occupants. "Enforcers coming. Time to go."

"Right." Maldynado jogged toward an alley.

Amaranthe bumped and bounced on his shoulder like a crate on a bicycle navigating cobblestones. "I can run on my own," she said, voice vibrating with Maldynado's every step.

"Promise you won't sprint back inside and try to drag that body out?" Maldynado asked.

"Yes." Unfortunately.

Maldynado lowered her gently. She scraped damp hair out of her eyes, wincing when she brushed against a knot the size of a chicken egg on the side of her head. She was surprised to find she still clutched the jacket she had pulled out of the carriage. Not exactly the chance for illumination the body would have provided, but maybe a pocket would contain a useful clue.

Several blocks away and back on the street following the waterfront, Amaranthe paused beneath a streetlight to examine it. The flame revealed heavy black material in the cut of an army fatigue jacket.

"What's that?" Books asked, stopping beside her.

Maldynado stopped as well, though he turned his attention the way they had come, watching for pursuit.

"It was in the carriage." Amaranthe checked the pockets and found nothing. So much for that hope. The rank pins had been removed, though the nametag was still sewn on above the breast pocket. She turned it toward the light. "Taloncrest," she read and paused. That name seemed familiar.

"Nobody I've heard of," Maldynado said.

"Nor I," Books said. "Amaranthe?" he asked when her thoughtful silence continued.

"Colonel Taloncrest," she murmured, an uneasy flutter vexing her stomach at the memory.

"Who's he?" Maldynado asked.

"He was the surgeon performing medical experiments on people in the Imperial Barracks dungeon when Hollowcrest had me thrown down there."

Memories of that miserable place flooded Amaranthe. The military could not be behind the kidnapped athletes and her missing men, could it? No, Sespian would not allow that to happen. Unless he didn't *know* it was happening. He hadn't known of the experiments in the dungeon the winter before. But he had been drugged then. The more likely scenario was that Sespian had learned of the experiments in the dungeon and ousted Taloncrest for being one of Hollowcrest's lackeys. That would mean Taloncrest was a rogue, perhaps hirable by someone else. Such as this red-haired woman.

"You're sure?" Books asked. "Medical experiments?"

"Dear ancestors," Maldynado said, looking back the way they had come, toward the dead woman. "That's disturbing."

Amaranthe tried not to think of Taloncrest standing over Sicarius, a scalpel poised. It did not work.

CHAPTER 11

When Basilard woke, his head ached worse than it ever had after a night out carousing with Maldynado. He opened his eyes to—thankfully—dim lighting emanating from a globe hanging beside a metal door. The entire room—cubby might be a better word—was made from dark gray metal. He lay on a narrow cot, staring at riveting running along ridges traversing the walls from floor to curved ceiling. He had never been on a steam ship, but guessed that was his location. Engines somewhere rumbled, the reverberations pulsing through the floor and up his cot.

Was he being transported somewhere? Though he had never sailed, he had seen maps of the empire and knew that one could travel from the Chain Lakes down the Goldar River and all the way to the Gulf. From there, one could go... anywhere in the world. Had he been captured to be sold into slavery once again? This time someplace far away? Someplace so far away there was no chance he would ever return home again to see his daughter?

The daughter you could have already gone to see if you weren't such a coward, he told himself.

Basilard sat up, and the pounding in his head intensified

so much he groaned and grabbed his temples. Toughen up, he told himself. Sicarius would not bellyache so.

He sneered at himself. Why was he holding Sicarius up as a model to emulate?

When the throbbing calmed enough to handle, he swung his legs over the edge of the cot and found the floor—the deck? Was that what ship people called it? The cold metal numbed his bare feet. With a twitch of surprise, he realized everything was bare. He patted himself down, checking for...he did not know what, but one couldn't trust people who kidnapped one and stole one's clothing.

Soft, rhythmic clangs sounded beyond the door. Footsteps.

A scratch and thud echoed through the door. Basilard slipped off the cot and dropped into a defensive crouch. One that could easily turn offensive, if the situation permitted it. Though he should perhaps figure out where he was before attacking people. Who knew how long he had been unconscious?

Another thud sounded, then a clank. Multiple locks being thrown? If so, they had secured him well.

The thick, metal door squeaked open.

A woman stood there, her long red hair pinned into a swirling dervish atop her head. Two men framed her. They wore the black fatigues of army soldiers, though no rank pins adorned their collars. One appeared to be "the muscle." He crowded the hallway with broad shoulders and tree-trunk arms that even Maldynado would have dubbed substantial. He aimed a pistol at Basilard, though the challenging sneer curling his lips said he would be happy to battle barehanded or perhaps with the sword sheathed at his waist. The surname stitched on his jacket read, LEV. The second man had neatly trimmed gray hair and wielded a clipboard instead of a gun. His tag read, TALONCREST. A warrior-caste officer involved in this scheme? Surprising.

The woman stepped inside first with no apparent fear of

Basilard. The men followed after, one at a time, ducking and stepping over the raised frame of the door to enter.

"Greetings," the woman said. "I have questions for you."

Though Basilard would not have been in a rush to answer their questions under any circumstances, he doubted it was a possibility here. The soldiers would not understand his sign language, and he did not think the woman was Mangdorian. Though fair-skinned, she was not as pale as his people, and he thought she might be Kendorian or perhaps from one of the island nations between Turgonia and Nuria.

He touched the scar tissue at his throat and shrugged. Maybe they would not think to ask if he could read, though Arbitan had insisted Basilard learn that skill before he took over as head of security for the wizard.

"You can't speak?" the woman asked, eyes narrowed.

Basilard shook his head and signed, *Who are you?* more out of habit than because he wanted a response. In reflection, maybe he should not have done that. Maybe it was better if they believed he could not answer their questions at all. Or would that mean they had no use for him?

The gray-haired officer's eyebrows rose. "The Mangdorian hunting code?"

Basilard nodded.

"That answers your question, Litya." Taloncrest scribbled something on his notepad.

"Yes, but race matters little for my experiments," the woman said in a lilting, almost musical accent Basilard did not recognize. "I prefer Turgonian stock, given the goals of my clients, but your people have such muddied bloodlines that no one will be the wiser as long as we breed the foreigners with darker skinned specimens."

Breed? Basilard caught his mouth dangling open, and he snapped it shut.

"If you don't need him," Taloncrest said, eyeing Basilard as he tapped his pen on his clipboard, "I'm sure I could use him."

"You can have them all for your cuttings after I've taken my samples."

"Excellent," Taloncrest said.

"I can move ahead with him as soon as my sister returns with the anesthesia ingredients."

Cuts were nothing new to Basilard, but Taloncrest's smile and the enthusiastic way he scribbled notes on his clipboard made Basilard uneasy. As did the talk of "samples" and "anesthesia."

"Your speed in the race," the woman—Litya—said, "is that typical for you, or do you believe it was a fluke performance? Your agility must have impressed our boy, because he'd had another pegged as our last acquisition. I have no data on you however."

Basilard clasped his hands behind his back. These people had nothing good planned for him, so he saw no reason to assist them.

"Taloncrest," Litya said, "can you understand his hand codes? Can you make him speak?"

Basilard raised his chin. They could *try* to make him speak.

The young soldier stepped forward at this, an eager smile tightening his lips.

"I don't know enough of the signs," Taloncrest said.

"Maybe he's learned to write Turgonian?" Litya asked. "Or does anybody here read Mangdorian? They're vaguely literate, aren't they?"

Basilard thought about waving for a pen, if only so he could attempt to stab the woman in the belly with it before the men stopped him, but it was probably better to pretend he could not write and did not understand much of what they were saying.

"When Metya gets back, we'll question him under the influence of *pok-tah*," the woman said. "If he knows anything, he'll be eager to share it with us then, one way or another."

"It didn't work on Sicarius," Taloncrest muttered, head down, scrawling notes again.

Had Basilard thought about it, he would have assumed

Sicarius was here somewhere, too, but hearing the name startled him. He covered his surprise quickly and hoped nobody noticed.

He waited, hoping they would say something that would indicate whether Sicarius was alive or if they had already... disposed of him, but nobody spoke again. After Taloncrest finished scribbling his notes, he nodded to the woman, and the trio left.

The door clanged shut, and the locks thunked into place.

Basilard could only guess at what these people were up to, but he knew he wanted to be no part of it. If he was on a ship, steaming away from the city, he could not count on Amaranthe and the others finding him and rescuing him. He would have to escape.

He eyed the solid metal walls and the sparse confines of the cabin. It would not be easy.

Amaranthe swept dust and food crumbs off the top of the lookout car. Despite the busy night, she had slept poorly when she, Maldynado, and Books returned to their camp in the boneyard. She had woken at dawn, the lump on her head throbbing, and frequent yawns had been tearing her gritty eyes ever since. Morning sun beat against her back, making the night's rain a faint memory, but the warmth failed to cheer her. Akstyr had not returned, and she was beginning to fear he had been captured, too. Or worse.

She could not stop picturing Fasha's dead body in her mind. Though the girl had never officially hired her team, or asked for protection, Amaranthe knew she had failed her. She should have kept better tabs on the girl, or at least warned her not to go hunting for clues on her own.

She swept more vigorously.

"Amaranthe?" Books called. "Are you up there?"

She swept a walnut shell off the edge, sending it clanging against the rail car on the far side of their camp.

"Must be a yes," Books muttered as he climbed up. He frowned over the top of the ladder at her. "I can see cleaning the cars we're dwelling in, but the tops of them? Is that necessary?"

Books held a napkin full of food, and Amaranthe stopped sweeping. Her stomach rumbled, reminding her that many hours had passed since her last meal.

"Someone ate walnuts up here and left shells everywhere," she said.

"Yes, but is it *necessary* to clean that?"

"No, it's not necessary, Books, but this is what I do when—" She broke off, not wanting to start ranting over nothing. He was not the one upsetting her; it was the cursed situation and the fact that she was losing men every time she turned around. "This is what I do."

"Sorry," he said. "I just thought...you should get more rest."

"I couldn't sleep."

"Ah." Books cleared his throat, glanced down, and seemed to remember he held food. "Breakfast?" He offered her a couple of hard-boiled eggs and a slab of ham.

Amaranthe drew her kerchief from her pocket, found it soot-stained, and sighed. She set it aside to wash later and grabbed the food barehanded. "Thank you."

"It's an all-protein breakfast," Books said. "I believe Sicarius would approve."

She tried to smile. "He'd add seeds and raw vegetables to counteract the saltiness of the ham. Or maybe they're to keep morning movements regular. I think I've finally got his diet down, but I can't remember all the reasons for all the rules."

"I just know we're lucky to have food at all with Basilard gone. What are we going to do next to find them?"

"I'm not sure." Which meant she had no idea. "They know we're looking for them now. I wish we had some soldier friends at Fort Urgot, so we could ask if anyone knew what Taloncrest was last working on." Amaranthe took a bigger bite of ham than normal, tearing it off with a savage chomp.

"Yes, soldiers have that tedious tendency to try and capture us when we get close. Or shoot us on sight."

"We were *this* close...." She held up her thumb and forefinger, a millimeter between them. "I don't know if that was their hideout or simply a transfer station, but the fire surely destroyed any evidence left behind. They must have realized there were witnesses to Basilard's kidnapping. Or maybe they intended him to be the last person they stole, and they didn't need the fire brigade building any more."

"I know it seems bleak now," Books said, "but we can't give up."

"Of course not. We're just..." Amaranthe touched the lump on her head, eliciting a stab of pain. "Recovering for a few hours."

"Anyone home?" a familiar voice called.

Akstyr. Amaranthe rose to her feet and stepped to the edge of the car roof. He slouched into camp, his spiky hair drooping, and dark circles beneath his eyes. He appeared uninjured.

Amaranthe knew it was uncharitable, but she wished it were Sicarius striding into camp instead. Akstyr might have information though. She waved for him to come up.

"Busy night?" she asked.

"Boring night," Akstyr said.

That didn't sound promising. "Did you learn anything?"

"Enh."

She circled her hand in the air, implying he could explain further.

"I spotted the woman and the man running out of the smoke and into an alley," Akstyr said.

"Woman and man? From inside the carriage?" Amaranthe asked. "What did they look like?"

"The woman had red hair and she was nice and curvy. The man was older. Short, gray hair. Looked like a soldier, but he was just wearing a black shirt, so it was hard to tell."

That sounded like Taloncrest and the woman the young thieves had described. Amaranthe nodded. "Go on."

"I followed them, figured you'd want to know where they went."

"Yes, I do. Thank you. And?" Sometimes she appreciated that Maldynado launched into the whole story at the tiniest prompting. Surely soldiers could get information out of prisoners of war more easily than she could dig it out of Akstyr at times.

"Stayed back in the shadows so they wouldn't see me. Almost lost them a couple of times, but I found 'em again on the docks. They went out on Pier Thirteen to a warehouse at the end."

Amaranthe frowned at Books. "That's the Bolidot's Imports warehouse, isn't it? She has a huge business with a big turnover, and cargo ships go in and out of there every day. Kidnappers needing to maintain a low profile couldn't use such a busy place."

"Agreed," Books said.

"They never came out," Akstyr said.

"That seems unlikely," Books said.

Akstyr stepped toward him, chest puffed out. "You thinking I'm blind? Or lying? While you were sleeping, I was sitting there watching and waiting for them to come back down the dock and they never did. I stayed until workers showed up and went inside. What'd you do? Come back here and snore all night?"

"Four hours, perhaps," Books murmured.

Amaranthe rested a hand on Akstyr's arm, drawing his attention to her. "Is it possible they slipped away in a boat?"

"Don't think so," he said. "I thought of that and checked how many boats were around. Didn't see any disappear."

"I guess we can take a look," Amaranthe told Books.

Akstyr yawned. "You two do that. I'm going to make it thunderous in the sleeping car." He emulated a noisy snore, then jumped to the ground.

"Akstyr," Amaranthe called. She stifled a twinge of annoyance that he had dismissed himself without asking if she needed anything else. He had to be tired after staying up all night, and he was surly even on a perky day. "We need you to come."

"What?" he called up in a whiny voice a five year old could not have bested.

"I'll bet you ten ranmyas Taloncrest and his foreign lady aren't working out of that warehouse."

"So?"

"*So*, if you didn't see them leave by mundane means, isn't it possible they used the mental sciences?"

"Oh," Akstyr said. "Well, yeah."

"Then we'll need you to stick your magic-sniffing nose in the corners," Amaranthe said, "see if you can catch a scent."

"I'm not a hound, you know."

"We *know*," Books said. "Hounds work a lot harder for a lot less incentive."

"You're not helping," Amaranthe said.

"We can't go until night, right?" Akstyr asked. "Lots of people will be working, so we can't sniff around until they go home."

Amaranthe leaned over the edge of the roof and smiled down at him. "I'll get us in. Have some breakfast, and we'll head over. You can sleep later."

Akstyr stabbed a finger at the open door of the sleeping car. "Does Maldynado get to stay here?"

"That wouldn't be fair, would it?" Amaranthe asked. "You better go wake him up."

"Good." Akstyr smiled for the first time and leaped into the car with zealousness.

"Misery is more palatable when shared with others," Amaranthe noted to Books.

"Indeed."

Amaranthe led Maldynado, Akstyr, and Books onto Pier Thirteen, her strides long and her chin high beneath the brim of her sunhat. It hid her face to some extent, and, on the trolley ride over, she had arranged her hair in a number of braids, then pinned them up in a creative bundle that looked nothing like the style on any of her wanted posters. She supposed she could look into cosmetics to disguise her facial features, but she *wanted* to be recognized when she was doing something good, something that might help her clear her name.

A massive crane belched smoke as it lifted shipping containers from the bowels of a merchant steamer and lowered them to the dock. Dozens of burly, bare-chested stevedores unloaded the cargo and ported it inside the towering warehouse. The shirtless workers seemed to be competing with each other for the role of Tattoo Emperor. Amaranthe decided the man with the kraken was the winner—its head emblazoned his neck while tentacles ran down his back, both arms, and his chest, with the largest pair disappearing beneath his trousers. Of its own wayward volition, her mind wondered how far beneath the waistband the tentacle motif might continue and what exactly it would be doing down there.

The tattooed man glanced her way before heading into the warehouse with a crate in his arms. He caught her eye and winked.

"If Deret doesn't turn out to be your dream man," Maldynado said, "we can always find you someone here."

"Don't be ridiculous, you dolt," Books said. "If Amaranthe must copulate at all, it should be with a man who knows how to read and preferably how to use the Imperial Locus System to pluck appropriately intellectual books from the library shelves."

"A skill that would be completely useless for satisfying her in bed," Maldynado said.

"Surely, finger dexterity has crossover applications."

"Gentlemen," Amaranthe said, wondering when such commentary had ceased to make her blush. "Let's go over our story."

"You're going to pose," Books said, "as the owner of an escort service, with Maldynado as your employee and—"

"*Star* employee," Maldynado said.

"Uh huh." Books stepped around a man carrying a massive ceramic jar and continued. "And you're shopping for imported silks and tapestries and such for your...office? Is that the correct term for a place where someone like Maldynado would be prostituted out?"

"Close enough," Amaranthe said.

"Costasce called her viewing room 'The Parlor'," Maldynado said.

They had reached the roll-up door of the warehouse, so Amaranthe stopped. None of the men streaming in and out spared her group a glance. Maybe they could simply walk in and snoop about without anyone caring. She peeped through the doorway.

A woman in spectacles checked off items on a clipboard and directed men toward different areas in the warehouse or toward a massive lift that could deliver cargo to an upper level. The men might not care about interlopers, but she would surely notice strangers strolling through the premises. The platform sandals crossing her feet with thin straps promised she wasn't going to wander far to do lifting or other work.

"As to our role," Books started, but Amaranthe cut him off with a raised hand.

"Akstyr?" she asked. With his disinterest for things non-magical, she never knew how much he was paying attention. "Your role?"

"We're your porters." He yawned. "Me and Books."

"Good," Amaranthe said.

"As long as we don't have to really port things."

"You just sniff about," she said.

"Are we sure this is wise?" Books ask. "Should this turn... confrontational, we don't have our two most proficient fighters here."

Maldynado propped his hands on his hips. "You have *me*."

Books looked him up and down, then focused on Amaranthe again. "We don't have our two most proficient fighters here."

"You believe Basilard a better brawler than me?" Maldynado asked. "*Truly?*"

"We'll be fine," she said and headed in.

The clipboard-toting lady's head swiveled toward the door before Amaranthe had gone more than three steps. No, this woman would not allow random snoopers, not without a cover story.

"Morning," Amaranthe said, strolling closer.

"What do you want?" the woman snapped.

Ah, the friendly sort. Wonderful.

"Hello, I'm Darva," Amaranthe said. "Darva Larkcrest." As long as she was making up names, she might as well attach herself to a warrior caste family. "Who are you?"

Amaranthe's invocation of warrior-caste status did nothing to impress the woman. In fact, she scowled more deeply. New money, perhaps, one who had no respect for the aristocracy. Still, if she was the owner, or someone high up in the business, she ought to be interested in pleasing clients.

"Ms. Setjareth," she said. "Partial owner. What do you want? This is my warehouse, and unless you're carrying in cargo, I'm not interested in talking to you. You, Squid Tat, take that one to the second floor."

"I'm interested in purchasing some of your inventory," Amaranthe said.

"Shop's on Third and Canal." The woman's gaze lowered to her clipboard again.

Amaranthe stepped closer so she blocked the woman's view of Akstyr. Behind her back, she flicked a finger to send him to snoop. "I thought it might save us both some money if I came directly to the source. No need for you to transport and stock your inventory when I can—"

"Shop's on Third and Canal," the woman repeated.

"I see. You're the half of the ownership team that *isn't* in charge of dealing with customers."

"Correct," the woman said without the faintest hint of an eyebrow to suggest she took reproach at Amaranthe's dry tone.

Akstyr had moved away from the group, but he had scarcely begun to search. Time for another tactic. Maldynado was leaning against a post nearby, an amused smile on his lips. She jerked her chin toward the woman.

Maldynado gave her a small bow and strolled forward. He crouched down so the woman could see past the clipboard to his face.

"Ms. Setjareth," Maldynado drawled. "I'll wager you've got the prettiest smile this side of Wharf Street. Why don't you give me a demonstration so I can more properly judge?"

"If I tried a line like that, I'd get stabbed in the eye with a pen," Books muttered.

"Ssh," Amaranthe whispered. "Let the master work."

"Master?" Books said. "Please."

"There are less than ten females this side of Wharf Street," Setjareth growled. "Not much of a competition."

Amaranthe grinned. Though it wasn't exactly an instant melting, the woman didn't order Maldynado to go away or leave her alone, so it was promising. There was no talk of stabbing eyeballs with pens either.

"Ah, but some of your stevedores might have attractive smiles," Maldynado said.

Setjareth snorted.

"Also my own employer stands a mere five feet away." Maldynado waved at Amaranthe. "Do you understand the risk I take to my livelihood by suggesting your smile might be prettier than hers?"

Setjareth's snort was mellower this time with a slight upward curl of her lips. Amaranthe eased a few steps backward to let Maldynado ooze his charms in private. She should have started with that.

"What are you doing?" Setjareth shouted.

The bellow startled Amaranthe, and at first she thought Maldynado had offended the woman, but that wasn't it. Setjareth was pointing into a corner of the warehouse where Akstyr stood, a trapdoor in the floor lifted.

He offered a blank look in response to the question.

"Don't worry about him." Maldynado slung an arm over Setjareth's shoulder and attempted to turn her about. "He's a dull lad. Got run over by a steam carriage as a boy and hasn't been strong in the head since. Harmless though. If—"

Setjareth shoved Maldynado's arm from her shoulders and stalked toward Akstyr. "What're you doing poking around my warehouse?"

Akstyr looked at Amaranthe. "Uhm."

"Are you spying on our inventory?" Setjareth asked, voice rising. "Are you reporting to Lady Devirk or Bucktooth?"

Several of the stevedores who had been on their way out the door to pick up more cargo stopped and turned around. Chests out, arms flexed and wide at their sides, the muscled men strode toward their boss.

"No, no, nothing like that." Amaranthe grabbed Akstyr's arm and tugged him away from the trapdoor. She caught a glimpse of a ladder and water less than a foot below. There was no way a boat could have waited down there. "I see you're not interested in easy sales, and that's your loss. We'll leave now."

"Not until you answer some questions." Setjareth snapped her fingers, and the stevedores loomed closer.

Amaranthe's instinct was to flee rather than risking injury to these people or her team, but Akstyr gave her a minute nod. He was onto something. Besides, it would be nice if Books realized he was capable of more than he gave himself credit for. She counted the men. Eight of them against her four. Thanks to their work, the stevedores were large and brawny, but they had the cultivated swagger of street bravos rather than the cool, competence of soldiers, and she doubted there were many distinguished veterans among the bunch.

"You wish us to stay?" Amaranthe asked. "Very well." She gave her men a single nod.

Books blanched, but he did not object. Maldynado grinned. Akstyr gave his "whatever" shrug.

"Wants me to grab 'em, boss?" One of the stevedores stretched a meaty hand toward Amaranthe.

She caught it by the wrist, twisted it over, and smashed the palm of her free hand into the back of the man's locked elbow. He blurted a surprised yelp. She forced him to the ground with a kick to the inside of his knee, and something popped in his arm.

"My shoulder!" he bellowed.

Amaranthe yanked the knife at his belt free and spun on a second man advancing upon her.

A few feet away, Maldynado had already thrown himself into three others and gone down with them in a tangle. Despite the chaos of flailing arms and scissor-kicking legs, he was on top, seemingly in control. Akstyr, his dagger out, was trading opening swipes with another man. Books had a blade in hand as well, though he crouched in a defensive stance, waiting for an opponent to advance on him, rather than jumping into the fray.

The man nearest Amaranthe lunged for her. He had chosen fists over blades, and he grabbed at her arm with his right hand while drawing his left arm back for a blow. She blocked the grasp, ducked the punch, and slammed the heel of her hand into his solar plexus, twisting her hips to throw her entire body into the move.

His hard sheath of muscle provided some armor for his torso, but she hit her spot. He hunched over, clutching his chest. His mouth gaped open, but his stunned muscles denied him air.

Eyes huge with concern, he did not see Amaranthe's knee

coming. She rammed it into his groin. His nose scraped his knees as his hunch turned into a collapse. The big man hit the ground and rolled into a protective ball next to the first stevedore Amaranthe had dropped.

That fellow lay on his back, eyes watering, his hand clutching a dislocated shoulder. He glowered at her and seemed to be considering whether to hurl himself back into the fight.

"I wouldn't," Amaranthe said. "I know how to dislocate other body parts as well."

He eyed his comrade who was still hunched on the floor, grabbing at his groin and moaning. "I don't doubt it," the stevedore muttered.

Amaranthe checked on her men. Maldynado stood next to three bodies stacked on each other like Strat Tiles. He had one foot atop the pile, as if to keep them pinned down, but none so much as twitched in an escape attempt.

Nearby, blood trickled out of Akstyr's nose, but he had dropped one man and was boxing with another. Akstyr dodged a swift series of punches, but barely. Though layers of blubber sheathed the towering stevedore's broad torso, he moved with the speed and precision of someone who had been the recipient of training at one time.

"Need help?" Amaranthe asked.

The big man glanced in her direction.

Akstyr's eyes narrowed in concentration. He clenched a fist and flung it open again when his opponent turned back.

Flesh never touched flesh, but the man staggered back, arms wide, face stunned. With flexibility that had greatly improved over the last few months of training, Akstyr launched a straight kick that smashed the stevedore beneath the chin. The big man toppled backward, felled like an oak.

"That was good," Akstyr told Amaranthe.

She did not know if he referred to the timeliness of her brief distraction or his ability to employ the mental sciences during a fight. The latter probably. He wasn't the sort to praise anyone.

"Yes," Amaranthe said, agreeing either way.

"Look out." Akstyr pointed over her shoulder.

She ducked and slid to the side, avoiding a stevedore's attempt at a grasp. A knife glinted in his hand.

Books stalked after the man. Surprising intensity burned in his eyes, and Amaranthe danced further away from the confrontation, figuring this was the middle of something between the two men.

"You think you can grab her and use her against us?" Books growled as the stevedore spun back to face him. "I don't think so."

The man limped backward, hands raised, and Amaranthe wondered what Books had done to him.

Movement to the side distracted her from the rest of the fight. Ms. Setjareth had discarded her clipboard and was scurrying toward the door, steps short and awkward thanks to those sandals.

Amaranthe ran over to cut her off. They did not need the woman calling for reinforcements—many more stevedores still labored on the dock.

Setjareth tried to evade Amaranthe but tripped, sprawling face first onto the hard floor. Amaranthe gripped the woman by the triceps and hauled her upright.

"One who has a personality that grates like glass paper should probably choose footwear sufficient for fleeing from irritated people," Amaranthe said.

"You're no business woman," Setjareth growled.

"Not true. I run a mercenary business."

"What do you want?" Setjareth tried to yank her arm away.

Amaranthe did not let go. After skirmishing with the brawny stevedores, restraining another woman was easy. "Tell the workers out there to take a ten-minute break, then close the door."

The woman leaned outside and filled her lungs. Recognizing the nascent scream for what it was, Amaranthe gripped the back of Setjareth's neck and dug her thumb into one of Sicarius's favorite pressure points. The would-be scream came out as a soft whimper.

"Listen," Amaranthe said. "Nobody's planning to harm you or your business. We just need a few minutes to look around to make sure you're not harboring fugitives." She decided not to point out that she was a fugitive herself.

"What?" Genuine bewilderment blossomed on Setjareth's face.

"A couple of suspicious folks took refuge in your warehouse last night."

With the sounds of fighting fading, Amaranthe checked on her men. They had routed the impromptu security team and were forcing the stevedores to sit against the wall in a neat row. Akstyr had returned to peering into corners and prodding at crates.

"Maybe that's why the lock was destroyed," Setjareth muttered.

"What?" Amaranthe asked.

"When I came in this morning, the padlock on the door was dangling open. It didn't look like it'd been forced, and it still works."

Amaranthe removed her hand from Setjareth's neck. Akstyr knew a few atypical methods of bypassing locks; maybe the red-headed woman was a practitioner herself.

"First time this happened?" Amaranthe asked.

"Yes," Setjareth said. "I spent two hours running inventory this morning." That might account for some of her dourness. "Nothing was missing, and I didn't find anyone inside."

"I'm sorry. Checking through all your inventory must have made for a tedious morning."

"Ancestors know that's true."

"And we must have fueled your suspicions," Amaranthe said, thinking she might yet win the woman's cooperation if she commiserated.

"You're mercenaries, you say?" Setjareth asked.

Books, who had been supervising the disarming and lining up of the men, looked in the women's direction at the question. A grin played across his lips. Pleased with himself, was he? He *had* done well. No falling apart as he had done in the past. Amaranthe smiled and nodded at him.

"More or less," she told Setjareth.

"Do you have a card?"

"A what?"

"A business card. My partner and I occasionally have problems the enforcers are lax about solving. They're professional and thorough when it comes to protecting citizens, but much less enthusiastic when they're tasked with protecting a business's interests."

As illogical as it was, Amaranthe still bristled at slights toward enforcers, but she had to admit that members of the predominantly male force did sometimes show resentment toward the growing power women in the city wielded. Maybe she should tailor her services to fill that gap. As the men—especially Akstyr—were quick to remind her, charity work done in the name of the emperor didn't pay well. Especially when the emperor never learned of that work....

Setjareth, waiting for an answer, lifted her eyebrows.

"Sorry, no card," Amaranthe said. "We find it prudent to move our base of operations often, but..." She retrieved the woman's clipboard, scribbled the name and address of one of their contacts on a page, and tore it off. "Either one of these fellows usually knows how to contact us. Uhm, take some of your stevedores—the big ones—if you go to that neighborhood. And don't go at night. Or without some alcohol to bribe your way out of..." Amaranthe leaned over and scribbled the name out. "Actually, just go to that fellow. It's usually safer. And if you get there before noon, he's usually sober."

"You might want to think your contact chain through a little, dear," Setjareth said.

"Yes, thank you."

Since the woman no longer seemed inclined to scream for help, Amaranthe joined Akstyr to see what he had found. He had returned to the trapdoor and was peering down the ladder again.

"Think they swam away?" she asked, though it seemed unlikely. Why go through the effort of breaking in when one could simply dive off the end of the dock?

"There's a residue here." Akstyr swiped a finger along the edge of the square hole.

"Something physically visible?" Amaranthe squinted but saw nothing more interesting than algae sliming the two ladder rungs visible above the water's surface.

"No, just a sensation. Someone used the—" he glanced about and lowered his voice, "—mental sciences. Remember when that Mangdorian shaman flew out of the lake with Books and there was a glimmering globe wrapped around them?"

"I was unconscious at the time, but Maldynado told me the story, yes. You think this practitioner lady enveloped herself and Taloncrest in magic?" She almost choked at the idea of a Turgonian army officer agreeing to such a mode of transportation, especially when the man had sneered at the idea of magic when he'd explained his medical experiments in the Imperial Barracks dungeon. "If so, where did they go? For a flight? Or into the lake?"

"I didn't see anyone fly away in a glowy sphere," Akstyr said.

"Glowing," Books said.

"What?"

"Glowy isn't a word."

"Books..." Maldynado groaned. "I was getting ready to compliment you on doing a decent job in that fight and being less of a pedantic know-it-all, but you're ruining my enthusiasm for the idea."

"Impressive," Books said.

"What is?"

"That you used the word pedantic. Correctly."

"You're always going to be a stodgy professor, aren't you?"

Books's eyes crinkled. "It does seem likely."

Amaranthe held up a hand to silence them. "Akstyr, are you suggesting the perpetrators have a hideout...*in* the lake?"

"I'm not wearing a diving suit again," Books said.

Amaranthe watched Akstyr, hoping he would suggest another explanation, but he merely shrugged.

"Is it even possible to have a hideout on the bottom of the lake?" she asked Books.

"If we were talking about something made entirely with imperial technology, I'd say no, but with magic..." He spread his arms. "I have no idea."

"All right," Amaranthe said. "This is all speculation at this point. We need to find out if there's anything to it or not."

"So...we need diving suits?" Books grimaced.

"Unless Akstyr knows how to make one of those bubbles to steer us around the lake depths."

"Nope," Akstyr said. "I'd sure like to learn from someone who could though."

"You're not thinking of apprenticing yourself to the enemy, are you?" Amaranthe teased, though it was not as much of a joke as she pretended. She watched him carefully for a reaction.

"Naw," he said. "Not unless... Do you think she'd have me?"

"She seems the type who would prefer a man who could grow a real mustache," Maldynado said.

"I can!" Akstyr probed his upper lip. "It's getting there."

Amaranthe nodded to Books. "I know you're not excited by the idea, but I think we're going to need those diving suits. Can you do some research and see where we might get some?"

Books sighed. "Why do I have the feeling nothing good is going to come of this?"

"Because you lack optimism?" Amaranthe suggested.

"That must be it."

CHAPTER 12

Footsteps rang on the other side of Basilard's door. He leaped out of his cot. The hours he had spent searching, pressing, pulling, and pounding his fists had not revealed any weaknesses in his prison.

The door opened, revealing the burly young soldier who had held a pistol on him earlier. An equally young and burly man accompanied him, though this one had a scraggily rat tail hanging down his back and wore no military clothing. Both pointed pistols at Basilard.

"Move," Rat Tail said.

Basilard measured both men as he squeezed past them. The tight doorway and corridor forced closeness, and he thought about trying for their weapons, but they watched him carefully. And what if he did overpower them? He had no idea where he was or how to get back to the city. Hoping he would not regret it later, he decided to wait for a better opportunity to escape.

The men pushed him through a corridor so narrow his shoulders brushed the walls, and he had to duck frequently for pipes that crossed overhead. He waited for a porthole that would provide a glimpse of their location, but nothing broke the monotony of the dark gray bulkheads. The glowing orbs provided the only lighting, and he had no idea if it was night or day outside. Oddly, though engines pulsed somewhere in the structure, he had no sense of forward movement nor the rise and fall of waves.

Clanks, clacks, and a rhythmic sucking sound came from ahead. The engine room? The corridor ended at a chamber, but a transparent barrier filled with glowing yellow tendrils that writhed about like snakes blocked the entrance. Basilard blinked, questioning his eyesight.

"Stop," one of the guards said before Basilard reached the entrance.

The man pushed him aside and stepped forward. He leaned into a bronze box mounted on the wall at head level, and he pressed his face close to a concave indention. A blue pulse of light washed over his face.

The shimmering tendrils winked out, and the guard stepped through. The second guard shoved Basilard from behind.

They entered a chamber cluttered with pipes, equipment, moving machinery, and tanks of yellowish blue liquid. Flesh-colored blobs floated in some. Machinery and pipes filled the center of the space and one could go left or right down confining aisles jammed with consoles and narrow tables, or perhaps those were beds. Some lay horizontal and others were tilted upward to stand against the wall. Trays near them held scalpels, saws, and scissors.

Basilard swallowed. He did not know what this place was, but it was nothing so innocuous as an engine room.

The men prodded him toward the far aisle. He rounded a tight corner and stopped. Two red-haired women leaned together, heads almost bumping. One wore her hair in a long braid and the other had hers pinned up in a wild swirl of hair. They spoke in soft tones. Litya and the sister.... What was the name? Metya.

One of Basilard's guards cleared his throat. The women turned in unison. They were twins, identical except for a few freckles and an old half-moon scar on one's temple. He picked Litya out as the woman without the marking.

As one, their eyes shifted up and down, studying Basilard. Under other circumstances, he might have flushed with embarrassment—he *was* naked, after all—but there was no sexual interest in their perusal. He struggled to keep from squirming under their scrutiny.

The aisle behind them held more beds, occupied by nude men and women. Most were propped upright against the wall, the people held tight by leather straps, but the bed behind the twins lay in the horizontal position with a muscular man on it, not strapped like the others but chained, the links so secure that he could do no more than lift a hand or twitch a toe, though he did neither while Basilard watched. Cords snaked from a machine to coin-sized, spider-like devices with the tips of the "legs" digging beneath the skin on the man's naked chest. Translucent tubing ran from a pulsing green globe, and a viscous fluid of the same color flowed through it and into a needle in his arm. Not just his arm. His vein.

"Put him on that table." Metya pointed to an empty one behind her. "I have the *pok-tah* solution ready." She stepped to the side, so the guards could shove Basilard past. "Once we hook him up, he won't—"

Basilard sucked in a startled breath when the view opened up and he saw the face of the man on the table. He should have guessed. Sicarius.

His eyes were open. That surprised Basilard again—he would have assumed, even with the restraints, someone would keep Sicarius unconscious if they dared to detain him. When those dark eyes swiveled toward Basilard, though, they were glazed and dull. No sign of recognition glinted in them.

The guard shoved Basilard, trying to force him around the end of Sicarius's table and toward the vertical one a few feet away. He balked and groped for a way to communicate.

"Wait." Litya pointed the pen at Basilard. "Do you know him?" She shifted the pen and tapped Sicarius on a bare toe.

Basilard choked on her audacity. He didn't think even *Amaranthe* would poke Sicarius's toe, and he tolerated more from her than anyone else.

"Well?" Litya demanded. She grabbed a clipboard from a wall where it dangled on a string, a pen attached.

Basilard did not know whether admitting he knew Sicarius would help him or hinder him. He just knew he would have to make his escape attempt soon—if these people strapped him down and drugged him, he might never wake again.

Basilard lifted his fingers and signed, *Can you understand me?*

"Why does it matter?" Metya asked. She stood near the second bed, tapping buttons beneath a dark orb identical to the green one at Sicarius's station.

"Aside from this one—" Litya waved her pen at Basilard again, "—the assassin is the only one here whose lineage we haven't been able to discover. He proved resistant to the truth elixir, and he's the one I'm most curious about."

"It's not crucial," Metya said.

"No, but the information could prove useful for our studies. He's already what our clients wish us to create."

Basilard lifted his eyebrows. Assassins? Gifted warriors? Superior athletes?

Metya sniffed. "I'm sure we can make improvements."

Litya gave her sister a slit-eyed glare and shuffled a blank page to the top of her clipboard. She held it out to Basilard. "Can you write? I can read Turgonian, Kendorian, Kyattese, and Nurian."

Which of those was her native tongue? He took the implements and wrote, *I know him. What's in it for me if I can extract the information?*

When he handed Litya the notepad, the other sister came over as well. Not a foot from Basilard, they bent their heads together to read his message.

If he could grab one, spin her about, and use her as a shield against the guards' firearms, maybe he could barter for his freedom.

Before the thought had finished, a cool pistol muzzle pressed against the back of his neck. He sighed. He would have to find a better moment, one when the guards were less attentive.

"Help us," Litya said, "and we'll let you walk out of here when we're done collecting specimens."

Purpose of specimens?

"Nothing you'd understand," Metya said.

"Stay focused," Litya said. "Are you willing to cooperate for your life, or not?"

All these other people will die?

Metya shrugged.

"Not by our hands," Litya said, "but our colleagues have more invasive experiments. Some of them prefer fresh cadavers. However, you were something of a bonus. We'd already collected our handful of chosen men and women." She laid a hand on Sicarius's bare leg and smiled.

Basilard shifted, uncomfortable with the entire situation and not certain how to read her. He had never had much of a knack for perceiving when women were telling the truth, but going along would prolong his stay amongst the upright and un-drugged.

What about him? Basilard nodded to Sicarius, then wrote, *Will you let him go as well?*

He wasn't sure why he asked it. If Sicarius met his death here, at the hands of these scientists, that would be a way to see the Mangdorian royal family avenged. It seemed cowardly to shy away from doing it himself, but if God had other plans, why should Basilard interrupt?

"Well..." Litya started.

"No," Metya said, throwing her sister a sharp look. "Why do you think we were trying to get him to show up at the stadium where we could snatch him? This is a long-term project, and the bounty on his head will fund the latter half of our work. It's far more than we're getting from our clients."

"*I* wanted him for research," Litya muttered.

The speculative gaze she cast Sicarius made Basilard wonder if this one had more than science in mind.

He wrote, *Research for what?*

"The main goal of our research is to—"

"Litya," a male voice said from the corridor. Footsteps thudded, and Taloncrest appeared at the head of the aisle. "I know you're a newcomer to our land, but here in Turgonia we don't explain ourselves to our captives."

The guards shuffled aside to let Taloncrest through, and Basilard took note of the pistols no longer pointed directly at him. Unfortunately, people fenced him in on either side, so his odds of getting by were poor. Besides, where would he go? He had yet to glimpse a door to an upper deck on this ship or even a porthole so he could see what lay outside. Footsteps sounded as other people walked in and out of the laboratory, and he suspected there were far more people on board than he had seen.

"We're not interested in adopting Turgonian tactics," Metya said. "Your people aren't known for their negotiating skills or anything else that doesn't involve bloodshed."

Taloncrest leaned against one of the tanks, apparently intending to watch. Though he carried no weapons beyond a utility knife at his belt, he towered over the women. Sensing they would be less forthcoming with Taloncrest there, Basilard pointed at Sicarius and indicated he was ready to start.

Can you lessen his stupor? He doesn't recognize me. I won't be able to get answers from him.

"I wouldn't," Taloncrest said, the first to respond to Basilard's scribbles. "You girls aren't from the empire, so you may not be that familiar with his reputation, but he's dangerous. That you got him at all was..."

"Impressive?" Litya suggested.

"Lucky," Taloncrest said.

Metya snorted. "We are highly trained practitioners. Setting a trap for a mundane warrior is easier than a first-year telekinesis test."

"Turgonian men are horrible at acknowledging that women can be skilled," Litya said, sharing a look with her sister. "One wonders why the intelligent women living here don't leave."

"Perhaps," Taloncrest said, "you'd have them go to the Kyatt Islands where they'd be kicked out if their research methodologies did not fit in with the humanitarian values of your Polytechnic?"

"We'll handle this," Litya said. "Go back to your research on your side of the lab, the lab that *our* gold funded and that we are graciously letting you work in."

Taloncrest stepped past Basilard to thrust a finger at the woman's nose. "Don't order me around. You presume—"

Metya closed her eyes briefly, then flicked her own finger. Taloncrest lurched to the side, his head cracking against the back of the machine he'd been leaning against. In the process, he bumped against Basilard.

Basilard feigned a stumble and used the movement to palm Taloncrest's knife. The ex-officer glared at the women and did not seem to notice. He clenched his fists and stood to his full height. The veins in his neck strained beneath the skin.

The twins smiled sweetly.

Basilard watched, hoping the confrontation would elevate into a worthy distraction for an escape, but Taloncrest took a deep breath and stalked back the way he had come.

"Tie him up next to the assassin," Metya said. "They can chat from adjoining beds."

Basilard wriggled his fingers to remind them he needed his hands free for talking, but Metya had already turned away. She stroked the globe controlling the liquid oozing into Sicarius's veins.

The guards pushed Basilard past her. He resisted the impulse to make their work difficult. If he cooperated meekly, they might be less prepared when he did strike. He kept his hand down, the knife pressed against the inside of his arm. It was not a small blade, and it would take luck to keep the guards from noticing it while they tied him. Should he strike before then? No, he would probably need Sicarius's help to escape, and Sicarius would need to be alert for that.

The guards pushed him back against the table while it was still vertical. Its cold metallic surface pressed against his bare flesh. One guard bent to strap his ankles and thighs to the table. Basilard inched the knife around his side.

He wondered if he was being a fool for waiting and letting them secure his legs. He glanced at the other table. Metya was still fiddling with the globe, and Sicarius's eyes remained vacant.

Basilard slipped the blade behind his butt and pressed his cheeks into the cold metal. A heartbeat later, one of the guards grabbed both of his wrists, yanking them before him.

"Leave them free for now." Litya held out her clipboard.

Basilard hesitated. Would it be a mistake to reveal that Sicarius could understand his signs? At the moment, they did not realize Basilard and Sicarius worked together. The writing would be slow, though, and the women would be able to read everything he shared.

He pointed at Sicarius, touched his own temple, and signed, *He understands*, figuring the women would get the gist.

Litya's eyes narrowed. "The assassin knows your sign language? Why?"

Basilard accepted the clipboard and wrote, *He's traveled to my country. To slay people.*

"I see." Litya took the clipboard away and flipped it back to her papers. "Give him a few moments, and he should regain a measure of cognizance. I mixed in some of my truth elixir, too. He resisted it before, but perhaps if he's familiar with you and doesn't see you as a threat..." She eyed him a little too knowingly. "The more you can get me, the more favorably things will turn out for you. I want to know his parents' names, whether they were distinguished warriors or athletes, and what mix of blood is in his veins. The Turgonians are mongrels through and through, but most of them are a combination of their ancient Nurian roots and the brawny tribesmen that roamed these lands before they came. He looks like he might have some Kendorian in him though. Find out as much as you can."

Basilard nodded. She propped her hip against Sicarius's table and waited. One of the guards at the head of the aisle yawned. No privacy for this chat.

Basilard waited for Sicarius to come around. Already his own toes felt numb from the straps around his legs and ankles. He was conscious of the steel of the knife behind him, its metal warm now from his body heat. It reminded him not to squirm, lest he drop it.

His gaze drifted toward the nearest of the strange tanks where a fleshy blob floated. Something nagged at the back of his mind, a feeling that he should have put the puzzle pieces together and figured things out by now. The women's words floated through his mind. *He's already what our clients wish us to create....This is a long-term project.*

Babies? He stared at the blob. Were they creating babies? Was that *possible?* Would that make the captured men and women the parents? Not parents. Brood-stock. Like hounds being used to whelp offspring with desirable traits.

One of Sicarius's fingers twitched. Basilard watched his face, waiting for a sign that the drugs were losing their hold. It came, not in an expressive show of recognition, but in a hardening of his features—a resumption of the stony mask he always wore. It replaced the blank stare, though his eyes were not as sharp as usual.

Basilard signed, *You recognize me?*

Sicarius nodded once. His eyes shifted from side to side, taking in the woman and the looming guards.

I got captured, too, Basilard signed.

Though Sicarius's wrists were strapped to the table like the rest of his body, he could manage some of the one-handed signs. The one he chose was, *Obviously*.

Basilard clenched his teeth, sensing condemnation in that brief gesture. Sicarius must assume Basilard had done something foolish to get here. He didn't even consider that Basilard might have been planted as part of a rescue plan from the team.

Basilard forced his jaw to loosen. He could not read Sicarius's thoughts, and, even if his guess were close, Sicarius would be right, wouldn't he? Basilard *had* been foolish and had gotten himself captured.

I was competing at the Imperial Games when they got me. How did they capture you?

Heartbeats thumped past with Sicarius doing nothing but gazing impassively. Maybe he had done something foolish, too, and was loathe to admit it. The thought pleased Basilard. Sicarius was too cursed perfect. Nobody should be so perfect that he never made mistakes. It wasn't human. Of course, Sicarius might not be responding because he could not explain with one-handed signs what had happened and did not want to speak of it with their captors listening.

Amaranthe is looking for us, Basilard signed. *She's concerned about you.* He did not know why he added the latter. Even as an incapacitated prisoner, Sicarius did not look like someone who needed bolstering, and he probably did not care if anyone ever worried on his behalf or not.

"I presume we have a limited time to talk," Sicarius whispered in flawless Mangdorian. "Stick to relevant topics."

Basilard winced, both because his offering of compassion was being shoved aside, and because he was all too aware of the reason why Sicarius had learned his tongue.

"I've learned little," Sicarius added, "only that we are in the lake, possibly deep enough that we'd drown before reaching the surface if we simply went out a hatch. I believe there are forty people in the facility, half scientists and half guards. Have you obtained any information?"

Litya glanced at the nearest guard.

The man thumped Sicarius on the temple with the butt of his pistol. "Speak in Turgonian."

Sicarius leveled a cold stare at his tormentor. Even though Sicarius was immobilized, the guard stepped back, shifting uneasily.

Even the dullest wolf knows it's not good when the moose and the rabbit conspire in a language foreign to the pack, Basilard signed.

It was an old saying that usually elicited a smile amongst Basilard's people. Sicarius stared at him without comment.

I'm supposed to be getting your lineage out of you, Basilard signed.

"My parents?" Sicarius asked in Turgonian.

Basilard suspected it was for the sake of those listening rather than a need for clarification. The guards relaxed at the words.

I just got here, Basilard signed. *If we're so deep, how do they travel to the surface?*

"I was never told," Sicarius said as his fingers twitched his real response. With his hands separated and restrained, he could not make the arm motions that accompanied many of the Mangdorian signs, and Basilard struggled to follow the words.

Mental sciences. No thing. Women create when need.

Thing? Basilard guessed he meant there was no magical artifact or other contraption they could snatch to travel to the surface on their own.

...unconscious...don't know how many days... Sicarius kept speaking as he signed, "Though I was given to understand it was an arranged mating, and my parents were chosen for their desirable attributes."

Basilard caught himself listening to the words. Were they the truth? Had Sicarius been bred like a hound? Basilard

had heard what Hollowcrest said in Larocka's mansion, that
Sicarius had been trained from birth to be a tool for the
empire, to *obey* Hollowcrest and Emperor Raumesys. Which
meant he had not likely had a choice about the assassination
mission to Mangdoria.

That didn't matter. He had still done it.

Sicarius was glaring at him, and for a moment Basilard
wondered if he read minds in addition to his other skills. But,
no, Sicarius signed slowly, with emphasis, and Basilard realized
the glare was for not paying attention.

Amaranthe know where we are? Sicarius asked.

Not when I saw her last, Basilard said, *but perhaps by now. It'd be
best to assume we must escape on our own.*

A few heartbeats passed without a word or a sign from
Sicarius. He seemed to be considering Basilard. His dark eyes
appeared black in this lighting, and Basilard felt them boring
into his soul. Was he suspicious of something? Did he think
Basilard had cut a deal with the women that would leave him
stranded?

Yes, was all Sicarius signed.

You know how many guards watch this room? Basilard rushed
to sign, wanting Sicarius's mind on escape, not anything else.

"Yes," Sicarius said and signed, *Four guards...split twelve-hour
shifts. These soldiers worked for Hollowcrest...now rogues.* "A cook
who used to give me balms after childhood punishments told
me my father was an army officer and my mother a university
professor." Sicarius's brow crinkled, as if he was surprising
himself with how much he was revealing, and he glanced at
the glowing orb controlling his drug dosages. *Many practitioners
here...only sisters and one male...transport surface.*

Basilard signed, *If we can capture one, perhaps we can force the
other to—*

"So," Litya said, "you don't know your parents' names?"

"No," Sicarius said.

"But they could still be alive?"

He hesitated, and Basilard wondered if he had ever considered the possibility. Any child without parents would speculate about that, wouldn't he? Maybe he didn't care about such things. Most of the time, he did not seem human.

"I was told not, but I suppose it's possible," Sicarius said.

"Hm." Litya stopped at his side and laid a hand on the hard ridges of muscle armoring his abdomen. "I've not seen you in action, but based on your reputation and what I see here..." Her hand roamed, and Basilard looked away. "I'd definitely be interested in researching your heritage further," she said. "We have extensive resources and could help you if you were so interested."

Sicarius said nothing.

"Your Commander of the Armies Hollowcrest disappeared last winter, did he not?" Litya asked. "He's rumored to be dead, but there's speculation that this may be untrue since the current emperor has not appointed a successor to what must be a vital position for you militant Turgonians."

She tilted her head, watching Sicarius. Basilard wondered if she found his unreadability as frustrating as most. She showed no sign of it. Too busy being intrigued by him, he supposed.

"If it's possible the man is still alive and incognito," Litya went on, "I'd be curious to speak with him, perhaps compare notes...."

"He's dead," Sicarius said.

"You're certain?"

"I killed him."

"Ah."

"It's possible he left notes," Sicarius said, surprising Basilard. Sicarius never volunteered anything, especially not to people on the other side. He must be angling for something.

"Oh?" Litya asked. "And you'd know where they were?"

"In his hidden office in the Imperial Barracks."

"I suppose you know where this office is and could retrieve such notes if properly motivated?"

"Even if I said yes, you would be foolish to believe I could be trusted to do so for you," Sicarius said.

Basilard frowned at Sicarius, wondering at his tactics. He ought to either stay silent—which suited his normal proclivities—or play along and try to get the woman to let him go.

"Thank you for the warning," Litya said.

"You let him off that table, and he'll kill you," came Taloncrest's voice over the sucking and clanking of equipment. "He's killed people for daring to do a lot less than capture him. Also, Hollowcrest hated the mental sciences, so you'd find little that interests you in his notes. Anything he did was of natural means."

"Much can be done with nature," Litya said, though more to herself than in response to Taloncrest.

"Hollowcrest used to keep notes on my training," Sicarius said. "He researched widely before I was born and applied techniques from many cultures, current and past." He tilted his head slightly. "If you intend to turn your fetuses into warriors, blood will only get you so far."

So, Sicarius had reached the same assumption about what these people were doing down here. Litya did not correct his assumption.

"Indeed," she said.

"Litya," Taloncrest said, "I told you your funds and assistance would win you my long-term advice on training."

"You're a doctor, not a legendary assassin," she said.

"I am—I was—an officer in the Turgonian Army. I've been training to fight since before he was born."

Litya snorted. "Perhaps I should let him go and you two could spar for dominance."

Yes, that would be good. Maybe they would be kind enough to release Basilard as well.

"Don't be ridiculous," Taloncrest said.

"You are right," Litya told Sicarius. "It would be foolish of me to release you. Unless there is a price at which your assistance—and your word that you will offer it faithfully—can be purchased."

Sicarius neither offered his usual blunt "no" nor proposed a deal. He ought to promise the woman to help if she would simply unlock him first....

Instead he remained silent. Almost...thoughtful. What could this woman have that he might want? But then, what did *Amaranthe* have that Sicarius wanted? Basilard reluctantly admitted that he knew the man very little, despite the six months they had worked together. If it was only some whim that kept him with the group, might not another come along that interested him more?

"There *is* a price," Litya guessed from Sicarius's silence.

Sicarius's expression never changed, but his eyes shifted to focus on one of the tanks.

What? Did he want a child? One born in some crazy scientist's laboratory? If so, *why*? Though Sicarius had the personality of a particularly bland, pointy stick, it seemed he could find a woman to bear a child for him if he wished it. Though maybe he did not want some random woman's blood for a child. Not if he could get some specially selected female "specimen" to help breed a babe who could be his equal— or perhaps more—one day. Basilard grimaced at the idea of Sicarius as a father, training some child with the same heartless techniques that had been employed on him.

It was hard to imagine Sicarius even *wanting* a child, but he met the woman's eyes and jerked his chin for her to approach.

Litya hesitated but leaned closer, her chest brushing his. She tilted her head so he could whisper in her ear.

The guards had stood mute through the exchange, but they tensed at this closeness.

Basilard signed, *Bite her!*

Nobody was watching.

Sicarius said something Basilard could not hear, and the woman leaned back.

"Interesting," she said. "I'll consider it."

She snapped her fingers and the guards clicked their heels, coming to attention.

"Fully secure the other man," Litya said. "We don't need him talking with his fingers any more, and I want to get samples."

The guards tromped toward Basilard. He let his hand drop, as if in defeat, but his fingers touched the edge of the knife pressed behind him.

While Litya gazed speculatively at Sicarius, Metya eased past the guards and brushed her fingers across an orb next to the head of Basilard's table. It had been dark and dormant, but it flared to life under her touch. She considered him for a moment, judging his weight for a dosage probably. Nothing about her gaze suggested *he* would get a chest caress or any deal offers.

She was close and this might be his last chance.

A guard reached for his wrist. Basilard balled his hand into a fist and jabbed it into the man's nose.

With half of his body secured, he did not get much power behind it, but his hand speed gave the blow force enough. The guard stumbled back, grasping at his nose.

The other man raised his pistol. Knife in hand now, Basilard leaned out and slashed the blade at the guard's wrist. Though swift, the blatant attack sent the man leaping back in time to avoid it. That was all Basilard needed.

Before Metya could likewise scurry away, he grabbed her arm. He spun her as he pulled her against his chest to use her body as a shield, and he pressed the knife against her throat.

The guards froze, one on either side of Basilard's station. They raised their pistols, aiming for his head. The one with the blood streaming from his nose gritted his teeth, finger tense on the pistol. He wanted to fire. Badly.

Basilard should have been terrified, but he had been in life-or-death situations too many times to fall apart when faced by one. Anyway, he did not think they would fire with Metya so close. Unfortunately, he could not bargain with his hands busy holding the woman. Nor could he imagine one of the guards offering him a clipboard to scrawl a note while he held a knife to their employer's throat.

Sicarius watched but did nothing. Strapped down, he could not help physically, but Basilard would have appreciated verbal assistance. He could speak and handle the bartering. But Sicarius said nothing. Basilard lifted his eyebrows expectantly. Sicarius gazed back.

"What do you want, Scarred and Mute?" Litya asked, her voice calm despite the blade at her sister's throat.

She stepped into view behind one of the guards. Remembering the mental blast her sister had hurled at Taloncrest, Basilard tightened his grip on Metya.

"Put your weapons down," he tried to say, but no sound came from his scarred vocal cords. Maybe the brainy science woman could read lips.

Litya lifted her hand, palm out. Basilard would have howled in frustration if he could. He knew what was coming. He cut into the woman's throat, determined to take out at least one of them before they dropped him.

Warm blood gushed down his forearm. A wave of energy crashed into his head from the left, and agony ricocheted through his body like a lightning bolt.

The woman dropped from his hands. Dead? Alive? He didn't know. Pain assaulted him from all directions, and he hunched over. If not for the bindings on his lower body, he would have fallen to the ground and curled into a ball.

With the last of his wherewithal, he threw a betrayed look at the man who *should* have been his ally in this.

Sicarius's eyebrow twitched. He knew. Even if he didn't know for certain, he had to know Basilard was a threat. While Basilard had been thinking of betraying him—of letting *him* die—Sicarius must have been considering the same thing. Basilard might never wake up, and the rest of the group—his *friends*—would never know that Sicarius could have helped him and chose not to.

Darkness ended Basilard's whirling thoughts.

Books returned from his research trip in time for dinner and sat down with Amaranthe and Maldynado around the fire pit of their camp. Snores wafted from the rail car where Akstyr rested. Yawns tugged at Amaranthe's mouth, but she focused on Books.

"I found two possible sources for diving suits," he said. "A privately owned fresh-water treasure-hunting tugboat called the *Tuggle* has been moored in Stumps for the last two weeks. It seems likely they'd have diving gear. Also, the *Imperial Saberfist* is coming into port tomorrow. It's a military vessel in charge of maritime rescue and salvage operations."

Amaranthe shook her head. Leave it to the empire to give even its rescue ships war-like names.

"During times of war," Books continued, "the *Saberfist* plies the Gulf, but it's currently stationed in the Chain Lakes and has been working the Goldar River alongside an archaeology team."

"Is there a reason I should do anything except dismiss the *Saberfist*?" she asked, surprised Books had bothered with all the details. Though Sicarius might find thieving from a heavily manned and well-guarded military vessel a good training exercise, she could not think of a reason to risk it when another option existed.

Maldynado scratched his jaw. "That ship sounds familiar."

"The commander of the marine vessel," Books said, "is one Captain Talmuk Mancrest, elder brother of Deret."

Maldynado snapped his fingers. "That's right. We got a tour of it when we were children. Not much firepower—only a couple of dozen cannons—but lots of other brilliant equipment. We got to swing on this crane that's used for—"

Amaranthe cleared her throat. "Let's save story hour for

later. This isn't the same brother who tried to arrange my capture at the newspaper office, right?"

"No," Maldynado said. "Talmuk's nearly twenty years older than Deret. Acts like he's forty years older. Stuffy old coot. Walks around like he's got a ramrod permanently lodged in his—"

"*Thank* you, I get the picture."

"I thought you might wish to try talking to your Mancrest again," Books said, "to see if he could get us on board to requisition supplies. Perhaps, since you spared his life in the pyramid, he'll be more inclined to listen."

"Depends on how long it took him to retrieve that key," Amaranthe said.

Maldynado snorted.

"I don't want to wait until tomorrow. Let's visit the treasure-hunting ship. If it's a civilian vessel, maybe there won't be more than a guard or two on board."

Or maybe there would be no one on board, and they could easily borrow the suits. For once, it'd be nice if something was easy and went according to plan. Somehow, she doubted she would be that lucky.

CHAPTER 13

No gas lamps burned near the narrow, rickety docks at the end of the shipyard. Far south of the broad, modern piers used for military ships and merchant vessels, these berths were some of the oldest in the city. Moorage was relatively cheap and apparently not enough to cover the expense of public lighting. A quarter moon hanging over the lake illuminated the silhouettes of smaller ships, a mix of old steamers, sailboats, and combinations of the two. Amaranthe questioned whether the vessels being tied to the creaking docks kept them from floating away or if it might be the other way around.

She led the men along the street, pausing at each sign to read the numbers. One might assume Pier 173 would follow Pier 172, but some docks had sunk over the years while others had expanded and branched out. They passed 169, 169B, and 169C, followed by a skip to 171.

Clothing rustled ahead of them, near a warehouse on the far side of the street. Five or six people loitered in the shadows, slouching degenerately against the wall.

"Friends of yours?" Amaranthe murmured to Akstyr, knowing this was the Black Arrows territory.

"Ain't got no friends left in the gang," Akstyr said.

"Your rosy personality didn't endear you to them?" Books asked.

"Ssh," Amaranthe whispered.

Though she could not see the eyes of those who lurked ahead, she felt the intensity of their attention. No doubt, they were calculating odds, deciding if she and her men looked like easy targets. She doubted it—Maldynado, Books, and Akstyr wore their swords openly—but, then, superior numbers and desperation could make a group brave.

A few muttered words reached her ears.

"...take them."

"That one's got an expensive..."

"...brandy for months."

Amaranthe shook her head at Maldynado, knowing he was the only one with something "expensive" that would tempt thugs.

"Looks like another fight," Books murmured, a resigned slump to his shoulders.

"Not necessarily," she whispered, a mischievous thought sauntering through her mind. "It's not contagious, is it?" she asked loudly.

"Huh?" Maldynado blurted.

"I touched you. We all did," Amaranthe said. "I just want to know how contagious it is. You should have known better than to sleep with that girl. Fresh out of the tropics with emperor knows what disease plaguing her."

"How was I supposed to know?" Maldynado played along, but he glared at her. "She looked all right to me."

"Thank my ancestors I'm not male," Amaranthe went on. "Did you hear what one of the customers said? Rumor is someone's peeper rotted up and fell right off after seeing her."

Murmurs and the sound of shuffling feet came from the posse across the street.

"I bet it's terribly contagious," Amaranthe said.

"Yes," Books said. "A new strain of pizzle rot out of the Gesh

Islands. Coitus isn't required for transmission. I expect we're all doomed just from walking beside this lout."

The dark figures in the shadows pushed past each other in an effort to be the first to sprint away. One tripped and fell in his haste to round a corner. Nobody stopped to help him up. Cursing, he scrambled to his feet and ran after his comrades.

"That's one way to deter bandits," Books said, a grin in his voice.

"You *would* approve," Maldynado said. "Boss, it's not right to joke around about a man's... Did you call it a *peeper*?"

"Too sanitized?" She pointed down a rickety dock with missing and broken boards. A sign magnanimously called it Pier 173.

"Not if your next job will be teaching small children."

"Will they be less vexatious than you?" Amaranthe led the way down the dock.

"Doubtful," Books said.

Three ships lined the dock, none with lights burning on the decks. She started to check the first one, but paused. The skeletal frame of a crane rose from the deck of the last ship, a steamer. It possessed a metal hull instead of wood and had the sturdy look of a tug. Other equipment bristled from the deck like quills on a porcupine, creating a strange silhouette against the moonlit sky. Gear for pulling treasures off the lake or sea floor, Amaranthe guessed.

She turned off her lantern, and darkness engulfed the dock. She padded toward the salvage vessel, stepping lightly on the warped, creaking wood. In the still night, she grew aware of the sound of her own breathing and a breeze flapping a loose sail a few docks away. The air stirred the omnipresent fishy scent of the waterfront, and for a moment Amaranthe thought she smelled something else. Something rotten. The breeze shifted, and the scent disappeared. Maybe it was nothing—a dead fish washed up to a nearby beach.

The starlight did not offer enough illumination to read the name on the bow, but she could not imagine this being anything except the ship they sought, the *Tuggle*.

"Must not be any treasure on there now," Maldynado said. "Nobody's on guard."

"Some of the crew might be sleeping below decks," she whispered.

They stopped beside the ship. No gangplank offered easy access, but Amaranthe had come prepared. She unwound a length of thin rope she had looped around her waist several times and dug out a collapsible grappling hook. She fastened it and swung the tool, releasing it toward the ship's railing. The hook clinked softly and caught on the first try.

"You're turning into a proficient burglar," Books said.

"Is that a compliment or a condemnation?" Amaranthe tested the secureness of the rope.

"It depends on whether we'll be leaving monetary compensation for the suits we're stealing."

Maldynado groaned. "You're wholesome enough to teach toddlers right alongside her."

"I was hoping to return the suits without doing any damage," Amaranthe said.

"Such as with the trash vehicle?" Books asked.

She winced. "When we have our men back, I'll see what I can do about compensating those we've wronged."

"I know," Maldynado said in response to a muttered comment from Akstyr. "They are the *worst* outlaws you'll ever meet. What criminals worry about such things?"

Amaranthe shushed them, then shimmied up the rope. Before climbing over the railing, she paused to listen for voices or movement on the deck. Only the soft lapping of the waves reached her ears.

She slipped over the railing and landed in a soundless crouch. Nothing stirred. She glided through the shadows, skirting the crane and capstans the size of huts. A single closed hatch allowed access to the lower levels. She collected the men before exploring further.

"Shall we light the lanterns?" Books whispered.

"Wait until we're below decks," Amaranthe said.

At this point, she did not think anyone was aboard, but she did not need someone on another dock noticing their light and coming to investigate.

Amaranthe pressed an ear to the hatch. Again, she heard nothing. She turned the latch and eased the door open.

A powerful stench rolled out, smelling of rotten meat and death. Her unprepared stomach roiled, and images of the dam—those eviscerated men and women—washed over her. She braced herself against the wall.

"Ugh," Akstyr said. "It smells like a half-eaten possum left to bake on the street in summer."

"Or dead people," Books said, his voice hoarse, as if he was fighting back the urge to retch.

"Really, boss," Maldynado said, "is it necessary to take us to such desecrated destinations all the time?"

"Apparently." Amaranthe wondered if the *Saberfist* might have been a better bet after all. "Books, is it possible these people brought back some sort of contagious disease from their explorations? Something that...killed them?"

"Pizzle rot?" Maldynado asked.

"I made that up."

"If it helps," Akstyr said, "it smells like more than pizzles are rotten down there."

"How does that help?" Maldynado asked.

"I read the dock master's report," Books said. "These fellows have been in port for a couple of weeks, and before that they were working Squall Lake."

"So whatever happened..." Amaranthe started.

"Happened after they arrived here," Books said.

"Do you think we're in danger of catching something if we go down?"

"If it is a disease, I'd guess we're finding them after the point of contagion, but I couldn't be certain."

Akstyr lifted a finger. "How about I stay up here and stand guard?"

"How about you go first?" Maldynado said. "You're the youngest. The most expendable."

"*What?*"

"Maybe they just brought back a treasure that someone wanted and someone killed them for it." Amaranthe mused that it was a strange line of work she found herself in when that was a cheery thought.

"And maybe not," Maldynado said.

"I'll go," she said. "Akstyr, you get to find out a way to heal me if I contract something."

"Uh, I don't know how to do diseases," Akstyr said. "It's not in the On Healing book."

"Get a shaman then. Sicarius has found them in the city before."

"Sicarius isn't here," Maldynado pointed out.

All too aware of that fact, Amaranthe pushed the hatch further open, descended three steps, and entered a dark corridor. Mosquitoes whined in the air. The scent of urine and feces lingered beneath the overpowering stench of death. She breathed through her mouth as she turned up her lantern. Closed cabin doors lined either side of the short corridor. She glimpsed metal and coiled rope through an open hatchway at the end. Storage?

A creak sounded from the steps behind her—Books following with a lantern of his own.

"You'll need help collecting all the equipment and hauling the suits out," he said, "The kits weigh over one hundred fifty pounds each."

She gripped his arm. "Thank you."

Her intent was to bypass the cabins and go straight to the storage area, but, in the confining corridor, Books bumped an elbow against one of the doors. It had not been fastened so it creaked open. He hesitated, then eased his lantern inside.

Whatever he saw arrested his attention for he stared for a long moment.

"Body?" A few steps farther down the corridor, Amaranthe could not see in, and she was not quick to run up and poke her head under his arm.

"Yes."

"Throat cut?" She doubted it.

"No. It does appear to be some sort of disease."

Reluctantly, Amaranthe went to take a look. If it *was* a contagious disease, it was probably too late for them to avoid it anyway.

The inert male body lay on a cot, his chest bare, his blankets thrown to the floor. A rough red rash covered the flesh, a rash Amaranthe recognized. Maybe it wasn't the same. Maybe the symptoms were just similar. Maybe...

"What is it?" Books asked, watching her face.

"Hysintunga," she whispered.

"That's one possibility, but there are other diseases with similar symptoms. The insects that carry Hysintunga aren't native to this area—they prefer hot, humid climates—and it's unlikely this man died of that malady."

"I've seen it in Stumps before," Amaranthe said. "I've been *infected* with it here before. By that colonel, Talconcrest."

Books closed the door on the dead man. "Hysintunga is always fatal, isn't it?"

"Unless you know a shaman who can heal it."

"But Sicarius is the only one who knows where to find one?"

"Yes," Amaranthe said. "It looks like these people are beyond help anyway."

"If those responsible for the kidnappings are also responsible for this...how could they have known we'd come here?"

"Maybe this has nothing to do with us. Maybe they just didn't want this crew poking around on the bottom of the lake. For these people to be dead now, they would have to have been infected days ago."

Amaranthe continued down the corridor. More narrow steps led down to the storage area where spindles secured to the deck held coils of rope and chain. Cabinets lined the sidewalls, and a low ceiling sloped down to a larger double-door cubby. She could stand straight, but Books would have to hunch low to keep from hitting his head on ceiling beams.

"Let's check these," she said.

Books took one side and Amaranthe unlatched the cabinet doors on the other. Hooks and chains occupied one cubby, rope another, and copper equipment she could not identify a third. No diving suits.

"Any luck?" she asked.

"Not yet." Books had reached the larger doors at the end. He unlatched them and tugged one open.

An angry buzz came from the darkness within. A familiar angry buzz.

"Close the door!" Amaranthe shouted, stumbling for the exit. "Get back!"

When Books tried to comply, he cracked his head on one of the beams, and his foot caught in a coil of rope. He dropped his lantern and stumbled to the floor. His light winked out. The door he'd thrust shut banged against the frame and bounced open again.

The glow of Amaranthe's lantern was enough to reveal a fat insect as long as her finger flying from the hold. A tail reminiscent of a lizard's streamed out behind it. Some utterly useless part of her mind remembered the Kendorians called them Fangs.

Wings flapped, and the insect veered straight toward Books. His feet were tangled in the rope, and he floundered.

Amaranthe tore her sword free and set the lantern down

in one motion. She darted to Books's side and swung at the insect. The blade sliced it in two. Its halves splatted to the deck, the long tail still twitching.

Before she could reach down to help Books to his feet, more buzzes filled the silence.

"Emperor's warts," she cursed. She started toward the cabinet, hoping to shut them in, but movement near the door made her jerk back.

Books extricated himself and leaped to his feet, his blade out before he stood fully upright. Four Fangs streamed out of the cubby.

"Back to back," Amaranthe barked. "Slice them or squash them beneath your boots, but you're dead if you let them bite you."

"Understood." Books lowered into a crouch, sword raised.

One Fang veered toward Amaranthe. She whipped her blade at it, but the insect sensed the threat and flitted upward. Her tip smacked into a beam instead, jarring her arm. The blade stuck in the wood, costing her precious time.

The insect arrowed toward her neck. She ducked, spinning and tearing her blade free. Books's sword sliced in, hacking a wing off the Fang. It spiraled toward a wall.

Before Amaranthe could thank him, she spotted two insects flapping toward him. "Watch out!"

The wingless one bumped against a cabinet door near her. Fear stole finesse, and she chopped at it like a logger with an axe. Wood chipped free, and bug guts splattered.

"Got one," Books said.

"Where are the other two?"

Amaranthe put her back against the cabinets and held her sword ready before her. She strained her ears, listening for their buzz, but she heard footfalls instead. Maldynado and Akstyr.

"Stay back, you two," she called, charging for the corridor. "The bugs are deadly."

She darted through the hatchway in time to see Maldynado ducking and flailing his arms. Akstyr lingered behind, and he backed away at her warning.

A Fang buzzed about Maldynado's head. Amaranthe ran toward him, sword poised for a strike.

He saw her coming and dropped to the deck. She never took her focus from the bug. It drew in its wings to dive at Maldynado, but she skewered it.

"Where's the last one?" she demanded. If it escaped into the night, it could buzz about the city, infecting countless citizens.

"Got it," Akstyr said in a strained voice.

He stood on the steps, his arm outstretched. A bug hovered in the air, inches from his open palm. The wings continued to flap, but it did not make any forward progress.

Amaranthe raised her blade. "Shall I?"

"Wait," he whispered.

Akstyr's eyelids drooped, almost as if he were falling asleep, but Amaranthe knew better. She did not lower her sword and debated on simply ending it, but Akstyr needed practice to master his art.

Seconds ticked by. Though she heard Maldynado rising behind her, she kept her eyes focused on the Fang.

She opened her mouth to question Akstyr, but paused when smoke wafted from the insect's wings. A heartbeat later it burst into flame. Amaranthe gaped as it burned to a crisp. Ashes trickled to the deck.

"It worked," Akstyr blurted, a grin on his face.

"That was...disconcerting," Books said.

"Can you do that with people?" Maldynado asked.

Akstyr shrugged. "Probably not yet."

Yet? The day he could do that would be the day Amaranthe feared Akstyr.

"Let's see what they were guarding," was all she said.

The large cubby in the back of the storage area held five diving helmets and suits as well as tubing and pumps.

"Now *that's* disconcerting," Amaranthe said.

"What is?" Maldynado asked.

"The fact that Taloncrest booby-trapped the very equipment we need?" Books knelt to inspect the gear.

"This does lend credence to our theory," Amaranthe said. "That something's down there in the lake and these people don't want it discovered."

"So they killed the whole crew?" Maldynado asked.

"It's possible this doubled as an experiment. When I met that colonel, he was quite cheerful about furthering his research and didn't seem concerned about deaths. Actually, he was looking forward to dissecting my cadaver."

"He sounds like a lovely fellow," Maldynado said.

"I'm not sure how experimenting with diseases could tie in with the kidnappings though." Amaranthe reached up and gripped one of the beams over her head. "But if it *is* connected, and if there *is* a laboratory or hideout on the lake bottom, it might be handy to have a tugboat specializing in underwater operations."

"You want us to steal a ship?" Maldynado gaped at her. "Oh, Books is going to give you an extra hard time for that. He was whining when you just wanted the suits."

"Actually," Books said, "if the owners of this vessel are all dead, I believe Maritime Salvage Law would be in effect."

"What?" Maldynado asked.

Amaranthe grinned. "Finders keepers."

"You mean we get to have our own ship?" Akstyr asked. "Nice!"

"Maldynado," Amaranthe said, "want to come find the engine room with me? See if things are in working order?"

"A tour through a part of the ship likely to be littered with more corpses? Nice of you to think of me."

"You could stay and help Books with the suits. Of course, I'd have to leave him in charge since he's the underwater adventuring expert."

"No, thanks." Maldynado headed for the door. "Last time he was in charge, he forced me to swim naked in glacial water."

A trapdoor in the center of the corridor led into the bowels of the ship. Amaranthe climbed down a narrow ladder, descending into a tight space crowded with machinery. Nothing clanked or whirred, and the cool temperature promised the furnaces had been dormant for some time. The air smelled less rank down there, though a faint singed odor came to Amaranthe's nose, reminding her of a smelter.

At the bottom, she took a step, lifted her lantern, and halted. "Uh."

Maldynado dropped down behind her. "What?"

She pointed at a contorted lump of metal that resembled melted candle wax. "That's the engine."

"It's, ah..." He touched an amorphous protrusion that might have been a flywheel once. "Hm."

"A brief but sufficient description."

Maldynado walked around the contorted mess. "It's melted right into the deck. You couldn't even replace it with a new engine."

"It looks like someone wanted to make sure this ship didn't engage in any underwater adventures while it was in town," Amaranthe said. "If they saw it come into port, they might have seen it as a potential threat. Even if the treasure hunters had no inkling of what lay below, someone could have chartered the boat and used it as a base of operations for investigating." She rapped a knuckle on the warped engine. "And, if this ship was a target, it stands to reason the *Saberfist* could be one too when it comes into port. We haven't had good luck dealing with Mancrest, but maybe we should warn him that his brother's ship may be in danger."

A clank answered. Maldynado had wandered to the far end of the engine room and was poking at a lock on a cast iron box set into the floor.

"Are you listening?" Amaranthe asked.

"Huh?"

She sighed. Maldynado or Books would call her crazy for missing Sicarius's company, but he always *listened* when she rambled on, speculating about their enemy's actions.

"Do you think we should warn Mancrest that his brother's ship could be in danger?"

Maldynado snorted. "I wouldn't worry about a military vessel. The marines can take care of themselves."

"Against practitioners?" Amaranthe nodded toward the melted engine again. "I suppose it's possible some sort of acid did this, but it seems more likely the mental sciences were involved." She thought of Akstyr's bug incineration trick above. She had seen him create a flame to light a candle, too. There must be an entire field devoted to heat and energy.

But Maldynado had turned back to the lock and did not respond.

"What's so fascinating?" Amaranthe squeezed past a knot of pipes and joined him.

"This is warm." He perched on a small stool bolted to the deck next to the two-foot-by-two-foot box. Rivets secured the corners, steel hinges fastened the lid, and a padlock hung from a sturdy steel loop.

Amaranthe touched the cast iron. A faint heat warmed the coarse metal. She checked to make sure the key was not dangling on a hook nearby, or something equally obvious, before fishing her lock-picking set from her pocket. "Scoot over."

"Ah, yes," Maldynado said. "Books mentioned that you'd acquired that skill from Sicarius."

She selected a pick and a torsion wrench and bent over the lock. "Did he mention it in a tone of chagrinned concern for my deteriorating morality?"

"Yes, but isn't that his usual tone for all of us? And the world in general?"

After a few minutes of wrangling the pins into submission,

the lock clicked open. Amaranthe hesitated, thinking of Books's advice. "It's imprudent to open a strange box that may be booby-trapped with magic, isn't it?"

"How magical can it be? It's part of a Turgonian ship." Maldynado removed the lock and shoved the lid open.

No explosions threatened to sear off their eyebrows. Good. Amaranthe peered inside, almost bumping heads with Maldynado.

A bronze-and-iron rectangular device rested inside. Two small bars—handles?—stuck out from the ends, levers and dials dotted the sides, and a red, multifaceted glass knob protruded from the top. There was no bottom to the outer box, and the device appeared to sit on the deck, but something beneath it kept it from resting flush.

Amaranthe tapped one of the handles. When nothing happened, she risked grabbing both sides and lifting. A collapsible pipe linked the bottom of the device to the deck beneath it, and she had no trouble raising it three feet. Two round concave pieces of glass set in the side closest to her made her think this was something one looked into. She was about to try it when the knob on top flared to life, emitting a soft crimson glow.

She dropped the device. It clunked back to the deck, but nothing untoward happened.

"That's definitely not standard Turgonian technology," Maldynado said. He had relinquished the stool to her and crouched at her side, his shoulders fighting for space amongst levers and gauges protruding from a control panel beside him.

"Maybe the *Tuggle* has been outside of imperial waters and acquired tools to help in its trade," Amaranthe said. "Could this be some sort of underwater version of the Turgonian periscope? Like the ones used on army trampers for seeing over trees and brush? Only this one lets you see down into the water?" If so, that might be just what they needed. "These knobs and levers could be controls for rotating it and raising and lowering it."

"You're an imaginative girl."

"Is that good or bad?" she asked.

"Mind if I wait to pass judgment until after we see if you get us blown up by playing with that thing?"

After giving the glowing knob a wary squint, Amaranthe pulled the device up again and leaned her face in so she could peer through the glass eyepieces.

Blackness greeted her. She fiddled with the knob, which she could raise, lower, twist, and push in different directions. The view wavered, but she still couldn't see anything.

"Because it's the middle of the night and dark down there," she realized. "Drat."

Amaranthe started to draw back, but her sleeve caught on a small lever beneath one of the handles. It clicked. A beam of light shot out from somewhere beneath the viewing display, and it illuminated the water.

"There we go," she murmured. The blue-painted hull of the ship came into view, taking up most of the rectangular display. Not sure which lever or knob to push, she started with the handles themselves. The box twisted, altering her view below. "Ah."

Turning the periscope allowed her to see to either side around the bottom of the ship. Nothing more interesting than a couple of fish and the wavy green algae on the dock pilings came into view.

"I wonder if this can go down deeper," she mused.

"Am I supposed to respond to your mutterings, or are you simply talking to yourself?" Maldynado asked.

"It depends on whether you have an idea."

Maldynado pressed on the glowing knob.

Bubbles of water streamed past the display until the view vanished in a swirl of sand followed by darkness.

"Crashing it," Amaranthe said, "isn't what I had in mind."

"Oops." He released the knob.

The darkness faded again, and the view drifted up from sand, to seaweed, to water, and finally back to the hull of the tug.

"Huh." Amaranthe played with the knob and figured out how to move the viewer, not just up and down, but laterally as well. She had trouble fathoming how the latter was accomplished, but reminded herself magic was involved.

She navigated the display farther from the ship and deeper as well, marveling as fish flitted through the light. Remembering their purpose on the ship, Amaranthe angled the view toward the bottom of the lake.

Ruins—the foundations of long sunken buildings—protruded from the sand and seaweed. Amaranthe remembered some childhood trivia about the lake level being lower a thousand years earlier and of previous civilizations that had called this area home and built places such as the pyramid.

Nothing more interesting occupied the floor, and she soon passed the last of the ruins. The sandy slope ended at a cliff plunging into blackness. She debated whether to back up and search north and south along the shoreline. Wouldn't the kidnappers stay close to the surface for convenience? The lake was hundreds of feet deep out in the middle. While she considered her options, the viewer's momentum, or perhaps a stray current, took it over the cliff. It dropped rapidly, and she decided to let it continue.

Maldynado shifted from foot to foot. "Can I play with it?"

"I'm not playing," Amaranthe said. "I'm scouting. Our comrades' lives are at stake. This is extremely important."

"All right. Can I *scout* with it?"

An orange glow emanated from somewhere beneath the viewer, and Amaranthe forgot the conversation. Her insides twisted. Nothing natural could be making that light; this had to be the spot.

As the device continued to drop, a great structure came into view, all painted metal and massive rivets running vertically and horizontally on the hull. Though the word hull came to mind, this construction looked nothing like a ship. It sat on the floor of the lake, reminiscent of a couple of mating octopi tangled in a tableau of passion. Tentacles—she did not know what else to call them—spread out on two levels, each tube large enough that, if they were hollow, men might walk through the insides. Here and there, bulbous protrusions—rooms?—stuck out. The two octopi "heads" were bigger, each the size of a house. Some of the larger protrusions had portholes, and she wondered if she could slip in close to peep through one.

Cannon-like bristles on the ends of the "tentacles" stayed her hand. Weapons.

Strange creatures swam about, too. Nothing she remembered from her science classes in school. A translucent golden fish glided into view, its sleek body pulsing with inner light.

Something stirred in the seaweed below. The fish's glow increased in intensity, and Amaranthe almost had to turn her head away, but then, with a flash, a streak of lightning shot from its body. The charred husk of some innocent lake dweller floated away.

A shadow fell over Amaranthe's viewer. She twisted the knob, pulling the device back and tilting it up for a look.

A massive purplish blue creature floated there, tentacles—*real* tentacles—waving around it. A kraken. She had read of them, but they lived in the depths of the sea, not in freshwater lakes.

A tentacle streaked toward the viewer. In the ship's engine room, Amaranthe flinched, jerking her own head away.

"Idiot," she whispered. She leaned back in, clamped her hand on the knob, and pulled it back as far as it would go.

But it was too late. The tentacle wrapped around the viewer, so large it easily blotted out the entire display. Amaranthe did not hear a crunch or snap—not with so much distance separating them from the device—but she sensed it. The view winked out, leaving only her reflection in the glass of the eyepieces.

She stepped back, lowering her hands.

"Do I get to use it now?" Maldynado asked.

"Uh, sure." Amaranthe rubbed her face. She hoped the kraken could not track the viewer back to the ship.

"Wait, it's broken." Maldynado frowned at her.

"Yes, and it's possible we shouldn't stick around. Just in case what broke it wants to visit."

Amaranthe jogged for the ladder.

"I can't believe you broke it before I got to play—scout—with it," Maldynado muttered as he followed her.

She almost gagged when she returned to the death stench of the corridor above. She glanced toward the storage area where she had left Books and Akstyr, but it was dark, so she headed outside.

"Over here," Books called as soon as she trotted onto the main deck. "We hauled four suits out, and we can go down tonight. This gear is brilliant. There's no tubing except to these packs, which can be filled with compressed air. They must be magic of some sort. I can't imagine we have the technology to—"

"Not now, Books," Amaranthe said. They had laid everything out on the side opposite from the dock. "It's defended. We're going to have to—"

The deck heaved, throwing Amaranthe into Akstyr. She bounced off him and almost tumbled over the railing. It caught her in the belly, forcing an "Oomph!" out of her lungs. The far side of the ship rose, slanting the deck further, and she wrapped her arms around the railing, clinging like a tick lest she be hurled into the water.

The men cursed, but the sound of wood cracking drowned their words. Everyone else had tumbled to the deck as well, and they were bracing themselves against the railing.

"The suits!" Books cried, wrapping an arm around one helmet and his legs around another.

"Blazing ancestors," Maldynado yelled. "What's going on?"

As abruptly as the far side of the ship had lifted, it crashed down. Amaranthe flew from her perch and landed with a painful thump on the deck. The ship rocked, and water surged over the railings. A suit threatened to float away, and she grabbed it.

"Get the gear and run to the dock!" she ordered.

A tentacle thicker than a man's body reared out of the water ten feet away. It stretched high, towering over the tugboat. The tentacle waved menacingly against the starry backdrop, then plummeted. It slammed onto the deck at the front of the ship.

Metal groaned under the assault. A wooden ship might have been destroyed right there. As it was, the tentacle wrapped around the base of the crane and snapped the metal support, as if it were breaking a pencil.

Amaranthe ripped her gaze away. The men were already scrambling across the rocking deck, slipping and flailing in the water streaming past. She grabbed the lone remaining helmet to go with the suit, groaning at the combined weight of the two items. On hands and knees, she clawed her away across the heaving deck after the men.

The tentacle lifted the crane into the air and flung it with an irritable flick.

The forty-foot metal arm flew out of sight, though Amaranthe heard it land. Wood smashed and cracked, and she feared another docked ship had been turned into a victim.

The tentacle reared for another attack.

She hustled faster. Fifteen feet to the railing and the dock beyond. Maldynado and Akstyr were already there, hurling their suits off the ship.

The tentacle smashed into the main cabin this time. Wood shattered, and shards flew everywhere, pelting Amaranthe's back as she continued to drag the heavy suit toward the rail. The tentacle thrashed. The roof caved in, and more waves rocked the ship. Beneath Amaranthe's hands, the deck trembled under the stress, and the hull quaked.

In seconds, the cabin was destroyed. The tentacle lifted from the wreckage and swept sideways across the deck.

Amaranthe flattened. It came so close, the breeze ruffled her hair and cold water droplets rained onto the back of her neck. As soon as it passed over her, she sprang to her feet and sprinted the last couple of paces.

Akstyr grabbed her helmet and tossed it onto the dock. "What *is* that thing?"

She winced when the helmet nearly bounced off and into the water on the other side. "I'll tell you about it when we're safe." She heaved the suit over the railing and gestured for Books and Akstyr to follow.

"Whatever it is," Maldynado said to Akstyr, voice muffled, "I'll pay you a thousand ranmyas if you can incinerate it with your mind." He was *wearing* his helmet.

Akstyr paused, his foot on the railing. "Really?"

"No." Amaranthe shoved him from the boat and nodded toward Books. "You next."

The tentacle grabbed the rail on the opposite side of the ship and pulled. The deck tilted thirty degrees, lifting Amaranthe's side high in the air.

She hooked her elbow over the railing, even as her feet skidded out from beneath her. Books was not as quick to grab hold. He hit the deck and started to slide away. Amaranthe thrust a foot out, and he caught it.

The jolt popped something in her hip, but she gritted her teeth and hung on to the rail. She caught it with her other hand and anchored herself, so Books could crawl up her leg and find purchase again.

The dock, previously ten feet below the deck, lay twenty feet down now.

"Go," Amaranthe told Books.

Without pause, he flung himself over the side. The deck rocked. The kraken seemed to know Amaranthe and Maldynado were still on board, and it was trying to shake them free. They pushed the last of the gear over the side.

"You go first," Maldynado said.

A new tentacle shot up between the dock and the ship, the gleaming purple skin not five feet from Amaranthe and Maldynado. Water sprayed everywhere and spattered her in the eye.

"Both of us," she said. The tentacle swept down toward them. "Now!"

They leaped over the railing just as the kraken smashed through it. A chunk of wood hammered Amaranthe on the back as she fell. Air whistled past her ears.

In the dim lighting, she struggled to judge the distance to the dock. Through luck more than skill she landed with a roll that kept her from breaking legs, but her momentum threatened to send her tumbling into the water on the far side.

A hand clamped about her collar, hauling her back before she flew over the edge.

"Thanks," she said.

"You're welcome," Maldynado said, head still ensconced in the helmet.

"*I* caught her, you dolt," Books said. "You're lucky you didn't land headfirst wearing that thing."

Amaranthe hustled to her feet and grabbed one of the sets of gear. "Let's chat later."

The dock lacked any sort of comforting sturdiness, and she ran for the street as quickly as she could while dragging the suit and helmet. The men raced after her. Wood cracked behind them, and the dock shuddered. She did not look back. Only when they reached land and the solid cobblestone of the waterfront street did Amaranthe feel safe enough to check.

"Emperor's warts," she breathed at the sight. Or the *lack* of a sight.

The *Tuggle* was missing, along with half of the dock. A ship that had been moored opposite the tugboat was tilted on its side, its wooden masts broken, with water flowing through a hole in its hull. Tangled sails smothered the deck. In the water, boards, rope, and other jetsam floated, the only remains of the salvage ship.

The tentacles were gone.

"That was a kraken?" Books shook his head. "That can*not* be here. The Aracknis Kraken is a deep-sea-dwelling relative of the giant squid that's native to the Trechara Trench, two thousand miles away. It feeds on large fish, squids, and other species found only in that environment. It's physiologically adapted to a saltwater habitat, and it can*not* be here."

"Thank you, professor." Maldynado removed his helmet, and his damp curls stuck out, creating a silhouette reminiscent of a dandelion gone to seed. "Perhaps you should swim into the lake and tell that to Lord Tentacles out there."

"That was brilliant," Akstyr said. "My first sea monster."

"Sea monsters can't be in freshwater lakes," Books muttered.

"They can if they're guarding a submerged magical fortress full of kidnappers," Amaranthe said.

"A fortress?" Books frowned.

"That's what I'd call it, yes."

He groaned.

"Does this mean we're not going diving tonight?" Akstyr asked.

Books groaned again.

CHAPTER 14

Though darkness had fallen hours earlier, light crept beneath the door of Deret Mancrest's flat. No lamps burned in the hallway outside.

"He stays up late for a respectable newspaper man," Amaranthe said.

"Maybe he's entertaining," Maldynado said. "Though I'd expect more thumping and moaning if that were the case."

Books was not there to glare at him. Amaranthe had sent him and Akstyr to slip into the library and research krakens—specifically how to kill them—and check for information on underwater habitations as well, though she doubted they would find anything there. She did not think the technology existed to create something like that without the mental sciences, and the curators of the imperial libraries would never put books discussing otherworldly construction on the shelves. Not if they valued their necks.

"Be ready. He answers the door with a sword stick." Amaranthe knocked.

"Naturally," Maldynado said.

Shuffling sounds came from within, along with a noisy yawn that could have woken half of the building. A moment later, the door opened. Mancrest stood inside, leaning on his sword stick, his tall form limned by candlelight coming from behind him. Papers scattered a desk, as well as a couple of quills and an old-fashioned ink jar.

Mancrest gaped at them, though he dismissed Maldynado with a glance and focused on Amaranthe. She tensed, expecting a barrage of imprecations.

"Ms. Lokdon!" he blurted.

"Yes...." She tried to judge his tone, but could only read the surprise. Given the hour, that was hardly shocking.

"Hello. I didn't expect you." Mancrest winced. "That's obvious, isn't it? What time is it? After midnight?" He peered at a clock perched on a fireplace mantle. "It is. Huh."

"Does he seem scattered to you?" Amaranthe whispered to Maldynado.

"His shirt buttons aren't in the wrong holes, so I don't think he's been entertaining," Maldynado whispered back, then he raised his voice. "Have you been drinking, Deret?"

"What? No?" Mancrest rubbed his eyes and yawned again. "Just been up. Thinking."

Amaranthe fought back a yawn of her own.

"Come in, come in." Mancrest shuffled to the table in sandals that slapped the wood floor with each step. The neighbors below probably loved that. "Since you're here," he said, "I might as well..." He poked through papers. Some were empty, some had a line or two on them, and some had more. A few crumpled balls occupied a nearby waste bin. "No, that's awful. Ugh, what was I thinking there?" He discarded those two pages and surveyed others. "No, I was closer on a previous draft. Uhm...this one isn't entirely horrible. It'll have to do."

Amaranthe exchanged eyebrow raises with Maldynado while Mancrest folded the selected page with care. He placed it in an envelope, melted the end of a wax stick over a candle, and sealed the missive with a smudge. He tugged on a golden chain around his neck, pulling a flat, oval signet out. Mancrest pressed it into the wax, leaving the image of a soldier holding a sword aloft—his family's crest.

Amaranthe was about to interrupt letter-crafting time—they had important matters to discuss—when Mancrest straightened, marched the envelope over, and handed it to her.

"Er, what's this?" she asked.

"It's in the letter."

"Did you...want me to read it now?"

Mancrest glanced at Maldynado. "Maybe later. When my ego isn't around to watch."

"Definitely drinking," Maldynado whispered.

Mancrest *was* acting strangely, or at least not in accordance to what she expected from him based on previous meetings, but no scent of alcohol lingered about him.

"All right." Amaranthe considered the creamy envelope. It was too large to stick into a pocket without folding, and she feared it was rude to treat a missive stamped with someone's warrior-caste seal so cavalierly. "Can we talk, Lord Mancrest? It's about your brother's ship, the *Saberfist*. And the missing people."

Mancrest's forehead crinkled—had he thought she'd come about something besides business? No, he was probably surprised to have his brother brought into things. He recovered and waved them to seats around a gaming table.

"No soldiers waiting to jump out?" Maldynado slid open the door of a credenza, as if a squad might be hiding inside.

"Not this time." Mancrest smiled. "I wasn't expecting you."

Amaranthe slid into a seat and launched into the story, sharing not only the information on the underwater structure, but everything that had led them to discover it. When she admitted to the garbage vehicle destruction, Maldynado choked and thrust an accusing finger her direction, claiming she "practically forced me to drive at knife point." Amaranthe swatted his finger away and continued on. She wanted to be honest since the head of *The Gazette* would have the resources to tease out any truths she left untold—especially truths that involved arsons and collisions. Mancrest merely stared at her through the recitation.

When she finished, he leaned forward, peering into her eyes from different angles.

"I believe," Maldynado said, "he's now wondering if *you've* been drinking. Or worse."

"No." Mancrest leaned back. "I just wasn't sure... Well, I don't know you that well, so I don't know when you're joking."

Amaranthe resisted the urge to tell him that he would know her better by now if he had not been so insistent on trying to apprehend her.

"No joke," she said. "I don't know if they'll attack the *Saberfist* or not, but this is a threat to Stumps either way, and your brother's ship is best equipped to deal with it."

Maldynado leaned close to her and whispered, "If *they* deal with it, what will *we* do? We're supposed to solve the problems and get credit, right?" Whisper or not, his aside was loud enough for Mancrest to hear.

"What's important," Amaranthe said, lifting her chin and meeting Mancrest's eyes, "is that the threat to the empire is vanquished. Who gets credit is immaterial."

Besides, her plan should let her team come out as heroes to people who mattered—those trapped in the submerged structure. She brushed a wayward strand of hair behind her ear, using the movement to hide a covert wink for Maldynado.

"The good of the empire," Maldynado said. "Right, right."

Mancrest stroked his jaw. "I'm not sure who would believe this story, but my older brother was a young lieutenant during the Western Sea Conflict, and he's seen magic being used. He knows the imperial stance is propaganda. But, you might not get a chance to tell your story. He and all his marines would be duty-bound to apprehend you as soon as you stepped aboard his ship."

"*I* wasn't planning to talk to him." She smiled at Mancrest.

"I was hoping you would."

"Oh. Yes, of course. I should have realized more prompted this late night visit than an interest in sharing a tip for the paper."

"I wouldn't interrupt your sleep—" Amaranthe glanced at the envelope, "—or midnight scrivener aspirations for something that wasn't important."

"Yes," Maldynado said, "she's not your average girl who shows up in the middle of the night to ply you with wine and sex in the hopes of being impregnated with a warrior-caste scion that your family would feel obligated to help raise, and, oh, maybe there'd be a stipend for the mother as well."

"Surely, that's not your idea of an *average* girl," Amaranthe said, though Mancrest's rueful smile might have meant he had experienced similar situations. "Are you willing to meet your brother at the docks in the morning?" she asked. "If he's been gone on a long voyage, he'll doubtlessly be eager to reunite with family and hear about what's been going on in town. And the lake."

"Doubtlessly," Mancrest said dryly. "Though even with his ecumenical background, I don't know if he'll believe any of this. Especially from his little brother, the writer, who *loved* to tell stories as a boy."

"He doesn't need to accept it as fact based on words alone. I'll give you the location. You just need to convince him to float over there and send divers down to take a look."

"And get eaten by a kraken?"

"Well-trained military men know how to take suitable precautions, do they not?" Amaranthe hoped Books would come up with a tactic to use against the kraken, but she knew very well she might be endangering lives with her request. If that was what she had to do to get her men back and rescue the captives, so be it.

Mancrest sighed. "Why do I have a feeling working with you will cause me as much trouble as trying to capture you did?"

"That's a given," Maldynado said.

Amaranthe merely folded her hands on the table and smiled agreeably. Mancrest had given in; there was no need to cajole him further.

Her smile faded a few minutes later when she was standing beneath a streetlamp, reading Mancrest's note.

Ms. Amaranthe Lokdon,

I have treated you unfairly, and for that I apologize. I had plenty of time to think over my behavior when I was failing to reach those keys and waiting for the soldiers to wake up and...rescue me. Yes, that's what it was, and I must confess it. For the second time, you left me helpless... but unharmed, though I deserved worse for trying to apprehend you without listening to your story or researching your situation.

I have done so now, and though I do not believe all the facts are out there to be discovered, I suspect you deserve to be exonerated. Of course, I am not in a position to grant you that, but I am open to listening, if you are still interested in sharing. You have no reason to trust me, but if you will give me another chance, I'd like to take you for a picnic dinner in the Imperial Gardens. I'll understand if you bring your bodyguard (but I hope you won't).

To the peace after the war,

~ Deret

"Guess you wooed him after all," Maldynado said.

Amaranthe twitched, jerking the paper away. She had not realized he had been reading over her shoulder.

"I thought there was no hope for the relationship once you dropped the keys in the pyramid hallway and left him locked up." Maldynado reached over her shoulder and tapped the page. "I agree. If we've got Sicarius back by then, leave him behind. He'll kill the sunset-picnic-mood faster than a swarm of mosquitoes."

"You know, people like privacy to read letters." Amaranthe returned the page to the envelope. She had too much else on her mind to worry about Mancrest's words. "Let's check on Books and Akstyr. We need a way to defeat that kraken."

"You mean the plan isn't to use the marines as bait while we sneak in from below?"

"It is, to an extent. I do want the soldiers there as a distraction, so nobody will notice us walking up in our diving suits, but I don't want them getting mauled either. We need to kill the kraken."

"No chance you can woo it with your tongue, huh?" Maldynado asked.

"Judging by our previous encounter, I think it'd be more likely to pull my tongue out, wrap it around my body like bacon, and swallow me whole."

"Such imaginative imagery."

"I get creative when I haven't had any sleep."

"The next few hours should be interesting then," Maldynado said.

"Likely so."

CHAPTER 15

Awareness returned to Basilard slowly. Memories of dreams wafted away like smoke in the wind. A dim blurriness met his eyes, and he blinked, struggling to focus. A face came into view.

Sicarius.

His features held no warmth or friendliness. Basilard tried to lift a hand, but bindings secured him to the table. Sicarius was free, though still nude. He wore his brace of throwing knives on his forearm and held two daggers, one the black blade he favored and the other one of Basilard's fighting weapons. Basilard's gaze lingered on the sharp steel, and he remembered his last thoughts; before he had succumbed to the drugs, he had been sure Sicarius knew of Basilard's plan for killing him.

Basilard turned his head from side to side. Other prisoners lay on the tables, some horizontal and others tipped vertical against the wall. None appeared to be awake. How much time had passed? Deep shadows shrouded the corners of the laboratory, and the lights were dimmer than he remembered. It must be nighttime, though one might never know the difference down here.

Sicarius lifted his hands and signed, *You are alert?*

That he signed instead of speaking meant he had escaped, not been released, and being quiet was important.

Had Basilard's hands been free, he would have responded with "vaguely," but, strapped down, he had fewer options, so he only nodded.

Sicarius slipped a key into the first lock, the one that bound Basilard's wrists to the table.

As soon as his hands were free, he asked, *How'd you escape?*

The woman. Sicarius's signs were as terse as his spoken words.

She released you? Because she wanted to... Basilard stopped. He had no interest in the details; he just wanted to know if Sicarius had won her over—or forced her over—and if she could take them to the surface.

She was unable to craft the sphere.

Was? Basilard asked. *She's dead?*

Yes. We have to find another way off. Only the other twin and a male telekineticist can make the protective bubbles. The woman is incapacitated from your attack, and the male isn't on board right now. We may be too deep to swim out. Regardless, a kraken guards this place. Our blades would be useless against it.

No, even firearms would be useless underwater. *The woman told you all this?* Basilard asked.

Yes. Sicarius's cool gaze told him to drop it.

Basilard swallowed, imagining Sicarius letting that woman think they had some connection, and then turning around, interrogating her, and killing her. True, Basilard himself had killed, but only in combat and only men. Not women. His eyes narrowed in remembrance. Or children.

Sicarius unfastened the bindings about Basilard's ankles, then continued with those tying his torso and thighs to the table.

Basilard tilted his head. *Why come for me?*

Sicarius flicked him a glance that could have meant anything and continued to unlock the bindings.

When the drugs were overtaking Basilard, he had not expected Sicarius's help, indeed had thought Sicarius might have set him up to die. Was it possible he had imagined everything?

Sicarius released the final straps and stepped back.

Do you know I know... Basilard stopped himself. If Sicarius had not figured it out, it would be foolish to alert him.

I know, Sicarius signed.

Basilard waited for him to continue, to offer some ultimatum or say something like, "If you make a move against me, I'll kill you." He still held all the knives. Sicarius did not add anything to his comment though. Maybe he figured it was all assumed.

You could get rid of me down here with no one on the team wise to it. And maybe Basilard should not be pointing things out. What if Sicarius was only releasing him because he needed help escaping? And what if he planned to kill Basilard on the way out? Or maybe... *Do you not see me as a threat?*

You are capable.

As scant an admission as that was, Basilard found it heartening. *Then why free me?* Basilard asked again.

Because Amaranthe would wish it. Sicarius flipped Basilard's knife and extended it, hilt first.

The answer, or perhaps the honesty of the answer, surprised Basilard. *So, I'm safe around you as long as she's alive?* He smiled, though he knew Sicarius would not return the gesture.

If you force me to defend myself, I will. Sicarius shook the knife, emphasizing Basilard should take it. Right, they had to escape before anyone noticed Sicarius missing and the woman dead.

Basilard took the knife and stepped into the aisle. He paused as one more thought occurred to him. *Is Amaranthe the reason you were captured?*

He thought of the way she had talked him into the Clank Race. Her intentions had been good—maybe that was what made her requests appealing—but he would not be at the bottom of a lake, stripped naked, and the latest specimen in some scientist's research experiment if not for her.

I got closer than I should have, Sicarius signed. *I sensed the Science being used, but... I did not want to return without answers to her questions.*

Huh, he had been right. Basilard was going to sign one of his grandfather's sayings, that many a male duck had been lured to its demise by the call of a female, but Sicarius turned away, as if to say, "Enough chit chat. Time for work."

He strode to the next table and cut the tubing leading to a young man's veins. He unlocked the bindings there as well, though he did not wait for the person to wake before moving to the next table.

Why free them? Basilard asked, not because he objected, but because Sicarius would not do it for altruistic purposes.

Distraction, Sicarius signed.

While we do what?

Take this—Sicarius twitched a hand to encompass the structure—*to the surface so we can get off.*

Take over the...tiller? Basilard had no idea if something like this had a tiller—probably not—but Sicarius would know he meant the navigation system.

Yes.

You know where that is?

But Sicarius had already turned back to the captives. Basilard helped with his own knife. Most of the other prisoners were young, in their teens and twenties. He hoped they would be able to escape themselves without being harmed. More harmed, he corrected himself, when he noticed freshly stitched scars gouging the abdomen and groin areas of more than one. Basilard glanced down at himself and was relieved to see no incisions. Sicarius must have found him before they got started with...whatever it was they were doing exactly. He shuddered.

Sicarius bumped him on the shoulder and jerked his head toward the exit.

The first captive was stirring.

Wouldn't it be better to work with them? Basilard asked. *A combined force to confront our adversaries?*

Athletes would be useless against practitioners.

Basilard was not certain what value he might have against a shaman or wizard either. He recalled the humiliation of his old owner, Arbitan Losk, plucking him from hiding and flattening him to the floor with a force he had been unable to elude.

A noise started up, a throbbing whine that vibrated from the walls loudly enough to wake any slumbering guards.

"Alarm." Sicarius jogged toward the exit.

Basilard remembered the invisible barrier and wondered if Sicarius had disabled it. He must have if he had come in from the woman's quarters or somewhere that direction, but it was up now, evinced by a strange sheen with yellow tendrils shimmering in the air.

Sicarius plucked a thin knife off a console near the hatchway. A bloody ball was skewered on the tip.

Though Basilard noted the gory thing, he did not realize what it was until Sicarius held it up to the eyeball reader. The recognition did not quite make Basilard flinch, but he did curl a disgusted lip. Given his background, he ought not be squeamish about such things, but he could not help but find it discomfiting. Maybe because his putative ally was the one who had removed it, and it might very well have belonged to that woman.

The shield wavered and disappeared.

Sicarius and Basilard passed into the long corridor outside, ducking their heads to dodge intermittent pipes along the ceiling. The glow of the orbs on the wall waxed and waned with each pulse of the alarm. The corridor curved in angled segments like some mechanical snake stretched along the lake floor. They passed closed hatches, but Sicarius did not pause to check any of them.

Rhythmic thumps sounded above them. Footfalls? Was there a second floor? Basilard had not noticed ladders on his previous trip, but that had been a short journey. They had already passed the cabin he had started out in.

Sicarius ran through a four-way intersection, then rounded a bend. A few feet before a dead end, a ladder rose to a closed hatch in the ceiling.

Instead of starting up, Sicarius smashed his black dagger into an orb on the wall. Shadows thickened in the corridor. He darted behind the ladder and crouched, his back to the wall. Basilard joined him.

Above, the footfalls started and stopped a couple of times, and Basilard had the impression of guards pausing to collect reinforcements.

Plan? Basilard asked.

If a manageable number of men come down, we jump them. Sicarius retained the eyeball-on-a-knife, and it made a grisly accent to his hand signs.

Would you have done that if Amaranthe were here? Basilard caught himself asking.

He thought Sicarius might give him a frosty look or tell him to pay attention to what they were doing. Instead a faint ruefulness softened his stony expression.

Doubt I would have needed to. She would have subverted one of the guards.

You can't subvert one? Basilard joked, not expecting a reaction beyond a glare.

Apparently, I lack charisma.

Basilard gaped at him, not certain if that had been a joke or not. Overhead, the footfalls clomped to a stop at the hatch, and he focused on the matter at hand. Sicarius, too, turned his attention upward.

The hatch creaked open. A pistol descended first, then a guard eased his head through. Basilard held his breath. Attacking the guards on the ladder would be the best spot for catching them by surprise.

Wariness stamped the man's face, though, and he checked

both ways, aiming the pistol without stepping onto the rungs. His eyes turned in Basilard's direction and paused. Maybe the shadows weren't deep enough.

"Hobarth." The guard squinted and shifted the pistol toward the shadows.

The only warning Basilard had of movement was Sicarius's arm brushing his. A throwing knife zipped between the ladder rungs and thudded into the guard's eye.

In less than a heartbeat, Sicarius darted out of the shadows and up the ladder. He grabbed the dying man by the shirt, hurling him to the floor below, then disappeared through the hatchway.

Basilard leaped out and grabbed the fallen guard's pistol. He clenched it between his teeth, tugged the throwing knife from the eye socket, and climbed the ladder with Sicarius's blade and his own balanced in his hands.

He pulled himself onto the next floor, landing in a fighting stance, ready to help.

Two guards were sprawled on the deck, their throats cut. Sicarius was patting one down for keys or weapons or, for all Basilard knew, something to eat.

Feeling useless, he took the pistol out of his mouth and checked the charge. With his hands full, he had to juggle the weapons to sign a question, *Should we take their clothes?*

The guards were all bigger than Basilard, but he felt vulnerable running around nude.

To what end? Sicarius took his throwing knife from Basilard and sheathed it.

Pockets?

Sicarius flicked an indifferent finger, picked up the eyeball knife, and headed down the corridor. Basilard stripped the fatigue jacket off the smallest guard and put it on, grimacing at the sensation of cloth sticky with blood pressed against his skin. He hustled to catch up.

Sicarius stopped at a barrier before an intersection to

fiddle with the reader. He glanced at Basilard's new attire but said nothing. Clothes or not, *he* probably never felt vulnerable. Between the eyeball in his hand and the streaks of someone else's blood smeared across his forearm and chest, he looked like nobody one would want to tangle with.

You better stick with Amaranthe, Basilard signed. *She humanizes you.*

The barrier dropped. Sicarius looked himself over and considered the gory eyeball before stepping through.

Agreed, he signed.

There was no time to mull over the response. More footfalls and numerous voices rang throughout the structure. The alarm continued pulsing. If all they met were soldiers, Basilard and Sicarius might be able to handle them, but Basilard expected practitioners at some point, and who knew what otherworldly obstacles.

The corridor sloped upward. Closed hatches marked the walls to either side, each with a reader set nearby at eye level. Sicarius did not slow to try any of these. He obviously had a destination in mind. Or maybe their eyeball only opened communal doors, not private laboratories.

They passed another ladder leading down, and Basilard tried to imagine a map of the place in his mind. They could no longer be above the tunnel they had run through on the first floor, because there had been no ladders leading up before the one they had taken. How much of a maze might this place be? He hoped Sicarius knew where he was going.

After the ladder, the corridor continued on in a straight line. Its riveted, gray walls offered no alcoves or niches for hiding in, should someone come out shooting at them.

The narrow passage ended at another barrier. In a chamber on the other side, the back of a large black chair was visible before a control panel and a horizontal, oblong porthole. Dark water pressed against the glass. It could be night or day at the lake surface and no one would ever know down here. Around the chamber, lever- and gauge-filled panels ran from floor to ceiling. Many held multi-hued glowing protuberances, all amorphous, more like fungi that had grown there naturally than mechanical devices. Was this the navigation area? Basilard struggled to imagine this unwieldy ship—if one could call it that—floating up a river, but it had to have arrived somehow. Perhaps it could become compact for travel.

Sicarius waved the eyeball before the reader on the wall, but this shimmering field did not fade away. He plucked a piece of lint from the floor and tossed it at the barrier. It burst into flame and disappeared.

Basilard stepped back, *far* back.

The owner of the eyeball didn't have access to that room? he asked.

Apparently not. Sicarius wiggled the eyeball about in front of the reader again. He must have expected it to win him entry.

The chair rotated, and Basilard jumped. He had not realized anyone was sitting in it. A tall, gray-haired man in a white coat scowled at them. The navigator, perhaps, and maybe a practitioner as well. Though he bore no weapons openly, he showed no fear at the prospect of intruders on his threshold.

Back? Basilard signed, aware of the alarm still throbbing, of shouts in the distance. It sounded like someone had discovered the dead guards.

Sicarius decided it was the time to engage in a staring contest. Maybe he thought the practitioner would wither under an unrelenting gaze—or at least come over and open the door.

The gray-haired man lifted a hand. A crackling yellow ball formed in the air before his fingertips.

Basilard backed further. That could only be a weapon, and if it could go through the barrier...

Sicarius crouched, ready to spring. He must believe the barrier had to drop for the man to launch the weapon.

Boots pounded in the corridor behind them. Basilard gripped his knife and nodded to let Sicarius know he would provide time for him—if he could. He did not know how he would dodge pistols in the tight corridor.

He ran down the passage anyway.

Before he reached the ladder, two guards stomped into view, one behind the other. In the narrow space, Basilard almost missed spotting a gray-haired woman in a blood-spattered white coat striding after them. She toted a two-foot-long cone, and, judging by the way she held it over the guards' shoulders, trying to target Basilard, it was a weapon. He had to focus on the first problem: the two guards and the pistols in their hands.

The first man dropped to one knee, pointing his firearm at Basilard, while the second remained standing and aimed over the first's head. The distance between Basilard and them was too far to charge before they could fire.

He focused on their fingers, trying to watch and anticipate when they would pull the triggers. One tensed. Basilard hurled his knife and threw himself into a forward roll.

Pistols fired.

One shot clanged off the metal floor, but another hammered into the back of Basilard's shoulder. Pain seared through him, as if someone had thrust a hot iron into his flesh. He gasped, eyes clenched shut, but managed to finish the roll and come up running. He had to, or they would have him.

The closest guard was on his knees, hunched against the wall, trying to work Basilard's knife free of his upper arm. The man in back dropped his pistol and drew a serrated dagger with a ten-inch blade.

"Move, Fiks," the woman barked in accented Turgonian. "Let me—"

Basilard charged. The second guard had one foot in the air to step past his comrade, and one ear toward the woman. It was Basilard's best chance, to attack before the men had time to plan something.

The guard wasn't as distracted as he appeared. He slashed

at Basilard to keep him at bay, then yanked a smaller pistol out of his belt behind his back.

Caught off guard, Basilard was the one who had no time to do anything but react. He lunged in and grabbed the downed man, yanking him to his feet. The injured guard roared in surprise and pain. Basilard punched him in the face, hoping to stun him and keep him as an obstacle. The movements stirred fresh agony in his shoulder, and he nearly dropped from the pain. He forced it aside and yanked his knife free from the man's arm, eliciting another howl.

The rearmost guard thrust his pistol over his comrade's shoulder. Basilard ducked and hurled his knife around the injured man's ribs. The awkward position gave the throw little power, but it was enough to slice into his target's thigh. The man bellowed and dropped the pistol.

Further up the corridor, Sicarius shouted, "Down!" in Mangdorian.

Basilard hesitated. To drop to the floor would be to put himself at a disadvantage.

Light flared down the corridor, as brilliant as a sunburst. Basilard dropped to the floor, dragging the closest guard with him for cover. Heat roiled down the passage, and brightness burned his eyes, even through the lids. The man above him screamed. The scent of burning hair and singed flesh flooded Basilard's nostrils.

He expected screams from the woman and the other guard but heard nothing. Had they been quick enough to hurl themselves to the floor?

The light blazing against his lids lessened, and he pried an eye open, hoping to find his opponents vanquished. The woman had not moved, except to fiddle with something at her belt. A transparent barrier, the same streaky yellow as those used in the corridors, hovered around her and the guard. Heat shimmering in the air parted around the defensive shield like water flowing past a boulder in a stream.

Safe behind the barrier, the guard clenched his knife and glowered at Basilard. Blood dripped from his thigh and splashed onto the floor.

Further up the corridor, Sicarius dropped from the ceiling where he had hung like a spider to avoid the blast.

Basilard scrambled out from beneath the singed—and now quite dead—man. Every movement brought fire from the pistol wound; he could feel that ball in his flesh, grinding against the bone of his shoulder blade, but he gritted his teeth and told himself he could deal with it later.

The remaining guard charged out of the protective barrier and slashed at Basilard's neck with the serrated knife.

Basilard had lost his own blade when he threw it, but he skittered back from the attack without trouble. He had faced many knife wielders without the benefit of a weapon. He watched the man's collarbone—not the eyes; the eyes could lie—and kept the blade and free hand in his peripheral vision.

The man stabbed at Basilard's chest. He saw the feint for what it was. The man's body wasn't behind it; he wasn't committed. Three more feints came, and Basilard began to wonder if the man would attack in earnest. Then he committed, legs crouched to spring and dart in close behind a swipe.

Basilard crouched low and blocked the striking arm, knocking it upward. He grabbed the man's wrist, pulling it toward him as he stepped closer. His other elbow swung up, pounding the underside of the guard's jaw. The man's head whipped backward with a crunch.

Basilard could have finished him on his own, but Sicarius slashed the man's throat and shoved him to the floor so he could leap over him and spring toward the woman.

Before he reached her, an invisible blast slammed him in the chest. The edge of it caught Basilard as well, a stiff blast of air so rigid it had the force of a battering ram, and it sent him stumbling against the wall. It hurled Sicarius a dozen feet.

Despite the power of the blow, he twisted and landed on his feet, light as a cat.

Basilard crept close to the woman and tapped the shield with the tip of his dagger. It buzzed and hissed at him. Hadn't Akstyr once said a practitioner could not attack and defend at the same time? The dual task certainly wasn't bothering this woman. Maybe because she was using a tool to attack instead of her own mind?

Sicarius sprinted back toward Basilard and the woman. "Go by her," he barked in Mangdorian. "Down the next ladder."

The woman flipped a lever on her cone. Sicarius saw the attack coming and dove to his belly this time. That had to hurt without clothes on, but it worked. He skidded under the cone's field of influence, and the wave did no more than ruffle his hair.

He jumped up, inches from the shield and jerked his arms up as if to attack, but he exaggerated the movements. Trying to startle her? To break her concentration so the shield would drop?

She watched him without flinching, then ominously reached for the lever on her weapon again. He tapped the barrier with his knife. It buzzed at him. He stalked about the shield, like a prowling tiger checking his cage for a weakness.

Basilard picked up his knife and tried to pass the woman in the corridor. The edges of the barrier extended to the walls, so he had to slither on his belly to find an unblocked spot.

A string of words came down the hall. Basilard did not understand the language, but it sounded like a question. Without taking her eyes from Sicarius, the gray-haired woman answered in the same tongue.

Basilard thumped the wall to get Sicarius's attention, *We should go.*

Where to he did not know. If the navigation area was out, what else could they try?

The woman lifted the weapon at Sicarius's chest again. Her

finger tightened on the trigger, but he anticipated the attack. He leaped over the woman, barrier and all, and avoided the blast.

Sicarius joined Basilard and they ran down the corridor.

Before they reached the ladder, two bronze-skinned men with long, thin braids of black hair came into view. They wore white coats and toted small canvas bags that bulged with balls. Each carried one of the balls in his free hand, pale green globes with the icy dark depths of a glacier.

The men were on the other side of the ladder, and Basilard thought he could reach it before they did. He increased his speed, running ahead of Sicarius. Had they been guards, Basilard would have challenged them, but he wanted nothing to do with practitioners.

When he reached the ladder, he dropped down, landing in a crouch, knife ready. A pair of guards running toward the ladder almost crashed into him.

One started to lift a pistol. Basilard knocked the arm up, and the weapon went off, the noise deafening in the metal corridor. The pistol ball ricocheted off the walls, and the guard flinched. Basilard feinted toward the man's face with his knife, drawing a block, then lowered his blade and thrust toward the unprotected gut.

The guard had fast reflexes and almost recovered quickly enough to block the attack, but Basilard was faster still. The blade plunged through flesh and organs before he pulled it free again.

He shoved the injured man at his comrade, eliciting a new blast of pain from his shoulder. He need not have bothered. As Sicarius dropped down, he hammered his black blade into the top of the man's skull. Bone crunched, and utter shock stamped the guard's face—his last expression ever.

"Run!" Sicarius sprinted up the corridor.

As Basilard turned to follow him, two of the pale green balls dropped down from above. Busy running, he did not see them hit the floor, but he heard cracks like breaking glass.

He hunched his shoulders, expecting an explosion. But it was a stench that assaulted him. He snorted, trying to expel any intrusive gas from his nostrils. After that, he held his breath as he raced after Sicarius. He might be fast on the Clank Race, but he had the shorter legs, and he fell a few paces behind.

The long, twisting corridor seemed to go on forever. Ahead, someone leaned out of a hatchway, a compact crossbow poised to fire. The attacker probably thought he was safe, that he could duck back behind a barrier as soon as he made the shot, but Sicarius dodged the quarrel and surged forward with startling speed. He grasped the crossbow wielder's wrist and yanked him out before he could duck back. Sicarius spun the man about, a hand going to his head, and broke his neck before he could so much as shout for help.

Basilard's lungs burned from holding his breath. Sicarius stopped to grab the crossbow and pat the man down for ammunition. It must be safe to breathe.

Basilard opened his mouth to suck in a gasp of air, but couldn't. His lungs were frozen. He tried again. And again. Nothing. It was as if he had taken a blow to the solar plexus and his system was stunned. He thumped on his chest, not sure what else to try. Panic encroached upon him. Would he die for lack of the air all about him?

Before he reached the dead body, Sicarius rose and headed down the corridor again. Basilard thumped on the wall.

Sicarius stopped and turned. For a moment, he simply stood there. Trying to ascertain what was wrong? Or thinking that, despite his earlier words, he was being given a chance to leave Basilard to die and to end the possibility of a threat?

Blackness crept into the edges of Basilard's vision, and the weight of a thousand pounds of sand filled his legs. He stumbled and pitched toward the floor.

Hands caught him. Air that Basilard wanted so much to inhale breezed past as he was hoisted from the floor and draped over Sicarius's shoulder. The darkness swallowed more of his vision, and his pulse throbbed in his ears. Vaguely, he was aware of the floor skimming past as Sicarius continued running down the corridor. He turned at an intersection and halted.

Another barrier to pass? Did Sicarius still have the eye? Basilard could not see, nor could he feel his limbs or move his head.

Metal squealed and they moved again, but only a few steps. Basilard felt himself being lowered to the floor. Its cool smoothness pressed against his cheek. He wondered if it would be the last thing he ever felt.

Abruptly, a massive spasm coursed through his body. His lungs surprised him by coming to life, and he gulped air in so quickly he almost threw up. He was so relieved he did not care. A temporary paralysis of the lungs, thank God.

Shots rang out nearby. Basilard rolled to his stomach and tried to get his hands and knees beneath him so he could help, but his body was too busy breathing to obey. He did manage to lift his head.

Sicarius stood beside the hatch, reloading a pistol. The crossbow leaned against his leg.

White-coated figures milled several meters down the corridor. One started forward. Sicarius sensed it somehow and leaned out, firing the crossbow. The figures did not even duck. The quarrel bounced off a shield identical to the one the gray-haired woman had used.

Sicarius slammed the hatch shut and spun a round wheel, causing a thick bolt to clang into place. Though it sounded sturdy, there was no way to lock it.

Basilard staggered to his feet. He and Sicarius were in a chamber dominated by an engine, boiler, and furnace. Giant pistons pumped, and a flywheel turned, and the place might have looked purely Turgonian, but unfamiliar tubes and sinuous pipes swept and twisted about the chamber like vines amongst trees. Domes of various sizes punctuated the dull metal at points, emitting orange and red pulses of light. Whatever burned inside the furnace emitted crimson flames instead of yellowish orange.

Welcome to the engine room, Basilard told himself.

Sicarius strode toward the engine controls, lifted a hand, but stopped a few inches shy of touching a lever. He gazed at it for a long moment, the way Akstyr focused when he was calling upon his science. Then he shook his head once and backed away. He grabbed a wrench out of a toolbox and tossed it at the control panel. It bounced off an invisible field and zipped across the cabin. Basilard ducked as it shot over his shoulder. It clanged into the bulkhead and bounced halfway across the room again before clunking to the deck. Singe marks blackened the tip.

If Sicarius had meant to take over the engines, the possibility of succeeding was not looking good.

He tore a pipe from a wall, and steam burst forth. He shoved the pipe through the wheel on the door.

A pipe against three wizards? Basilard signed.

"Six," Sicarius said.

What?

"There are six practitioners out there now. At least."

What's the plan?

"The *plan* is to come up with one."

Basilard searched his face, wondering if that was a joke, but no hint of humor softened Sicarius's stony expression.

Amaranthe tugged at the thick water-repellent material pooled around her boots, boots two inches too large. If there were such things as diving suits for women, she had not encountered them yet. Maybe it would not matter. In the water, the material ought to float, right? Or it would cause her to become hopelessly tangled in seaweed where she would be an easy-to-catch snack for a kraken.

"Less pessimism, girl," she muttered, then raised her voice for Maldynado and Akstyr. "How are your suits fitting?"

They were gearing up around the trapdoor in Ms. Setjareth's warehouse. Amaranthe had agreed to give the woman a discount on future work in exchange for the use of her building for a couple of hours—a deal to which Setjareth had magnanimously agreed, possibly because no shipments had been due in that morning. Fortunately, she was not around to see the pile of harpoons and hand-held launchers sitting next to her trapdoor. The tub labeled Skelith Poison was probably not a typical warehouse store either. Books promised the tar-like substance, which they had smeared on the harpoon tips, would survive the water, at least for a couple of hours.

"This thing weighs a thousand pounds." Akstyr tugged at the collar.

"Only one-eighty, including the helmet," Amaranthe said, "or so Books tells me." Saying his name prompted a glance toward the door. They were waiting on him to return with another weapon to use against the kraken. He had rushed off before sharing the details, and Amaranthe had a hard time not worrying. Six months later, she still had nightmares of that printing press careening down the icy street with Maldynado riding it like a contestant in a log rolling competition. That had been one of Books's ideas, too.

"My helmet is fabulous," Maldynado said, "but the suit binds across the chest. Whatever runty treasure hunter commissioned this piece lacked my substantial musculature."

"And your ego, too, I'd imagine," Amaranthe said.

Wearing everything but the helmet, she shuffled over to a high window facing the lake. She had to clamber atop a crate to push open the shutters and peer outside.

Early morning sun glittered on the calm lake water. A few fishing boats meandered away from the docks, heading out for the day's work. Given what was going on below, Amaranthe thought the scene should be less idyllic.

She stuck her head out, twisting her neck for the view she wanted. Dozens of docks away, the *Saberfist* floated in its berth. Plumes of smoke rose from its twin stacks and a thrum of excitement ran through her. Had Mancrest done it? Convinced them to send divers down to investigate? Marines bustled about on the deck, and the activity had doubled since the last time she took a look.

"Books is back," Maldynado called. "And he didn't bring anything useful."

Amaranthe hopped down in time to catch the scowl Books sent Maldynado's direction. Books was carrying a wooden keg labeled SALT into the building. Amaranthe's earlier excitement faded. Harpoon launchers might harm a kraken, but salt? There had to be more to it than that.

"That's your secret weapon?" she asked, joining the men. "Salt?"

"Actually, it's empty," Books said.

"So you brought a wooden keg?" Maldynado asked. "Genius strategy, professor."

Amaranthe frowned, aware that this might be their only chance to retrieve Sicarius and Basilard. If the *Saberfist* was en route, and it found and attacked the underwater structure, the kidnappers would flee. She couldn't imagine them sticking around once they knew they had been discovered. And who knew where they would go after that?

"Tell us," she prompted Books, who was scowling at Maldynado.

"As it turns out," Books said, "krakens are quite difficult to kill. There are more stories of them sinking ships than there are of people slaying them."

"How comforting," Maldynado said.

"My idea is to fill this keg with poison," Books said. "I tinkered with the design, so it'll implode when squeezed. There are also razor-sharp caltrops inside to cut the kraken's flesh to ensure the poison enters its bloodstream."

"How do we convince the creature to grab it?" Amaranthe asked. "And will a little poison injected at the end of a tentacle really incapacitate it? It's quite...large."

"Ah, but we won't target the tentacle. Squids, and presumably krakens, travel by sucking water into their mantel cavity, then streaming it out behind them in a jet, much like a fireman's hose. Perhaps if we could propel this keg toward its mantle, the creature would inhale it, so to speak, and it'd be like getting pepper up your nose."

"Couldn't we just use pepper?" Maldynado asked.

"Do you want it to sneeze or to die?" Books asked.

"Maybe if it sneezed hard enough, it'd go flying into the air, land on the *Saberfist*, and the marines could hack it to pieces with their swords."

Books threw Amaranthe an exasperated look. "Is it necessary to have these louts present during planning?"

"This mantle cavity," she said, trying to imagine Books's scenario, "is up under all the tentacles? I can't imagine anyone being able to get close without getting killed."

"We could send in someone expendable," Books said, eyeing Maldynado.

"Oh, no," Maldynado said. "When I get my statue, I don't want it to be an image of me going up a squid's butt."

"All right, gentlemen." Amaranthe lifted her hands, struggling not to snap at them for being silly. It must be the lack of sleep stealing some of her patience. "We'll go down with the keg and harpoons. With luck, the marines will figure out a way to kill the kraken through attrition, and we won't need to implement any of this."

"When have we ever had that kind of luck?" Books asked.

"I don't remember any," Amaranthe said, "but we ought to be due, eh?"

The men traded skeptical looks. She forced a smile. Someone had to be optimistic after all.

Basilard waited with a rag pressed to the back of his shoulder, watching as Sicarius shoved equipment against the hatch. Soon everything that could be moved, or torn free, blocked the only entrance. Like the pipe in the lock wheel, it did not seem enough against wizards, but maybe they wouldn't want to risk destroying their own engine room.

Basilard dropped his hands so he could sign, *What now?*

"Back up plan," Sicarius said over the grinding and chugging of the engine. "If we can't steer to the surface, we may be able to float there."

Float? Basilard stared at him. He could not imagine this sprawling maze of tunnels and chambers moving at all, much less bobbing about at the surface of the lake.

"The air you're breathing would typically make us buoyant," Sicarius said, "so this craft must have ballast tanks."

Basilard occasionally found Books too verbose for his tastes, but he wouldn't have minded more of an explanation just then. Sicarius turned his back to study symbols on panels—writing presumably, but not in Mangdorian or Turgonian, the only two languages Basilard could read.

He walked about, in part to see if he could find some way to help and in part to distract himself from the metal ball grinding against his shoulder blade.

He found a storage locker holding a pair of flintlock muskets that appeared only a model or two up from the old matchlocks. More weapons that would prove useless against practitioners who could generate shields. There were a couple of axes, too, and he suspected this was a supply the engineer and his mate were supposed to use to defend their station.

Which raised a question: where *was* the engineer?

Had he fled the room at the sound of the alarm? It still throbbed in the corridors outside, along with a few bangs and scrapes. The practitioners up to something, no doubt.

Basilard took one of the axes—they had a satisfying heft, and he imagined smashing some of the machinery with it. If Sicarius could not find these ballast tanks, perhaps they could convince the structure to rise to the surface by destroying the engines. At the least, they could make sure this vessel never navigated into imperial waters again to harass its citizens.

That thought made him freeze mid-step. When had he come to care about the empire and its citizens? This place had done little enough for him, and the old emperor had been responsible for the ruthless assassination of Mangdoria's rulers.

But Amaranthe, Maldynado, and Books were Turgonians and they were the first friends—the first family—he had been allowed to have in years. He wished he could see his daughter again someday, but, coward that he was, he feared her reaction. She would see his scars, know the violence he had been involved in, and would condemn him. She had to. That was his people's way. It pained him to think that he might have more in common with these warmongering Turgonians these days than his own kin.

He flexed his fingers around the axe haft, bringing his attention back to the moment. This was no time for daydreaming. He prowled around the flywheel to consider an angle of attack and almost tripped over two bodies in Turgonian army fatigues. Their throats were slashed. Basilard glanced at Sicarius. He supposed it had been a matter of defense, but if they were alive, they might have been coerced into helping with the engines. Basilard shrugged and stepped past them.

A glint of light near the ceiling caught his eye. A small, transparent cylinder floated in the air beneath a grate—no, a vent. It was filled with something yellow. The same stuff that had incapacitated him in the stadium?

Basilard crept closer. It hung in the air for another moment, then dropped, as if the invisible hand holding it let go.

He dove for it, hitting the deck chest first. A fresh wave

of pain erupted from his shoulder, but he flung his arm out and caught the vial before it smashed to the floor. He opened his fist, worried he might have cracked the glass. It remained intact but now what was he supposed to do with it? For all he knew, the practitioner who had levitated it in could snap the glass with his mind.

"What is it?" Sicarius asked.

Basilard showed him the vial, then pointed at the furnace. *Should we burn it?*

"That'll release the fumes, and the furnace isn't airtight."

Sicarius found a flat sheet of metal, then fished in the toolbox again and pulled out a screwdriver. He held a hand out for the vial. When Basilard gave it to him, Sicarius slid it back into the duct from whence it had come and screwed the metal sheet across the vent to block it.

They'll try again, Basilard signed.

"Yes. Continue to stand watch while I read."

You're welcome, Basilard signed.

"What?"

For saving you—both of us—from a trip back to the laboratory tables.

"At this juncture, it's more likely they'd kill us." Sicarius bent his head over a manual he had found.

Basilard remembered how he had not thought of him as one of the people he considered friends or family. No mistake there.

You're an ass, you know that? he signed, sure Sicarius would not see with his head bent over the book. *I can't believe I'm planning on not killing you when you are so deserving of being killed.*

Basilard scowled at himself. That didn't even make sense. Before he could stalk away in disgust, Sicarius spoke.

"What changed your mind?"

Basilard froze. Er. He lifted his hands, but hesitated. Trying to explain his emotions would be futile. Sicarius had saved his life in the corridor, and possibly on the laboratory table as well, but Basilard did not want to admit to any feelings of gratitude, not to someone who would brush them aside. He signed, *Because Amaranthe would never forgive me if I was successful.*

"Huh."

With that, Sicarius went back to reading. Basilard sighed and found a spot where he could watch the duct and the door. He wished Amaranthe were there with them. If nothing else, she would have convinced Sicarius to find clothes by now.

CHAPTER 16

There was water in Amaranthe's boot. With every step, her toes sloshed about in it. At least she could *take* steps. The size and heft of the suit on dry land had worried her, but the air inside her pack and helmet made her surprisingly light as she walked—*sloshed*—down the lake's steep slope. Indeed, the suits required weights to keep one from floating to the surface.

Maldynado, Books, and Akstyr strode at her side. Well, it wasn't "striding" exactly. Between the swords belted at their waists and the harpoon launchers in their arms, they were not the most agile creatures moving about in the lake. Books carried his keg instead of a launcher, but that was just as awkward, and he had already stumbled twice. Each time somebody slipped, Amaranthe's heart jumped into her throat. If anybody cut themselves on the harpoon tips, the poison would kill them as quickly as it would kill a kraken—much *more* quickly in fact.

The helmets made it difficult to speak to each other—though sometimes a muffled curse reached her ears as someone slipped on the seaweed-slick lake bottom—but they were managing with Basilard's hand signs.

When they reached the cliff, Amaranthe crept to the edge. A dark expanse yawned below. She had little feel for how far the viewer had dropped, but no hint of the orange glow she remembered seeped up from below. Since these suits were self-contained, there was no tube connecting them to the surface, and the idea of stepping off and falling a hundred feet or more made her hesitate.

Four hundred feet, Books signed.

To the bottom of the lake? Amaranthe asked.

It's a thousand at its deepest, but this first ledge has been measured as a three- to four-hundred-foot drop, depending on where you step down. He tilted his head. *We'll be fine, but we should go slowly to acclimate our bodies to the pressure change.*

I was more worried about coming back up, Amaranthe signed.

Just remove the weights when it's time, and you'll float up.

If there wasn't a kraken waiting in the middle to eat her.

Amaranthe took a deep breath and stepped off the ledge. She kept her gloved fingers near the cliff, using the rough stone to slow her descent.

Time trickled past, measured in the soft inhalations that echoed in her ears. Fresh air whispered into the helmet, brushing her cheek, while her used air escaped through an exhaust vent, creating tiny bubbles that floated away. Her ears popped, and pressure built in her sinuses. Had this been a trip for mere fun or adventure, she would have turned back.

An orange glow grew visible below, and she exhaled in relief. They were getting close.

She touched down in a bed of silt, stirring a cloud of fine dust. The strange, two-story fortress waited some twenty-five meters away. Translucent fish still swam about the perimeter, but Amaranthe did not see the kraken. With luck, it and the crew of the vessel had turned their focus toward the *Saberfist.*

Something ticked against the back of her helmet. Maldynado. He pointed overhead.

She tensed, expecting the kraken, and flexed her finger on the trigger of the harpoon launcher. No tentacles waved in the distance though; Maldynado was pointing to divers descending. Six of them. Two carried waterproof lanterns and wore swords. Two others bore weapons she could not name—they had the appearance of arm-sized cannons, but black powder would be useless down here. The final two carried harpoon launchers.

Did they believe us and come expecting trouble? Amaranthe signed. The nearby illumination provided enough light for the hand gestures.

They're marines, Maldynado responded. *I bet that's their typical underwater exploration gear.*

She snorted, fogging her faceplate with the breath. Probably true.

Akstyr came up between them and pointed at a school of the guardian fish. Amaranthe grimaced, remembering how one had charred some sea critter into a blackened husk. She hoped they lacked the firepower to harm full-grown humans.

Let's try to find a door, she signed.

Little seaweed grew this far down, so their boots stirred sand and silt as they advanced. Amaranthe kept an eye toward the ground, thinking that those fish would blend in against the beige surface.

Even prepared, it caught her by surprise when one swooped up from the sand right before her. Golden scales shimmered, and an inner light pulsed, building toward a discharge.

Figuring the poison-smeared harpoon would be overkill, Amaranthe slid her sword free and slashed at the fish. The water drag slowed her swipe, and the foot-long creature flitted aside easily.

Maldynado lunged, his rapier leading. Poking was faster in the water than swinging, but the agile fish still slithered away, undamaged. Its tail fins fluttered, and it swam back a few feet before facing them again. It started pulsing again, more rapidly now.

Amaranthe pushed off the bottom, sword raised again. She tried to be subtle, to hold the weapon back so the fish would not see the attack coming, but it moved again. Or started to—it froze in the middle of a fin flap.

Quick to take advantage, Amaranthe skewered it. The fish's inner light winked out.

You're welcome, Akstyr signed.

She removed the creature from her sword and gave him a salute. *You're turning into a useful young man.*

I know. I should get more respect. Akstyr glowered, not at her but at Maldynado.

It's hard to respect someone who can't grow a decent mustache, Maldynado signed.

Akstyr pointed at Amaranthe and propped his fists on his hips.

True, Maldynado signed, *hers hasn't come in yet either.*

I imagine you'll stop trying to set me up with men when it does. Amaranthe continued forward. She left her sword out, but she hoped no more trouble hid on the lake floor. She would hate to admit to Sicarius a fish had gotten the best of her.

The thought of him sent a twinge of anxiety through her. She had missed him more than made sense these last couple of days. It was not as if he were some cheery, warm presence in her life. Certainly the group had survived a few adventures without him, proof that, for all his skills, he was not some nucleus they could not do without. Professionally, she knew they could go on without him, but personally... Her heart cringed at the idea of infiltrating this structure, only to learn they were too late.

They neared one of the tunnels of the structure, and she pushed stray thoughts from her mind. "Focus," she told herself.

They had no trouble creeping up to the hull of the fortress, and Amaranthe worried that things were going too easily. She sidled over to a porthole, pushed off the ground, and rested a hand on the metal, intending to peer in.

Energy surged up her arm, thrusting her back even as an electric jolt surged through her body. Spasms wracked her muscles, she couldn't breathe, and she swore her heart stopped. Panic flashed through her.

The convulsions ended as abruptly as they began, and her heart started beating again. She recovered with a gasp, the experience leaving her shaken.

"Too easy?" she muttered. "I take it back."

A hand gripped her shoulder. She realized she had fallen back to the lake floor—and that she was clutching her chest as if to keep her heart from bursting out of it. She lowered her arm and nodded to Maldynado before he could ask after her health. Or perhaps after her sanity for presuming to touch something here.

I sense energy about the exterior, Akstyr signed.

Now he told her.

Amaranthe grabbed a rusty tin can sunken into the silt and tossed it against the hull. Lightning crackled about it as it bounced off.

"Probably should have done that first," she muttered, picking up the can and tossing it again, this time at the porthole.

It clunked off without any sparks of electricity. She grabbed it and pushed off the bottom again. With it in her hand this time, she prodded the clear window material—she was hesitant to think of it as glass, since it might be some magical creation. No lightning coursed through her body, so she dropped the can and rested her hands against the surface, kicking lightly to stay in place.

An empty, dimly lit corridor stretched in either direction. She waited for a moment, in case a crew member walked through or something otherwise enlightening happened. It didn't. She dropped back to the lake floor.

Maldynado had moved a few meters away and was looking around a bend. He waved and signed, *There's a hatch over here. Maybe we can get in.*

Without getting electrocuted? Amaranthe signed.

Maybe...not.

I'll look at it, Akstyr signed. Still carrying his keg, Books trundled after him.

Amaranthe popped back up for another look into the porthole. A naked woman darted into a nearby intersection, and her hopes rose. Was that one of the kidnapped athletes? Surely the practitioners wouldn't be running around nude.

She tried to press her cheek to the porthole for a better view, but her helmet clunked against it. The woman must have heard the sound, for she crept closer. She came forward in a slow, wary crouch. Snarls and knots tangled her hair, and her wide, wild eyes darted from side to side. Fresh scars marred her abdomen.

Amaranthe tapped on the glass.

The woman spotted her, and leaped back, eyes wide. She sprinted down the corridor and disappeared around the intersection.

Emperor's bunions, that woman better not set off an alarm.

Maldynado tapped Amaranthe on the shoulder. He was treading water beside her and grinning. *You do look like a scary monster in that helmet.*

Even without a mustache?

Oh, yes. Maldynado's grin widened.

A tapping noise came from inside, and Amaranthe spun back toward the porthole. The woman had returned. She crouched in the corridor like a rabbit poised to flee. Narrow eyes regarded Amaranthe with suspicion, but hope, too.

"We're here to help," Amaranthe said, exaggerating her words in hopes the woman could read her lips through the face plate. "Can you let us in?" She pointed in the direction of the hatch.

The woman sprinted away, not toward the hatch but back toward the intersection, and disappeared around the corner.

Amaranthe sighed and clunked her head against the porthole.

Maldynado patted her back. *They're athletes. They don't have to be bright to win the races, just fast.*

Several moments passed, and Amaranthe was about to give up and check other portholes when the woman jogged back into view with a crowbar in her hands. She nodded curtly and continued past, heading toward the hatch.

Amaranthe pushed away from the porthole and swam in the same direction. When she rounded the bend, she found Akstyr sprawled on his back in the sand, a dazed expression on his face.

Problem with that energy you sensed? she signed.

He struggled to sit up. *I got a little close.*

Amaranthe helped him to his feet. The five-foot-wide square hatch in the hull had a wheel-style door opener, so it seemed one could get in if the defenses weren't up. She wondered if the woman would be able to bypass them. Her snarled dark hair and bronze skin had appeared Turgonian, so she probably knew nothing about the Science.

Scrapes and clunks came from the other side of the hatch.

If she opens it, Maldynado signed, *won't water flood in?*

Amaranthe shrugged. *I don't know. It's my first underwater-fortress infiltration.*

A shadow passed overhead. Dread sprang into Amaranthe's limbs, and she knew they were in trouble before she looked up.

The kraken glided over the structure, its tentacles streaming out behind it. The creature had to be more than seventy-five feet long from arrow-shaped head to tentacle tips. An eye the size of one of the dive helmets rotated until it fixed upon them.

Something that might have been a string of curses came from Maldynado. Amaranthe almost grabbed the wheel on the hatch in a vain hope the woman had turned off the defenses, but she did not need more lightning knocking her on her backside.

The kraken's great mantle flexed, and its tentacles flared outward, allowing it to alter course toward them.

Wait by the hatch, Amaranthe signed, then pushed off the lake floor before the men could object.

302   ☙ Lindsay Buroker ☙

Books shouted something. The helmets and the water made it indistinguishable, so it was doubtlessly her imagination that she heard the word "prudent."

Amaranthe kicked and paddled one-armed—holding the harpoon launcher made her strokes awkward—to the porthole, then treaded to maintain a position in front of it. She waved her arm, trying to draw the kraken's attention. She need not have made the effort. The beast had already spotted her. Hungry black eyes bored into her soul, as if they might freeze her by the might of their stare alone. The tentacles spread out, suction cups lining the dark purple flesh, and two long limbs stretched toward her.

On the floor below, Maldynado and Akstyr raised their harpoons. Though Amaranthe knew they would not like it, she lifted a hand, telling them to wait. She wanted to see if her idea worked first. If not...they could fire everything they had into those tentacles. Each one was as thick as Maldynado's chest and could wrap her in a grip she could never escape.

One darted toward her. Amaranthe kicked out, pushing off the porthole glass, angling down toward her men.

The tentacle clipped the fortress wall. Lightning streaked up the purple flesh, and sparks danced over the suction cups.

A high-pitched squeal assaulted Amaranthe's ears. The tentacle jerked away. Black ink clouded the water, and the kraken retreated.

Two harpoons flew from below. With the kraken already swimming away at top speed, Amaranthe did not expect much, but one blade did clip a tentacle. It was hard to tell if the poison had any effect on the creature.

She landed on the lake floor beside the men. *Got that hatch open yet?*

We were busy trying to protect you. Maldynado frowned at her.

Yes, Books added. *Didn't we discuss how you were going to partake only in prudent actions going forward?*

Is there a prudent way to fight a giant squid? Amaranthe signed.

Hide behind someone tastier looking than you? Akstyr suggested.

Before they could discuss it further, a sucking noise sounded—a seal being broken. The hatch swung outward.

Amaranthe started for it, but Maldynado bumped her aside with his hip, gave her a pointed look, and went first. Feeling protective, was he?

She followed right after, careful not to touch the outer frame of the hatchway, lest it be electrified as well. They entered a tiny chamber full of water. Another hatch, identical to the first, waited on the inside.

Maldynado reached for the wheel-shaped opening mechanism, stopped with his hands inches away, drew back and poked it with his sword. No sparks or branches of lightning ran up the blade.

Metal conducts electricity, you twit, Books signed. *If the door had been charged, that wouldn't have helped.*

Maldynado sheathed his rapier and managed to elbow Books in the process. He tried the wheel, but it did not move.

Maybe we have to close the outside door first. Books eyed the walls. *There must be a way to make the water drain out before one enters the main structure.*

Akstyr pulled the outer hatch shut. The light from outside disappeared, and blackness dropped over them.

"Well, that's lovely," Amaranthe said.

Since the helmets and the water precluded talking, she had to imagine the sarcastic comments from the others. It was a strange sensation, being in the dark with water swirling about her. Inside the helmet, her breaths echoed in her ears. Somewhere in the distance, a throbbing *woo-wah* noise pulsed.

A clunk sounded, reverberating from within a nearby wall. Water tinkled, as if running down a drainpipe, but nothing happened quickly. When she reached up, Amaranthe found only a two-inch-high pocket of air at the top of the chamber.

When the water lowered to chest level, she removed her helmet, figuring it would be better to talk to the naked girl looking like a human being, not some mad tinkerer's person-shaped walking machine.

With the helmet off, the *woo-wah* sound rang more loudly in her ears. An alarm? And if so, was it for her team, or for the marine ship overhead? The latter she hoped, but there could be a squad of guards waiting with rifles on the other side of the hatch, especially given how long it was taking the chamber to drain.

Water splashed behind her—someone else removing his helmet.

"Are we shooting people?" Maldynado asked, and Amaranthe imagined him hefting the harpoon launcher.

"We should save the poisoned harpoons for the kraken," she said. "We don't have many, and I suspect we'll have to deal with it before this is over."

"Are we *stabbing* people then?" Maldynado asked. "Or is this like with soldiers and enforcers where it'd be bad for our image to kill them?"

Amaranthe winced at the idea that it was only their image that kept her from killing people, but she knew what he meant. "I doubt we'll run into any enforcers down here, and we can assume any soldiers have gone rogue." She thought of the message these people had sent to the enforcers, claiming they would be turning a dead Sicarius in for reward, and she had little trouble hardening herself toward them. "We don't need to go out of the way to butcher anyone, but...we're going to be outnumbered. Don't let mercy get you into trouble."

"Understood," Books said quietly.

When the water level dropped to her knees, Amaranthe figured it was low enough. "Time to go," she said, though her fastidious streak made her wince at the idea of water gushing into the corridor, leaving the enemy's floor in need of a mopping.

Maldynado grunted a few times. "The wheel's not budging. How do we get out?"

"Never overlook the obvious." Amaranthe knocked.

He snorted, but the hatch creaked open. A foot of water flowed into the corridor. Though dim, the lighting was bright after the darkness of the chamber, and Amaranthe squinted. After a few blinks, the nude woman came into focus. She stood in the corridor, ignoring the water dampening her bare feet. She alternated glancing both ways down the passage and plying Amaranthe with questioning looks. One of the men stirred, and the woman jumped away, pressing her back to the wall.

Lowering her harpoon launcher, Amaranthe stepped into the corridor and raised a friendly hand. "We're here to help."

The men crowded out behind her. Maldynado and Books had the maturity not to gape openly at the naked woman—even in her frazzled state, she had a tall, athletic form with curves enough to interest any man—but Akstyr was another matter. Amaranthe elbowed him, and he closed his mouth.

"I'm Amaranthe," she told the girl. "I assume you're one of the kidnapped athletes?" The alarm going off made her want to grab the woman by the arm and demand to be taken to the others immediately, but they would get farther with a cooperative guide.

"Yes, I'm Merva."

"A pleasure to meet you, ma'am." Maldynado managed a graceful warrior-caste bow even in the confining corridor, with the bulky helmet beneath his arm. "Are you perhaps—"

"Able to show us where the other prisoners are?" Amaranthe asked, giving Maldynado a please-wait-to-seduce-her-until-later look.

"And can you let us know," Books added, "if that's an alarm? Are they trying to find you?"

"I—probably." Merva touched her mouth with her fingers. "I think they're after those two men though."

Amaranthe stood straighter, eyes riveted on the woman. "A blond man and a scarred one?"

Merva shrugged without dropping her hand. "I'm not sure. I've been..." She touched her head with her other hand. "I don't remember anything since... Two men grabbed me in my bunk at the athletes' barracks and thrust a vial under my nose. After that... I don't know how long I've slept. I woke up a little while ago, like this. Someone had cut straps holding me to a table."

Someone? That sounded too beneficent for Sicarius, but Basilard perhaps? She wanted to pump the girl for answers, but they had best find someplace less open for planning the next step.

Merva leaned past her and pointed into the staging chamber. "Can I get out that way? We're underwater, right? Are we in the ocean?"

"Nah," Akstyr said. "We're just—"

"We can help you escape," Amaranthe said, cutting Akstyr off before he could reveal how close to the city they were. She did not want the girl swimming out there, only to drown trying to reach the surface. "But let's get all the prisoners out first. Have you seen others since you woke up?"

Merva tore her gaze from the chamber. "We started out together, several of us, but then we ran into those soldiers, and one of them fired at us. Everyone scattered, and—"

A man in military fatigues jogged around the corner and skidded to a halt. His eyebrows flew up when he spotted the diving suits. "Intruders!" he shouted and grabbed for a pistol, but he seemed to realize he was outnumbered. Instead of shooting, he whirled for the cover of the corner.

Grimly, Amaranthe fired her harpoon launcher. They couldn't let him run off and gather reinforcements.

The projectile zipped down the corridor and sliced into the man's shoulder before he disappeared around the corner. He stumbled and landed belly-first on the deck. His pistol flew free and clanged against the bulkhead, going off with an echoing bang.

Amaranthe winced at the noise.

Maldynado ran past her and checked the corridors leading from the intersection. "No one else. Yet."

The guard tried to crawl away. Maldynado stepped on his arm to pin him. The man scrabbled for a knife at his belt, but Maldynado took it from him easily.

"Want me to...?" He made a throat-slashing motion.

Amaranthe sighed. The poison should kill the man in a couple of minutes, but she had no idea if that would be a more merciful end than a dagger to the throat.

The man twisted his neck to look at her. Fear haunted his eyes.

"Sorry," Amaranthe said quietly.

A part of her was tempted to ask Akstyr if he could do anything to keep the man from dying, but there was no time. Someone would come to investigate that shot.

"Leave him," Amaranthe told Maldynado. "After that entrance, I'm sure the whole vessel knows we're here."

She waved for Merva to come forward. The younger woman gave her the same wary look Amaranthe had seen so many people use on Sicarius. Having such an expression directed at her made her uncomfortable. I'm not a monster, she wanted to say. I'm just trying to do the right thing....

"Can you take us to the navigation area?" she said instead. Finding the captain—or whoever was in charge of this place—would be better than wandering around randomly. If they found someone important, perhaps they could use him or her as a hostage and avoid more bloodshed.

"I think it's on the second floor," Merva whispered.

They hid the harpoon launchers in the transition chamber, drew their swords, and headed away from the fallen guard. They passed numerous closed hatches and ducked under and around knots of pipes. Another four-way intersection came into view ahead of them, and, beyond it, a ladder rose to a second level. Voices drifted from the corridor to the left of the intersection. Agitated voices.

308   Lindsay Buroker ↞

Amaranthe lifted a hand for silence and passed Merva. As if by magic, the clomps of her men's heavy boots softened to imperceptible footfalls. She glanced back, intending to sign an order for someone to watch their hindquarters, but Books was already doing it. He stalked backwards, his sword at the ready.

At the intersection, Amaranthe poked an eye around the corner. She almost yanked her head right back. Not ten feet away, six white-jacketed men and women stood before a closed hatch marking the end of the corridor. Only the fact that all their heads were turned away from the intersection kept her there for a longer look.

Their hair ranged from blond to black, straight to wiry and tightly curled. Representatives from several nations and, Amaranthe feared, practitioners as well.

They were gesticulating and talking, more than one at a time with frequent, emphatic points at the hatch. Were her men inside? Or other escaped prisoners?

Symbols were etched in a plate above the doorway. Amaranthe waved for Books to take her spot and decipher the language.

Engine room, he signed after a peek.

Amaranthe fingered the hilt of her sword, but she did not want to attack practitioners. They would have far more tricks than Turgonian guards. Besides, she did not know if what lay behind the hatch was something that should concern her or not.

Let's sneak past, Amaranthe signed, then put a finger to her lips and pointed to the ladder for Merva's sake.

She waited until all of the practitioners' heads were turned and eased through the intersection, figuring sudden movement would be more likely to draw someone's eye.

A clang sounded down the corridor behind Books. Guards searching the vessel? The practitioners were too engrossed in their argument to notice.

Amaranthe waved for Maldynado and the others to follow,

one at a time. A bead of moisture slithered down her ribcage. More than nerves made her sweat; now that they had left the icy water, the suit kept her far warmer than she needed.

Akstyr slipped across without incident. Good.

Out of habit, Amaranthe lifted a finger to her mouth to nibble on a nail, but the gloves stopped her. Books crossed, and Merva stepped into the intersection. Amaranthe curled her fingers into a fist. It was working. Everyone would—

A thunderous boom erupted, and the corridor heaved.

Amaranthe stumbled back and threw an arm out, trying to keep herself from falling, but the smooth walls offered no hand holds, and the suit affected her balance. She hit the floor, her helmet flying from her fingers. It clanked down the corridor, bouncing as it went, and she cursed under her breath.

Quakes rattled the fortress. Half of her team had fallen to the floor as well, making her glad for her decision to leave the harpoon launchers behind; someone might have cut himself on a poisoned blade.

Curses in foreign languages—*multiple* foreign languages— spilled from the adjoining corridor.

Amaranthe rolled onto her knees and grabbed her helmet. She waved and pointed toward the ladder, silently urging her team to hurry. She hoped the commotion had kept the practitioners from hearing them.

Merva and the men filed up the ladder. Amaranthe went last, her oversized boots making the ascent awkward.

Clomps sounded in the corridor she was leaving. The practitioners? No, Turgonian words punctuated the footfalls. Those were guards coming.

Ignoring the awkward boots, Amaranthe flew up the last few rungs. She rolled into the corridor above just as a man below demanded, "Have you seen the intruders?"

Her first ludicrous thought was that he was talking to her, but the voice was not that close. The guards had to be at the intersection. She was tempted to stick around to listen to the conversation, and see if she could find out what was going on in the engine room, but those men would soon move on with their hunt.

At the top of the ladder, another hatch-filled metal corridor stretched.

"Which way to navigation?" Amaranthe whispered.

Merva spread her hands, palms up.

"That way." Maldynado pointed down one corridor. "Or that way." He pointed the other direction.

"Twit," Books said.

Amaranthe chose a direction at random. The passage angled to the left, and a well-lit chamber opened up at the end. Something shimmered in the air before it. Some sort of magical hatch?

Books pointed to a plaque above the doorway. "Navigation."

Amaranthe slowed as they approached. She did not see anyone inside yet, but such an important station should be manned.

Another boom rocked the fortress, though not as fiercely as the first, and she remained upright this time.

What is that? she signed to Books. *Some kind of attack from the marine ship?*

Charges dropped in a waterproof container? he suggested.

Amaranthe inched closer to the chamber. The far wall held an eight-foot-wide oblong porthole above a console filled with levers, gauges, and a head-sized illuminated dome. Water pressed against the porthole, and an orange glow from the lights outside bathed the silt and rock of the lake floor. A school of the translucent guard fish flitted past.

One man walked into view from the side, and a second rose out of a high-backed chair that had hidden him from sight. They leaned over the controls and argued in their own language. One pointed at the porthole. Muskets leaned against the console between them.

Amaranthe used their distraction to inch closer, though she

was careful not to touch the shimmering field. Energy crackled in the air and nipped at her cheeks.

On a side wall, an open weapons locker held cutlasses and the empty musket slots. A row of yellow vials hung in a small rack. If those contained the same concoction that had rendered so many people unconscious, they might prove useful.

The voices of the two men grew more agitated. Outside the porthole, a metallic box floated into view. It couldn't be heavy since it drifted down instead of plummeting. Amaranthe squinted, trying to decipher a black stamp on the box. An oil can over crossed swords, the symbol representing the army's engineering division.

Books grabbed her arm and tried to pull her further back into the corridor, but too many others occupied the space. Before they could organize a retreat, the metallic box exploded with a blinding flash.

The force hurled her backward. Someone caught her, but they tumbled to the deck in a tangle of limbs anyway.

In the chamber, the navigators also toppled, and their muskets clattered to the floor. One man lunged to his feet and pointed at the porthole, curses flowing from his lips. At least, Amaranthe assumed they were curses. Nobody said happy things in that tone of voice.

She spotted the reason for their ire: a hairline crack streaked across the porthole glass.

Amaranthe climbed off of Books, and he touched her arm, nodding for them to retreat to speak. The rest of the group followed.

"You know what they're saying?" she whispered when they had backed to the ladder. Voices still floated up from below, but she could not tell if any belonged to the guards searching for them.

"They're cursing the Turgonian devils outside and the blond devil inside," Books whispered.

Blond. That *had* to be Sicarius.

"They want to move this vessel," Books went on, "but he's killed the engineers and barricaded himself in the engine room."

Those *were* her men inside, giving those practitioners trouble. But if they were trapped, they needed her help. Amaranthe rubbed sweat from her brow and ignored an urge to claw off the stifling suit. They might need to flee outside again.

"All right," Amaranthe said, "here's the plan: you and Akstyr take Merva and find the rest of the athletes. Maldynado and I will get inside navigation and deal with those two." And maybe the practitioners in front of the engine room, too, if she could pilfer a couple of those vials.

Books lifted a finger, as if he meant to object—or perhaps warn her of the lack of prudence in her scheme—but shouts came from the level below, and he dropped his hand. "Very well."

"One more question," Amaranthe said. "I know these helmets are waterproof. Are they air-proof, too? If one chose to wear them in here?"

Books's brow crinkled. "I imagine they'd have to be. So long as you don't run out of the air in your dedicated supply, you should be fine." He nodded to the tank on her back.

"Thanks." Amaranthe waved for him to take off with the others. "Be careful."

Books, Akstyr, and Merva left, leaving Amaranthe and Maldynado alone to face the practitioners. She took a deep breath and pointed toward the navigation room. "I'm going to distract those two while you grab a couple of the yellow vials in the weapons locker, got it?"

"Got it, boss."

Amaranthe returned to the barrier and knocked on the wall. The two men, who had been arguing over the crack, whirled and gaped. She spoke quickly, wanting to head off any lunges for weapons—or magical attacks.

"Greetings. It looks like you gentlemen could use some help. Do you speak Turgonian?"

"Help!" one man yelled. He wore spectacles that rested so low on his nose that Amaranthe could not imagine them offering anything more than an enhanced view of his own pores.

"Was that a question," Amaranthe asked, "or a call for assistance?"

"Are you with *them*?" He stabbed a finger toward the ceiling with such vigor that his spectacles fell the rest of the way off his nose. He caught them with a growl and thrust the frames back over his ears.

The second man, a rangy fellow with pale hair combed over a balding pate, watched the exchange in silence. Long, bony fingers flexed at his side, as if he might be thinking of hurling some spell at Amaranthe.

"With the marines?" she asked, her eyes wide. "No, they want us dead. I'm Amaranthe Lokdon. I run The Emperor's Edge mercenary outfit. Haven't you heard of us?"

The two men exchanged blank looks. That was fine. As long as they weren't thinking of attacking her.

"I assumed you had," Amaranthe said, "because you kidnapped two of my men."

"Oh," Spectacles growled. "Sicarius. You run with his group?"

"He runs with *my* group." Amaranthe turned to Maldynado. "I make all the decisions and do all the planning. Why is nobody ever aware of that?" She hoped her whining made her sound innocuous, like someone who wasn't a threat, like someone who could be invited in to chat further....

"Because you're friendly and nice, and he's...someone who likes to kill people who are friendly and nice?" Maldynado suggested.

"That must be it." Amaranthe faced the practitioners again, empty hands spread. "Gentlemen, it looks like you're in a dungeon with few prospects for escape. Am I correct in deducing that my men are making trouble in your engine room?"

"We're taking care of them," Spectacles said.

Another boom rattled the fortress. The men's wary eyes lifted toward the ceiling. If the marines kept dropping charges, one was bound to land on top of the vessel eventually.

"I could get them to walk out right now," Amaranthe said, "and you people could amble in, fix up those engines, and escape this lake before the marines get lucky."

"The kraken will handle their ship," Spectacles said. "Even now, it's attacking them. They will either sink or flee to the docks, wetting their trousers on the way."

"Uhm," Amaranthe said, "you speak Turgonian very well, but you don't seem to understand the warrior mentality of our people. The captain will be tickled at the idea of facing a kraken. A training exercise, if you will. If they thought the beast a severe threat, they'd be too busy facing it to drop charges over the side." That story sounded plausible, anyway. In truth, there were probably a couple of lowly privates up there, assigned the task of sending the explosives down in hopes that destroying the fortress would make the kraken lose interest in defending it. "Once they dispatch your little pet, they'll be able to focus all their attention on this vessel."

"We'll be fine on our own," Spectacles said. "We—"

The balding man stopped him with a raised hand, and Amaranthe wondered if he, despite being the quiet one, might be in charge. "What are you proposing, woman?"

"Amaranthe," she said, figuring they'd be more likely to see her as an ally if they were on a first name basis. "May we come in to discuss this? Some of your guards have been looking for us, and we'd rather not get shot in the back while we're talking to you."

The men frowned at her. Despite her attempt at wide-eyed innocence, they seemed to think she might be up to something.

Annoying when the villains had a modicum of intelligence.

Spectacles murmured a few words to his boss in their language. Amaranthe hoped it was something like, "They're simple fighters and not a threat to our magical greatness."

"Drop your weapons and kick them back into the tunnel," the leader finally said.

"Kick?" Maldynado said. "One doesn't *kick* a Teldark and Brook blade."

"Ssh." Amaranthe tossed her short sword onto the floor behind them.

Maldynado gently laid his rapier next to her weapon.

Spectacles walked to the wall to the left of his side of the barrier where a box emitting a soft green glow perched at face level. He lowered his spectacles and leaned forward to stare into it. The barrier shimmered and winked out.

Amaranthe waited for the man to step back and gesture for them to enter. She eased inside, hands open and spread. Maldynado did the same, but he stepped to her side, a couple of feet closer to the vials in the weapons locker.

"Stay there," the leader said. "What's your proposal?"

"I'll get my men to leave peacefully," Amaranthe said, "and you let us walk, or swim, out of here unmolested."

"Sicarius is worth a million ranmyas."

"Yes, and if you wanted that, you should have kept him unconscious." She assumed that was how they had captured him in the first place, no doubt thanks to her sending him off to snoop. Someone must have caught him with a whiff from one of those vials.

"Litya woke him up," Spectacles said. "We told her not to. She paid for it, too. Your *men* have killed many of our guards and some of our practitioners. Letting them walk away unpunished isn't acceptable."

"I see. Are you two in charge?" Amaranthe asked, wondering if she was negotiating with someone who had the power to do anything.

"We're on the committee."

"Committee? As in shared powers? And votes?"

"We're not savages like you Turgonians," Spectacles said. "We run a democracy here."

"Well." Amaranthe clasped her hands and strolled to the porthole. Their gazes followed her, leaving Maldynado unobserved. "I'm not going to talk Sicarius into walking out if your intent is to capture—or shoot—him," she said.

"Suppose we take you prisoner and use your life to barter with the assassin?" Spectacles mused.

"That'd be a gamble on your part." Amaranthe leaned her back against the console, ostensibly so she could chat face-to-face with both men, but she was more interested in checking on Maldynado's progress.

He was leaning on one arm that happened to rest on the wall near the weapons rack, but his quick headshake said he had not yet palmed the vials.

"The problem for you, gentlemen," Amaranthe went on, "is that Sicarius doesn't care enough about anyone in the group—about anyone at all—to risk himself on their behalf. He's like that kraken out there."

She twisted and leaned toward the porthole, gazing up as if she had spotted the beast. The men leaned forward, too, no doubt worrying their prize kraken was idling about instead of terrorizing the marines.

Amaranthe thought about signaling to Maldynado to sneak up on the men and bash them both on the backs of their heads, but practitioners seemed to be good at sensing bodily threats.

"Sicarius is pragmatic and practical and out for his own interests. He'll crush you if you inconvenience him." She faced the men again and, in her peripheral vision, saw Maldynado nod once. She hoped it meant he had the vials, not that he agreed with her assessment of Sicarius. "Don't let greed lead you to disaster," Amaranthe urged the practitioners. "Money isn't what brought you here in the first place, is it?" In truth, she had no idea, but it sounded like a promising guess.

"Our research requires funds," Spectacles said. "Ultra modern mobile labs don't build themselves."

"Why do you need to be mobile?" she asked, figuring the more they chatted with her, the less likely they would be to hold a knife to her throat as part of a bargaining ploy.

The men's lips grew flat.

"Your research isn't sanctioned by your government?" Amaranthe asked, her tone not one of accusation. No, she gave them her best brotherhood-of-folks-beleaguered-by-oppressive-government-policies smile.

"You could say that," Spectacles said. "Most of our funds won't come through until we deliver the babies, and that's a long-term project, obviously."

Babies? What *were* these people doing down here?

"A project that will be more difficult to complete without Litya," Spectacles added.

The quiet man whispered something in a string of vowel-rich syllables. A warning not to reveal so much? Whatever it was, both men scowled at her. Litya must have met the sharp side of one of Sicarius's daggers.

"Out of curiosity," Amaranthe said, pretending not to notice their flinty stares, "were you hired or told to come here by a group called Forge?"

The men exchanged sharp looks.

"We have Turgonian customers, but your people didn't fund our mission," Spectacles said.

That...wasn't quite what she had asked. That they recognized the organization told her much though.

"Forge is just a client, then?" Amaranthe asked.

Spectacles shrugged. "Who in Turgonia *couldn't* find a use for a child gifted enough to win at the Imperial Games or excel on the battlefield? That's the only way to join your archaic aristocracy, is it not?"

Amaranthe said nothing. Was *that* what the miners had been planning? If they combined funds to *buy* a son who could one day gain entrance into the warrior caste through merit, the parents would share the family honors: land, entitlements, access to the emperor. Though businesses had brought common citizens many opportunities, no amount of money could buy what the warrior caste received as a birthright.

Something clunked against the hull of the vessel. A flash of light appeared outside the porthole, and a massive boom coursed through the fortress.

Amaranthe grabbed the console and managed to stay upright, but Spectacles tumbled to the floor, cracking his head on the seat. A wailing reminiscent of an injured bird started up, creating a cacophony as it competed with the ongoing alarm. The rangy man gripped the console with both hands, and his eyes closed to slits as he concentrated on something.

Maldynado crept toward Spectacles. Amaranthe nodded, thinking this might be a chance to subdue these two.

From his hands and knees, Spectacles flung his fingers outward. An invisible force hurled Maldynado back, and he hit the wall with a resounding thump. His helmet dropped from his hands, hitting the floor with a clatter. He slid down the wall and onto his backside, then slumped into a stunned heap.

Amaranthe bit her lip. Maldynado looked like he would survive, but if his crash had cracked one of the vials, they might all end up unconscious.

"I'll thank you to keep your bodyguard by the door," Spectacles growled. He had his feet under him and was straightening his jacket.

"That wasn't necessary," Amaranthe said. "I told you we'd work with you if you release my men."

"That brutish behemoth was going to *work* my face into the floor."

"*Brutish?*" Maldynado had recovered enough to manage an indignant tone. "*Brutish?* I'm a child of the warrior caste, descended from generations of noble warriors and distinguished matrons of exquisite manners and taste. I'm no brute."

"I'm sure he was only coming to help you," Amaranthe told Spectacles.

"Er, yes." Maldynado staggered to his feet. "That's right."

"Stop blathering," the rangy man said. "The hull has been breached in the upper port wing. I've closed it off from the rest of the *Areyon*, but if we take on too much water, we'll never be able to leave the bottom of this Akahe-forsaken lake."

"It's time to accept your losses and escape while you can," Amaranthe said.

The two men argued with each other in their own tongue. Another explosion went off, this one too far from the porthole to view the flash, but Amaranthe felt its power in the tremors that rocked the vessel. The accompanying groans and creaks of the structure sounded ominous. How much damage was the fortress—no, *laboratory* was the better term—designed to take?

"We agree," Spectacles told Amaranthe. "You can have your two men, but we will keep the rest of the test subjects."

If you can find them, Amaranthe thought, but she kept her sneer inward and shrugged. "I'm only concerned about my people."

Spectacles strode to the barrier again. He leaned into the box, and the field winked out again. "You first," he said.

"Very well." Amaranthe lifted her helmet and fastened it as if it were a typical Turgonian thing to do. She caught Maldynado's eye and gave him a nod. He put his helmet on as well.

Spectacles watched with a frown. "What are you doing? We're not going outside to get to the engine room."

Amaranthe pointed at the ceiling. "With those marines dropping charges, I'm not taking any chances. What if one lands right on top of us?"

The men gave her exasperated looks. That was fine. So long as they didn't find her suspicious.

"Mind if we collect our weapons?" she asked before the group started down the corridor.

"Yes," Maldynado said. "It'd be unforgivable to leave my fine blade on that grungy floor."

"No weapons," Spectacles said. "Walk."

Though the two practitioners stood more than an arm's length away from her, Amaranthe felt a nudge of pressure against her back. The sensation sent an uneasy tingle down her spine, and she worried they could do much more than "nudge" her with their powers.

When they reached the ladder, Amaranthe waved for Maldynado to descend first. The helmets made it hard to see one's feet, and she had little trouble feigning a clumsy climb. At the bottom, she deliberately missed a rung and tumbled into Maldynado. He caught her and pressed a vial into her hand. Thank his ancestors for hiding a brain beneath all that arrogance.

She straightened before the practitioners reached the bottom. "Perhaps donning the helmets wasn't such a good idea after all."

"Nah," Maldynado said. "This way if you trip and hit your noggin, it'll be protected."

"Stop dawdling," Spectacles growled.

Amaranthe headed for the intersection. Low, excited voices came from around the corner. She imagined the foreigners saying, "We're almost in...."

She stopped to wait for the two practitioners to pass her, but Spectacles said, "You first," and applied another invisible nudge of force.

Unwilling to walk into a den of wizards unannounced, Amaranthe called out, "New allies coming around the corner. Don't shoot or incinerate us or do other unpleasant wizard-ish things, please."

That drew snorts from the men behind her. Arms spread, and the vial pressed to the underside of her hand with her thumb, she stepped around the corner.

Six faces stared at her. Six *practitioners'* faces, she reminded herself. Suddenly her plan with the vial seemed ridiculously simple and doomed to failure. As soon as she dropped it, they would figure it out and raise magical defenses.

"Good morning, all," Amaranthe said. "I heard you could use help getting a couple of pesky escaped prisoners out of there."

"Just talk to your men," Spectacles growled.

The practitioners parted to let her pass. The man closest to the door held some sort of baton that was spouting a stream of fire. It had burned three sides of an access panel into the hatch, leaving smoke drifting from perforated singe marks.

Amaranthe tried to see through one of the tiny holes, but the room appeared dark behind it. Or maybe something else blocked the door. If her men were barricaded inside, it would take time for them to come out and help if a fracas started. She had to assume she and Maldynado were on their own for this.

As she drew closer to the door, she wiggled the cork loose with her thumb. The gloves stole some of her dexterity, and she fumbled, almost dropping the vial.

Inside the stuffy helmet, a bead of sweat rolled down her nose. Too bad she had no way to wipe it.

The cork came free in her hand. Yellow smoke curled between her fingers, and she lowered her arm, swinging it to hide the evidence.

She pointed at the hatch. "Should I knock?"

"Stop him," someone blurted behind her, then switched to another language.

Cursed ancestors, they must have seen Maldynado opening his vial. Two men reached for him, and a woman stepped back, her eyes growing glazed.

Amaranthe threw the vial at her nose. It bopped her between the eyes, breaking her concentration. The two men had tried to grab Maldynado's arms, but he thrust them away. He *did* tower like a behemoth over these people. Too bad it wasn't going to be a solely physical confrontation. But if they could keep the practitioners busy until the smoke kicked in...

A man grabbed Amaranthe's wrist even as a prickle on the back of her neck alerted her to a magical attack from elsewhere. She kicked her captor's shin and twisted her arm, yanking it free from the man's grip. She jammed her knee into his groin and spun about, seeking the practitioner targeting her.

The man with the baton torch lunged at her. She ducked and whipped her arm up in a hard block. The baton flew from the man's grip, hit a wall, and spun into the fray. Someone screamed.

Nearby, a glassy-eyed male practitioner raised a hand toward Amaranthe. She lunged and launched a punch, twisting her hip to put her whole body into the maneuver. Her fist smashed into the man's nose with bone-crunching force. He hadn't made an attempt to block, and he went down like a brick. He wasn't the only one with slow reflexes.

The vials. They were working.

Relief welled and caught in her throat. No, not relief. Something was tightening her airway. Though the helmet protected her neck, a force pressed in from all sides, as if someone were strangling her.

Amaranthe stumbled back, fighting the urge to clutch at her throat. That would do nothing. She whirled about, searching for her attacker.

Six of the eight practitioners were sprawled on the deck. Maldynado had crumpled to his knees, his face contorted in a rictus of pain behind his mask.

The rangy navigator stood in the intersection, his focus on Maldynado. A gray-haired woman had a fist clenched as she stared at Amaranthe with fierce concentration. Neither appeared affected by the smoke that wafted from the vials.

Lightheadedness swept over Amaranthe. Lack of air scattered her thoughts, and desperation crept in. She wheezed, groping for a plan while her body cried out for oxygen.

She tried to stalk toward her attacker, to stop the assault, but she bounced off a barrier protecting the woman. Hadn't Akstyr always said practitioners could only concentrate on one thing at a time? That they couldn't attack and defend simultaneously? That was why Arbitan Losk had conjured up that deadly soul construct to watch his back. Maybe someone down here was working on protection tools—artifacts, that's what Sicarius called such things—and the woman had some physical object that could be destroyed.

Blackness crept into the edges of Amaranthe's vision as she squinted, searching for some sign of a tool on the woman's person. There. A blocky square jutting against the fabric inside her jacket. Little good the knowledge did. As long as the tool was *inside* the barrier, Amaranthe could do nothing to it.

A tight smile curved the woman's lips. She had Amaranthe and she knew it.

We'll see, Amaranthe thought. She glanced toward the fire baton. It had gone out when it hit the deck, but maybe she could turn it on again. And maybe one artifact could fight another.

She dropped to one knee, pretending defeat—it wasn't much of a pretense—and rested her hand near the torch. She gripped the smooth material, using her body to hide the action.

Involuntary gasps for air tore through her, but they were ineffective and nothing could pass her constricted throat. She did not have long. If her attack failed...

Another charge exploded near by, and the corridor rocked. The lights flickered. For an instant, the pressure on Amaranthe's throat disappeared.

She gasped and jumped to her feet, forcing air-deprived legs to support her. She thumbed the only thing that felt like a switch on the smooth baton, and a six-inch flame streamed from the tip. Amaranthe jabbed it at the invisible shield.

The baton didn't pierce the barrier, but the flame flared in a brilliant flash, startling the woman. She backpedaled, tripped over a fallen comrade, and crashed to the deck. Something crunched beneath her. The tool?

Amaranthe dove in, hoping the shield had failed. Out of the corner of her eye, she spotted a dark shape arcing toward her—the male practitioner's boot.

She flung herself to her belly, but hurried to find her feet again as soon as the kick whispered overhead. She dropped the baton and caught the man's boot as he was retracting it. She sprang up, heaving his leg into the air. The man tumbled onto his back.

"Maldynado," Amaranthe rasped through her aching throat. "Keep that one busy."

He was on his back, panting, but he rolled onto his side to obey.

The woman had found her knees and was trying to rise. Amaranthe planted a foot on her back—the barrier had disappeared—and forced her flat on the deck. She snatched the baton and raised it, but paused. Maybe she need not kill anyone else.

She spotted the vial Maldynado had dropped, grabbed it, and held it to the woman's nose. Already the practitioner's eyes were glazing and her struggles were weak, so the effects of the powder must not have faded yet.

A thump sounded behind Amaranthe. She leaped to her feet and whirled, baton in hand, ready to thrust the flame up an attacker's nose.

"Easy, lady grimbal." Maldynado raised his hands over his head. The male practitioner lay at his feet, gasping—and inhaling—the lingering odor from the other vial. "You'll need that for getting in if Sicarius won't answer the door."

"True." Amaranthe lowered her hand, but she did not relax until she had ensured nobody was in a position to trouble them. The practitioners all lay prone. One was snoring. Good.

"You might want to do it before this stuff wears off and these magic-spewing people wake up," Maldynado said.

"Yes, but how do we know when the air is clear? We don't want our men to walk out and pitch over, snoring."

"I wouldn't mind seeing Sicarius snore," Maldynado said.

"Do you want to sling him and Basilard over your shoulders and tote them out of here?"

"I could. I've carried many women on these broad shoulders."

"Many women at the same time?"

"On occasion, yes." He winked.

"Just watch them, please." Amaranthe nodded to the slumbering people and knocked on the hatch. "Sicarius? Basilard? You can come out now. We're pushing the unconscious people into neat piles."

The clomp of footsteps came from around the corner, and she winced. Maybe calling out had been foolish. If there were still guards around, someone must have heard that brawl....

The people who tromped around the corner were not guards however. Books and Akstyr led the way, wearing their suits but not their helmets. Seven, no, eight nude men and women trailed them. More than one naked body sported smears of blood, and several people gripped knives or pistols. Books carried a familiar black belt full of daggers.

Amaranthe lifted a hand, intending to warn everyone to stay back, but she *did* need to know if the air was still tainted. Nobody dropped to the ground and started snoring.

"What took you so long, Booksie?" Maldynado asked.

"We took the tour and beat some heads in." Akstyr grinned at one of the girls, but she showed no inclination toward returning it.

"Why are you wearing...?" Books started, but stopped to study the inert forms. "Should we *all* be wearing helmets?"

"I think it's worn off." Amaranthe unfastened her helmet. "Tie these people up, will you? No, we need more than that. They can use their minds to choke us—as I have reason to know. Akstyr, is there a way to keep them unconscious?"

"Shoot them?" Akstyr said.

"You're supposed to be a Science advisor," Books told him, "not a Sicarius acolyte."

Maldynado cleared his throat. "For the record, that would have been my response, too."

"How surprising." Books handed Sicarius's knife collection to Amaranthe.

She struggled to hold all the blades and the baton, so she settled for dumping them into her helmet.

"We can strap these bastards to the tables and sedate them the way they did us," one young man said.

"Can we cut them open, too?" another growled.

Amaranthe grimaced, wondering what manner of experiments the practitioners had been conducting to create those future warrior-caste babies. Thoughts for another time.

One of the young women caught her eye, a tall blonde with facial features similar to Fasha's. She must be Keisha, the athlete whose disappearance had started everything for Amaranthe and her team. Keisha would need to know about her sister's death, but now wasn't the time.

She knocked on the hatch again. "Sicarius, if you don't come out, we're leaving you here."

The athletes stirred and traded whispers of, "Sicarius?"

Something scraped on the other side of the hatch. Equipment or furniture being moved? Bangs, thumps, and more scrapes followed. A light poked through the perforations in the hatch.

Amaranthe crouched and peered through only to find herself staring into a dark eye that gazed back from the other side. She twitched in surprise, but did not draw back. Was that—

"Basilard believes we should have code words you could speak so we would know if you were giving us legitimate orders or talking under duress." Sicarius spoke the words as blandly as if they were discussing the men's training regimen, and no hint that he had missed her or was relieved to see her seeped into his tone.

By now, Amaranthe should have known better than to feel stung, but the emotion encroached upon her nonetheless. She pushed it aside and conjured a smile. "Basilard is a wise fellow. We'll schedule it for discussion during the next team meeting."

The eye disappeared, metal squealed, and the hatch tottered open on wobbly hinges.

Basilard exited first, his legs and feet bare, though he wore some guard's fatigue shirt. He grinned and stopped to give Amaranthe a one-armed hug before moving on to greet the others. Blood stained the back of his shirt.

"Basilard, did you get shot?" she asked.

Yes. I fashioned a bandage. It is fine for now.

The pain lines creasing the corners of his eyes belied the statement, but they did not have time to perform more extensive first aid, so Amaranthe let it go.

Sicarius strode out, utterly naked except for a technical manual in his hands. He didn't bother to wield it strategically to hide...anything.

Amaranthe gaped at him. After a startled moment of surprise, she forced herself to keep her eyes focused on his face. Mostly. "Sicarius. I, ah..." Have always wanted to see you like this, she thought. No, she couldn't say that. Was wondering if you were blond all over. No, definitely not that. "I hope that's not your suggestion for the team uniform," she decided on as she handed him his gear.

"The lack of a place to hold weapons makes it impractical," he said in his usual monotone.

Behind Amaranthe, Maldynado leaned close to Books and whispered, "So many jokes the man could have made, and he goes with that."

Sicarius strapped on his weapons belt, which, combined with the throwing knives sheathed on his forearm, created a style that would have earned anyone else a round of mocking. Nobody made a comment.

Sicarius lifted the manual. "If the way is clear, we can adjust the ballast tanks to bring this craft to the surface." He opened the manual to a diagram. "They're located here, here, here and here."

Straight to business. No hug or, "Thanks for coming for us." Professional as always. But then, she was the one who had sent him on a task that resulted in his capture. Maybe he was holding a grudge.

"Do you know how to do it, or do you need Books?" Amaranthe asked him.

"I can do it," Sicarius said.

"All right. Books, do you want to take your team to handle the practitioners?"

"My *team?*" Books eyed the young, bloodthirsty athletes. "How lovely."

"Akstyr and Basilard, go with him, please. Maldynado, you're with Sicarius and me."

"Double lovely," Maldynado said after a glance at Sicarius's nude state, or perhaps at the streaks of dried blood smearing his arm and shoulder.

"Wait," Books said. "The plan is to go to the surface in this? The enemy vessel? With the marines sitting up there with all their weapons firing?"

"We'll surrender," Amaranthe said.

"We could swim out before we get to the top," Maldynado said.

"With the kraken waiting out there?" Books asked.

"Kraken?" Sicarius asked mildly.

"Er, yes," Amaranthe said. "Did you not know about that?"

"I thought you'd have to slay it to get in here."

"No, the kraken-slaying is still on my to-do list."

Sicarius's eyebrow twitched.

"Don't worry. We have a plan. Sort of. Books, meet us back

at the transition chamber once you have these people secured. Sicarius, let's go see to these tanks."

CHAPTER 17

Basilard led the way to the laboratory from which he and Sicarius had escaped mere hours earlier. Books, Akstyr, and the athletes followed, grunting and panting as they toted the unconscious practitioners. Clunks and thumps sounded as limbs—or heads—collided with pipes and bulkheads. Despite the damage the vessel had taken, the barrier remained in place, blocking the laboratory entrance.

"Do you know how to get past?" Books asked.

Basilard stared at the eyeball-reader thoughtfully. He had no desire to try Sicarius's method.

"Akstyr, do *you* know how to get past?" Books asked over his shoulder.

"That work's beyond me," he said.

"Can we hurry up?" a man asked at the rear. "This bloke's stirring. I think they're going to wake up soon."

Basilard pointed at an unconscious woman strung between Books and Akstyr. *Lift her up, pry her eyelid open, and wave her face in front of that device.*

"That'll work?" Books asked skeptically.

The alternative is to gouge her eyeball out and wave it on a stick.

"Let's...make the first thing work," Books said. "And please don't tell me if you know for a fact the other method works."

He and Akstyr jostled the woman into place. Basilard used his good arm to pry her eyelid back and held his breath. Nothing happened. The iris was rolled back in her head. Grimacing—and worried she would wake up—he used his finger to slide her eyeball downward.

The barrier winked out.

Before he could let his breath out in relief, something tinkled to the deck inside. Basilard had no idea how many of the crew had been accounted for. Not everybody, apparently.

He drew his knife and motioned for the rest of the team to wait inside the threshold.

Only tables and equipment occupied the first aisle. Basilard tiptoed toward the second and paused at a tank on the end.

In case someone waited around the corner with a pistol, he stuck his hand out as a decoy, then whipped it back. No shots fired. He listened but heard nothing. Knife in hand, he peeked around the corner....

Only to find it empty. He ducked to see if someone might be hiding beneath the beds. Nothing. The hairs rose on the back of his neck, and some instinct told him to look up.

A pair of black boots swung toward his face.

Basilard dropped into a crouch so low, his rump smacked the deck. He bounced up instantly, whirling as a gray-haired soldier hanging from the ceiling pipes swung past him. Taloncrest. Before he could release the pipes and drop down, Basilard jammed his knife into the man's kidney.

Taloncrest snarled as his boots hit the deck, and he whirled, a pistol in hand.

Basilard dropped again, this time hurling himself onto his back. He kicked up, sending the pistol flying with surprising ease. Taloncrest stood there, face slack, a bulky tote slung over one shoulder, papers fighting to escape the flap.

His eyes grew glazed, and he toppled forward.

Basilard scrambled backward in the tight aisle and barely

avoided having the man land on top of him. A second knife protruded from his back.

Akstyr stepped forward and removed it. "You're welcome."

Thank you, Basilard signed.

"This goon's waking up," someone said.

A loud thump sounded.

"Never mind," someone else said.

Let's get these people strapped to the beds, Basilard signed.

Books stuck his head around the corner in time to see the message. "Do you know how to sedate them?"

Basilard pointed to one of the globes that perched beside each table. *I saw it done.*

"So, that's a yes?" Books asked.

Basilard hesitated. *Not really.*

"This should prove interesting then."

After retrieving their swords, Amaranthe and Maldynado wound through the corridors, following Sicarius. She focused on carrying her helmet, not tripping over her oversized boots, and watching for guards; she most definitely did not focus on Sicarius's bare rear end as he jogged ahead of them.

"If Deret's on board the *Saberfist*," Maldynado said, "he might be able to keep the marines from shooting us when we pop up."

"Why would Mancrest be there?" Sicarius asked, his tone as friendly as the edge of that black knife of his.

"His brother is the captain of the marine salvage and rescue vessel dropping explosives on us," Amaranthe said. "I had to chat with Deret to make that happen." Another charge blew nearby, and the corridor trembled. "Which has been a boon and a bane, I'll admit."

A second blast went off, this time right outside the wall. The floor heaved, pitching her sideways. A light on the wall bounced out of its holder and shattered on the deck. Sicarius caught Amaranthe before she smashed against the bulkhead— nothing so mundane as a shock wave would throw him off his feet—and she nodded a thank you. It was good to have him back even if the return look he gave her was on the cool and disapproving side. She hoped it was because of Deret and not due to her own clumsiness.

"Don't worry about Mancrest," she said. "You *were* right about that meeting at Pyramid Park being a bad idea, but we've come to an agreement since then."

If anything Sicarius's gaze grew cooler.

"He gave me his word," Amaranthe said. "He's not trying to turn me over to the military any more."

"No." Maldynado snickered. "He's just trying to date you now."

Sicarius threw a sharp look at him.

A snap sounded, and a hairline crack formed in a wall seam next to Amaranthe. A bead of water appeared at the bottom.

"We better go." She grabbed Maldynado and Sicarius by the elbows, trying to hustle everyone down the corridor. "There's a lot of pressure down here. I don't want to be around if anything implodes."

Sicarius strode forward, breaking free of her grip. He led them around two corners and past a massive bulkhead sealing off a corridor. Water pooled on the floor before it.

"Must be that wing they closed down," Amaranthe said. Too bad nobody was left in the navigation room to drop more doors in case other sections flooded. "Is it possible these ballast tanks won't be enough to lift us if too much of the interior has taken on water?"

"Very possible." Sicarius stopped before a panel filled with levers and smaller versions of the wheels that opened the hatches. Though it looked like Turgonian technology, the words etched on plaques were nothing she could read.

Sicarius handed her the manual, turned a wheel, and

twisted one of the levers in a half circle. A grinding noise came from behind the wall, followed by a muffled hissing. Air being forced into the tanks? Her thoughts tangled as she tried to grasp the science — or perhaps Science — behind the system.

"It's working." Sicarius tapped a gauge. "But there's another tank along the other main corridor, and then two more used for leveling the ship. We may need to open the flood valves on those, too."

Before he finished talking, he was jogging again. Amaranthe and Maldynado hustled to catch up.

"What happens if we've taken on too much water and this doesn't get us off the bottom?" Maldynado asked. "Everyone without diving suits drowns down here?" He seemed to realize he was talking to someone without a suit, for he added, "And, er, just so you know, this wouldn't fit you, Sicarius, so there's no need to stab me in the back for it."

"I wouldn't do that," Sicarius said as they turned into another corridor.

"That's a relief," Maldynado said.

"It would compromise the suit."

Maldynado grew pale, as if he were imagining Sicarius forcing him out of the suit at knife point and *then* stabbing him.

Amaranthe elbowed him. "I think that was a joke."

Maldynado shook his head. "Given the source, I doubt it."

They reached a set of controls identical to the first.

"How deep are we?" Sicarius asked as he checked the gauges.

"Books estimates three to four hundred feet," Amaranthe said.

"I've studied free diving. I can make it out."

"What's free diving?" Maldynado asked.

"Employing mind-body control techniques to maximize the effectiveness of the mammalian diving reflex."

Maldynado's brow furrowed and he mouthed, "What?" at Amaranthe.

"I think it means he's good at holding his breath," she said. "Oh."

Sicarius twisted a wheel, turned a lever, and they moved on.

Amaranthe was about to ask him if the vessel should be lifting yet when they rounded a corner and entered an occupied corridor. Two guards stood before a set of controls similar to the other ones.

The men carried pistols, but Sicarius never slowed. He strode toward them as determined as death. One of the guards reached for his firearm, but he took one good look at Sicarius and backed away. Both men turned and ran.

Sicarius must have deemed them no threat, for he stopped at the controls without bothering to hurl knives into their backs. Maybe Amaranthe's influence was mellowing him. Right. Or maybe their situation was so dire there was no time for knife play. As far as she could tell, the vessel had yet to budge.

"How come no guards turned and ran from us when we were infiltrating the place?" Maldynado asked.

"Their employers were conscious," Amaranthe said, "and their ship wasn't half-destroyed, so they had higher morale."

"Oh, good. I'd hate to think that even naked, Sicarius is scarier than us."

Sicarius finished with the controls and took off.

They threw the last lever in the forward section of the vessel and returned to the transition chamber where the team had first entered. Akstyr, Books, Basilard, and some of the athletes waited there. All of Books's charges had found clothing, if only the white jackets the practitioners wore, which left Sicarius as the sole nude member of the group. He did not seem to care.

"Are the practitioners subdued?" Amaranthe asked.

"You mean those stinking wizards?" one athlete asked with a sneer. "They're taken care of."

"They're strapped down so the marines can pick them up when they board," Books said. "We weren't sure how to operate the drugging mechanism, but we tossed a couple more of those vials into the room before we left." He shrugged. "Best we could do. I left a couple of women there to warn us if anyone stirs. I didn't know if one of us should stay or if you'd need us for the next phase of your plan."

The next phase of her plan. That sounded very official and organized. If only that were the truth.

"Thank you, Books. Sicarius, how long should it take for air to fill the tanks and for us to rise?" *If* they were going to.

"Soon," Sicarius said.

Some of the athletes stirred again at the mention of his name. They were probably wondering why the city's most notorious assassin was helping them. Maybe it was time to make sure her charges could tell the journalists about their rescuers.

"I'm Amaranthe Lokdon," she told them. "We're an outfit called The Emperor's Edge. I bring this up in case you want to mention it to someone later on."

Books chuckled. She wondered if she should further tout their merits. There wouldn't be a chance once they were on the surface and the marines were swarming onto the foreign craft. Amaranthe certainly wasn't planning to stick around then. Just because Deret had talked his brother into checking out the laboratory did not mean—

The floor tilted.

Amaranthe caught herself on the wall. Was it another attack? No, she had not heard an explosion.

"We're rising," Books said.

The floor titled further, and Amaranthe braced herself.

"Lopsided as a drunken marine," Maldynado said. "Who's driving this boat?"

Basilard signed, *Are there still people in navigation?*

"No," Amaranthe said. "We convinced them to come out and join the others on the deck in front of your hatch. It seemed logical at the time."

Convinced? How?

Amaranthe twitched a shoulder. "A little palavering."

Basilard lifted an eyebrow at Sicarius and signed, *No eyeball required.*

Amaranthe frowned, wondering if she had misread a sign. Eyeball? That did not sound right.

Sicarius's eyes glinted though, and he signed back, *As predicted.*

It felt strange to be on the outside of a joke between Sicarius and someone else. More than strange—a twinge of jealousy reared its head. She stomped it down. It was good for the men to bond, those two especially.

The vessel left the lake bottom with a scrape. Amaranthe checked the nearest porthole.

The orange exterior lights still shone, but a cloud of sediment was rising with them, and dust swirled about. A startled school of fish flitted close enough to the porthole to see, but more than a few feet away, the haze obscured everything.

Amaranthe started to return to the group, but her men had come to join her. She rapped her knuckles on her helmet. "Everyone with suits, get ready. We'll assume the kraken is troubling the marines and take the harpoons out to help with it. We'll exit roughly twenty feet before reaching the surface." Assuming the dust cleared and they could *tell* when the surface drew close. "Based on what I've seen of this place from the outside, it's the sort of craft most sane people would shoot at on sight and wait to investigate until it's capsized and dragged up on a beach. Any questions?"

"If the marines are handling the kraken, we can use that as a distraction and swim away," Sicarius said. "There's no need to risk ourselves against it."

"We've already had a run-in with the thing," Amaranthe said. "It may be more than the marines can handle unless they get creative with their thinking."

"Like we're going to." Books smiled.

"Explain," Sicarius said.

Books launched into his spiel about the poison and how they meant to get the kraken to suck the keg into its vulnerable core. Amaranthe checked the porthole again. The sediment cloud still swirled about, though the density had lessened. They were making progress, albeit slow progress. She hoped the ship didn't get stuck mid-ascent.

"That plan is dangerous," Sicarius said. Though he was responding to Books, his gaze settled on Amaranthe.

She spread her arms. "They usually are."

"What if I can't swim?" a young woman asked.

"Find someone who can and who thinks you're cute," Amaranthe said.

"Why does cuteness matter?" Books asked.

"Would you let a woman drown if you thought she was cute and would be utterly grateful to you for saving her life?"

"I wouldn't let a woman drown under any circumstances," Books said.

Amaranthe arched her eyebrows.

"But especially not ones such as you described," he admitted.

Sicarius took Amaranthe's arm and guided her several steps from the athletes. "I assume you are planning on this course of action regardless of what I do or say."

Amaranthe thought of Books's advice. Was she being reckless again with this plan? "We'll only do it if the marines look like they need help."

"I'll take the keg then. You'll be clumsy and slow in that suit."

"Thanks," she said dryly. "Me specifically, or anyone in a suit?"

"Anyone, but you were planning on taking the risk, I assume."

She blushed. True.

"Since I have no suit to drag at me," he said, "I'll be the logical choice."

"So that's why he's insisted on running around naked all day," Maldynado muttered to Akstyr.

Sicarius leveled a cool back-out-of-our-conversation stare down the corridor. Maldynado lifted his hands and turned to gaze out the porthole.

"All right," Amaranthe said, drawing him a few more steps away, though part of her did not want to let him take the role. Emperor's teeth, she had just rescued him, and now he wanted to risk his life again. But he was her most skilled man, not some vulnerable neophyte. It made sense to use him for the dangerous work. "You'll take the keg, but be careful, please. Don't risk holding your breath so long that you pass out and sink to the bottom."

"You don't believe I'm cute enough to rescue?" he asked, deadpan.

"Oh, you're decent." She gave him a once over before remembering how nude he was. Her blush belied her offhand tone. "But we'll be busy shooting harpoons into this beast to distract it for you. At least take someone to help you."

Sicarius raised his voice to say, "Basilard." He pointed upward.

Amaranthe would have picked someone who wasn't injured, but they exchanged nods of understanding. She wondered what the two had talked about while incarcerated down here.

Maldynado cleared his throat. "Just in case anyone was concerned we wouldn't get to play with the kraken, it's still alive, and—" he leaned closer, cheek pressed against the porthole, "—it's got the marine ship wrapped up tighter than lovers tangled in the sheets."

Amaranthe darted to the porthole. The sediment cloud had disappeared, and they were thirty or forty feet from the surface. The depth did little to mute the brilliant morning sunlight, and she had no trouble making out the black hull of the *Saberfist*. It had to be a substantial ship to do its job, but the tentacles curled along the bottom of it made it appear insignificant. To the side of the vessel, more tentacles swirled about like live snakes in a pit.

The current brought something large in to thump against the porthole. It must have bumped the hull, too, because lightning streaked out, surrounding it and illuminating it all too well.

Amaranthe's stomach curdled. It was a body in a marine diving suit, one leg torn off.

"Ew," Akstyr said. "That one's a kraken snack."

Annoyance flared within Amaranthe, and she almost snapped at him to show respect. But she bit her lip. Though she had arranged this "distraction" and felt—*was*—responsible for any marines who died down here, Akstyr had no reason to care about them.

"Ready your suits. We're going out." Amaranthe plunked her helmet over her head and started screwing the fasteners together. "Everyone who's not on my team, stay here and wait for the marines to get you. And don't forget. When they ask you who came down to help you, I'm Amaranthe Lokdon, that's Sicarius, and we're The Emperor's Edge. You can tell that to any journalists who happen by, too."

Maldynado cleared his throat, probably planning to deliver his own parting words, words that touted his copious merits. Amaranthe opened the hatch to the transition chamber and pushed him inside. She handed him a harpoon launcher and grabbed one for herself. The rest of the men piled in behind her. Helmets clanked against each other as everyone squeezed to fit inside. It had been tight before, with the four of them, and now they had two more men squished amongst them.

Sicarius stood next to her, holding the keg. Maybe she should offer some heartfelt parting words, in case...

"Be careful," was all she could manage with so many witnesses around.

He gazed into her faceplate and gave her a solemn nod. He understood.

"Basilard," Amaranthe said, "open the door when you're ready. The water will come in fast."

He nodded and squeezed between Maldynado and Books.

"Easy," Maldynado told him. "Watch what you're grazing with that harpoon."

"He doesn't have a harpoon launcher," Akstyr said.

Maldynado stared at him.

"Oh," Akstyr said. "I get it."

With his dagger clenched between his teeth, Basilard gripped the wheel to the hatch. He took a few deep breaths in preparation. Beside Amaranthe, Sicarius took a different approach. He stood still, body relaxed, eyes hooded, like some Daikon mystic deep in a meditation routine.

Basilard opened the hatch, and water flooded into the chamber. Amaranthe waited, making sure Sicarius and Basilard slipped out before she maneuvered for the exit.

Sunlight filtered through the water from above. Their rate of ascent had slowed, and they were still twenty feet from the surface. Another of the thick, dark purple tentacles had snaked beneath the *Saberfist*. Even as she watched, one of the free ones thrust out of the water. From her viewpoint, she could not see what it did on the deck, but two men flew overboard on the opposite side of the ship.

Amaranthe hefted her harpoon launcher and gestured for her team to fan out around the laboratory. They would have to convince the kraken to leave the *Saberfist* and swim for Books's plan to work. Sicarius and Basilard were already angling toward the surface. Maldynado, her strongest remaining swimmer, headed in to make the first shot, to lure the beast downward. Books, Akstyr, and Amaranthe treaded water near the top of their vessel and waited, harpoons ready.

CHAPTER 18

Cold water streamed past Basilard. He followed Sicarius toward the surface, kicking and stroking with his good arm. For the moment, he carried his dagger clenched between his teeth. Clear water surrounded him, but, without a mask, images were blurry and indistinct, though he had little trouble making out the kraken's massive form.

Someone—was that Maldynado?—was swimming toward its underbelly. He stopped ten or fifteen feet below the kraken and lined up a shot. He ignored the tentacles—though he was careful not to swim too close to them—and fired at the creature's giant mantle.

The harpoon streamed toward it and sank into the purple flesh. Though it appeared small next to the creature—like a toothpick protruding from a bear's hide—the kraken must have noticed it, for it whipped a tentacle up and batted at the intrusion. The harpoon fell out and sank, disappearing into the lake depths.

Another tentacle dropped away from the bottom of the ship and snaked toward Maldynado. On land, he could have dodged the attack, but Sicarius was right. The water and suits made people slow. Despite Maldynado's quick kicks and strokes to the side, the tentacle clipped him on the shoulder. He spun backward in a clumsy somersault.

Basilard grabbed his dagger, thinking to go in and help, but Amaranthe and Books were kicking toward Maldynado's position. Sicarius tapped Basilard and pointed to the surface.

Basilard grimaced. His lungs were starting to hunger for air, but he hated to leave if his teammates needed help.

Sicarius saw his hesitation and stroked for the surface himself. Thinking he had some plan to share, Basilard went after him. They were deeper than he realized, and he gasped in a great lungful of air as soon as they broke the surface.

A cannon boomed, the sound pummeling his eardrums. They had come up less than ten feet from the bow of the ship. A broken wooden rail floated by, scraping Basilard's injured shoulder. Fresh pain flared, and he gasped, almost dropping his dagger.

Fortunately, the marines were too busy to notice him. To their credit, the men shouting to load guns and bring the ship about sounded calm and competent rather than terrified.

"I'm going in," Sicarius said. "Watch my back."

That was all he said before taking a deep breath and submerging again.

Basilard inhaled, tipped his legs up into the air, and dove.

Below the kraken, Maldynado had recovered and was loading a new harpoon. Amaranthe, Akstyr, and Books fired their own launchers, timing it so the weapons released simultaneously.

Akstyr's harpoon skimmed a tentacle and did no damage. Books's projectile flew wide, but Amaranthe's sank into one of the creature's eyes.

The body reared back, and the tentacles released the *Saberfist* and stiffened. Ink clouded the water, obscuring the ship and the creature.

Basilard watched, hoping Amaranthe's shot might prove the killing blow.

The kraken dropped below the ship, tentacles streaming out behind it as it dove.

Sicarius was already swimming toward it. This was their chance.

Basilard hurried to catch up. What he could do with his insignificant dagger, he didn't know, but he had to try to help.

The mantle flexed, and the kraken shot forward on a stream of water. Sicarius stroked after it, but the powerful creature outpaced him. It swam straight for Amaranthe.

Basilard cut across. He couldn't catch up with the body of the thing, but maybe he could slice into a tentacle and distract it.

Suction-cup-covered flesh streamed past. He tried to grab the tentacle, but the slick rubbery flesh offered a poor handhold. Nonetheless he managed to thrust his dagger into it near the tip.

The tentacle moved past so quickly, it nearly tore the weapon from his grip. As it was, his blade ripped a foot-long gouge into the flesh.

The tentacle flicked, an annoyed gesture that caught Basilard in the chest. Despite the off-hand nature of the attack, it thumped him hard, and precious air escaped his lips. Bubbles streamed upward before his eyes. At least he had kept the dagger.

Basilard debated on going up for air again, but the kraken slowed as it neared the laboratory vessel. He did not see Amaranthe. Sicarius was weaving through the tentacles, avoiding them instead of attacking them. He approached the hole water shot from, and Basilard could see the current pushing against him, making the swim difficult.

Forgoing air, Basilard swam downward.

The kraken wouldn't cooperate and hold still. Apparently incensed by the eye wound, it whipped about the fortress, seeking the one who had struck the blow.

When the beast switched from blowing out water to sucking it in, Sicarius dove in, aided by the current. Basilard swirled through the tentacles, trying to swim closer without letting the kraken know he was there, and could easily be captured—or killed.

Sicarius reached the interior of the mantle and thrust the keg into the dark orifice. Basilard thought that was it, that they had accomplished the mission, but the keg gushed right out again on the kraken's next burst of forward motion. It bounced off a tentacle and dropped, unharmed.

Sicarius dove for it. Another tentacle clipped Basilard in the back, stirring pain again, and he swam away from the writhing limbs. He worried the kraken would turn on them, but it was still intent on its prey—Amaranthe.

With quick efficient strokes, Sicarius retrieved the keg before it disappeared into the depths below.

Basilard paddled down to join him. Even here, underwater, Sicarius maintained his neutral facade with no hint of disappointment stamping his face. He had to be surprised or annoyed at the least. Hadn't the keg been designed to implode?

Above them, the kraken swooped beneath the laboratory. Amaranthe was swimming there, hiding beneath the corridors and rooms of the vessel. The rest of the team appeared to be out of harpoons. Maldynado was chasing after the kraken with his sword. Basilard's gut clenched. They had to stop the creature soon, or it was bound to catch Amaranthe.

Basilard's lungs called out for air again, but he swam closer to Sicarius and waved his knife. He pointed at the keg and made a hammer motion. If they pierced a hole in it, the poison might flow out when the kraken sucked it in next time. Enough of the poison to affect something.

Sicarius nodded and held out the keg. Basilard rammed his dagger through the wood. He started to pull it out again, but Sicarius stopped him.

He mouthed something but swam away before Basilard realized what. The dagger hilt stuck out of the wood, and he left it there. Ah, cork. Yes, he could pull it out at the last moment.

Basilard wanted to stay and help, but he needed air.

Maldynado and Akstyr swam past as he headed upward. He hoped they would survive without him.

Amaranthe circled the vessel and swam beneath its belly, following one of the corridors. Its ascent had slowed to a crawl, and she wondered if it would ever break the surface. All too aware of the kraken weaving after her, she stayed in the craft's shadow. She was out of harpoons and had dropped the launcher. She still had her sword, and, though it made swimming hard, kept it in hand.

She hoped she was giving Sicarius and Basilard the time they needed.

Something batted her ankle. One of the tentacles. It moved in to get a grip, but she bent double and sank her short sword into it.

It jerked away and bumped against the hull of the laboratory. Streaks of lighting ran up its length, dancing between the clear cups on the underside of the tentacle.

The kraken jerked that limb away, but another snaked in from the opposite side. Amaranthe pulled her legs up, barely evading the grasping tentacle. She tried to spot Maldynado and the others, but couldn't see anyone. Ink and blood—all the kraken's, she hoped—muddled the water. With the creature so obviously targeting her, she dared not swim out from beneath the vessel. Besides, with the electrified hull so close, the craft offered more than a hiding spot.

A tentacle swooped in five feet ahead, and she reversed her strokes to halt herself. The two sinuous limbs had her trapped; she could not evade them without swimming into the open.

Amaranthe gripped her sword, a notion of making a stand in her head. She stroked forward, eyes focused on the tentacle blocking her route. It swept back and forth like a cat's tail, though it was careful not to touch the hull this time. She timed the movements and stabbed the rubbery purple flesh. Too bad she did not have poison on the tip. The tentacle did not seem to notice her attack.

She tugged her sword free, intending to search for a more vulnerable target.

Something wrapped around her leg. The other tentacle. She'd taken her eye off of it for too long.

Amaranthe tried to yank her leg free, but the grip tightened, applying bone-crushing force that smothered her from calf to thigh. Her knee creaked, and she hissed in pain.

An image flashed through her mind of a shattered knee with her unable to walk for the rest of her life. If she *had* a rest of her life. Where was the rest of her team?

She twisted and slammed her sword into the tentacle. Though her blade sank in a few inches, the kraken tightened its grip instead of releasing her.

Maldynado swam into view, but he carried only that thin rapier, not a harpoon launcher. What would *that* do?

He stabbed gamely at the creature, but the tentacle ignored him. The kraken pulled her from beneath the vessel, its movements slow, almost leisurely.

Amaranthe hacked at the appendage, no grace to her movements. She was like a logger hewing at a tree. A tree that wanted to kill her.

Something snapped in her knee, and she screamed, the noise half pain, half rage. She tore into the tentacle with even more vigor.

Her breaths came in short gasps. She could not get enough air.

Under her rain of blows, the tentacle stiffened, then loosened. Had the creature finally had enough? Or maybe it was only shifting its grip.

Amaranthe looked up, trying to spot the kraken's eyes, hoping she would find defeat there.

It hovered, ten feet below the *Saberfist*. Her harpoon still protruded from the right orb, and the tentacles on that side of its body floated limply. Basilard and Sicarius were weaving between them, approaching the underside of the creature. The keg was still in Sicarius's arms.

Hurry, she urged.

He swam the last few meters, yanked something out of the keg, and thrust the poison into a dark orifice.

Amaranthe hoped that was it, the death blow, but a spasm coursed through the tentacle restraining her. It tightened about her leg, and she gasped as fresh pain erupted from her knee. She fought back tears of frustration. What if Sicarius had delivered the killing blow, but the kraken ripped her in half in its death throes?

She hacked at the tentacle with renewed vigor, determined to free herself or die trying. Inside her helmet, sweat dribbled down her face, stinging her eyes. Dozens of perforations marred the tentacle, and blood clouded the water, but still it would not release her.

Finally, the limb relaxed. Amaranthe shoved at it to pull her leg free. She stroked away from it and almost lost her sword as lightheadedness overcame her. She was breathing too hard, sucking in more air than the suit was designed to deliver.

But the tentacle remained limp and unmoving.

Two suited figures and one naked one were treading water a few feet away.

Problem? Amaranthe signed, cheeks warming with sheepish chagrin, knowing Sicarius had observed her wild hacks. Mercenary leaders were supposed to remain calm and rational during a crisis, not descend into an animalistic frenzy.

It's dead, Maldynado signed, *but if you want to keep at the blade practice, we can wait.*

She checked Sicarius's face, wondering how long it had been since he had taken a breath. He appeared fine, if more serene than usual with those hooded eyes.

No, she signed. *That was sufficient.*

Amaranthe started to swim toward the men, but the first attempt at a kick sent fire flaring from her knee. Someone gripped her upper arm. She lifted a hand to sign that she could make it on her own, but it was Sicarius, so she stopped. No doubt, he wanted to go up for air, not discuss her independent streak.

She stroked with her arms, letting her wounded leg hang limply, and he helped her toward the surface. He angled away from the *Saberfist* as they rose. Good idea. No need to tempt any marines by popping his million-ranmya head up in the middle of the activity.

The top of the laboratory vessel was creeping out of the water. That ought to keep the marines busy for a while.

When she broke the surface, sun blazed into her eyes. Morning sun. It seemed as if they had been underwater all day, yet it must have only been a couple of hours.

Amaranthe squinted and tried to lift a hand to shield her face, but, with her left leg dangling uselessly, she needed both arms to stay afloat. Her eyes adjusted, though, and she made out the marines scurrying about on the deck of their ship, preparing their salvage crane and dinghies for boarding. The kraken was floating on the surface now, too.

She struggled with the fasteners for her helmet. She wanted the thing off, so she could breathe fresh air again.

Sicarius caught her by the armpit with one hand and unclasped her helmet with the other. He had no trouble staying afloat using just his legs, but then both of his legs were working. As soon as her head was free, she flung the helmet aside, not caring if it floated away. She had had enough of suits and krakens and underwater practitioners. Though she could not complain about the outcome, she decided not to put subaqueous activities on their official list of mercenary services.

"Your knee?" Sicarius asked, his gaze roving the deck of the ship and the surrounding activity.

"Yes. I don't think I'll be joining you for a morning run anytime soon."

"Akstyr can fix it."

"Surely, I'll need to rest it for a couple of weeks."

"Days."

Amaranthe spotted Maldynado, Akstyr, Books, and then Basilard closer toward the shore. She waved for them to head inland. It was time for her team to disappear.

"Aren't I entitled to a vacation now and then?" she asked. "Look, there's a nice beach over there. If we swim that way instead of meeting up with the men, we could enjoy the summer day." She nodded at Sicarius's bare shoulders. "You're dressed for it."

"You are not."

"True." She plucked at the heavy suit. "But I've been wanting to get out of this. Whether that's back at the docks or on a secluded beach doesn't matter to me." She smiled playfully.

He did not answer promptly, and she thought he might actually be considering it. Until he said, "With Akstyr's healing, two days should be sufficient rest for your knee. Then your training can commence again."

Amaranthe sighed. "You're an unrelenting taskmaster."

"Yes."

A wave washed over them, and he wiped his face. She eyed him, half-suspecting him of using the movement to hide the barest hint of a smile. But surely that would be too jovial for him.

"Ready to go?" she asked.

Something on the *Saberfist* caught his attention, and he did not answer. Someone on the ship leaned against the railing, someone in civilian clothing and a hat.

Amaranthe lifted a hand toward Deret, the best "thank you" she could manage at this distance. He started to wave back, but glanced at marines jogging past behind him and kept himself to a nod.

"Ready to go?" Amaranthe repeated.

"Yes." Sicarius's humor had evaporated, and his unreadable facade returned.

CHAPTER 19

Amaranthe straightened the crimson, braided-hide band across Basilard's chest. Following in the Turgonian style, he wore it diagonally across a crisp white shirt with silver piping. According to imperial lore, the band was symbolic of the across-the-back sword scabbards the original conquerors had worn, a throwback to the days when the size of a man's sword had indicated...well, no man had dared carry one any less than five feet long.

How do I look? he asked when she stepped back.

"Maldynado picked out your clothes and dressed you," Amaranthe said. "How do you think you look?"

Fabulous?

"Correct. How's your shoulder?" They had taken him to a surgeon to remove the pistol ball, and Akstyr had applied his healing fingers, but she was still surprised he had been able to compete in the final Clank Race. Compete and win. He'd said he had realized his purpose—or perhaps remembered it—down in that laboratory and had been motivated to kill himself, if that's what it took, to earn dinner with the emperor.

Basilard rotated his shoulder. *Good enough. How is your knee?*

Amaranthe grimaced. "Also, good enough. Unfortunately. I was hoping for more of a vacation from our training regimen."

She glanced toward the doorway of the rail car, though she doubted Sicarius was anywhere nearby. He had been scarce the last three days, and she wondered if there was something he had not told her about the events below.

Sicarius does not know what a vacation is.

"I've noticed." She could use one though. Earlier that day, she had talked to Keisha about Fasha's death, and the weight of that failure, along with so many others, hung heavily about Amaranthe's shoulders.

When I get to talk to the emperor, Basilard signed, *what should I say about the team?*

Everything, Amaranthe wanted to blurt. Basilard should tell Sespian how much they'd done for the empire, that they were responsible for stopping his assassins, for fixing the water supply when it was poisoned, and for saving the athletes. And he should let the emperor know Sicarius wasn't the demon he once knew.

Amaranthe exhaled slowly. "Don't say anything about us. That'll get you thrown in the dungeon. You didn't enter the Imperial Games using the name you go by now, so, with luck, he won't know you're part of a team of criminals. Wrongfully accused criminals, but criminals nonetheless. Just talk to him about what's important to you."

Basilard held her gaze for a long moment, then nodded. *I understand.*

Amaranthe waved to Books, who was sighing dramatically and repeatedly as Maldynado fiddled with his clothes. Since he no longer had a bounty on his head, Books would go with Basilard to act as a translator. Sending two members of her team to see the emperor was risky, but this was Basilard's dream. Besides, they were the quietest and least notorious of her crew.

What if we get thrown in the dungeon? Basilard asked, as if he had been reading her thoughts.

"We'll rescue you, of course." She patted him on his good

shoulder and debated a moment before voicing her next thought. "I'm glad you chose...to set aside the past to try to improve the future."

He stared at her. *You know? That I meant to kill...*

He did not finish. He didn't need to. Amaranthe knew.

"You'd been glowering suspiciously in his direction for months," she said quietly, so the others would not hear, "and then suddenly you were avoiding looking his way at all. And spending an inordinate amount of time with Akstyr."

Oh.

"You don't have to forgive people for their past crimes, but if you believe they can do future goods, perhaps it's worth helping them along that path."

Perhaps. It's hard for one man to make those kinds of choices. Normally a priestess would advise.... Basilard grimaced. *It doesn't matter. No priestess will advise me any more. Even if I avenged our people, it wouldn't make a difference. Not for me. I have no chance at redemption.*

Amaranthe blew out a slow breath. What could she say to that? "I've noticed...every culture has a different notion of what the afterlife entails, which makes me think nobody's all that certain. Maybe your best bet is to find fulfillment here, in this life."

Basilard raised a single eyebrow. *You think I can find fulfillment with Sicarius?*

Amaranthe smirked. "Perhaps not *him* specifically, but if you can get him on your side, he's pretty useful for helping achieve goals."

Basilard stroked his chin, and she left him like that. Considering her words, she hoped, and not dismissing them as the ravings of a Turgonian heathen.

Amaranthe headed for the doorway, but Maldynado stopped her with, "Don't go far, boss. We've got to get you into *your* outfit and do something with your hair."

"My outfit?" She cringed and wished she had not mentioned

that she was meeting Deret that evening. She only intended to tell him her team's side of the story, but Maldynado believed that, because this discussion was taking place in the Imperial Gardens and involved a picnic basket, it should be treated as a tryst.

"I picked out something tasteful for you," Maldynado said.

"Tasteful?" Books said. "You? That's doubtful."

"You doubt *my* fashion sense?" Maldynado asked. "You who, most days, wear the same rumpled clothes as you slept in? And who..."

Amaranthe left them to bicker. Maybe she could sneak out of camp before Maldynado finished with Basilard and Books.

When she hopped out of the rail car, she turned and almost stepped on Sicarius's toes. He stood by the door, his back to the rusty metal siding.

"Something you wish to discuss?" Amaranthe could not imagine him eavesdropping on a conversation about clothing.

"We should move the camp tonight. If Basilard is recognized and interrogated, he could lead the imperial guard right to us."

Always the positive-thinking pragmatist.

"We *have* been here for a while," Amaranthe said. "We can move tomorrow."

"Tonight would be better."

"I don't believe Basilard would give us up, even if he were taken prisoner. Besides, tonight everyone's busy."

"Busy," Sicarius said.

"Sorry, but after the last week, I think a few days of relaxing and recuperating are in order. You're welcome to do so, too."

"Relax."

"Yes, it's something most humans need to do. It involves getting one's mind off one's troubles, putting away one's extensive knife collection, and not stalking about in a hyper-alert state all the time."

"Sounds like a way to get killed," Sicarius said.

Amaranthe pointed toward the rail car doorway. "Maldynado

and Akstyr do it at brothels all the time, and nobody's bothered to stick daggers in their backs yet." She realized how that might be construed and winced. "Not that you need to visit brothels to relax. I mean, unless that's what you prefer, because it's not my business if you do, but you could, uhm, take a nice moonlit stroll on the beach." Oh, sure, like any man would choose that option. "Or play Tiles or gamble a bit, or, uh..." Dear ancestors, she could not imagine what he might do for fun or relaxation. Practice throwing knives? "Well, you should do something you'd like to do tonight, as the rest of us are, and we'll worry about moving in the morning."

Sicarius, as usual, regarded her with the blandness of a particularly featureless rock, then walked away.

The dress Maldynado had chosen wasn't entirely appalling. The V-neck and sleeveless nature left more skin showing than Amaranthe was wont to do, but it *was* summer. Though the sun floated low over the horizon, it still beat against her shoulders, and the faint breeze felt good whispering across her bare arms. She enjoyed the rustle of the silk swishing about her legs, too. She never could have afforded such a garment on her enforcer salary. No doubt Maldynado had wheedled it from some businesswoman for free.

For once, she wore her hair down, though a braid on either side of her temples pulled the locks away from her eyes. Pleasant evening at the Imperial Gardens or not, one had to be prepared should one need to defend oneself. She could kick off the sandals if she needed to run away—or drive a heel into someone's crabapples.

Amaranthe chuckled sadly at herself. "Turn down the boiler, girl. Relax."

As she crunched along the park's main gravel pathway, she vowed to enjoy the summer evening. She inhaled the floral scents that wafted from flower baskets hanging from lampposts alongside the path. She passed a group of teenage boys competing at draftball in a sandy arena while younger children played hide-and-seek amongst the tall, dense shrubs of the Emperor's Maze.

Deret had suggested they meet at Lookout Vista at the center of the park, but she spotted him before reaching the base of the hill. He leaned against the waist-high lip of a fountain. Above him, Vlem the Valiant held a sword aloft, and a curtain of water streamed from the granite blade. Amaranthe smirked, thinking of Maldynado's concern about a statue being made of him swimming up a squid's hind-end. That wouldn't likely make center stage in an imperial park.

"Good evening, Ms. Lokdon." Despite having the sword stick in one hand, and a bulging canvas tote in the other, Deret performed a graceful bow. He wore a sleeveless tunic that accentuated muscular arms, which he managed to display nicely during the greeting. "You are looking lovely this evening."

The suave greeting was somewhat diminished when the head-sized draftball from the boys' game sailed into the fountain, sending a splash of water into Deret's face. He stepped away and awkwardly rearranged his belongings so he could wipe his spectacles with his shirt. A nervous boy trotted up to retrieve the ball amongst numerous utterances of, "Sorry, my lord."

"Good evening, Lord Mancrest," Amaranthe said to rescue the boy from any backlash, though Deret did no more than give the lad a faintly peeved glance.

"Please, call me Deret. Now that you've had me at your mercy a couple of times, I feel you've earned the right to call me by my first name." He winced. "That sounded arrogant, didn't it?"

"Yes, but I'm used to that from warrior-caste types. I've been working with Maldynado for several months now."

"He's...not exactly someone to whom I'd wish to be compared."

"Because he's disowned?"

"Because he's *Maldynado*."

"Ah." Good answer.

"May I call you Amaranthe?" Deret looped the tote over his opposite wrist, eliciting a clinking of glassware within. He gripped his sword stick with the same hand and offered Amaranthe his free arm.

"Yes, though you've been particularly troublesome, and I'm not sure *you've* fully earned the right yet." She smiled to let him know she was joking and accepted his arm. Sadly, she could not remember the last time a man had offered her his arm. Though she appreciated the gesture, a twinge of guilt ran through her, as if she were betraying Sicarius. But this was just a dinner related to work. A chance to further their cause. Besides, it was not as if Sicarius had given her reason to hope anything might happen between them.

"You're most kind." Deret guided her toward the path leading up the hill to Lookout Vista. "I'm glad you came. I wasn't certain you would after you read the article in *The Gazette*. I'm sorry it said so little about you and so much about the bravery of those on the *Saberfist*. I could only report what I witnessed with my eyes. I know you and your team were down there and may have been the ones responsible for destroying that strange ship, and the kraken as well, but..."

"It's fine," Amaranthe said. "You mentioned us, and you didn't imply we were behind everything." It was nothing short of their most visible triumph yet.

"Still," Deret said, "I'd like to hear your story and about everything that happened. Maybe we could do an interview for the paper."

"I'd be happy to tell you about it, but perhaps it'd be better for us—and your health—if you didn't come out too openly in favor of my team."

"My health?" He frowned.

"You've heard of a group called Forge?"

Deret's jaw tightened. "Yes."

"We've irked them a couple of times, and it sounds like they had an interest in this venue, too." They had reached the crown of the hill, offering a view of the lake beyond the trees and warehouses, and she nodded toward the sunset-streaked water to indicate the laboratory vessel. It had sunken back to the bottom as soon as the athletes were pulled out. She had thought the *Saberfist* might want to salvage it, but the marines had seemed happy to have it disappear. It would be hard to continue denying the existence of magic with a ship full of evidence to the contrary. She wondered what Sespian thought of the whole event.

"I'm not one to run from a threat." Deret thumped his sword stick into the gravel path and grimaced at it. "Or hobble from a threat either."

"But if you have a facade of neutrality, or even come out in favor of business in the capital, then you won't likely be targeted, *and* you'll have an easier time getting information from various enemy sources. Perhaps you could even share some of that information." She gave him her best winsome smile.

"Ah, so you want your own personal spy at *The Gazette*?"

"Are you offering to work for me?" Her smile broadened.

"Er, no. I mean..." He poked at the gravel with his sword stick. "You're good, you know that, right? Since the day I met you, it's been hard for me to think of you as an enemy to the empire."

"That's because I'm *not* an enemy to the empire."

They reached the top of the hill where stone benches waited for those wishing to watch the sunset. A meditation pit and a pair of wrestling rings occupied the area too.

"No, it's because you don't seem like... You know those sexy, dangerous women who you can tell just want to manipulate you to their own ends? You don't seem like that at all."

Amaranthe raised an eyebrow at him.

Deret stopped. "What?"

"You said I wasn't sexy. I hope you weren't expecting a kiss tonight."

"Oh! I didn't mean, uhm..." His bronze skin took on a suffused hue that matched the crimson warblooms in the planters framing the benches. "I just meant you seem nice. And wholesome."

"*Wholesome?*" This time both of her eyebrows flew up. "That's what my father used to say about broccoli."

"Wholesome isn't bad," Deret said. "I *like* wholesome."

"Hm."

He set the tote on a bench, withdrew a blanket, and spread it on the sand of the meditation pit. Deret was avoiding her eyes, and his cheeks were redder than ever. He removed a bottle of apple wine, glasses, a covered dish, and slices of flatbread for dipping in oil.

He cleared his throat. "This kiss, was that on your mind for tonight?"

"Uhm." Amaranthe had only blurted it out as a joke. She could easily see liking Deret, but more? Maybe that wouldn't be so bad. Being with someone who would take her on picnics to parks and share laughs with her.... It was not as if she could see Sicarius ever doing those things. Dear ancestors, she had never even gotten a true smile out of him. "Let's just see if we can make it through the evening without you trying to turn me over to some marines."

"That sounds like a good start."

Deret maneuvered himself onto the blanket with a faint wince, and she sensed irritation in the stiff way he set the sword stick aside. Though war wounds were common in the battle-seeking empire, he was young to have to deal with a permanent disability. He converted the wince into a smile and lifted a hand, inviting her to join him.

She sat cross-legged beside him.

"So," Deret said as he dug out a corkscrew, "are you going

to give me the full story of what happened down there, or am I going to have to go into aggressive interviewer mode?"

"Does an aggressive interview involve threats and punches?"

"Usually only with prospects that are male and criminal." He poured two glasses of wine and handed her one.

"And female criminals?"

"I have to bludgeon them into talking using my wit." He grinned, and she found herself responding in kind. "But," he went on, "I'm told it's not—emperor's warts!" He gaped at something on the other side of Amaranthe.

Sicarius stood there, hands clasped behind his back. Her first thought was that he had been running and stopped by to check and make sure Deret wasn't up to no good, but he was freshly shaven and had also combed his hair, though tufts still stuck out in spots, a result of him choosing to cut it on his own...with a knife. He wore his typical fitted black with his shirt neatly tucked in. No red dust from the lakeside running trail smeared his soft boots. He was as tidy and presentable as ever, if one ignored the throwing knives adorning his arm.

"Problem?" Amaranthe asked.

Deret had sloshed wine on his arm, and he wiped it while he glowered at their intruder.

"Yes," Sicarius said.

"Back at camp?" she asked.

"No."

Amaranthe waited for him to explain his presence. He simply stood there, watching them. He hadn't decided she needed a bodyguard, or, emperor forbid, a chaperone, had he?

"What *is* the problem?" she asked.

"Besides his presence?" Deret muttered.

"I wish to speak with you," Sicarius said, ignoring Deret. *Wish?* Not "will" or "must?" That was...polite for him. Yet, if it wasn't an emergency, surely it could wait.

"Now?" she asked, pointedly tilting her head toward Deret.

Sicarius flicked a dismissive glance toward him, but said, "I can wait until you finish here."

He made no move to leave. Did he intend to wait right *there?*

"I didn't bring enough food for three," Deret told him.

"I am not hungry."

Amaranthe never would have considered Sicarius the type to be deliberately obtuse, but he certainly seemed to fall into that category tonight. She sighed and told Deret, "I better see what he wants."

"Aren't you in charge of the group? Can't you tell him to run along and sharpen his knives?"

For the first time, Sicarius turned his gaze on Deret, and it was an icy one. Amaranthe did not think he would attack someone simply for annoying him—surely, Maldynado would be dead thirty or forty times by now if that were the case—but Sicarius might decide Deret represented a threat, and do away with him the callous way he did away with other threats.

"My wholesome charms don't work that well on him," Amaranthe said, climbing to her feet as she spoke. Best to separate the two men before Deret sent any more jabs at Sicarius.

"You're coming back, right?" Deret asked.

"Yes," Amaranthe said at the same time as Sicarius said, "No."

"I'll be back," Amaranthe said with a cool look of her own for Sicarius, then she followed as he led the way down the hill.

The sun had dropped below the horizon, and twilight darkened the park. Gas lamps glowed, but Sicarius avoided the paths they lit, striding across the grass toward the towering hedges of the Emperor's Maze. Amaranthe's heart sped up, and an uncertain flutter of anticipation danced through her gut. If this were any other man, she'd assume he was leading her into the hedge maze for a private tryst, but this was *Sicarius*. He'd be more likely to lead her off for a private evening of weapons practice.

Though her sandals and dress made her gait slower than usual, he was careful not to outpace her. He wound his way into the maze. Giggles and low conversations drifted from the alcoves. On such a lovely summer evening, it might be hard to find a private spot anywhere in the park.

They padded down a long aisle of lush grass surrounded by the smell of freshly watered hedges and flowers, and he seemed to find a spot he liked. He turned into an alcove with a bench and a small fountain tinkling softly.

"Romantic spot," Amaranthe said. "Are you bringing me here to seduce me?" She kept her tone light, so he would know she was joking, but that nervous flutter teased her insides again. What if she wasn't? Or he wasn't? Or—erg, she had to stop thinking.

"You're dressed for it," Sicarius said, surprising her.

Her first thought was that he was implying disapproval at her bare-armed attire—he certainly had been insulting about the *last* dress Maldynado picked out for her—but his tone lacked any sort of edge, and he looked back and nudged her when she drew even with him.

Ah, that was teasing, if one could call it that. He was quoting her line from the lake.

"You're not," she said, quoting his line.

"No?" Sicarius stopped before the bench and examined his clothing. He smoothed a non-existent wrinkle and brushed an imaginary fleck of dust from the hilt of one of his daggers.

Actually, the black, however unimaginative, *did* accentuate everything nicely, and he'd have little trouble stirring a woman's fantasies in that outfit...or anything else. But that was far too honest to admit aloud. "In my experience," she said, "seductions usually involve fewer knives."

"Huh." Something in that single syllable made her believe that hadn't been *his* experience. She supposed anyone with the guts to proposition him...liked that it took guts to proposition him and found the blade collection an appealing part of the package.

Sicarius sat on the bench and held a hand out, offering her the seat beside him.

Amaranthe ought to tell him to hurry up and say what he had to say because Deret was waiting on her, but she couldn't bring herself to mention him. She didn't want to go back to Deret, not when she actually had Sicarius in a romantic spot, and he wasn't discussing work. Well, he wasn't discussing anything yet. She didn't know what to expect. It was bizarre of him even to sit on a bench; usually, he'd nod for her to sit while he remained standing and alert, surveying their surroundings as they spoke.

It was not a large bench, and when Amaranthe slid onto it, her leg touched his. The tall shrubs must have protected the stone seat from the afternoon sun, for its coolness seeped through her dress. It made her hyperaware of the heat from Sicarius's thigh.

"You mentioned a problem?" she asked, cringing when her voice cracked. She cleared her throat.

"Yes."

Someone giggled in another alcove. A small creature rustled through the undergrowth beside them.

"And that problem would be...?" Amaranthe prompted.

"Your plans to kiss Mancrest."

Amaranthe bolted up from the bench. Her tongue tangled under the assault of words that flooded into her mouth. Part of her wanted to deny any such thing, and part of her wanted to berate him for eavesdropping. All of her felt like a child caught reaching for a forbidden bag of candies. She had nothing to be guilty over though. She hadn't betrayed Sicarius. They had no agreement of fidelity. And besides, she hadn't said she was going to kiss Deret. She'd only been in the earliest stages of thinking *maybe* he *might* be someone with whom she could see having a relationship.

She settled for crossing her arms over her chest and saying, "How long were you skulking about the gardens, spying on us?"

He gazed up at her. The deepening twilight hid the nuances of his features, and she couldn't tell if anything other than his usual mask occupied his face. "What do you consider 'long'?"

"A period of time during which a normal, *considerate* person would feel ashamed for listening in on someone else's conversation."

Sicarius did not answer.

Amaranthe sighed and dropped her hands. "What are you doing out here? Checking up? Do you still believe Deret is a threat to me?"

"No."

Crickets sang to each other in the shrubs while Amaranthe waited for him to explain further.

"I do not like you seeing him," he finally said.

"Because...?"

"You know why."

She spread her arms. "With any other man in the world, I'd be positive, but this is you. Lord General Unreadable." Besides if it was what she thought, she wanted to hear him say it.

His sigh was so soft she might have imagined it. "It makes me jealous."

Dear ancestors, she might have *wanted* him to say it, but she had not truly expected him to admit it. "But I've told you how I feel about you, and you chose not to do anything about it."

"I told you why."

Amaranthe was torn between rolling her eyes in frustration at him and being tickled it bothered him to see her having dinner with another man. She took a few steps to the fountain and leaned her hands against the damp stone rim. "Let me see if I've got this. You're not willing to have a relationship with me, but you don't want me to have a relationship with anyone else either."

"Yes," Sicarius said. "Is that acceptable?"

She snorted. "No, it's not."

Sicarius joined her by the fountain. "I thought not, but you raised my hopes."

Amaranthe rubbed her face to hide a smile creeping onto her lips. She *ought* to be furious, but this was progress for him. Incredible to think it from a man over thirty-five years old, but he had probably never been jealous of anyone in his life, nor told a woman he cared. "I wouldn't have thought you were the type to do something so frivolous as hope."

"A recent development." Sicarius extended his arm, a hand out to her.

She stared at it, not sure what he was offering. She tried to read his face, but the darkness hid what few cues he gave. A warm breeze whispered through, ruffling his short hair.

Amaranthe stepped toward him, and he drew her into a hug. At first, she could only stand there, shocked. Despite the chiseled muscles beneath the thin fabric of his shirt, his embrace was gentle. She grew aware of his scent, of shaving soap and weapons cleaning oil, and inhaled deeply. Closing her eyes, she leaned into him and slipped her arms around his waist. Her knuckles bumped against the hilts of knives, and she smiled in bemusement. Only Sicarius would bring all his weapons to the smooching corner of the Imperial Gardens.

He lowered his head and rested his cheek against her temple. His soft exhalations warmed her neck, and heat curled through her body. She wanted to see if he might be interested in a little more than a hug, but she didn't. He always seemed like a feral animal in moments like this, and she feared any show of enthusiasm would send him stampeding back into his den where he'd hide behind a wall of emotionless stoicism.

"You're the only person who's ever wanted to give me happiness," Sicarius said.

That puzzled her until she remembered when she had said that, in her talk with Basilard the week before. "Do you eavesdrop on *every* conversation I have with other men?"

"You can't call it eavesdropping just because you don't notice me in the area."

She snorted again. He sounded like he was enjoying himself. Probably because he had gotten away with stealing her from her evening with Deret, and she was not giving him a hard time about it. "You're stealthier than a cat's shadow. You can't possibly expect me to notice you when you're lurking."

"Perhaps you have not been assiduous enough with your training."

"I can't believe you're blaming me for the fact that you're a chronic eavesdropper."

"What did you expect from an assassin?" he asked, tone teasing—or as close to it as he got.

Sicarius drew back, and Amaranthe caught his wrists before he could step away completely.

"We haven't resolved anything, you know," she said.

He extricated one hand and pointed to the bench. He probably wanted to sit and discuss the situation, as if it were some battle plan they were concocting. Shaking her head, she returned to her seat.

"Just to be clear," Amaranthe said, "this jealousy of yours, it arises from the fact that you'd like to be...uhm..." She groped for a word. With anyone else, she would say lovers, but that implied emotions she doubted he would ever admit to—if he could feel them at all. "...Bed friends," she said, then rolled her eyes. Lovers would have been better. "It's not just some territorial dog-peeing-on-a-lamp-post thing, right?"

"Bed friends?"

Yes, he probably thought she was silly because she didn't simply say what she meant, but, curse him, he wasn't saying what he meant either.

"Are you voting for that one or mocking the term?" Amaranthe asked.

"Yes."

Someday she was going to learn not to give him those sorts

of questions. "Somehow, I think things would be going easier for me if I'd stayed on the hill, drinking Deret's wine."

"You like a challenge."

She grew aware of the warmth of his thigh again. "Would it truly be so detrimental if we...were a we? If it's about the men being jealous that two out of the six people in the group get to have...bed friends, that's not really a problem when we're in the city, right? They can go off and find their own partners. They wouldn't even need to know. You're about as demonstrative as a rock, and I think I can manage to keep my hands off of you while the others are around."

"Really," he said dryly.

Though she doubted Sicarius would fail to miss spies in the bushes, she lowered her voice to a whisper to say, "If it's about Sespian, I can understand you not wanting more obstacles between you two, but it would be *my* choice. Even if he does still have feelings, which is unlikely."

"You might decide he's a better choice."

"Oh, I'm certain he is." Amaranthe grinned, though the deepening darkness probably hid it. "But, as you pointed out, I like a challenge. Why would I want to spend time with some adoring, warm youngster when I could have a stiff, aloof assassin whose idea of romance involves throwing knives and running up stairs together?"

"That's not romance; that's training."

"Is there a difference for you?"

"Slight."

Sicarius stood, breaking the contact between them.

Amaranthe sighed. Cool evening air whispered past her arms, and dew-touched grass flicked at her bare toes. "I guess this means you're not going to demonstrate what that difference might be?"

"Not until this is over."

"*This* being our...exoneration? And you having a chance to talk with Sespian?"

"The latter in particular."

Amaranthe fought down a grumble. So, she got him *if* she found a way to put him and Sespian together, so he could have his chance to explain everything to his son. Setting that up had always been her intent, but she was not sure how long it would take.

She supposed she ought to find it encouraging that Sicarius cared enough about righting things with Sespian not to want to steal his girl, but, cursed ancestors, she *wasn't* his girl. And he had surely gotten over that fleeting infatuation by now anyway. He had been drug-addled at the time after all.

"In the meantime," Amaranthe said, "I get to spend my nights sitting chastely in the team hideout?" How...wholesome.

"We could add an evening training session to your regimen."

She groaned and dropped her head in her hands. "You have a disturbing sense of humor."

A long moment passed before he said, "Offer a proposition."

"I don't know." Amaranthe shrugged helplessly. "I can wait. I just need to know.... Well, we've never even kissed. How am I supposed to know if all this is worth it?"

She winced as soon as the words came out. She hadn't meant to imply that *he* wasn't worth waiting for, just that she didn't know if they'd actually have a physical connection when they actually—

"*Worth* it?" Sicarius asked, sounding, for the first time she could recall, offended.

Amaranthe groaned. She was making a mess of this.

She stretched out an apologetic hand. Sicarius took it and pulled her off the bench. Her feet tangled, and she stumbled into him. His other arm came around her, and he pulled her against him with none of his earlier gentleness.

He wouldn't hurt her—at least she didn't *think* he would— but her heart quickened, a jolt of concern coursing through her. Maybe she had pushed him too far. The arm wrapped around her tightened, mashing her against his chest. The fabric of his shirt did nothing to soften the ridges of granite muscle beneath it, and the thought crossed her mind that if she ever truly did anger him, all her training would be no use.

Amaranthe swallowed and opened her mouth to speak, though she was not sure whether she meant to apologize or blurt some sort of bravado. It didn't matter. His mouth found hers, open, demanding, and she forgot about talking. And breathing.

The kiss crackled with intensity, and she thought of the hull of that fortress, its electrical charge knocking her on her backside. She wriggled her arms around him and returned the kiss.

His fingers tangled in her hair, caressing the back of her neck. An ache grew inside, and her toes curled around the edges of her sandals. She thought of kicking them off, of kicking *everything* off and—

Sicarius released her and stepped back, leaving her stunned and breathless, her heart galloping in place behind her ribs. Then, without a word, he strode away.

Amaranthe, legs wobbly, collapsed on the bench. "He's right," she croaked. "It *is* different than training."

EPILOGUE

Basilard told the nerves fluttering in his belly to be still. The stubborn things refused to obey.

Tall, broad-shouldered imperial soldiers in blue uniforms with gold trim strode along the brick paths of the Oakcrest Conservatory, their boots so polished they reflected the flames of nearby gas lamps. The men's expressionless faces reminded him of Sicarius, and so did those dark, cool eyes as they scrutinized the civilians and servants who crossed their paths. Youths carrying trays of lemonade, iced tea, and wine paid the soldiers no mind. Of course, they had no reason to worry about being detained, captured, or killed.

Basilard sucked in a deep breath, grateful a number of overhead panels were open, letting in fresh air. With sweat already trickling down his spine, it would have been unbearably stifling without the evening breeze. He adjusted his collar. Maldynado's outfit was far more constricting than the loose garments his people favored.

"Problem?" Books asked.

There are as many soldiers as athletes, perhaps more.

"I don't think you need to look so concerned," Books said. "We made it past the phalanx of vehicles and soldiers outside, and the door guards let us in, despite much eyebrow raising over the fact that you brought a man as your one permitted dinner companion."

Basilard smiled. *I didn't think the empire had issues with that sort of thing. Are you sure it wasn't that they were surprised a victorious athlete wouldn't have a younger, prettier man for an escort?*

"I'm going to forgive you for that because of all that time you recently spent with—" Books glanced around, "—a certain disreputable sort. You probably feel the need to unleash your sense of humor."

Or distract himself. Basilard feared their admittance had been too easy. Though Books had received a few questions about Basilard's need for a translator, another soldier had jogged up during the interview and whispered something in the guard's ear, resulting in Basilard and Books being waved inside. Could the soldiers have recognized them and let them in as a trap? Were they even now waiting to see if Amaranthe and Sicarius waited nearby?

Basilard and Books walked toward a long wooden table with sixty or seventy place settings laid out. Athletes and their companions chatted in pairs or small groups near trellised vines and citrus trees potted along the way.

"There he is," Books said.

A glass door beyond the table had opened with two soldiers in black entering, the emperor's personal guard. Sespian came next in blue, quasi-military attire. Unexpectedly, a gray-haired woman in a sapphire dress strode beside him. Not exactly beside. Basilard had the impression Sespian was trying to keep space between them.

"She's old to be his escort," Books murmured, also watching the woman. "A chaperone?"

Four more soldiers trailed after the pair.

The emperor gazed about alertly. Though his position must cause him a great deal of stress, he appeared no older than his nineteen years, perhaps even younger, and Basilard wondered how much power he commanded around the Imperial Barracks.

Could Sespian do anything about the empire's underground slave trade? About the fact that Mangdorians were often targeted?

Though the cadre of guards about him could have made the emperor seem unapproachable, he strode up to the first group of athletes and greeted everyone with a friendly smile. After the three young men managed flustered bows, Sespian started asking questions.

"This may be a good time to talk to him," Books said. "Before he grows weary of people pestering him."

Let's meander that way, Basilard signed.

The other athletes seemed content to wait. They probably lacked his agenda.

As he and Books strolled over, the nerves tormenting Basilard's stomach redoubled their flutters. If this was a trap, the soldiers would spring it before Basilard got close to the emperor.

Books plucked an iced tea from a server's tray. He was either more comfortable here than Basilard, or he was doing a good job of hiding his nerves. Basilard took a drink without looking to see what it was; ice cubes clinked in the glass.

The emperor moved to a second group of athletes, this one made up of young ladies. He was courteous and professional, and Basilard did not get the impression he was searching for bed partners—a vibe warrior-caste men often exuded, whether they were married or not. The emperor's older chaperone never said anything, and Basilard had the feeling she was there only to keep an eye on Sespian.

"Think that's someone from Forge?" Books murmured.

Would they have someone here so openly?

Amaranthe had mentioned her belief that Forge had a toehold in the Imperial Barracks, but Basilard had not realized it might run so deeply.

"If so, that's...a concern," Books said. "They might restrict his access to information and certainly his ability to take action."

So, he might not be reading the papers and be aware of our heroics?
"If so, all our work would be for naught."

Sespian looked over the women's heads, his gaze coming to rest on Basilard and Books.

Basilard twitched, flushing guiltily. Had the emperor overheard Books's half of their conversation? They were speaking quietly. He shouldn't have, but who knew?

His first instinct was to look away and pretend no interest, but that might appear more suspicious. He forced himself to hold the gaze and nod.

After finishing his conversation with the women, the emperor strode toward Books and Basilard.

Basilard glanced left and right, expecting a legion of soldiers to stampede them at any moment. Books thumped a fist to his heart and bent at the waist, his sword arm stretching wide with the palm open.

"A pleasure to speak with you, Sire," he said.

Basilard mimicked the bow and signed, *Most respect, Chief.* He hadn't worked out hand signs for honorifics for emperors yet. Books would know what he meant though.

Oddly, when Books translated, he left the word for chief instead of correcting it. Perhaps he wanted Basilard to sound quaint—and unthreatening—thanks to his Mangdorian vernacular.

"Good evening." Sespian pressed his own fist to his chest in response. "Temtelamak, isn't it?" His eyebrow twitched.

Basilard swallowed. The emperor recognized the name for a pseudonym and possibly knew Basilard had something to hide.... Curse Maldynado for picking out something silly.

"Congratulations on your victory," the emperor went on.

Thank you, Chief.

The woman glided over to join them, and Basilard signed, *Evening, ma'am.*

"This is Ms. Rockvic," Sespian said, his face difficult to read. "She's...trying to find me a wife, I think." He arched an eyebrow at the older woman. Her lips thinned, but she said nothing.

Basilard exchanged concerned looks with Books. Amaranthe would need to know about this new development.

I'd hoped to talk to you about something, Chief, Basilard signed. Sespian would not chat forever, so he had best make his request.

Sespian blinked. "Yes, of course. Go ahead."

I escaped slavery here in Stumps last winter. I was one of hundreds taken out of Mangdoria and sold in your underground market, where business owners in particular save money by buying slaves instead of using day-paid laborers or paying for expensive machines. Some slaves, like myself, are forced into the pit-fighting circuit where they must battle for their lives every night.

He paused so Books could translate, and he watched Sespian's face, trying to judge whether this was new information for him or something he was aware of and had dismissed. The emperor's eyebrows climbed as Books spoke, and more than once he glanced at his chaperone. The woman's face was closed and hard. If she *was* a member of Forge, Basilard hoped he was not making trouble by revealing these facts in front of her.

I'm particularly concerned for my people, Basilard went on. *I believe they're targeted because they're pacifists and not strong Science practitioners.*

For the first time, Books edited the translation, leaving off the last few words.

"I see," Sespian said through a tense jaw. "I wasn't aware of this problem. My ignorance is not an excuse, and I apologize for the ruthless way you were brought to the empire. I will look into this slavery as soon as I'm able." He glanced at Rockvic, and his lip twitched in a brief grimace. He was being open about his displeasure at having this companion. Was it possible he wanted Basilard and Books to know? That made no sense.

Thank you, Chief, he signed. He wished he could do more—

elicit a promise of some kind—but the emperor did not seem to be in a position to promise much right now.

Sespian extended his arm and clasped Basilard's hand. The action surprised Basilard because the standoffish Turgonians did not make physical contact during their greetings. Maybe the emperor knew Mangdorian hunters clasped forearms as a gesture of friendship? But it was Sespian's hand that pressed against his, not his arm, and something poked into Basilard's palm. Paper?

When Sespian withdrew his grip, he left the object in Basilard's hand.

"Have a peaceful evening," the emperor said.

Basilard pressed his thumb into his palm to keep the object in his hand and dropped his arm to his side. It felt like a piece of paper folded numerous times into a small square.

"I don't know if he'll be able to do anything for you right now," Books said after the emperor had moved onto the next group, "but perhaps someday. If not, maybe *our* team could tackle the slave trade."

Basilard barely heard him. He was searching the conservatory, looking for an empty but lighted place where he could unfold the paper, but two soldiers were frowning in his direction. He ended up waiting through dinner and a theater show during which university students reenacted some of the great moments from the Games, often with amusing asides. All too aware of the note in his pocket, Basilard had a hard time conversing or enjoying the festivities. He let out a deep breath when they exited the conservatory without any guards accosting them.

"Something wrong?" Books asked. "You've been quiet all…"

Basilard strode toward a winding but lit path. Books hurried to catch up. When they were out of sight of the soldiers, guards, and other dinner-goers, he stopped, finally unfolding the message.

"What is that?" Books asked. "Did the emperor give it to you?"

Basilard already had the note open, and, after another check of their surroundings, he held it out so they could both read it.

Amaranthe Lokdon:

I wish to hire your outfit to kidnap me. I can offer 100,000 ranmyas.

No signature marked the page, but there was hardly a need, not when the emperor had personally handed the message to Basilard.

Books let out a low whistle. "This could change everything."

Or get us all killed, Basilard signed, thinking of all the security they would have to get through to abscond with an emperor. If it were easy to elude those guards, Sespian would have escaped on his own.

"Yes, it could be a trap," Books said, "designed to rid the empire of Amaranthe and Sicarius. For all we know, that woman might have forced Sespian to slip this to you."

Either way, this autumn should be interesting.

"Indeed so," Books said. "Indeed so."

THE END

CONNECT WITH THE AUTHOR

Have a comment? Question? Just want to say hi? Find me online at:
http://www.lindsayburoker.com
http://www.facebook.com/LindsayBuroker
http://twitter.com/GoblinWriter
Thanks for reading!